THE GENERAL'S COOK

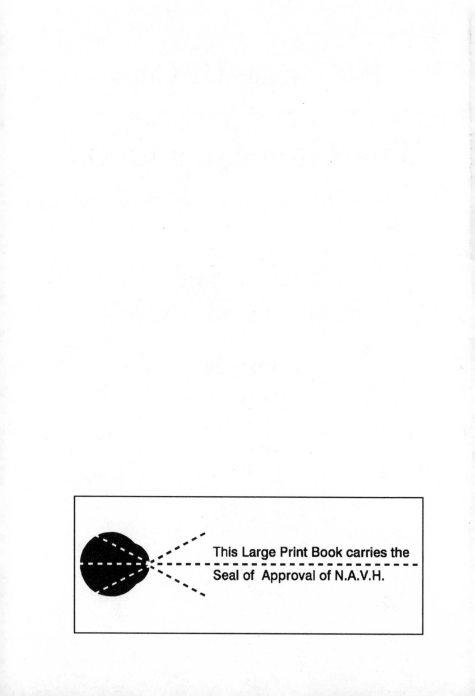

This Large Print Book carries the
Seal of Approval of N.A.V.H.

THE GENERAL'S COOK

RAMIN GANESHRAM

THORNDIKE PRESS
A part of Gale, a Cengage Company

Farmington Hills, Mich • San Francisco • New York • Waterville, Maine
Meriden, Conn • Mason, Ohio • Chicago

LIBRARY OF CONGRESS CIP DATA ON FILE.
CATALOGUING IN PUBLICATION FOR THIS BOOK
IS AVAILABLE FROM THE LIBRARY OF CONGRESS

ISBN-13: 978-1-4328-6101-8 (hardcover)

Published in 2019 by arrangement with Skyhorse Publishing, Inc.

Printed in the United States of America
1 2 3 4 5 6 7 23 22 21 20 19

AUTHOR'S NOTE

In an effort to accurately portray the historical language and sensibilities of late eighteenth century America, I have used the terms "colored," "African," "Negro," and some of their derisive derivatives throughout the book to refer to both the free and enslaved African Americans portrayed. By no means should the reader take this usage as agreement with or sanction of any historical or modern use of these words. No offense is meant in using this terminology and the author hopes that none is taken.

For S.P.V.

The chief cook would have been termed in modern parlance, a celebrated *artiste*. He was named Hercules, and familiarly termed Uncle Harkless . . . Uncle Harkless was, at the period of the first presidency, as highly accomplished a proficient in the culinary art as could be found in United States. . . . It was while preparing the Thursday or Congress dinner that Uncle Harkless shone in all his splendor. During his labors upon this banquet he required some half-dozen aprons, and napkins out of number. It was surprising the order and discipline that was observed in so bustling a scene. His underlings flew in all directions to execute his orders, while he, the great master-spirit, seemed to possess the power of ubiquity, and to be everywhere at the same moment.
— George Washington Parke Custis, *Recollections and Private Memoirs of Washington*, 1859

A man is either free, or he is not. There cannot be an apprenticeship for freedom.
— Amiri Baraka (1934–2014)

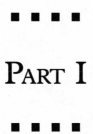

PART I

CHAPTER 1

Philadelphia, Winter 1793

The man who stood, legs firmly apart, his gold-headed walking stick planted in front of him with his beefy hands resting on top, smiled slightly even though his eyes were half closed as though he might doze off. He was undisturbed by those who walked around him speaking in hoarse whispers. Nor did he note the rage and bustle of the marketplace in front of him and the roil of docks behind. His shirtsleeves, white against his dark skin, were rolled up to show forearms layered with muscle and snaky veins.

He breathed deeply, nostrils flaring out and then in again. The stench of rotted fish and putrid vegetables mingled with the coppery smell of the animal blood that ran out of the market sheds and in between the cobbles around his expensive boots.

Along with the aroma of the unwashed beggars colliding with that of the expensive toilet water of the society ladies, these were the smells of Philadelphia — the smells of freedom. Hercules would take them over the fresh hay and magnolia of Virginia any day.

Behind him stood a boy and girl of about thirteen or fourteen. The boy wore the same tasseled cap as all of the Washington servants and the girl was dressed in a plain brown cloak and coarse linen mobcap. Her wide blue eyes darted around the busy market while the boy's light brown ones rested only on her.

Ignoring them, Hercules looked toward the market shed and the most agreeable posterior of Mrs. Polly Haine, the pepper pot seller, as she bent over her cauldron and he smiled broadly. He often enjoyed the delights of Mrs. Haine's famous stew as well as those of the freedwoman herself.

Around Polly, the buzzing of the crowd pitched high and then low, only to be cracked open by the yell of vendors hawking wares as Hercules began walking toward the market shed.

"My dear Mistress Haine!" he boomed as he drew near, the children trailing after him. "The view is agreeable, but not as much if I might look upon your lovely face."

Polly straightened, smiled, and walked

over to Hercules, who brushed at the long white apron buttoned to his chest and hanging low over his britches. Like the scarf around his large neck and the white shirt buttoned close at the collar, he wanted to ensure it remained immaculate. When he was done he leaned on his gold-headed cane and took her extended hand.

"If it isn't General Washington's cook!" Polly exclaimed. Hercules bowed over her hand as though he were a fine gentleman and she a lady. A clerk sipping his stew at the stall stopped with his bowl halfway to his lips to stare at them.

"Madam, it is no other," Hercules said, straightening and smiling. "I — we — are returned as you see."

"I heard the General was in Germantown these past weeks," said Polly. "Were you not there? We had hoped to see you here in town from time to time."

Hercules's eyes clouded over as he remembered being stuck in Virginia, flying hither and yon on Lady Washington's whims. President Washington and his household had gone to his Mount Vernon plantation in September to avoid the fever that was gripping the city. Now here December was almost gone before they had finally returned to the President's House at the other end of

High Street.

It was only a second before he smiled again. He had learned long ago the importance of never giving away one's thoughts. His eyes flickered over the clerk, who had given up eating altogether to ogle him.

"I was needed more at Mount Vernon," he said smoothly. "With Mrs. Washington and the family there, it was more important for me to stay. The General hired a cook for the time he was without us."

"No doubt not one as good as you," said Polly, turning to dish him up a bowl of pepper pot soup. Handing it over, she addressed her other customer.

"Will that be all then?" she asked, her tone skirting the edge of rude.

"Oh, er — yes," he said, drawing out the words in a long country drawl. He set the bowl on the table before turning reluctantly away.

As she turned back from watching the man go, Hercules reached into the small tapestry purse tied to the front of his apron.

"Oh, no, Master Hercules — no money from you," she said.

"You are kind, Mrs. Haine," he said, accepting the soup and taking a deep sip. It was rich and thick and the spices were balanced and well blended. His cook's mind cataloged the ingredients: beef, allspice, hot pepper, onion. The meat fairly melted on the tongue. "Beyond satisfactory, madam. As always," he said.

Hercules slurped with gusto, murmuring appreciatively, set down his bowl, and glanced over his shoulder at the young ones who stood there in his shadow.

"Nate, take Margaret and collect the items I need," he said. His voice was not unkind but matter of fact. It was best for these two to learn his way of doing things straightaway. "You'll need to show her the vendors we like and who we don't. Remember — don't buy the new apples from anyone but Mrs. Shapely."

"Yes, sir," Nate said, but the girl just stared at him fearfully. It was not until her companion put his hand gently on her arm and murmured that she jumped and moved on after bobbing a herky-jerky curtsy to Hercules.

"Is she slow-witted?" Polly asked when the pair had moved off.

Hercules sighed. He'd asked himself the same ever since the girl had come to the President's House. She didn't say much; mostly just stared at him with terrified cow eyes. "No. At least I think not," he answered. "She's new to us — an orphan — the

17

almshouse sold her into indenture."

Polly raised her eyebrows. "Since when is the General taking on indentures? He has you all —" She stopped abruptly, embarrassed.

Hercules shrugged. Her slip didn't trouble him because he made a point of facing facts square. It was a fair question — why indeed would a man who owned slaves take on the trouble of an indenture?

"Not many of us there now," he answered. "Him and Mrs. Washington are too worried that we'll all run off and take advantage of the freedom law. Sent most of us back to Virginia."

Hercules smiled mildly as Mrs. Haine sucked her teeth. Even though he counted her as a friend, he wouldn't show his true feelings for Washington to anyone. Safer to keep those to himself. He thought back to that summer of '91, when Mrs. Washington had wanted him to travel back to Mount Vernon "to cook for the family." She'd been afraid of him taking advantage of the freedom law that said any slave in the state more than six months could claim his or her freedom, and it had made her nervous and shrill. Hercules had only smiled at her pleasantly, then gone to Mr. Lear, the General's secretary.

"I'd never leave the General, Mr. Lear, sir!" he'd said, wringing his hands childishly as he had never done in his life. "The General — he been good to me!"

To his satisfaction, Lear had apologized and promised to tell the First Lady just what an ideal slave Hercules was and to allow him to stay past the six months as a proof of their faith in him. Better still, they showed their returned affection by allowing him to sell the kitchen slops and earn a good two hundred dollars a year by it — twice what a white Philadelphia workingman earned in as much time.

That was two years ago and since then he had come and gone as he pleased, spending his money on nice clothes and his own amusements. Except for the trips to Mount Vernon it was near as good as being free, and there had been nothing to tempt him away from the life he enjoyed at the presidential mansion — yet.

"But tell me, Mrs. Haine," he said, giving his cane a good thump on the market floor. Leaning close, he allowed his eyes to rake her up and down, "Tell me news of Philadelphia. Any worthy entertainments to speak of?"

A quarter of an hour later, he left Polly

Haine and searched for the two young ones, spotting them three sheds beyond where they had started. Margaret was grasping at Nate's sleeve as he walked purposefully through the market with the basket swinging at his side. She had to fairly skip to keep near him through the frenzied rush of activity around them.

"Melons! Last of the season! New potatoes! Wethersfield onions!" The yells of vendors all around joined with the snorts of pigs and bleating of sheep near the butchers' stalls to make one cacophonous roar.

Hercules had nearly caught them up when Nate stopped; the girl almost crashed into the young kitchen hand, she was walking so close. Hercules slowed again. Something about them bothered him. They were almost too familiar, though they'd known each other only a matter of weeks. It wasn't an association that would serve either of them well. Hercules approached carefully so that he could catch their conversation without being observed.

Nate put his arm out across where Margaret stood. "Halt a moment," he said, peering down the open roadway that intersected the market. There were six such avenues west of the river that crossed through the market sheds, offering halos of light at the end of each long wooden building. A heavy cart pulled by two large bay horses was clattering down the avenue in front of them, faster than was necessary.

"Drunk, no doubt," the General's cook heard Nate mutter as he took a few pointed steps backward. When Margaret tried to look over at what he saw, his movement forced her back as well.

"Why's he driving so fast?" she asked.

"From the looks of it, he's a farmer who's spent some of his day's earnings at a tavern," said Nate, shrugging. "Happens all the time. Once they're in their cups, they act the fool, drive crazy, and —" He paused. "And, well, other things."

Margaret nodded slowly, as though she wasn't quite sure what he meant. Hercules remembered her chatter as they walked to the market. She'd told them that her father had been a farmer and sometimes he came into town to sell the brewers extra barley from their farm in Northern Liberties.

Now the girl looked stricken, as though she might start to cry. Her parents had died of the yellow fever, leaving her orphaned, with indenture the only option to earn her keep. She bit her lip and stared ahead at the commotion the driver was causing as he tried to maneuver his large cart through the street crowded with people, animals, and vendors.

When the housekeeper, Mrs. Emerson, had brought Margaret to his kitchen, she had told Hercules that after the girl's parents had died, she had walked the city searching for work she did not find, sleeping behind an old crypt in Christ Church's yard. After three days, her pride exhausted from fear and hunger, she found her way to the almshouse, where after a few weeks of hot meals she was fit again. Being young enough to work hard, they sold her for eight years' indenture to Washington.

The girl had nearly fainted the first time she saw the president, and she looked like she swallowed a rock when Lady Washington came into the kitchen daily to discuss the meals with Hercules and the steward, Fraunces. Hercules stopped himself from laughing out loud thinking about short, fat, nervous Mrs. Washington clucking around like a high-strung chicken, and Margaret like a skinny worm, wriggling desperately to be out of her sight. Hercules knew how to handle the old woman. He spoke to her in a special voice he only used for her — low and soothing, like he was calming an angry mother hog in the slop yard.

"Come on," Nate said now. The commotion with the cart was over — the driver eventually parting the sea of people around his vehicle by heaping curses on them along with a few snaps of his whip.

Nate was already walking ahead and Margaret scurried behind him into the next block of market sheds. They walked past the cheese vendors toward a fruit stall in a corner, where Nate stood, looking confused. Hercules watched as the boy turned around slowly as if he did not know where he was. He turned back to the fruit vendor's stall where a thin man in a worn brown vest sat on a barrel.

"Is this not Mistress Shapely's stand?" Nate asked the man.

"T'were," he said.

"Where is she?" Nate asked, narrowing his eyes.

"Taken in the fever," the man answered, shrugging. "I'm here now."

"Oh." Nate picked up an apple and set it down, then picked up another and set it down.

"Surely these look fine, Nate?" Margaret said, touching his sleeve.

The fruit man raised his eyebrows.

"You buying or what?" he barked, although his stand had no other customers.

"Not much trade coming your way," Nate

said to the man. "Maybe your wares aren't so good."

The man gave him an evil look and opened his mouth to reply, but then spotted Hercules, who had covered the distance between himself and the pair and now stood behind them.

"Nate!" his deep voice rumbled. The boy turned to look at Hercules, who was leaning on his stick in an amiable pose, but when he glanced from Nate and Margaret to the vendor, his expression was hard.

"Why are you dawdling? Where is Mrs. Shapely?"

Nate swallowed. "Gone, sir. That is —"

"T'was the fever what took her," the vendor snarled.

Hercules continued to look at Nate, ignoring the vendor. "Ah, a shame. Let's be on our way."

"*I'm* here now," the man said again, this time to Hercules's back as he started to leave.

He turned back and regarded the man. He knew the type — lowborn with little desire except for enough chink to fill his cups and maybe his bed. He was scraggle-faced and dirty headed but sure of the position granted by his pasty skin. How delightful it would have been to poke the man in the chest with the tip of his cane. But, of course, he could not.

Instead he only said, "Ah, so you are, sir. So you are," before strolling away. The man was mistaken if he thought Hercules were some kowtowing nigra. He was Washington's man, and that made him untouchable, no matter how black he might be.

Hercules grasped Nate near his neck with his powerful hands and propelled the boy along, leaving Margaret to scurry after them as they walked past at least ten fruiterers before Hercules found one whose apples he liked. When he did, he bargained unflinchingly before loading Margaret's basket with the red and green fruit.

Then they doubled back to the cheesemongers and he walked past them all, studying their wares.

Finally, he paused in front of one in the middle of the shed row.

"Ah, here is a man with finer tastes," said the proprietress, eyeing him. His lips curled in the hint of a smile. She was a plump woman with huge bosoms pouring out of the top of her tight blue bodice. Her red hair escaped the lace-ruffled mobcap she wore — a cap far too fancy for a day at the market.

"Cut a slice of that sage cheddar for

General Washington's cook," she said to the young girl standing beside her, never taking her eyes off Hercules. The girl was small and skinny and maybe a year or so younger than Nate and Margaret. She looked at him with interest, her mouth hanging slightly open. Hercules ignored her.

"Don't catch flies, girl! The gentleman is waiting!" the proprietress snapped.

The girl appeared to be confused and Hercules knew what she was thinking: that he was a Negro, and everyone knew the Negroes in General Washington's house were slaves. Why was her mistress calling him a "gentleman"?

She cut a slice of the cheese and speared it with her knife, then stuck it out to Hercules. He looked down at it as if it were a snake on a stick, then stared at her coldly until she shrank back.

"Amanda!" her mistress snapped. "That is not how we treat our esteemed customers!" She grabbed the knife from the girl and plucked the slice of cheese off it, handing it to Hercules herself, leaning forward as she did so that he might get a better look at her powdered cleavage.

"Ma'am, ain't he a slave?" the girl mumbled loud enough for them all to hear.

The cheesemonger looked sharply at

Amanda. "Go turn those cheeses over," she said, indicating the other side of the stall. "Now!" she snapped when the girl continued to stand staring at him.

"Master Hercules — apologies," the lady said, simpering.

Hercules's bemused look now became a full smile. "Not at all, Mrs. Radcliffe. Not at all." He delicately plucked the cheese from her fingers and took a small bite.

"Delightful!" he said, looking openly at her breasts. "As your wares always are." He smiled again.

Beside him, Margaret stared agog, but Nate resolutely stared straight ahead. Clever boy.

"I'll take two pounds of that cheddar, Mrs. Radcliffe," said Hercules, while drawing a kerchief from his pocket and delicately wiping his mouth. Being the General's cook always had certain advantages.

Once they had their cheese, they stopped to collect tea and then some sweetmeats at the confectioners. As they made their way to the north end of the market at Fourth Street, people stopped to talk to him while others whispered as he passed. Hercules reveled in it. Each look and murmur, each greeting was filling the well of his soul, replacing the dry dullness of the many months at Mount Vernon. Margaret scurried beside him, her face growing redder at all the attention, but Nate continued staring straight ahead. This amused Hercules, who sailed on imperiously while the basket-laden pair struggled to keep up in his wake.

Outside the market the early winter wind had taken on a bite, blowing into the trio as they started up High Street. Hercules walked on in his shirtsleeves and apron as if it were a summer day, past Mr. Franklin's print shop and post office and the Indian Queen tavern, where loud conversation crashed out the door in waves. He paused about a block from Sixth Street, where the President's House stood on the corner.

"Set those down a moment," he said, gesturing for them to step closer into the sidewalk.

Hercules reached into his purse and pulled out a small paper package. Pulling open the string, he held it out to them.

"Go on, have one each. The others are for the rest in the kitchen," he said.

Six glistening sugarplums — pink, purple, and yellow — sat on the paper. Margaret's eyes grew wide. She reached her hand forward and then hesitated.

"Go on then," Hercules rumbled impatiently. Margaret snatched up a pink one and took a bite. "Oh!" she exclaimed, mouth full. "Thank you, sir!" she said, bobbing.

Nate chose a yellow one and took a slow bite. He seemed to be thinking hard each time his teeth came together.

"That's right, son, think about what you are tasting," Hercules said.

"Sugar, of course . . ." said Nate. "Anise . . ."

Hercules nodded.

"Something else . . ."

"Take your time. Think."

Margaret swallowed what was in her mouth and watched the exchange. Nate took another bite.

"Cinnamon?" he asked, looking at Hercules for approval.

Hercules crossed his arms over his chest and shook his head.

"Nutmeg?"

Hercules shook his head again.

Nate took another bite. "It tastes — like mint leaf somehow but then again —"

"Cardamom," Hercules said. "A seed from the East. I'll show it to you when we return. Now finish your treat."

Nate smiled happily and began nibbling again. Margaret looked at the confection in her hand and took a smaller bite. Hercules could see her mind working, brows knitting together until she gave up and nibbled the rest down.

After they finished, Hercules jutted his chin toward their baskets and they hurried to take them up. He strode ahead of them, tapping his cane on the ground at regular paces as he went. Out of the corner of the eye, he spotted the hatless man leaning back into the shadows of the Messrs. Miller and Cline's shop across High Street. His chestnut hair escaped its braid in wild waves and he hunched down in his old paint-spattered coat. He looked like a madman. Hercules had seen the man there when they'd left for the market hours ago. It was the third time in as many days that he'd noticed him hanging around the shops across the way.

As Hercules watched, the man leaned forward out of the shadows and squinted his eyes to better see them. Drawing a small pad and pencil out of his pocket, he scribbled madly, glancing at them and back down at the paper as he did, following them with his eyes until they slipped through the door in the garden wall. It made Hercules uneasy.

As the others walked toward the kitchen, Hercules pulled the wooden door behind him, staring through the grate at the man until he had committed him to memory.

CHAPTER 2

"Reverend Allen means to make his church today!" Oney rushed into the kitchen and panted the words out. She held one of the First Lady's shawls. "Jane, boil me some water, will you?" she said to a scullery maid peeling vegetables at the other end of the long table. "I need to wash out the perfume oil Mrs. Washington spilled on this before it sets into the weave. Ask the laundress for some lye soap too."

Hercules set down the knife he was using to cut paper-thin slices of the smoked ham sent up from Mount Vernon. The First Lady was serving it as a cold plate this evening at her weekly Friday night soiree for the women of Philadelphia society. Mount Vernon ham was a particular favorite of the president, who always dropped in on the evenings with a gaggle of ladies, who invariably gave him plenty of attention — the admiration of the finer sex was the one kind of social event Washington enjoyed.

"Oney Judge, you are not the master of this kitchen," Hercules growled. "And I'll thank you not to charge in here and order people around. You know good enough where the pots are and the well pump, and the lye too, for that matter. See to your water yourself."

Oney went to fetch a small iron pot, glaring at Hercules as she passed, although he had gone back to slicing the ham as though nothing had happened. She filled the pot with water from the pump that stood by the stone sink near the window, then set it among the coals on the hearth.

While she waited for the water to boil, she went to the laundry house and came back holding a small cake of lye soap and a long wooden fork. When the water boiled, she grabbed a cloth and carefully hoisted the small pot onto the worktable near Hercules and slowly lowered the shawl inside.

Hercules silently watched Oney lift the shawl out, soap it well, and drop it back into the pot.

"What exactly are you doing, Oney Judge?" he said, his voice low and dangerous. "How is it that you don't have the good sense to do that in the laundry room and not here where I'm preparing food?"

Oney flopped into a chair.

" 'Course I do," she said. "But I also have the sense to know that all of you in here will sure want to know about Reverend Allen's church. I reckon Fanny don't care much about it either way seeing as how she only gets paid on how much washing she gets done and not for listening to stories."

Hercules made a sound like a grunt, then took the platter of meats to the larder and placed it on a wooden bench and covered it with a clean linen cloth. When he returned he picked up the ham bone and scraped it down with his knife. He put the bone in a large footed kettle that was simmering gently in the fire, then went to the other side of the kitchen.

"Well, go on, then," he said, coming back with three eggs in a bowl.

"Richmond, bring me a half cup of sugar, two cups Indian meal, and a nutmeg with my grater," he called over his shoulder to his son, who sat husking dried corn by the open kitchen door. "You, Margaret, I need a molded crock — the one with the corn stalks on it."

Margaret nervously leapt up when she heard her name, knocking over the low stool she had been sitting on, shelling peas. Beside her, Jane — the youngest and lowest

ranking of the hired scullery maids —
snickered. She came with her mother Mathilda on Fridays when soiree preparation
required more hands. Hercules didn't care
for either of them because they didn't seem
to understand how things were in this
house. He knew they saucily called him
"General Kitchen" behind his back.

"Something amusing, Lady Jane?" Hercules said sharply, staring at the bony girl
hunched over the wide pan of peas.

Now it was Jane's turn to jump. "No," she
mumbled.

"What was that then?" Hercules said,
louder this time, his voice ominous enough
to cause Mathilda to look up from the
corner table where she was kneading bread
and for Mr. Julien, the hired French cook,
to pause and glance over from where he was
shucking oysters.

"Begging your pardon, t'were nothing,"
she answered him sullenly, looking down at
the peas she continued to shell, sliding her
thumb down the length of the split dry pod.
The kitchen was so silent the chink of each
pea hitting the tin pan echoed loudly.

Hercules let his eyes sweep around the rest
of the staff in the kitchen, challenging
anyone to step out of line. Jane looked over
at her mother, whose eyes warned her to

mind her tone. Here in this kitchen Hercules was master. It wasn't for them to question the manner in which the president or Mrs. Washington kept their house. Hercules saw Julien, in his corner, shake his head. He'd often told Hercules how odd he found Americans with their talk of liberty and freedom and yet they continued on with this business of holding slaves.

"Chef," Julien said. "Would you taste this sauce before I pour it over the oysters?"

Hercules knew that Julien didn't really need his opinion — the man had worked in some of the finest houses in Paris. As his eyes met Julien's, a small smile of appreciation played at the corners of his mouth. It was the Frenchman's way of showing the little slattern her place. It had been Julien who, in the French manner, insisted on calling him Chef. Hercules was indebted to him for that. Julien was the first white man who treated him like a true equal. The Frenchman was inspired by James Hemings, Mr. Jefferson's cook, who was also called Chef, having been educated to cook in Paris.

"Certainly, Mr. Julien," said Hercules, going to the Frenchman's corner. "Although I know that your taste is far superior to mine."

He leaned over and dipped his pinky into the thick white sauce in a small iron pot that Julien had brought over from the hearth. He thought a minute.

"A bit more salt, I would say — but only a bit," he said.

Julien smiled and said, "Just so, Chef. Just so," and added a pinch of salt to the sauce from the box on the table and stirred it vigorously.

"Now then," said Hercules to Oney, as he returned to his own table where Richmond had set down the dry goods before returning to husking the corn. "What is this about Reverend Allen and his church?"

"Not just Allen, but them who has started the Free African Society are going to make a real and proper church for black folk," she began while peering into the pot and giving the shawl a swish with the stick. "They're moving that old abandoned blacksmith shop from the prison yard down to some property that Mr. Allen owns at the end of Sixth Street."

"Huh," Hercules replied, looking down at the bowl into which he was cracking the eggs with one hand. "You said today. Are they moving the building today?"

"That's what I'm trying to tell you — they doing it now!" Oney sat up, excited. "If you had stepped outside this morning you'd have heard the noise clear to here." She lowered her voice to a whisper that only Hercules could hear. "I managed to get away from Lady Washington for a moment and nip out to see the men lifting the building onto some rolling logs. Mr. Dexter is there to lead the horses."

The free coachman, Oronoko Dexter, was one of the most trusted horsemen in the city. Along with Absalom Jones and Reverend Allen, he had started the Free African Society to help those who were recently liberated. Hercules had seen his share of these newly freed Negroes around town, wandering like specters unable to fend for themselves without the master's yoke around their necks. They reminded Hercules of a dog that had been tied too long in one place — even when the rope was cut, the dog didn't know better than to stay put.

Hercules glanced toward the kitchen door where Nate had stepped around Richmond, carrying the last small potatoes and carrots from the garden, and hesitated a moment before forcing himself to turn toward his son.

"Fetch some milk from the larder and scald it in a small pan, Richmond."

While Richmond rushed to do the task, Nate scrubbed the vegetables before peeling them with sure, careful strokes. Hercules caught Richmond scowling in Nate's direction while he aggressively stirred the heating milk so a little slopped over the edge of the pan. If the other boy marked the look, he didn't show it. Richmond was forever jealous of the interest his father took in Nate — Hercules knew that — but Nate had abilities where Richmond did not.

Still, Hercules was bound and determined to get his son to learn. If he didn't, where would the boy wind up? Back in the fields for sure. The kitchen, hot as it usually was, was far better than working morning to night bending, picking, plowing so the dirt worked its way deep into your skin and even your palms became dusky brown like the rest of you. And all the while an overseer was eager to use the whip to skin your flesh right off no matter what the General said because the General wasn't there to see it, was he?

No. He had to do everything he could to keep his son in this house.

Hercules grated some nutmeg into the eggs, added the sugar, then mixed it powerfully with a birch whisk. "How far have they got?" he said to Oney.

"It's taking a long time, to be sure," she said. "I'd be surprised if they make it before sundown."

"Hmmm."

They worked in silence for a few minutes, Hercules whipping his concoction until it started to swell and take on a paler yellow hue. Richmond approached with a long-handled metal pitcher in which he had heated the milk.

"Pour the milk in by small measures," he directed the boy. "Make the stream thin as you can, thin as a needle."

Richmond gripped the pitcher handle with both hands and began to turn the pitcher forward. His hands shook.

"Steady, son," said Hercules, laying a hand on Richmond's shoulder. "Don't grip so hard. You're not pulling back an ox by the horns. Watch."

Hercules moved his hand to Richmond's wrist and gently angled it forward to pour a thin stream of the hot milk into the bowl while he continued to whisk his eggs. "Now, you continue like that until I say stop."

Richmond tried to slowly pour, but then he faltered. Hot milk slopped over the pan and splashed into the bowl, sending its contents flying high.

"Take care!" exploded Hercules, grabbing Richmond's wrist and forcing it back. Richmond looked at his father, stricken, then his face contorted with anger. He moved forward again with the pitcher, but Hercules put his hand up.

"Leave it," he said harshly.

"I can do it now," said the boy, trying to raise the pitcher again.

"No, you won't," said his father. "You've ruined it. Just go and get me more eggs."

Richmond slammed the pan down and stormed off. Everyone looked down at their tasks as he came back from the larder, thrusting the eggs out at his father.

Hercules gave him a hard stare before taking the eggs and once again began whipping them with nutmeg.

"Go heat me more milk," he said.

When the milk was ready, Richmond again stepped forward, ready to pour.

"Set it down there," Hercules said without looking up. "Nate, come here, please."

His son didn't move as the other boy moved forward. Hercules had to swallow his exasperation. "Go on and finish husking that corn," he told Richmond. "You can start grinding it after you've picked out all the kernels."

Richmond opened his mouth to argue, but Hercules ignored him and turned to Nate.

"Now, son," he said. "I want you to pour that milk slowly and carefully into this bowl while I whisk. Did you see how I did it before?"

"Yes, sir," said Nate, glancing at Richmond's back as he stormed away.

"Let's go then," said Hercules, taking up his whisk.

Nate held the handle of the pitcher and took a deep breath before lifting it to pour out the milk. He angled the pot so slightly that hardly any milk came out.

"A little more, boy, you're doing fine," said Hercules. "Just be easy."

Nate angled the pitcher a little more. Everyone in the kitchen stopped mid-chore to watch as Hercules moved his whisk so fast it was just a blur.

"Good," Hercules finally said, and Nate eased up the pitcher. "Give the rest of that to Mr. Julien for his potato cake and then boil those potatoes you peeled for him too. Mind you salt the water properly, Nate."

"Yes, sir," Nate said, returning to Hercules's side.

"How salty then?" asked Hercules as he opened the crock containing the cornmeal and peered inside.

"Salty like the sea — Chef," said the boy, looking at him nervously. A small smile that started at the bow of Hercules's lips flowed out to the corners of his mouth.

"Just so — salty like the sea. Very good, son."

Hercules took up a scoop and started to dip into the bowl of meal that Richmond had brought earlier, then barked, "Richmond! This is corn flour — I wanted meal!" The boy immediately set his corn aside and stood up to head back into the larder. "No," said Hercules, not trying to hide his exasperation. "Margaret will do it."

Margaret rose quickly and set her pan of peas on her stool.

"Yes, sir," she said, heading toward the larder. She tried to catch Nate's eye when she came out with the cornmeal, but he was busy with the potatoes.

Hercules poured cornmeal into the mixture in his bowl, then took up his spoon and began to stir the whole thing in smooth, even strokes.

"Now, girl, I need you to grease that crock," he said, nodding at the mold she had brought him earlier. She brought a small piece of lard from the larder.

Hercules scooped up the ham bits he had scraped from the bone, added them to his pudding, then sprinkled in some dried thyme he had plucked from the string of herbs hanging on the wall behind him. When Margaret finished greasing the pudding pan, he poured the corn mixture inside it, covered it snugly, then set it in a large footed Dutch oven he half filled with water. He squatted to nestle the heavy cast iron pot in the embers of the fire and then stood, brushing ashes from his apron.

Oney stood too, hoisting the cast iron pan with the shawl in both hands and heading out toward the laundry building.

The kitchen settled back into a comfortable silence with everyone doing their own tasks. Hercules went into the cellar and came back with a small barrel that he set down on the worktable with a heavy thump.

"Mr. Julien, should Mr. Fraunces come down, please tell him that I've brought up the Madeira he asked for."

The Frenchman nodded from the hearth, where he now squatted turning the spits of the four tin roasting ovens lined up there, each holding two or three squab he had dressed and stuffed earlier in the day. Between turning the spits, he carefully fried the potato cakes he had made from the leftover scalded milk and Nate's potatoes.

Hercules untied his apron and placed it neatly over a chair near the door, then gave Richmond a quick rat-a-tat on the head as he passed him into the garden. He did not offer where he might be going, nor did anyone dare ask.

Outside, the waning sun cast a deep orange glow over the street. The red brick of the roads and the buildings that dotted Sixth Street glowed like irons in the fire, belying the chill wind that whipped down the avenue. Beyond Sixth the city opened up to wider country. The cold air raced over the flatlands and quickly cooled Hercules's skin, still sweat-soaked from the heat of the kitchen, but he didn't mind. Being away from the house was worth any discomfort of weather.

He walked past the State House and Congress Hall at the corner of Walnut, with the prison yard just across the street to the south. The crowd had gathered maybe a block and a half beyond the far end of the prison yard, barely moving as the ramshackle old blacksmith shop inched along on its rollers toward Reverend Allen's property at the furthest end of the street. A team of ten massive horses patiently walked a few steps then halted, led by Oronoko Dexter, who stood in front of them and coaxed them along. He held his hand aloft as he walked backward, a warning to the other coachmen who walked alongside the team at regular paces, whips in hand, ready to force them along.

Eyeing the crowd, Hercules wished he had had the time to grab his fine coat from the attic quarters he shared with Richmond and Nate — not for the warmth but for the appearance of the thing. It was a fine cutaway coat as good as — nay, better — than any worn by the free black men here. But there was no call for him to be in the upper quarters in the shank of the day; it was too risky to even attempt it. Better to slip out of the kitchen here and there and return quickly, even in his shirtsleeves. There was time enough of an evening to set out for the city's pleasures once every last morsel was plated and brought into the dining room by the footmen. Blacks and whites gathered to watch the spectacle. Some young gentleman jeered from the second-floor window of a fine house along the route, trying to spook the horses. Hercules spied Bess, the pickpocket, taking advantage of the chaos, weaving in and out of the crowd like a confused old woman. She'd earn a good take today.

Hercules passed close to the wall and nearly stepped on a pile of stench-filled rags. The rags shuffled and groaned near his foot. Old Ben lifted his head as if he were looking around even though there were just holes in his eye sockets.

"Alms? Alms?" he lisped automatically,

running his tongue around his toothless gums and holding out his hand.

Hercules reached into his purse and pulled out a coin to press into the old man's hand. He knew his story. Blinded by his master for trying to run away, and when he couldn't see to work, the man had pulled every tooth in Old Ben's head to sell to the dentist who made dentures for rich white folk.

Old Ben still tried to escape, once, twice, but blind as he was, he never got far, and each time the beatings crippled him worse. In the end, the master used him for stud on the slave women he owned, to increase their numbers and his profit. When Ben had gotten too old for that, he'd turned him into the street.

Hercules supposed that made the man now free — at least according to the abolition law — but what good was freedom when all he could do was beg and hope not to be robbed or abused for the amusement of drunks pouring out of the taverns that choked every block?

"Why have you left your corner, Ben?" Hercules asked. Normally the old man sheltered in the garden wall where the Reverend Allen lived.

"Is that the General's cook?" said Ben,

putting his head back and sniffing the air.

"None other," said Hercules. "But, tell me, why have you moved?"

"Thought I smelled that bay rum off you," Ben chuckled. "Mighty fancy you are . . ."

"Ben, do you want me to take you back?"

"Heh? No, son, I came here hoping the crowds will be generous." He groped under his mass of rags and brought out a little tin cup and shook it. "Not too much yet, though . . ." His voice trailed off.

"Can you get back on your own?"

Now Old Ben lowered his head. "Get back . . ." he mumbled.

"Miss Ollie done said the babe was still-born but I reckon maybe massa already eat him by the time I got back . . ." Old Ben was gone into some mad recess of his mind. Hercules straightened and pushed down the fury that rose in his gullet, seeing the Bens of the world. If he gave voice or form to his anger he'd be raging every minute of his life, there were that many like the old man in the streets of Philadelphia, battered and used until they were nothing more than a husk.

As bad off as they were, Hercules was sure there those who'd had their share of worse because that's how the whites were — they'd get all they could from you until there was no more. If there was a market for your very blood, bones, and skin after you were gone, they'd take that too, he thought grimly. Since there wasn't, you'd just as likely become like Old Ben, a pile of rags waiting to die and be flung in some unmarked pit in the Negro Burial Ground.

His clamped his jaw down tight so his mouth was a hard line as he moved away from Ben and walked ahead toward the front of the crowd, where the Reverend Allen stood to one side of the team. He was talking to someone Hercules presumed was a free woman. He spent enough time at the tailor's for his own clothes to know fashion, and this lady's clothes were plain but well made in the English style and very clean. She wore a dark blue silk bonnet, rather than a head kerchief, and matching slippers. Both the bonnet and the slippers were embroidered with silver thread in a simple design. The five-button kid gloves and the lace ruffles at her elbows and on her petticoat were not numerous, but were enough to tell him she was a person of at least comfortable means.

She stopped mid-sentence as Hercules walked up and smiled politely. Reverend Allen, his head inclined to hear what the lady was saying, also looked over to him and a smile broke across his face.

"Ah, Master Hercules!" he said, extending his hand.

"Reverend," Hercules said warmly, taking the hand into his own.

"And may I introduce you to Mrs. Harris?" Allen said, turning slightly to indicate the lady. "Mrs. Harris, this is General Washington's cook — Master Hercules."

Mrs. Harris offered her hand and Hercules bent over it politely.

"What brings you out today?" inquired Reverend Allen. The rest of his question was left unsaid. Allen, like everyone, knew that a black person in Washington's house was an enslaved person who was not strictly free to come and go except upon the General's business.

"Why, this!" Hercules said, choosing to ignore their unspoken question and instead sweeping his arm expansively across the scene beside them.

"It is quite something, is it not, Master Hercules?" Mrs. Harris said, smiling. "I myself have been drawn away from my work to come and look."

"Your work, madam?" Hercules asked. She was probably a milliner or a seamstress, which would explain the clothes.

"I am a school teacher," she said.

50

"Mrs. Harris has a school in Cherry Street," Reverend Allen explained, answering the question in Hercules's raised eyebrows. "She teaches our brothers and sisters their letters and arithmetics."

"Other things too," said Mrs. Harris, her eyes shining. "History and Latin. Natural sciences, even. Of course, I leave the religious education to you, Mr. Allen."

The minister smiled. "The Lord's army needs many soldiers, Mrs. Harris. God wants us all to teach the good word."

"Whom do you teach, Mrs. Harris?" asked Hercules, who had never met a black schoolteacher, much less a woman. Shopkeepers, mariners, artists even — but a schoolteacher? There had been the white Quaker, Anthony Benezet, who taught slaves and free people of color, but he died back in '87. There was the Association for Free Instruction that held meetings Sunday afternoons, but those were run by whites also.

"Anyone who cares to learn, sir," she said. "Young, old, free, or . . ." She paused a moment and looked at him carefully. "Or not."

"Whoa! Steady!" Oronoko Dexter called out toward the rear flank of the team. One of the horses had gotten spooked and tried to rear up after a man in a window dropped a white kerchief so that it fluttered before the animal's eyes. Dexter gestured to a younger man walking alongside the third horse to come up to the front and put his hand on the bridle of the blue roan he had been leading, before he himself walked toward the back to soothe the nervous horse. Reverend Allen excused himself and headed toward the commotion.

"We hold classes every day, just as they do in the white schools," Mrs. Harris continued, drawing Hercules's attention back from the scene.

"Quite an undertaking, I imagine, madam," he said.

"I would call it more of a mission," she said, meeting his eyes.

Hercules smiled at the prim lady and bowed slightly. "And no doubt one at which you excel," he said. There was something disturbing in the way she eyed him, like a fresh joint of meat. "If I may beg your leave, Mrs. Harris — I must, ah — I must get back. Will you please give the Reverend my apologies for running off?"

Mrs. Harris inclined her head. "Certainly, Master Hercules," she said.

As he turned away to head down the street he heard the teacher call behind him, "Do come to Cherry Street some time! Look for the gray clapboard building in the alley."

The General's cook slipped down the narrow alley behind the stables at the rear of the presidential mansion. The orange that had set the streets aglow less than an hour before had faded into a pale indigo that bathed the white bricks of the stables a gentle lavender. From within the stables he could hear a series of snorts followed by the murmurs of Austin, the coachman. Just as he walked through the gate and around the corner, the large white head of the president's favorite horse, Prescott, poked his head over a stall door. He tossed his head toward the breeze and his black nostrils flared as he caught the scent of Hercules. The blue twilight turned his white coat silvery-gray.

Hercules stepped toward the horse and put his hand on its nose. "There boy," he said in his deep, buttery voice. "I don't have anything for you now." Inside the stall, Austin was brushing down the animal.

"He up there?" Hercules asked, nodding to the president's study on the second floor.

"Yep, none too happy neither," said Austin without turning from his work. "Met Mr. Adams as he was riding in and was obliged to see him upstairs."

Prescott nudged Hercules's hand, now lying still on his nose. More catlike than horse, he was. He absentmindedly began to rub the horse's nose again, his thoughts dwelling on the odd Mrs. Harris before they settled on the General. If he was in with company he might have sent to the kitchen for refreshment. He hoped that Mr. Julien or even Nate had been free to see to it without calling attention to his absence.

"Oney told me about the Reverend Allen's church. You been over to see it?" said Austin, standing straight now to brush Prescott's mane. Lighter skinned than even his sister Oney, Austin cut a fine figure decked out in his livery in the coachman's seat or standing on the running board of the presidential coach. Where Oney could be sharp and sassy, Austin was always quiet and pleasant.

"Yep, they're moving slow. Won't make it before sundown but they'll make it," Hercules said, giving the horse a final pat on the nose.

"Black Sam were looking for you," said Austin, bending forward again to brush out Prescott's rear flank. "Near kicked a fuss when he found you weren't in the scullery."

"Did he now?" Hercules said. He met Austin's eyes calmly but his heart pounded a bit. Samuel Fraunces was no ally. Light-skinned and free, it was like he sometimes forgot that he wasn't actually white and that he certainly wasn't a Washington.

"Right then," said Hercules giving Prescott a final pat between the ears. "Evening, Austin."

"Evening, Hercules," said Austin going back to currying the horse.

Hercules stepped through the kitchen door and tied on his apron, relieved that Fraunces hadn't caught him walking in. He opened the Dutch oven and removed the crock with the corn pudding. It was golden and even. Later, after unmolding it, he would sprinkle some fine orange peel over it.

Samuel Fraunces came into the kitchen carrying a tray of used tea things and a small plate with one or two Shrewsbury biscuits just as Hercules returned to his worktable.

". . . knows better than to stop in on a Friday evening." Fraunces was muttering to himself and shaking his head. "Ate near a dozen biscuits too."

He set the tray down on the table. "Where were you?" he snapped.

"Evening to you too, Black Sam," Hercules answered. Nothing would make

Fraunces angrier than the nickname that reminded him of his race. Fraunces glared at him before stepping outside to the cellar door and calling down.

"You there, Margaret, come and wash these things."

Hercules looked at him as he returned. Small and slight, the steward was always impeccably dressed. From the fashionably styled silver wig to the buckles on his shoes, not a thread was ever out of place. It was the only thing that Hercules appreciated about him.

"I've sent Nate to the docks to see if the ship from Alexandria might have arrived," Fraunces said curtly. "Richmond is helping arrange the dining room for the party."

Hercules didn't respond. He hoped that, for once, his son did his work well and didn't give Fraunces reason to call him out. Richmond's place here was far from secure — a fact that worried him daily because he knew the boy could be maddeningly inept. With these thoughts on his mind, he went into the larder and began bringing out platter after platter. There was the ham he had sliced so thinly and stuffed eggs they had prepared that morning. Between trips he grabbed one of the last biscuits from the plate. The crumbly shortbread melted easily in his mouth, leaving behind the pleasant tinge of caraway that flavored them.

"Those are not for you," said Fraunces sharply.

Hercules paused midway to the larder and turned to face Fraunces. He popped the remains of the biscuit in his mouth and chewed slowly. When he was done he wiped his mouth with the back of his hand — a rough gesture he would normally never affect — so Fraunces would know that he meant it as a challenge.

Hercules was well aware that the General favored him — that had become clear to all when Fraunces wanted to bring his own cook into the President's House. He narrowed his eyes as he remembered the day. The General had actually come down to the kitchen to see how he was settling in, which had irked Fraunces something awful. After the steward had bowed deeply, he had asked the president for a word.

"Sir — I don't believe he will do," Fraunces had said in a low voice, as if to make sure that Hercules, who was busy pretending to examine the cookware, would not hear.

Washington had only raised his eyebrows in his customary way, waiting for Fraunces to go on.

"He is not versed in the French ways . . ."

"Then teach him," Washington had answered curtly.

"I am not at all sure he can be made to learn," Fraunces had answered, straightening proudly. "I've worked with the best trained cooks in the country and —"

"And I've eaten in more houses and taverns in the country than I ever cared to — no one yet has answered as well as my cook," said the president. "No one." With the last he'd given Fraunces the withering look he gave anyone who contradicted him.

"You will make do with Hercules," said Washington, walking around the steward, who inclined his head and bowed — not so deeply this time.

"You traveled well from Virginia?" Washington had asked, approaching Hercules.

"Yes, General, thank you, sir," he'd answered, politely, but without any hint of the deference he knew Fraunces wanted him to show.

"Good, good," Washington had said. "I've been missing your hoecakes. I'd like them for breakfast tomorrow."

"My pleasure, sir," said Hercules. Fraunces stood to the side and fumed, the thoughts plain on his face.

The rest of the kitchen staff, the scullions

and the day workers, stood by agape. Washington hadn't even acknowledged they were there.

"Good man," said Washington, smiling in his tight-lipped way. "Fraunces," he said, the smile vanishing as he acknowledged the steward and left the kitchen.

Later, when the General left, Fraunces had sidled up Hercules's side and hissed at him about who did Hercules think he was conversing with the General as if they were two gentlemen in a parlor instead of him just a nigra slave? Why didn't Hercules have the sense to duck his head or look at the floor?

"The General may not show an inclination to correct your ways but I will — mark me," Fraunces had said in a growl. Hercules knew better than to respond and give Fraunces cause to complain to the General. It was smarter to keep his own counsel because Hercules knew that the value of his cooking was clear enough to the president. Clear enough to garner him favors and freedoms — and keep him safe from any punishment Fraunces might have for him.

"Well," said Fraunces, turning away from Hercules now. "I'll send the boys down for the platters." There was little he could do. He could hardly complain to the president about such a little matter. Besides, they both knew that it had been a long while since General Washington had ordered any slave whipped or sold off as punishment — not even down at the Virginia farm.

Hercules continued onto the larder, saying over his shoulder, "There are some Chelsea buns, made fresh today. I've done them smaller than usual so the ladies might eat them in two bites." Emerging, Hercules held out the small cinnamon raisin buns, arranged on a delicate porcelain cake plate, for Fraunces's review. Submitting something for his approval was the surest way to get back into his good graces.

"Hmmm," the steward said approvingly. "Very pretty indeed. I'm sure they will be quite well received. I'll take them up myself."

Hercules nodded and put the plate on the smaller table near the door to the passage into the main house before turning his attention to carving the squab that Mr. Julien had left cooling on the bench.

CHAPTER 3

The lemony aroma of thyme always put Hercules in good spirits. It smelled fresh and clean, like the limewater and bay rum he used to perfume his going-out clothes. He hummed a little as he gathered the delicate stems into a bouquet along with some sprigs of juniper, the powdery blue berries still clinging to the thin branches. He tied the little bundle with a soft sprig of marjoram and arranged it with four others at the head of the platter, where he had butterflied a large poached salmon. He stood back and studied it.

"Nate!" he called out so suddenly that the scullion jumped from where he was washing down the chopping block with ash and lye.

"Chef?" he said, stepping forward, the rag dangling from his hand.

"Get me a bottle of pickled lemons — you'll find them on the back shelf of the larder. Third shelf from top, four jars in."

Nate ran to his task and Hercules turned to a tray of standing pork pies. He opened the pastry lid of one and examined the contents, then closed and opened it again. Walking to his chopping board where minced herbs lay, he placed a pinch upon the meat filling of each pie and then grated some nutmeg on top.

He took a bottle of cooking brandy from Fraunces's cupboard as Nate came back with the jar.

"Ah good," said Hercules in his rumbling voice without looking at the boy. "Finish with the chopping board, then take out three of those lemons and slice them thinly on the round."

Nate sluiced water over the cutting block and patted it dry before slicing the lemons on it. Hercules returned to the pork pies and carefully began adding the merest amount of brandy.

Nate watched him, glancing up as much as he could from slicing the lemons.

"Best mind what you're about rather than minding me," said Hercules, bent over his pies. Again, the young servant jumped. Soon enough he'd learn that Hercules made it his business to know everything that went on in the kitchen even when he didn't seem to be looking. Around them the kitchen buzzed with activity.

Nate put his head down and continued with the lemons. When he finished he brought them in a bowl to Hercules, who was bending down over the fire, holding a long handle attached to a small iron plate. When it was good and hot, he turned back to the pork pies and held the burning hot salamander over their open mouths until the layer of fat began to bubble and fry the herbs, their smell filling the kitchen. The brandy briefly caught flame and released its aroma into the air. When he was done, Hercules hung the salamander on its hook next to the hearth and nestled the pastry lids back on the pies before looking in Nate's bowl.

"Did you taste them?" asked the head cook, looking the boy in the eye.

"Taste them, sir?" Nate looked around nervously to see if anyone had heard. If they had, they gave no sign, but as Hercules followed Nate's gaze around the room he caught Margaret's eyes, widened in surprise.

"Yes," said Hercules, his voice beginning to rise. *Taste them.* He spoke as if Nate were a dullard. The boy had promise of being an excellent cook if only he learned to use all his wits. "If you don't taste them first, how do we know they've not gone off?" he continued, knowing that, as a slave, it would never occur to Nate to eat the General's food. "Would you serve spoilt food to the General?"

"N-no, sir," stammered Nate. He gingerly reached into the bowl and pinched out a thin slice of lemon. Just as he was about to place it in his mouth, Hercules grasped his wrist.

"No."

Nate looked at him, his mouth halfway open, his eyes nervous.

"Sir?"

"Look at it first. Hold it to the light. Do you see blemishes? Marks?"

Nate did as he was told. The lemon slice was the palest yellow and translucent. He shook his head.

"Good, now try it."

Nate cautiously took a bite.

"It seems fine, sir."

"Fine or good?" said Hercules, swallowing an agitated sigh.

Nate thought about this for a minute.

"It's good. It's salty and sour, pickled through, as it should be. It will be good to cut the grease of a fish like that one with so much fat to it."

"Now watch me," Hercules said, placing a

lemon slice next to the fish. He placed another and another, overlapping them in a perfect fan before he stopped a quarter of the way down the plate. "Now, you continue," he said, wiping his hands on his apron. "And mind, hold up every one of those slices to the light before setting it down."

Nate, fingers shaking, attempted to copy what he had done. Hercules stood next to him, watching.

"Slower, boy, go slower. Do it right, not fast."

Nate slowed down, bending closer to the fish, arranging the slices just so.

"Good," said Hercules and went to attend to another task. The boy was a quick study. Given enough time, he could command a kitchen himself. Once, Nate glanced over his shoulder at Margaret, who had stopped polishing the copper pots and stood absorbed in his progress with the lemon slices. Margaret was biting her lower lip. Hercules still wasn't sure about her — she was obedient enough but, he feared, something of a half-wit.

Just then, the steward came in with his usual rush and scurry. He was wearing the General's livery and his wig had been freshly powdered.

"How are the preparations proceeding, cook?" he asked.

"As always, Sam," said Hercules, without looking up. He was working with Mr. Julien to lay mutton chops on a large charger while the Frenchman ladled sauce over each, then sprinkling them with currants and fresh herbs.

Samuel Fraunces sighed in exasperation. "And what might *that* mean, Uncle Harkless?"

The kitchen became quiet. The Washington family often called Hercules "Uncle Harkless." It was a term of endearment for them, and of course he had to smile and bear it, but the name was too demeaning for him to tolerate from anyone else. The kitchen servants had started to call him Chef following the lead of Mr. Julien, and the day servants knew enough to call him Mr. Hercules or sir, at least, even though many of them resented giving that particular kind of courtesy to a Negro.

And, of course, Fraunces knew — especially Fraunces knew. Just a week ago a footman told Hercules that the General had coldly chided a latecomer to one of his receptions, "Sir, we are too punctual for you. I have a cook who never asks whether the company has come, but whether the hour has come."

Hercules finished the chops, wiped the rim of the platter, and nodded to Mr. Julien.

"Never to worry, Mr. Fraunces," he said smoothly, deliberately smiling so his white teeth flashed. His kept his eyes hard and he imagined himself as a fox moving in for a chicken's throat. "Uncle knows what he's about and the General knows what Uncle's about too."

Fraunces narrowed his eyes as if he were weighing how to respond to the challenge.

"And so it would seem that you do," Fraunces finally answered, even-toned. "Thank you for apprising me of your progress. Carry on."

Fraunces headed for the cellars, snapping his fingers at Nate and Richmond and gesturing for them to help bring up some casks of wine and Madeira, his face worried and drawn.

No one looked up during this exchange — not so as they could be caught at it anyway — but they knew who had won the battle. The steward's words fooled no one, but it was a neat turn at saving face.

Hercules moved over to the table lined with dishes for the footmen to serve course by course. It was important not to let

Fraunces or the others see his fury. Keep your cards close was his motto. He didn't mean to be baited into showing his hand.

The soup tureens sat ready to be filled, followed by the mutton and another platter of partridges wrapped in lard and roasted. Plates of fish were next: the salmon that Nate had finished decorating with lemon slices, some boiled salt cod with potatoes, dressed sturgeon, and three platters of fat oysters — the General's favorite. Several fruit pies, a pumpkin pudding, and fruit jellies rounded out the dessert.

Entertaining days had everyone in a state of high anxiety. The entire household was well aware of how much the General disliked social events. Washington was not a man for small talk and he rarely made or allowed toasts. They'd all heard that it wasn't uncommon, by the end of a meal, to find him tapping his fork against the table to some drumbeat in his own head.

While the household ran to and fro, as if movement and purpose could smother the president's agitation like a blanket over a fire, only Hercules remained calm, attending his dishes in measured paces that hardly seemed fast enough to produce the sheer volume of food that overfilled the table by midafternoon.

Footsteps echoed in the passageway from the house and then the footmen appeared in the kitchen. Fraunces took his place by the table. Each footman stepped up and held out his white-gloved hands for the dishes that the steward placed carefully into them. Here in Philadelphia where folks did not hold with slavery, the servers were most always white, or light-skinned enough to pass for white. Each of the tall men, outfitted smartly in the white and red Washington livery, towered over Hercules, but they knew to keep their decorum in his kitchen. Down to a man, none smiled or looked anywhere but straight ahead, turning quickly with their platters to follow Fraunces's barked orders.

When Fraunces had followed the footmen out with the first courses, Hercules unbuttoned his apron and pulled the kerchief off his head. His time was his own now, and he meant to make best use of it. Walking over to the bench by the kitchen door, he took his waistcoat from the peg, along with the cockade hat and cane that sat on the low shelf nearby. Lifting a basket he had prepared earlier and covered with a clean cloth, he turned smartly back to the kitchen staff and raised his hat to them before placing it carefully on his head.

"Ladies, gentlemen," he said, without any hint of irony. "I bid you good evening."

CHAPTER 4

The federal city into which Hercules emerged that midafternoon was noise-filled and laden with aromas that tickled and tormented the nose — just as at any hour of day. Philadelphia didn't mark time like other towns. What was dinner for some was breakfast for others, and the city buzzed with a low and constant hum like a hive. Hercules no longer jumped as he once had at the bursts of sudden sound as carriages, dray carts, and teamsters clogged the streets, their drivers shouting greetings or, more often, curses at one another.

Closer to the docks, barrels rumbled down wooden planks to crash into waiting carts. The noise of public minstrels mixed with hogs snorting and squealing as they rooted freely in the gutters, and the blacksmiths' constant striking of metal on metal rose above it all like a steady backbeat to the insane melody of the city. Hercules tapped his cane regularly to the noise as he walked east toward Front Street, the rough-and-tumble music of the place filling his head and his lungs.

When he had first arrived here three years ago, he had longed for the quiet Virginia countryside and the tamer, more predictable movements of Alexandria. Now the longing inched into his chest less and less in this place where it was hard to find men and women permanently hunched from a life in the fields. He loved this city where a man couldn't be whipped and chained like a horse and he could stand up and stretch in the sun with no one to say a word about it.

Philadelphia lured him like a high-class lady of pleasure inching down her bodice for him to get a better peek at the edges of a pink nipple, or raising her skirt just enough for a flash of ankle. Whenever he thought he had become accustomed to its delights, the way you could get used to the same woman, Philadelphia had a new parlor trick sewn into the stays of its encircling corset, waiting to be revealed at the right moment, lest he lose his ardor. Philadelphia wasn't going to let Hercules go — even when the General meant to return home for good — of that he was sure. And he didn't want her to.

There was nothing that couldn't be bought or had or tasted or borrowed in Philadelphia, and Hercules knew just where the best wares were found. There was no pressing himself against walls to let white gentlemen pass, there was no averting his eyes from the white ladies in their finery. He took up as much room as he cared to on the brick walks that bisected the city, tapping his cane in pace with his step and tipping his hat to whomever he chose, leaving it squarely on his head just as often too.

As Hercules moved down Lombard Street toward the byways nearest the docks, the press of people seemed to double. In Philadelphia, free people of color far outnumbered slaves, and at every turn of his head, Hercules saw more and more of those who looked like him but lived in a different world. Black children played in the roadways, often just missing a cart's wheels as they darted in and around the press of people and beasts. The washing lines were strung three deep in the small yards behind homes that bulged with many times their intended number as black families crowded together, generation upon generation, sometimes with no blood between them. Here and there women squatted in their kitchen gardens, now meager as the ground properly froze, pulling from it what they could for the evening meal as the stench of the privies used by a score of dwellers washed over them and into the street.

He knew their type, huddled together in the shelter of each other's company. The sea of public sentiment was always against them. A simple veering off-course, a misstep or misinterpreted look, might mean arrest and twenty-eight years of indenture for their bond.

As a man bound to the president, Hercules was untouchable by any other white man in the city — or in the nation, come to that. Oddly, it made him feel freer. The General gave him rein to roam unhindered, taken up as he was with his own daily affairs. As long as a better-than-fine meal was on the dining board, as long as Hercules was at his worktable in the day and under his roof at night, behind lock and key, Washington did not keep track of his whereabouts.

Moving about as he did gave him access to a world filled with any number of people, white, African, free, and enslaved, who eagerly shared bits of gossip. Of course, those who reported *to* him could report *on* him too. A well-placed gift to seal the bonds of loyalty was never amiss. A sweet-cake here or a choice joint of meat there went far among those who had too little or only just enough. These little tidbits of information were beyond value in keeping him aware of what went on outside the house — and sometimes inside as well — like the fact that Fraunces was looking to open a tavern like the one he'd had in New York.

Hercules stood fast in the roadway and tapped his cane thoughtfully on the ground. Black Sam didn't know that Hercules was aware of his plans. The General himself probably didn't know, and if Sam Fraunces had his way it would stay that way. The General didn't do well with changes to the household, and while he couldn't stop Fraunces from leaving he'd surely put upon every persuasion to entice him to stay if plans were not already well laid and underway. Washington was not one to try to reverse the course of a thing already done.

How, then, to ensure that Fraunces's plans went along smoothly so Hercules could be free of the interfering steward? He pondered this, blocking the pathway. A cordwainer cursed as he shoved his way past, his dyestained hands grasping a roll of raw leather on his shoulder, leaving the raw stink of tanning in his wake.

Untroubled, Hercules took up his pace. In

the distance, the State House bell burbled its tinny toll for the half hour. He needed to press on.

His destination was more than ten blocks yonder at Stampers Alley where it met Third Street. Witcher's boardinghouse, one of the few remaining clapboard buildings in the district.

Clearly it had once belonged to a prosperous man, but Mrs. Witcher divided the front rooms into guest bedrooms, leaving only one common room to the front and the wide kitchen in the back. Hercules knew the cook there — a freedwoman called Sally — and she obligingly turned a blind eye whenever he came in and made for the back stairs that led up to the small rear bedroom where French Thelma lodged.

Leaning over the half-opened Dutch door, he saw Sally at the opposite end of the kitchen skimming the cream from a milk pan. He tapped delicately on the doorjamb with the tip of his walking stick and she looked in his direction. With a swift rise of her eyes, she indicated that Thelma was in her room upstairs, and then her eyes darted toward the front of the house to let him know that Mrs. Witcher was at home as well. He would have to be fast. Even the president wouldn't be able to protect him

— or want to — if he were caught in a boardinghouse seeing a "white" woman in her private chamber.

Reaching into his basket, he drew out a small cone of fine sugar wrapped in its indigo paper and then quickly unlatched the door. He stepped in and crossed to where Sally's cloak was hooked on the wall, her own market basket sitting on the bench beneath. He placed the sugar in the basket, then entered the narrow stair — payment for her silence and her lookout.

As low as the stairwell ceiling was, Hercules still barely had to bend his head. Through the wall he could hear Mrs. Witcher at the front speaking to some ladies of the "better sort."

The hour of the day meant that most of the lodgers would be about their afternoon business, taking advantage of the waning light before hurrying to be indoors for the night. Supper would not be served until at least eight or nine, if it ever was in such a place. Most of the guests would probably go out to one of the middling taverns to take the light evening meal.

When he reached the landing, the hallway was blessedly empty. He walked quickly to the small door under the gambrel eave of the house and tapped on it with the pads of his fingers.

He opened the door a slight crack, eased himself inside, and strode over to where Thelma stood by the small shuttered window, a piece of artist's charcoal loosely held between her fingers. The room was small enough to cross in five or six steps, less if a man had a long stride. He looked down at the paper on the table, where she had drawn the heads and shoulders of a variety of people — wealthy, poor, dusky, and pale. There were even some Indians, their faces slashed with their tribal marks, and some whose faces had been maimed, perhaps by plague.

"You are making yourself as dark as I with this black coal," he said, picking up the delicate hand and kissing where the stick had stained her pale skin.

Thelma only smiled and drew her hand away.

Hercules set down the basket on a small square of free space on the table.

Thelma was one of the hundreds of refugees who were flooding the federal city from France and its blood-soaked revolution and from Saint-Domingue after the slave uprising. Her skin was only a bit darker than ivory and her reddish-brown hair held in tight long curls. She, like her mother, was the property of her slaver father, who had been killed in L'Ouverture's rebellion back in '91. While he had lived, he'd allowed his pretty half-breed daughter more finery and attention than any of the other slaves, and she received the hand-me-downs of his legitimate white children. She'd been allowed to linger in the schoolroom up at the big house, and had learned to read and draw and even speak English with her half siblings' private tutors.

After the slaves had taken over the island, her mother, fearing for Thelma's life given her near-white looks, gathered the coins she had saved over decades and bought the girl passage on a ship to Philadelphia. And so she came to be at Witcher's, which was both respectable and affordable, with a proprietress who could tell a fine gown and a quality upbringing when she saw it. Luckily for Thelma, Mrs. Witcher wasn't one of those worldly Philadelphians who was able to pick out those telltale signs that marked Thelma as a mulatto rather than a white woman.

Thelma tutored the lady's two daughters in French and classics, and even managed to obtain a few students among social-climbing white merchants who chose not to examine her too closely. She also earned a secret living among the tiny, elite class of free Negroes in town, including the children of the exceedingly rich confectioner Charles Sang, at whose home Hercules had met her last June.

Hercules had been to Sang's to order three of the beautiful swan centerpieces the candy maker carved from sugarloaf. They were to decorate the dessert table at the season's last levee before the Washingtons returned to Virginia for the summer.

Upon taking his leave, he noticed the girl coming from the front door of the house next to the shop. She had a look not unlike his friend James, slave to Jefferson, whose wavy black hair had a hard curl and his fine straight nose a delicate flair. His skin, while fair, browned like a nicely done roast chicken in the summer sun, making his green eyes appear all the paler. Like James, the young lady's shiny curls fell tightly on her shoulder and the gentle, pretty swell of her lips belied her heritage. Hercules knew she was not white.

"A fine day, is it not?" he said, falling into step beside her.

Instead of walking along faster or admonishing him for being so brazen, the girl had surprisingly stopped and turned to face him, her eyes sweeping from the top of his head to his boots. She looked for what seemed a longer time than was strictly appropriate before she said in her heavy French accent, "Who are you?"

Hercules smiled slowly then and made a deep bow since he had no hat to doff, his hair wrapped tightly in the scarf he wore while cooking.

"Mademoiselle, I am General Washington's cook," he said, straightening up and returning her gaze.

She put out her hand. "I am Thelma . . ." She paused for a moment as if uncertain. "Blondelle."

"Honored to make your acquaintance, Miss Blondelle," he had replied. "May I walk with you a little?"

Thelma had inclined her head to indicate her assent and the two set off in the direction of her boardinghouse, many blocks in the opposite direction from the presidential mansion. After that, he made it his business to meet her at Sang's whenever he could contrive to do so until she finally took him to her bed. When the General left Philadelphia for Germantown at the height of yellow fever in August, he was obliged to leave quickly with Mrs. Washington's retinue without stopping to tell Thelma where he was going; being unable to write, he could not send her word.

He was not in love with her, but it did sicken his heart to think that she might have been back in Philadelphia overcome with the foul fever — perhaps even turned out in the street, as so many had been, to die of their ague and thirst. The Reverend Allen had told Hercules that a terror had come over the city and it had torn at all bounds of human decency like a wild animal gnawing its prey. The healthy showed inhuman cruelty to the sick as they became crazed with desperation to distance themselves from disease.

It was a stroke of luck that Thelma had been spared — she had been fortunate enough to travel out of the city into the cleaner air of the countryside with the family of one of her white pupils. Hercules happened upon her in the market just a week after his return. From that moment on the nature of their acquaintance became more intense, each aware of how the only moment they possessed was the moment they were in. If Thelma was upset about Hercules's lack of word when he departed the capital, she did not show it. He had been too ashamed to tell her that he could not read or write.

Now, in the deeply shadowed little room, he kissed her upturned hand, then placed his arm around her waist, solidly encased in its corset. His wife, Lame Alice, had never worn one — what would a slave need with such restrictive finery? Alice had spent most of her life at sitting tasks since her crushed leg didn't allow much more. He remembered her slight little form, no bigger than that of the children she minded while their parents worked in the fields until they were big enough to do small chores and show their worth. Before then, Lame Alice kept them from being underfoot, delighting in their silly games, or teaching them skills like shelling peas or plaiting each other's hair while she sewed patiently, hour in and hour out, the large basket of cloth at her feet never seeming to diminish even while the shirts, nightdresses, napkins, and petticoats for the big house piled neatly in rows on the long wooden table.

Hercules pushed the thoughts of his dead wife from his mind. Alice was gone some six years now and Thelma was here. He pulled her close and buried his nose in her swelling bosom. Her skin smelled sweetly of the French lavender toilet water she used.

Thelma sighed and pushed into him. He nuzzled there for a time before she gently pushed him back and untied the bodice of her gown, letting it fall to the floor in a pool around her feet. Reaching into her corset, she popped out one pale beige breast, its fullness overflowing the hand in which it was cupped, inviting. Hercules leaned in and put the reddish-brown nipple in his mouth, suckling steadily until the sigh became a soft moan. After a moment, she pulled the breast from his mouth and leaned into him, her hand feeling the front of his britches. Then she led him to the bed, the small feast he had brought in his basket to wait until later.

That evening he walked into the yard of the president's mansion to find the cellar door propped open and the faintest flicker of light coming from within. As he passed he could hear the murmurs of Margaret's voice and Nate's occasional answer. The girl chattered endlessly when she was nervous, which, as far as Hercules could tell, was nearly always. They must be sorting the potatoes. The coolness of the root cellar, so welcome on the hot summer days, would be like the grave on this early winter evening. Hercules imagined the pair huddled close as they sorted potatoes in the weak column of light thrown off by the candlestick between them. He had begun to tease the boy about his "pale shadow," hoping to shame him into keeping his distance from her.

Scowling now, he paused to listen. He could hear the rhythmic *plunk* of the spoiled potatoes being tossed into a bucket punctuated by the gentle scrape as the good ones were rolled into wicker baskets to be covered over with dry hay and stored.

It took a moment for Hercules to identify the other sound that bounced off the field-stone cellar walls as coming from Margaret. The low steady singsong echoed eerily up the cellar stairs like a creeping fog.

"A was an Archer who shot at a frog . . ."

From where he stood, Hercules could just make out the words, but even knowing what she was saying, it seemed like gibberish.

"B was a butcher who had a great dog . . ."

The words sounded like a desperate chant to Hercules and he wondered what Nate could be thinking, beside her.

"C was a captain all covered with lace, D was a drunkard and had a red face . . ."

Hercules imagined her, pale lips in her even paler face, almost feverishly spilling out the words. The shadows cast from the flickering light would make the dark circles under her eyes appear darker and the hollows in her cheeks more pronounced. Margaret looked quite young, but Hercules wondered whether Nate had noticed the rise of the breasts beneath her bodice as he had. They were probably near the same age, he reckoned, remembering back to the year the boy had been born back at Mount Vernon — the same year as his own boy Richmond. Nate's mother had been a laundress, working eighteen hours a day in the tiny washhouse, winter and summer, wet down with water and lye that chapped and split her skin. She had been a friend to his own Lame Alice, and they had died less than a year apart.

"What's that you're saying, Margaret?" he heard Nate say.

The girl paused for a few beats.

"I . . ."

A longish time passed before Margaret continued,

"It's an alphabet rhyme. My mother taught it to me so I could learn my letters."

Nate said nothing.

"Don't you know it?" she ventured shyly, then she exclaimed, "Oh!" as if realizing what she was asking. Hercules supposed that if he could see her, she'd be blushing as she often did, the pink flush starting around the edges of her hairline that peeked from under her mobcap, then washing over her face like scalding water.

"I'm sorry," she said, and Hercules could

hear in her voice that the tears might burst through.

They were silent a few moments as they worked on sorting the potatoes.

"Would . . ." Margaret ventured, drawing her breath again before continuing in a stronger voice. "Would you like me to teach you?"

Hercules started, alarmed. Now this was truly dangerous territory.

"Shhhh!" the boy hissed and nothing more was said for a few minutes.

Finally, he heard their footsteps and the scrape of the bucket. Hercules heard nothing again for too long. He began to move toward the stairs to see what mischief they were up to when he heard the boy whisper,

"Yes — I would."

CHAPTER 5

Early 1794

The booth in front of the State House rattled with the loud snores of the watchman inside. Seven o'clock had only just gone. Hercules tapped lightly on the booth with his cane as he passed and the snoring abruptly stopped.

"Morning, Mr. Brooke," he said loudly enough for the watchman inside to hear and poke his head out, bleary-eyed. He was a thin and ragged Negro, only recently out of the almshouse, but Hercules knew him as a decent type, always ready with the tales of who came and went from the back garden of the president's mansion. More than once Brooke had given him fair warning to dally in order to avoid Mr. Lear or Fraunces.

If Brooke were caught asleep at his duties, calling out the time and keeping an eye out for fire and petty crime, he'd lose the job that he desperately needed — and that

Hercules desperately needed him in.

"Ah, Mr. Hercules," said Brooke, squinting in the sunlight. He raised his hand to his hat.

"Seven has just passed, sir," said Hercules amiably. He pulled out his pocket watch.

"Just a minute past, Mr. Brooke," he said again, pointedly, when the man continued to look at him dully.

"Ah, er — yes," said the wiry man. He stepped out of the box and straightened his coat. He held a watch lamp in one hand. "Thank you, sir."

Hercules inclined his head before he headed off toward Dock Street and the watchman walked in the opposite direction toward Sixth Street, calling the hour loudly.

As Hercules hurried on, his stomach grumbled when he passed the food stalls that lined the edge of the road opposite the State House. He had only gulped some beer before he left this morning, eager to get down to the docks to inspect the oysterman's first catch. The free Negro women who sold pasties and small cranberry tarts called out to him by name, but he paused in front a small, dark-skinned girl who was selling meat pies. The pies were not the best looking and the child sitting on an old crate was no more than eleven, wide-eyed, with plaits in her hair. Her dress was old and too short and her toes stuck out from her broken-down shoes. His heart tugged — she reminded him of his own Evey back home. Evey would already be working in the fields or, if she was lucky, in the house at Mount Vernon. There was no childhood for those such as them.

Tossing her a coin for a pasty, he walked on and ate as he went. The pie was more grease and gristle than meat. Pausing a block from the wharfs, he pulled out his handkerchief and wiped his hands and mouth. In the doorway of a small narrow house, a filthy skirted woman with stringy blond hair looked at him with interest. Hercules inclined his head politely, earning a black scowl before she retreated into the darkness of her hovel. Her outrage amused him.

To the unknowing observer, the docks appeared like nothing short of bedlam. It was impossible to tell what was what as the press of men with carts, carriages, and the frenzy of travelers mixed with mariners loading boats, cleaning the decks, or generally prowling the taverns along the shore.

Hercules could make out where each mast stood apart from the other, no longer seeing it as the great mash of timber as he had when he first arrived, bewildered, in the city. Now, he could discern the finer ships from the lesser and the professional seamen who treated their ships like a beloved wife versus the scoundrels who turned to the ocean to escape a wretched life on land.

A plainly but cleanly dressed Negro woman stood near one of the wharf buildings, clutching a mulatto boy in front of her, her arm clamped protectively across his chest. She looked fearfully around, jumping visibly every time a barrel crashed onto the dock or someone yelled across the wharf. Passersby — mostly burly men — deliberately stepped in her path, laughing when she shrank back. Some bumped her hard as they passed, guffawing — the presence of the clearly half-white boy like an unspoken abomination they wanted to rub out whether they be black or white.

Hercules shook his head and walked on, tipping his hat to her as he passed, her eyes widening in surprise. She looked as though she might speak, but he pressed on, unwilling to get wrapped up in her particular sad drama. There was naught he could do for her or her boy, so better not to be troubled by them, sympathetic though he might be.

As Hercules approached Atwood's wharf, he scanned the crowd for Ben Johnson, the

91

oysterman he favored, and squeezed through to place his order before heading off in the direction of the Man Full O' Trouble tavern, which was situated on the thin stream of filthy water that marked what was once Dock Creek.

Hercules paused in the doorway and let his eyes fall upon the crowd. Those who earned their keep working the seafront crowded the benches around the bar cage, but here and there, low-level clerks shared a table and one of the neighborhood merchants dined alone. Their presence testified to Widow Smallwood's attempts to raise the standards of her newly acquired establishment.

From across the room the proprietress saw him and squeezed between the chairs, her ample form bedecked in blue satin and an elaborately high wig in the fashion of twenty years past.

"Welcome! Welcome!" she said when she reached Hercules. He could see that she was clearly aware of who he was and knew that she'd figure his presence at Man Full could only publicize the place as a more genteel establishment instead of just another watering hole for the lower sort that swarmed the docks. No doubt that was true, but she'd be mad to think that he, Hercules, would be frequenting her tavern. He glanced disdainfully around at the moneylenders and junior clerks sipping cheap beer and cider. The fact that there were no wine or spirits on offer meant there was little chance of one's pockets being pilfered or of being dragged into a drunken brawl. He supposed that was one point in Man Full's favor, but it was a small point to be sure.

Now, Hercules turned his attention to Mrs. Smallwood, looking her up and down. Clearly, she was a lady who was striving to be more than she was. He couldn't fault her for that — they were all trying to better themselves in some way, but it was hard to take her seriously in her outrageous outfit.

"Mistress Smallwood," he said, inclining his head slightly — enough to be polite but not deferential — a trick he had seen the General use.

"Is it a meal you're wanting, sir?" she said. "I can have a nice table set up before the fire. I'll just scoot those young men along a bit . . ."

"Er. No," Hercules said with measured finality.

He was gratified to see Mrs. Smallwood blush. Surely, she couldn't believe that General Washington's chef wouldn't be taking a meal in a middling tavern.

"Of course," she began and stopped. If she considered it odd for a slave to be in a tavern so early in the morning, she dared not voice it. Naturally she'd know that his time was not his own nor were his hours as oddly kept as the men she served, fresh from their ships or on their way to sea again.

"I meet a friend, here, madam," he said pleasantly, sensing her question. "He has informed me that your establishment is clean and decent, and I see that he is right." He smiled at her. It did not hurt him any to give the woman a compliment.

"Oh, well then," she said, tittering at the kind words. "Come, do sit down." She gestured at one of the boys collecting used cups from the tables and told him to bring two chairs and a small bench to the fire.

"Follow me, sir," she said, sweeping forward as if she were entering a grand ballroom. Hercules followed her through the crowd. Pipe smoke mingled with sooty black wisps of smoke from the fire. Even though it was early morning, voices were raised over a game of cards in the opposite corner of the room.

Hercules sat in one of the chairs and settled back with both hands upon his cane as the proprietress herself went to fetch him a cider. She returned carrying a tankard and set it down in front of him with a large wooden spoon and a small bowl of what looked like a blancmange.

"The cook just made that there, sir," she said. "I'm sure you are used to much finer — that is, can *do* much finer — but we'd be honored to have you taste it." She stood there and watched him expectantly. "That is to say, *gratis* of course, Mr. Hercules."

Hercules looked at the pudding jiggling in the plate, but before he could comment, a figure appeared behind Mistress Smallwood.

"There you are, Hercules," said James Hemings, his tall form towering over the short squat lady.

Hercules rose to shake his old friend's hand. "Indeed, here I am," he said, smiling. "Mistress Smallwood has just offered a taste of this new pudding, James. Perhaps another spoon for my friend? He is Mr. Jefferson's own cook." Mistress Smallwood was fairly jumping with excitement. "Imagine — two such well-known cooks in my humble little tavern!" she simpered and snapped her fingers at one of the serving wenches. "Quickly! Another spoon and tankard of cider if you please!"

The girl returned and set down the cider, but Mrs. Smallwood snatched the spoon from her and held it up to examine it before rubbing it furiously with the lace apron covering her gown. She handed it over to James with a curtsy. He took the spoon with a slight bow before giving Hercules a curious and amused look. Hercules suppressed a laugh.

Mistress Smallwood stood expectantly looking at the two men until they were forced to turn their attention upon her again.

"Madam —" Hercules began, "Perhaps you might . . . er . . ." He paused, at a loss for just how to tell the woman to be about her business without seeming rude.

"Mistress," James cut in smoothly. "We would much like to savor this treat, and even discuss its fine preparation between ourselves. Could we beg your indulgence of a little time? We shall be sure to seek you out before we depart."

"Oh!" said the taverner with the good grace to blush. "Yes, of course. I shall be at the bar should you need me." She curtsied again. "Gentlemen," she said, nodding first at James and then Hercules. They nodded politely back before contemplating the blancmange before them.

"Well, we may as well get it over with," said James, taking up his spoon. "She is watching us." He took a bit of the pudding and raised his spoon in a toast.

"Yes," said Hercules, lifting his and taking some as well. "Hmmm, it's very light. Though not much real taste to speak of."

"True," said Hemings, swallowing. "The cook has too light a hand with the spice, to be sure."

"I detect no gaminess of gelatin about it, though," said Hercules thoughtfully. "How do you think he managed it?"

James Hemings thought about this a moment, and then he motioned the proprietress over.

"Madam, please ask your cook if he has thickened this with carrageen?" he said.

She pressed her hands against her apron.

"It is very good, Mistress Smallwood," Hercules hastened to say. "We are just curious about the method."

The lady, visibly relieved, rushed off to the kitchen.

"I would wager it *is* carrageen," said James thoughtfully.

"Carrageen?" asked Hercules.

"A type of seaweed," said James. "I encountered it in Europe. The Irish make good use of it. It has a gelatin in it — just as a cow or pig foot would."

Hercules contemplated this for a bit. He

would have to remember this interesting fact and see if he could put hands on some of the stuff himself.

Mrs. Smallwood returned breathlessly and James asked her if it was indeed the Irish seaweed.

"Yes, sir. How did you know?"

"From my travels in Europe," he said, smiling. To this she raised her eyebrows slightly.

"James has been to Paris with Mr. Jefferson, Mistress," said Hercules, relishing the surprise that registered upon her face.

"Oh, I see," said Mrs. Smallwood, recovering. "She — the cook that is — is newly arrived from Ireland. An indenture."

"Ah, I see," said Hemings, his smile moderating slightly. Although their time was limited, while bonded an indentured servant was enslaved. Hercules watched as his friend composed himself and gazed at the now even more abhorrent Mistress Smallwood.

Once again, Mrs. Smallwood stood there for an unnecessarily long time. This time it was Hercules who spoke up.

"We shan't detain you, madam," he said using the low, resonant voice that so charmed Mrs. Washington. "Clearly, your other customers long for your attentions."

He paused to smile while saying a silent apology to his fellow tavern-goers who would be forced to endure the woman's courtesies.

"Well, then, I suppose you are right," she sighed and sashayed back to the bar.

Hercules and James suppressed bemused smiles before leaning closer so their discussion might remain private.

"We'll be leaving for Virginia in a few days' time," James said.

Hercules studied his friend's face. James had told him that after the freedom of Paris and Philadelphia, he couldn't bear the thought of going back to that multilayered hell where little boys were whipped like mules in Jefferson's blasted nailery and overseers were studded on Negro women to ensure Jefferson's "increase." He felt James's revulsion in his own gullet and didn't understand how he could stand it, having tasted proper freedom in France. Why, he asked, hadn't James stayed there, where slavery was illegal?

"Because of my sister Sally," James answered bitterly. Sally wouldn't remain in Paris with him, and James knew that Jefferson would punish her viciously for her brother's treachery if they returned to Virginia without him.

When his own day came to go home, Hercules couldn't see himself back in Virginia either — even though Mount Vernon was less harsh than other plantations. In Virginia he wouldn't be able to take a step without Washington's leave and the boundaries of the plantation would be as far as he could ever go. The General had been saying for the last year or so that he longed to be home, but every time he tried to give up on the presidency, the others — Adams, Hamilton — pressed him to stay. Hercules owed the men a debt of gratitude for that, but he knew the General. There would come the day that he would refuse to be detained any longer, and then even God Himself would not stop him, much less Mr. Adams or Mr. Hamilton.

The knowledge of it weighed heavy on him, but for now Hercules focused again on his friend.

"So the scoundrel did not make good on his promise —" said Hercules.

"He did — eventually," said James. "After much badgering on my part." He reached into the breast pocket of his waistcoat and drew out a paper, which he handed to Hercules.

"Go on, read it," said James, taking up the tankard gain.

Shame rose up in Hercules's throat as he looked at the paper. He could make out a few letters here and there followed by a scribble larger than the rest and near the wax seal, so he knew it must be a signature.

Hercules glanced up quickly at James, then down at the letter a little more, letting his eyes rove over it as if he were studying the words carefully.

"I see," he said, handing it back and hoping his friend didn't notice his failure.

James eyed him as he took the letter back.

"It says I can have my freedom after I've taught my brother to cook in the French way," James said carefully.

Hercules considered this a moment. "How long will that take?" he asked.

"It's hard to say, but Peter is a quick learner," said James. "I hope no more than a year or two."

Hercules drew his brows together. "How can you be sure he'll keep his word? What if he never agrees that Peter is good enough?"

James sat back and shrugged. "I can't," he said. "But it's better than nothing." The two took up their drinks and had a few sips while they stared at the fire, each lost in his own thoughts.

"Read it," Hercules said suddenly, sitting up and squaring his shoulders as if ready to take a blow.

"How's that?" said James, eyebrows raised.

"I, I can't —" Hercules paused and swallowed, then began again, this time looking straight ahead over his friend's head, unable to meet his eyes. "Will you read it to me?"

"I guess so. If you like," said James putting down the tankard and drawing out the paper again.

Having been at great expense in having James Hemings taught the art of cookery, desiring to befriend him, and to require from him as little in return as possible, I hereby do promise & declare, that if the said James should go with me to Monticello in the course of the ensuing winter, when I go to reside there myself, and shall there continue until he shall have taught such person as I shall place under him for that purpose to be a good cook, this previous condition being performed, he shall thereupon be made free . . .

Hercules held up his hand and Hemings paused.

"Do not say more," he said. "It's so like Mr. Jefferson to be so . . . grudging, is it not?"

At this James smirked. "Your words are kinder than he deserves, my friend."

An idea flashed into Hercules's mind, stunning him with its quickness like a rush of rum into his throat. But acting on it seemed, suddenly, a very urgent thing to do.

"James," Hercules said, abruptly leaning forward so that his friend looked at him in some surprise. Hercules edged forward in his chair, leaning heavily on his cane so he was inches from Hemings's face and the younger man could hear his words, now spoken barely above a whisper. "I want to learn to read."

James's eyebrows shot up and then a smile broke across his handsome face, his green eyes avid and eager.

"Do you now?" he whispered. "Well, that's a fine thing! But how —"

"I met a woman in the company of Reverend Allen. She says she is a teacher," said Hercules. He didn't mention that since he had overheard Nate's conversation with Margaret in the cellar, the idea had been troubling him. Even his young assistant, ignorant to the ways of the world, wanted to read badly enough that he was taking risks to do so. And risky it was. The pair didn't think he noticed them, heads together at every chance, but he did. And the others did too. It wouldn't do.

"This teacher," Hercules said, "she has a school in Cherry Street for colored people."

"Slave as well as free?" said James critically.

"Yes, she said so," said Hercules. "Although not in so many direct words."

"But how can you go to school?"

"That far, I have not planned," said Hercules, his whisper becoming hoarse and his eyebrows drawing together. "But I'll think of something."

CHAPTER 6

From across the table, Hercules watched
Samuel Fraunces take a sip from the pewter
goblet and grimace. The president insisted
there be no wine at the second table because
of the presence of Hercules and the other
slaves. He didn't want to indulge them with
strong drink, so even on this, the president's
birthday, when all the city was celebrating,
so they sipped weak cider or water. Hercules
knew this rankled the steward particularly.

He watched, bored, as Fraunces smiled at
Mrs. Emerson, the housekeeper, who sat on
his right with Oney, Lady Washington's
maid, beside her. Mr. Julien sat next to
Hercules. The two cooks usually ate on their
own, chatting companionably, and Hercules
felt sure that Oney and her brother Austin
would be happy to do the same rather than
sit at a table with Fraunces and the housekeeper in some bizarre imitation of white
staff at the other great houses, whose

behavior Fraunces pompously tried to imitate in the president's mansion.

On special days — Christmas, Easter, the Day of Independence, and today, the General's birthday — Fraunces insisted that the house of the president of the United States would function no less correctly even if the peculiar institution of slavery, in this most peculiar city of Philadelphia, made their second table a singularly strange affair. And so it was they came to sit here mostly in silence, politely answering the questions Fraunces put to them but without elaboration. Here and there Mr. Julien told an amusing story about the grand kitchens in France where he had worked, while Oney made faces or rolled her eyes at her brother when she was sure neither Fraunces or Mrs. Emerson were looking. Austin just smiled and shook his head.

The waves of music and laughter rolled out of the house and landed dully against the plaster walls of the servants' hall. Occasionally, a burst of cannon fire could be heard from the harbor along with yells of both well-wishers and hecklers just outside the garden walls.

Mrs. Emerson cleared her throat. "Mr. Julien," she said, leaning forward slightly to look down the table at the Frenchman, "I wonder, perhaps, if you have had word from France? One hears frightful things about the situation there."

Hercules raised his eyebrows, interested in how the other cook might answer. For a moment the Frenchman's usually pleasant face clouded.

"I have not, madam," he said politely. "For once in my life, I find myself happy that I am without relations for, as you say, the situation there is dire."

"Miss Nelly says that the newspapers report the pavements in Paris are always blood colored now," said Oney, who was always full of the latest gossip from Mrs. Washington's granddaughter, to whom she had been a companion from the time she was nine and the younger girl just two. "And that they've gone mad dragging folks to the guillotine."

Hercules sipped his cider to hide his smile. Fraunces would not like that, and as if on cue, Fraunces looked meaningfully at Mrs. Emerson, whose duty it was to manage the housemaids.

"Oney!" she said sharply, causing the girl to snap her mouth shut from whatever further she meant to say. "Let us be more sensitive to Mr. Julien's feelings," she continued.

"And to the decorum of this table," said Fraunces, pointedly looking around. Julien looked at his plate. Hercules laid his napkin on the table and began to stand. He'd had more than enough of Fraunces's little charade.

Fraunces snapped his attention to Hercules. Before he was fully out of his chair, Fraunces scraped his own chair backward and stood to his feet, raising his glass.

"To the president on the occasion of this Birth Day," he announced. Around him chairs scraped back and fabric rustled as all made to follow suit.

"The president!"

"The General!"

"His Excellency!"

"The father of us all," said Hercules with a smirk, one beat behind the rest of them. He raised his glass to the others, who had already sipped from their own glasses.

Fraunces looked around the table, only glancing at Hercules from the corner of his eye. "Well," he said loudly. "I'll grant you all leave if we are finished here. I imagine you will want to contemplate this great day in your own ways." He bowed slightly to Mrs. Emerson, then faced the table again. "I will bid you all goodnight." Suppressing a laugh, Hercules headed out the door as soon as the steward had left the room and strode across the garden to the gate in the wall. Before he went through, he glanced back at the house. Every room was lit up and every window presented a tableau. In the dining room, a press of people mingled. Women with tall feathers in their hair brushed up against men in silk frock coats. Music tinkled out of the windows cracked to let in the cool air. Hercules could easily make out the General through the bay window at the back of the dining room, his head rising well above the crush of merrymakers.

In the scullery windows he could see Nate scrubbing out the large three-legged fry. Margaret approached, took up a copper boiler, and began to wipe it dry. As she worked, she talked to Nate and Hercules saw him answer, his lips moving slowly. Margaret nodded occasionally and spoke once more. Again, Nate's lips moved slowly in response. Hercules frowned, wondering what they were discussing so intently, and then watched curiously as they both stopped talking and looked out the window to the other corner of the yard.

Following their gaze, he saw Fraunces emerge from the other side of the house. Hercules stepped farther into the shadows beyond the garden gate and watched as the steward scanned the yard, then glanced back at the house as Hercules had done. He seemed to be deciding something and again turned to scan the yard, his gaze resting on the gate Hercules had just passed through.

Hercules stood a moment longer, waiting to see if the steward would move farther toward him. When he did not, Hercules let out the breath he hadn't realized he was holding and moved farther down the alley toward the street. He'd have to be more mindful of the old fox from now on.

CHAPTER 7

Hercules crossed the High Street and pretended not to notice the man standing with his back to the trunk of a large tree. His tricorn was tilted to the side of his head as he tried to scribble in a small leather-bound book until he was knocked off-kilter by one of the crowd of jeering French-supporters that had gathered across the street. The hat was sent flying into the road and, abandoning his post, the scribbler dashed after it.

The cook hoped the man would not notice him emerging from the president's garden and then heading rapidly down Sixth Street. Hercules walked on, determined. Even if the man were to follow, he'd lose him soon.

But the streets were crowded that night, making it hard for Hercules to move quickly enough to lose the scribbler, and he sensed him not far behind. As Hercules walked, the crowd seemed to part for him, nodding at each other knowingly. Here and there men wearing the French cockade upon their own hats would hail him elaborately, and though he bowed back graciously, he kept on his way.

Hercules stopped at the corner of Cherry Street and looked left and right. Here, away from High Street, the crowd had thinned and residences lined the small road. Within these few short blocks was a trim though modest little community. Many of the city's Jews made their homes and businesses here and their church banked the street at its eastern end. Just beyond was the border of Helltown with its vagrants, brawlers, and prostitutes living their tumbled-over, picked-over, throwaway lives.

Finally, Hercules slowed as he approached the end of the street and stopped in front of the Jews' house of worship. Mrs. Harris had said to look for a gray clapboard house in the alley, but so far the street had not presented any break between the buildings. Finally he saw it — where Cherry Street almost ran into Third and the gates of the Moravian church. Tucked next to the Women's Hospital was a small alley. He scanned the road behind him to see if the scribbler was still behind but didn't see him. He made his way down the narrow passage toward the house at the alley's end. He scanned the road behind him to see if the scribbler was still behind but didn't see him.

The door opened before Hercules could reach it. Mrs. Harris stepped out and turned to lock the door with a large key she drew from her bag.

"Oh!" she exclaimed when she turned toward the alley to find Hercules a few paces away.

"Mrs. Harris," he said, removing his hat and bowing deeply to hide his nervousness.

"Master Hercules, is it not?" she said, frowning. "What brings you here this night?" Then, considering that she might have sounded rude, she smiled and said, "Of course, I am delighted to see you. It's a welcome surprise!"

"I thank you, madam," he said, returning his hat to his head. "I wonder if I might have a word."

"Why, yes of course. Will you walk with me?" she said. "I was just heading to the harbor to see the fireworks for the president's birthday."

"I'd be delighted to escort you, Mrs. Harris," he said, smiling. "But what I've come to say will take but a moment and —" Hercules paused to look anxiously back down the alley and back to the teacher. "And I would prefer to speak . . . privately."

Mrs. Harris looked at him a moment, then reopened the door and stepped back in. Hercules followed her into the small, plain hallway with a stairway at the end. She opened a door on the right and held it for him to enter. The room was set up with rows of benches. Small slates sat evenly spaced upon them. A desk sat against the wall near the door, and a bookcase filled with volumes was by the window facing the alley.

Mrs. Harris stood, patiently watching Hercules as he took in the room. Finally he turned to her.

"I would like to make use of your services, Mrs. Harris," he said.

She raised her eyebrows.

"I should be delighted to welcome you to our class," she said. "We meet every morning, but not everyone stays of a whole day. Many students like yourself may only steal away a few hours —"

"A thousand pardons, madam, but that is not what I meant," he said.

Now Mrs. Harris's eyebrows shot up near the rim of her bonnet.

"Sir, I cannot begin to think what you mean but perhaps your needs might be better met a few streets down —"

Hercules, realizing that the schoolteacher

had mistaken him, put his hand up.

"No, no, madam, you misunderstand — no impropriety intended," he said quickly. "I meant that I want to learn to read from you."

He stopped and took a breath. Baldly stating the fact out loud was, itself, an act of physical effort. He'd run the ways to approach her over and over in his mind. Now that he'd said it out loud, he felt almost giddy-drunk with the actual doing.

"But I cannot come here in the day — at any time," he continued. "My circumstance, ah . . . my circumstance makes that quite impossible."

Mrs. Harris composed her features. She turned away, walked to the desk, and tapped gently upon it as she thought.

"Then I do not see how I might help you, Master Hercules," she said, looking at him at last.

He took another step forward. "I am in a position to pay for your services as a private tutor," he said. "And I'm free to come and go in the evenings as I like. Perhaps you might teach me then?"

Mrs. Harris considered this for a moment.

"It would make for a very long day, Master Hercules," she said.

"I am prepared to pay for your trouble,

madam," he said, leaning with both hands upon his cane and drawing himself up to take full advantage of what little height he had. "And," he continued, "your discretion."

"That, my dear sir, goes without saying," she said, looking at him thoughtfully.

Hercules noticed her dark green gown. Like the one he'd seen her in the day they'd met, this one was plain but well made. Her gloves and shoes matched, as did the dainty spray of feathers on the hat perched neatly at the back of her head. The heavy cloak she wore was of sturdy gray wool, but he could see the inside was lined with the same pale gray silk as the tassel ties that held it closed.

He could see that this was a woman who was not in need of money.

"I will not press you for an immediate answer, mistress," he said smoothly, realizing it was best to let the matter lie for now. "Perhaps you will give the matter some thought and we might speak of it again?"

Mrs. Harris looked at him curiously, but before she could say anything he said, "Will you still allow me to escort you to the fireworks?" He bowed slightly and she, in turn, gave a small curtsy. He opened the door and she went through it and the small hall and front entrance.

After she had locked the door, Hercules donned his hat and offered his arm. She took it and they made their way down the alley and Third Street to cut through Church Alley and then follow Pewter Platter Alley to the riverfront.

As they walked, Hercules was irritated to note that the scribbler was back dogging his moves, trailing behind them down to Girard's Wharf where a crowd had gathered to watch the pyrotechnics. When they had stopped walking he found a spot just close enough to be able to observe them, no doubt believing that Hercules had not observed him in kind. Out of the corner of his eye, he noticed the man drawing out his sketchbook and mechanical pencil and moving it crazily around the page.

Hercules forced himself to ignore the scribbler and focus on the fireworks bursting above, illuminating the forms and faces around him. He said something to Mrs. Harris, who smiled and leaned down to hear better, for she was a full head taller than he was.

There was a light bobbing in the kitchen when he entered the yard well past midnight. The light, held aloft, was stationary for some time and then seemed to wander aimlessly through the darkened room like a will-o'-the-wisp.

Walking swiftly toward the kitchen, Hercules paused to pick up a stout log from the woodpile. Crossing quickly to the kitchen door, he flung it open, raising the log high with one hand.

"Halt!" he boomed in a voice graveled with rage that an intruder would prowl freely his kitchen.

Instead of faltering or stepping back the light moved closer, purposefully. His pumping heart pushing him on, Hercules moved in closer too. Suddenly the General's tall form glowed in the yellow lamplight.

"Sir?" said Hercules, startled, dropping the log quickly over his shoulder. "I'm sorry, sir, I didn't know it was you."

"Nor I you, Hercules," said Washington, breaking into a small chuckle. "We would have done for each other, I fear."

"I'm sorry, sir," Hercules said, stepping forward, silently cursing his haste. "I didn't mean —"

"Nothing to apologize for, man," said the General. "I'm gratified to see you take up arms in defense of my . . ." He gestured with the hand not holding the lamp and took in the scope of the kitchen. "My . . ."

He paused, seemingly at a loss for words. "My home," he finished.

"Yes, sir," said Hercules uncertainly.

"Are you just come in, Hercules?" asked Washington, stepping back so the other man could walk properly into the room.

"Yes, sir," he said carefully. From his ever-mild tone it was impossible to discern whether Washington was displeased. "I was enjoying the fireworks in your honor, sir."

"Ah, that," said Washington, sighing slightly. His mouth tightened into a stern line. For a moment nothing was said. Hercules suddenly wondered why the General was in his kitchen of all places.

"Sir? Is there something you need?" he said.

"Actually, yes," said the president. "One of the overnight guests — a young Englishman — he seems taken with a bad cold. I thought I'd bring him a cup of tea."

"Did no one answer the bell, sir?" asked Hercules. "Where is Jacob?"

"The bell?" said the president thoughtfully. "No, I didn't ring it. It's late — Jacob is asleep and I didn't want to bother anyone. I was going to bring it myself."

Hercules studied the president, standing there in his britches and shirtsleeves, the cuffs rolled nearly to the elbow. Was he joking? Was this some sort of trick to see what his slaves were up to? He didn't seem agitated and he had always given leave for Hercules to come and go as he wished.

"I will bring it up, sir," he said finally. "Which room is he in?"

"No, Hercules," said Washington, moving toward the table and taking a seat. The lamp encircled him in a small halo of light. "I will do it. I *am* still capable of carrying a small bowl of tea." He smiled more to himself now, amused by his joke.

"As you say, sir," said Hercules, removing his hat and coat and hanging them on the peg near the door. Sometimes the General had odd ideas, to what purpose no one knew. Rolling up his sleeves, Hercules headed out the door to the woodpile and gathered the smallest kindling and log pieces he could find.

Hercules walked over to the hearth and squatted down, passing his hand over stone floor. Feeling that it was cold, he shook his head, then rose and walked over to the brick and plaster stove on the far wall and passed his hand over the square openings there. When he found one with still-warm coals, he added the kindling and blew on it until it lit. Next he walked over to the water pump to fill the smallest copper kettle and nestled it among the hot coals. In the chilly kitchen, Hercules was aware of Washington's gaze following him as he worked, following him to the larder for chest of tea and a small china pot, which he opened and checked carefully before setting it next to the tea chest.

Hard to believe it was more than twenty years since he had first seen Washington on the crest of the hill above the river that flowed through the president's land at Mount Vernon. Nearer twenty-five, mused Hercules, remembering the day. It had been early spring and dawn only just broken. He'd been at his cook fire near the small dock, the rising sun illuminating the land in swathes around him. It was the best time to think and plan.

The smoke from the cook fire had chased up the slope on a breeze that was still cold and raw. When it cleared, there had been Washington, cresting the hill on a large charger that whinnied just at that moment. Hercules had startled and leapt to his feet, dropping his small leather sack from which he had just pinched out some spices to sprinkle on the fish he had speared and held over his cook fire.

Washington had jumped down from the horse and started down the slope. Behind

Hercules, the sound of the corn cakes sizzling in bacon grease in his three-legged fry pan was loud in the morning quiet.

"Are you Posey's ferryman?" Washington had called out as he approached.

"Yes, sir. Hercules, sir," he had answered, watching Washington make his way down the slope. "As was. Guess I'm *your* ferryman now."

Washington had paused and looked at him curiously. Hercules knew his words were bold, but he'd done his best not to sound rude. Everyone in those parts knew that Washington couldn't stand insolence from a slave, and in those days he'd have had Hercules horsewhipped if anything he said had the slightest whiff of sass.

But Hercules had just said his piece simply — he was only saying truth after all: His old master Posey had lost Hercules to Washington, along with the ferry across the Potomac, as mortgage for an unpaid loan.

The General had surprised him by smiling. "Yes, I suppose you are," he said, heading over to the fire.

"Breakfast?" he asked mildly.

"Yes, sir."

"Don't let me keep you from it," said Washington, gesturing for Hercules to sit down as he sat on the rock opposite and watched closely.

As Hercules cooked that day, as now, they hadn't spoken. Washington just watched him roasting the fish and turning the corn cakes over in the pan.

Now, he slid a mug toward Washington. The president looked up questioningly.

"The cocoa-shell tea you like, sir," he said, lifting the teakettle and pouring hot water into the little teapot. He swirled the hot water in a smooth, elegant motion before turning it out and spooning in tea leaves before filling the pot with the boiling water.

The day he'd first met Washington, the General — the Colonel back then — had watched intently as Hercules had plucked the roasted fish from the stick and laid it on a wooden camp plate. He'd speared the two hoecakes and laid them next to the fish, then held the plate out to Washington, who had hesitated.

"Plenty here, sir," Hercules had said, holding the plate farther toward him. Once Washington had taken it, Hercules had speared a fish for himself, then set about dropping more corn batter into the pan.

Washington had accepted a fork from Hercules, who ate with his knife. The fish was smoky and succulent, falling away from the bone, and the hoecake had a bit of spice.

"What did you do to this fish?" he had asked.

Hercules had regarded his new master across the fire, the smoke intermittently marring the view between them, and he thought how odd it was that Washington would be so interested in how Hercules prepared the fish. But then folks said he wasn't like other men.

"I stuff it with wild herbs I gather in these parts, sir," he said, hoping the question was not a trick of some kind. "Learned it from some of the Indian folk."

"And the hoecake?"

"Black pepper, sir."

"How'd you come by the hominy?" Washington asked casually, but Hercules could see his eyes harden with suspicion. He wanted to know if Hercules was a thief. If he were, Hercules knew that Washington would sell him quick as he could rather than have trouble on his hands.

"Traded, sir," he said, busying himself with his pan. He made himself speak easily and without hesitation. It was important not to let Washington know that Hercules had read his thoughts.

"Widow Farley on the ridge, she trades me corn and suchlike for whatever game and fish I can bring her," he said. "She can't do for herself and all."

Hercules looked up at Washington, steady and clear-eyed. Farley, the barrel maker, had been crushed on the docks at Alexandria when a dray cart collapsed on him. His widow was lame and had three small children to feed.

Washington had gone back to eating. When he was finished he stood up.

"Thank you kindly, Hercules," he said. Hercules also stood quickly.

"Sir," said Hercules, nodding. He wouldn't stare at the ground when Washington spoke to him, but he wasn't insolent either.

When Washington had mounted his horse, he turned back and called down the slope of the hill, "Do you like to cook, Hercules?"

Hercules had been surprised. Another odd question. He gave it a moment of thought.

"Well yes, I suppose I do, sir," he finally answered.

Washington had nodded to him then and turned his mount on his way.

A few weeks later he had sent for Hercules to be apprenticed in the kitchen. Washington ate simply and didn't give much thought to food, but he expected the meal to be well prepared.

"I was just thinking of that first breakfast

I made you, sir," said Hercules now, setting the lid on the teapot. He had been a different man then, or barely a man, truth be told. Those few days on his own, when he had left Posey's house and before he was properly taken up by Washington's, had been a blessing and a curse, caught as he was between being merely invisible and actually free. When Washington had ridden up to him, he had almost died from fright but worked hard not to show it.

Washington smiled in his close-lipped way.

"Still one of the best meals I've ever had," he said and took a sip from the cup Hercules had set before him, then glanced at the contents and took another.

"What's in it, Hercules?" he asked curiously. "It tastes different — though not unpleasant."

"Yes, sir," he answered, pouring the steeped tea into a deep cup with a wide saucer. "I put a bit of ground clove in it. Soothes the gums, they say."

He did not look up as he said this and Washington did not answer. Instead he drank the rest of the tisane, holding the warm liquid in his mouth for a few seconds before swallowing.

"Thank you, Hercules," he said, setting

the mug down and standing. "I believe it does."

Hercules poured tea for the guest and, before handing it to the president, said, "Sir, I am happy to take this on up."

"No, Hercules," Washington said and rose, taking the saucer. "You go to your rest now. I'll take it up. Thank you for the drink." He picked up the lamp in his free hand and made for the door.

"Sir?" said Hercules. Washington turned at the door, his face quizzical. "Happy birthday, Excellency."

The president smiled his small smile and gave an almost imperceptible bow and nod before heading back into the main part of the house.

CHAPTER 8

The kitchen was abuzz with activity, with scullions running around with full bowls and empty bowls, lugging baskets of vegetables, stoking fires. In one corner Mr. Julien was whipping something in a bowl. At the sinks two maids scrubbed pots and cooking wares as fast as they piled up.

In the midst of it all, Hercules stood at the wide, worn worktable in the center of the kitchen, watching Nate slice a roast. Occasionally, he had to grab the young man's wrist and move it forward or back slightly before he began slicing so each piece was exactly the same as the last.

To Hercules it felt as if they floated along on a bubble of calm in the busy storm around them. The wide table was a raft that anchored them steady and absorbed them in their work. He was focused on Nate as if he were his own son; his own son sulked lazily on the edge of things, in the way most of the time. Whenever Hercules glanced his way, Richmond glared at them in between dodging others' purposeful movements around the kitchen. The boy was proving more troublesome every day.

His thoughts were broken when Reverend Allen rapped hard on the doorframe before coming into the kitchen proper.

"Afternoon, Master Hercules," he said loudly. Hercules was gratified to see there was no pause in the scullery activity beyond a few glances Reverend Allen's way.

Hercules had looked up slowly, reluctant to take his eyes away from the carving of the roast. He grasped Nate's wrist to prevent him from cutting any further.

"Reverend Allen," he said in a business-like voice. "Come in, sir."

The minister stepped farther into the kitchen, holding his hat in his hand.

"I've come to see if you are in need of a sweeping," he said. In addition to ministering the word of God to the black people of Philadelphia, Reverend Allen ran a successful chimney sweep business.

Hercules looked at him quizzically. They had just swept the chimneys a month before.

"Why —" he began.

"Thing is, you'll remember that part of the chimney where the points were worn down, those rough edges caught a lot of soot and whatnot," said Allen. "Here, let me show you."

"Ah yes," Hercules said, catching on. "I remember. It was on the oven side, was it not? You're in luck — there are no embers in there yet, so we might look in."

Allen made his way to the oven.

"Nate, go into the pantry and find me some dried sage," said Hercules as he turned to follow Allen. "Patsy, you can go on and help Margaret peel those asparagus now," he said to the hired girl turning various small birds on a spit at the fire. Now they were alone on this side of the kitchen.

Allen was at the oven, pulling away the wooden door.

"It's just here, you see," he was saying, putting his arm and shoulder into the oven. "If you reach in and follow my hand you'll be able to make it out."

Hercules stood close to the taller man and reached his arm into the oven as well. Their bodies nearly pressed together.

"Mrs. Harris says yes," Allen murmured in a low voice when Hercules's head was just below his chin.

"That's right, just follow where my finger is pointing, Master Hercules," he said in a normal tone, for the benefit of anyone who might be listening.

"I see, yes," said Hercules also in a regular tone. "Can you send your man, the brick-layer, to see to it?"

"Yes, I can send that message," said Allen, pulling his arm out of the oven. Hercules did so too.

"Good, when do you think he'd be willing to start?"

"I hear he has some time starting Wednesday next," said Allen, wiping his hands on his handkerchief. "He will be finishing a big project then. I'll go around to look for him at his quarters after the evening meal."

"Good," said Hercules, making his way back to the table and gesturing to Nate to come back over.

"Come to think of it," said Allen as if he were remembering something, "you may know of him, he has his digs in Cherry Street?"

Hercules nodded at Nate to let him know he should begin his work.

"No, I can't say that I know anyone in Cherry Street, Reverend," he said without looking up. "But if he comes with your good word I'm happy to recommend him to the steward."

"Very good," said Allen. "I'll be going then." He crossed the room toward the door in only three or four of his long steps.

"I thank you for looking in, Reverend," said Hercules.

"Day's work, master cook! Day's work!" said the minister cheerfully, waving his hat as he walked through the door.

So, thought Hercules, excitement trilling a beat in his chest, Mrs. Harris had agreed to teach him to read, starting next Wednesday evening at her school on Cherry Street. He smiled, but then looked around the room quickly. All were at their tasks and took no notice. He began to hum a little as he watched Nate carve the rest of the roast.

The evening meal had long since finished, and after a small delay answering Fraunces's questions about preparations for the next night's political dinner, Hercules finally made his way to Cherry Street. His shadow, the tall scribbler, was not far behind.

As he moved purposefully forward, he passed two men who stood at the mouth of an alley and gave him the hard eye. He didn't pay them much mind. Their kind was everywhere around the city — low-class bumpkins who no doubt had come into town looking for laboring work. They were similar stock and height, with bushy black beards, and wore their hair uncommonly short. Even their clothes were of a kind. It was nearly impossible to tell them apart. Hercules inclined his head politely as he passed but they only stared at him, their eyes hard and unblinking.

He didn't give them another thought as he moved on and within moments he reached the narrow alley in Cherry Street and ducked down the passage toward Mrs. Harris's door. He knocked lightly upon it with the tip of his cane, then turned on the stoop and looked down the alley toward the road. To his surprise, the men he had passed stood just at the alley's edge but stepped abruptly back when they realized he had seen them. Across the street, his shadow, the scribbler, watched from shadows of the Moravian Church's doorway. Before Hercules could consider this any further, Mrs. Harris opened the door and stood aside to allow him to enter.

"May I take your hat and cane?" she said politely.

He smiled graciously and handed her both. She stood there studying him a minute too long, until a bemused smile started to twitch at the sides of his mouth.

"Madam," he said in his smoothest voice, flashing his best smile. He realized she found him amusing, a fact that would normally irk him, but he was determined not to let it trouble him now. He was here with a purpose from which he would not stray.

"May we sit? I find that my neck begins to ache looking up at your statuesque form."

Mrs. Harris made a sound like a snicker, then smiled.

"No need to flatter, Master Hercules," she said. "You are not the first man to take exception to my height, which I assure you I had no more to do with than you with yours."

Hercules raised his eyebrows slightly, then smiled again. Mrs. Harris was proving, yet again, a woman to be reckoned with.

"Well said, madam. Well said."

The teacher led him into the same room as when he had first come to see her. She gestured to one of the benches and when he was settled sat beside him.

"I received your message from Reverend Allen," he said simply.

"Yes," she answered. Her hands were folded easily in her lap.

"I am most eager for your instruction," he said, leaning forward slightly and peering into her eyes, willing her to see how very serious he was.

Mrs. Harris looked at him for a time, her

eyebrows furrowing. After a moment she spoke. "Why?"

"Why?" Hercules repeated.

"Yes. Why are you eager for my instruction? Why do you want to learn to read?"

Hercules narrowed his eyes. What was the woman playing at?

"Reading — knowledge — it is power, is it not, Mrs. Harris?" he said, the light mocking tone dropping from his voice. "If a man can read he can manage his own affairs, he can learn the affairs of others, he can move through the world more easily. Is that not so?"

"Yes, it is so," she said simply. "But what need have you of those things? Do you not live well? Better than most working men, from what I hear. You move through the world easily enough, do you not?"

Now it was Hercules's turn to look at her thoughtfully.

"Easily enough, yes," he said warily.

"So then, what more can being able to read grant you?" she said.

"It can open a door, madam," he said.

"A door to what, sir?"

Hercules leaned closer to the schoolteacher, closing the gap between them so tightly that their thighs nearly touched.

"A door, madam," he whispered, low and

hoarse, "to being free."

Eleanor Harris looked steadily into Hercules's eyes and he could feel her light breath on his face. He did not blink.

"I see," she said before leaning away and standing. She walked to the other side of the room, gathered up something, and then fairly flew back to his side. She sat down again, so close that their bodies again nearly touched. In her lap she held a slate. She made a quick mark on it.

"That, Master Hercules, is an A . . ."

CHAPTER 9

"I don't understand why you have to live there," said Hercules, propping himself up on his elbow and looking down at Thelma lying beside him. He kept his voice calm, although he was agitated. The gold-tinged late afternoon light set off the reddish undertones in her hair. He reached out and twisted one of the long curls around his finger and drew it out slowly before releasing it to bounce back.

"It is an opportunity," she answered, looking up at the tattered canopy above the bed. Moths had eaten large holes in the sheer white cotton.

"Working for the Chews is an opportunity," Hercules said, teasing out another curl. "I grant you that readily — but why must you live there?"

Thelma shrugged. "That is what Harriet wants. She wants the" — she faltered, looking for the English word — "a companion.

x

137

She wants me to be there always for her company." When he didn't answer she lay back and began to tell him about that day she had met Harriet Chew in the park.

She'd been sitting on a bench, trying to sketch Carpenter's Hall between blowing on her hands to keep them warm in the chill March evening.

As she worked, she wondered what her mother was doing now. Before the revolt, they'd have been walking back together from the big house where Maman sewed fine gowns for the mistress and Thelma sat by her side with her lace pillow making the intricately fashioned trim for the ladies' mantuas and sleeves.

She'd turned back to her picture and tried to block out the thoughts. The charcoal had slipped from her chilled hands again and she leaned forward awkwardly, her tight corset holding her back, when a tinkling female voice said behind her,

"You're very good."

Thelma looked over her shoulder at a young woman in an expensive cloak lined with fur, its wide hood settling easily on long black hair that fell to her shoulders in thickly coiled curls, only slightly looser than Thelma's own.

"You are quite good," she said again, looking down at the sketchbook lying open on Thelma's lap. "Who is your teacher?"

"I have no teacher," said Thelma.

The young woman raised her eyebrows. "Then how did you learn to draw so well? I'm hopeless and I've had ever so many tutors try to teach me —"

She stopped abruptly and blushed faintly at Thelma's surprised stare before quickly coming around the side of the bench and sitting down.

"Do forgive me. I prattle, I know." She smiled and dimples appeared in each cheek. "I'm Harriet Chew," she said, as if that would explain everything. She examined Thelma's sketchbook again.

"So tell me, did you *actually* teach *yourself* to draw like that?" She searched Thelma's face.

Miss Chew had barely given her time to answer before she launched into more questions. Was she French? Did her family escape from the terrible revolution there? Was she alone here?

Thelma murmured answers that said neither this nor that, letting the other girl make her own assumptions.

"But how do you live?" Harriet finally exclaimed, blushing deeply. "Oh! I'm sorry, how very rude . . ."

Thelma had shrugged. "Do not trouble yourself, mademoiselle," she said, smiling. "I teach French to —" She stopped short before grasping a suitable answer. "To my landlady's daughters in return for board."

Harriet's eyes had fairly glowed. Thelma could tell the other girl was both scandalized and delighted by the drama of the tale.

"I must get back to my sister and mother," she said, standing and gesturing to the pair strolling at the other end of the park. "It was nice to meet you."

Thelma had turned back to her sketch as Harriet walked away. The light had become too dim to work and, she told Hercules now, she felt a surge of annoyance as she began to gather her things, but in another moment, Harriet once again appeared before her. "I don't know your name," she said abruptly.

"Thelma Blondelle."

"Will you call on me, Thelma Blondelle?" she said. "My father is Benjamin Chew and we live in Third Street. Just ask anyone in the city — they'll direct you."

And when she had finally gone to see Ms. Chew, the impetuous young lady had surprised her with an offer of employment as her tutor and her companion.

When she finished her tale, Hercules

sighed, sat up, and folded his arms across his chest, flexing them so Thelma could see the throbbing veins in the bulging muscles. If Thelma took up chatty, foolish Harriet Chew's offer of a job, then these trysts would stop. He took too much pleasure in her to be happy about that.

"But what if she asks you about France?" he said crankily. "What do you know of France? Will you tell her what your father really was to your mother?" he finished nastily. Thelma had told him that she was the product of the master's union with her mother, a slave.

Thelma shook her head firmly and stroked his arm.

"It is ever so much money, *ma chère,*" she said. She traced the lines in his forehead with one slender finger. "Do not make the scowl like so. Money, it is freedom — you know this."

"There will be no more meetings," he said sullenly. "Not like this."

"Perhaps *non,* but with enough money we can, perhaps, leave all this one day . . ." She gestured in the air.

"I'm not in need of money," he said, his voice low and angry.

"And the more the better," she murmured, nuzzling into his neck. "Imagine where we

141

could go . . ."

Hercules stiffened. "It is not so easy as you imagine," he said. "Money is not the only thing." Sometimes he couldn't tell if she were naïve or willfully stupid — no amount of money would make it easy to escape the General's house.

Thelma smiled and spread her hand across his bicep. *"Un tel pouvoir, comme un taureau,"* she murmured.

"What does that mean?" he said peevishly.

"It means . . ." She paused, thinking. "Such power — like a bull."

At this he smiled wolfishly.

She trailed her hand across his abdomen, where a jagged scar puckered the skin near his navel.

"How did this come?" she asked, her accent becoming thicker and her English more confused as it did when she was aroused.

His smile disappearing, he put his own hand over her fingers tracing the pink skin. "My old" — he hesitated for a moment trying to stanch the flood of memories that came quick and unwanted — "master," he finally said. "He used to beat me with a hot fire poker."

Thelma's eyes narrowed.

"I was a lad," he went on but then stopped talking, remembering the drunk bastard who took out his anger at his failing farm on Hercules with a well-placed kick in the guts or the head — but only after he had gotten through beating and raping his cook, Maggie. The girl had hung herself after he had used her, then wiped the shit from his chamber pot across her face and pissed on her huddled back as punishment for her cries.

The day Posey lost his mortgage on Hercules to Washington was the greatest day of Hercules's young life. When Washington didn't beat him or take up women from the quarters to rape, he felt like he had won a pot of gold. And then the day the General sent for him to come up to the kitchens — that day. Well. It was like the heavens opened up.

He sighed and ran his hand absently along Thelma's back. No, there was no need to run just yet. Her hair smelled like lavender.

"How will we meet?" he said again.

Thelma shrugged. "*Je ne sais pas.* I do not know." She lifted her head and looked at his face a long time, then put one long cream-colored leg across him and slid herself up on top of him. She leaned down, her hair falling forward and covering his face.

"We will find the way," she whispered

hoarsely before she covered his mouth with her own.

It was still warm when Hercules stepped out of Mrs. Harris's house, though it was near ten o'clock. The unusual heat of the April day had sent people out and about much later than they would have done on a Wednesday, and as he made the turn up Cherry Street toward Sixth he could hear the loud laughter and quarreling coming from Helltown behind him.

The softness of the air made Hercules want to draw a deep lungful of it, but he knew better. The stink of cooking and privies and bodies pressed close in the shabby little homes that lined the alleyways would taint its sweetness.

As he walked along, Hercules reflected on the last month. Mrs. Harris was a patient teacher and now he was near to knowing the full alphabet without pausing to think. She said she would teach him to spell short words next. It was an amazing thing to even consider.

His mind pleasantly occupied, Hercules didn't hear the footsteps behind him, rapid and heavy. By the time he registered the sound they were close upon him and he stepped aside, pressing his back to the brick wall of the nearest house so that the men could pass in their hurry, no doubt running from a bar brawl or some other nonsense.

They came upon him fast, each grabbing an arm roughly as though they were trying to pull them from their sockets.

They were white men, alike in every way, down to their closely cropped hair and black beards. Recognition surprised him enough that he didn't react right away. Though their hats were jammed low on their heads, he realized they were the same men who had followed him to Mrs. Harris's house some weeks before. Now they crowded in on him so close that he could smell the whisky stink of their breaths. The one on his right had thick whitish stains on his lapel. Hercules felt his guts lurch and his head spin as they tugged at him like children fighting over a rag doll.

Hercules hardened his stomach and marshaled the ball of rage that was forming there. With a huge roar he brought in his powerful arms and felt his right shoulder wrench with the effort. The men felt themselves pulled off their balance as they knocked toward each other. The one on the left let go and he lurched forward, only to feel a sharp sting across his forearm where the other man, who still held on, had pulled a knife and slashed him.

Now fury made him blind and he could barely make out the forms of people gathering around them in the street. Hercules made a fist and swung around to level a blow against the man's head, but was stopped by a fist to the belly from the other, who had regained his wits.

"This here is a runaway nigra!" the other bellowed at the crowd. He had pulled a piece of paper from his jacket and held it forward, jutting it at onlookers as if it were a torch. "It is our lawful right to take him back to his master!"

Some people in the crowd stepped back. Hercules opened his mouth to protest but a punch to the jaw stopped the words.

"Back up!" the man with the paper screeched. "Back up! We're executing our legal duty! This nigra's a runaway from Georgia!"

Another man now ran into the fray, fighting for his way between the two captors who still held Hercules by his arms as he doubled over for breath. He could see their scuffed and filthy shoes against the pebbled boulevard.

"This man is the cook of President Washington!" The new man yelled louder than the one with the paper. Hercules cocked his head upward and squinted. The man was tall with shaggy hair. His fingers were stained with ink and coal. It was the scribbler who had also been following him these many weeks.

"He is known to many of you by sight! Do not stand by!" He pointed to a young boy. "You! Run to the President's House! Quickly!" The boy hesitated, mouth open, looking from Hercules to the slave catchers and back to the scribbler. "Go! There's a shilling in it for you!"

"It's true! This man belongs to General Washington!" a female voice called out. Mrs. Harris. Hercules let his head hang again, this time shame washing over him as much as the pain from his blows. There was a murmur in the crowd.

Hercules felt the hold on his arms loosen and then drop. He leaned on his knees and breathed hard before willing himself to straighten. His hat had been knocked off and lay in the gutter nearby.

He stood for a moment, eyeing the men who glared back at him as if they were ready to attack the scribbler.

"Run! RUN!" the scribbler yelled at Hercules, and then at the attackers, "We are many against you — I suggest you don't try that treatment with me!"

The men looked at each other and with a signal known only to them bolted in the same direction, past Hercules and away from the crowd. A few men ran after them.

Hercules bent and retrieved his hat, which was too filthy to wear now. He drew a deep breath — his nose and lungs were filled with all the putrid stench of the road. Still, he willed himself to nod silently at the scribbler and bow to Mrs. Harris before he turned and walked unsteadily away.

Only when he was a good two blocks south of Cherry Street did he break into a run.

When Hercules limped into the yard, Fraunces already stood watching him from the kitchen door, silently stepping just to the side to let him pass through. Oney sat at the table, mending something of Lady Washington's and chatting and laughing with Nate and her brother, Austin. Richmond was scowling in a corner whittling on a piece of wood and Margaret, equally silent, hovered close to Nate as she always did, his silent shadow.

It was Margaret who saw him first, glancing away from Nate toward the door. A gasp escaped her throat and then, seconds later, the quiet hum of talk exploded. A chair fell to the floor with a smack, shoved violently backward with the force of Austin standing abruptly.

"Lord!" Oney cried out, stepping around the table to meet him.

"Pa, what happened?" Richmond yelped and ran toward him. Hercules put his hand on the boy's shoulder.

"A scuffle, that's all," he said, looking at his son and then the others. He was overcome with the urge to grab his boy and hold him close, but he didn't lest he scare the lad further.

Fraunces hung back. Margaret's wide and terrified eyes shot around the room, a pale specter among them.

"Over what?" Oney demanded.

Hercules gestured to Richmond to bring a chair. He sat down hard, wincing. When the boy rested his hand on his injured shoulder, he drew a sharp breath but did not move away.

"Some men took me for someone else," he said to their expectant faces. "Someone they had business with."

Oney raised an eyebrow and Austin seemed confused, as did Nate, that shadow of a girl behind him looking more terrified than usual. Hercules brought a hand to his jaw and touched the bruise there.

"Oney, put together a poultice, if you'd be so kind?" he said.

Oney put down the sewing she had been wringing in her hands.

Fraunces watched her go and stepped forward as if he were about to speak but held his tongue. Nobody spoke, waiting for Hercules to go on.

"Ah, good girl," he said when Oney returned with the herbs for the poultice wrapped in linen. She went over to the hearth and pulled up the kettle nestled in the ashes. She wet the poultice and brought it back to the table but then stood by Hercules, unsure what to do.

"Give it here," he said, holding out his hand. He applied it to his jaw and closed his eyes.

"Who did they think you were, Pa?" Richmond asked.

Hercules opened his eyes a little and studied his son. Dammit, he did not want to discuss this now. They were all looking at him. He could feel Fraunces hovering, quiet in a manner that was much out of character.

"A runaway," he finally said.

There was total silence for a few seconds before Richmond's angry voice loudly broke it to pieces. "You mean another slave!" he exploded. "Someone else's *slave* — just not

150

the General's slave!" He spit the words out like they were fouling his mouth.

"Enough!" Hercules said, his voice low and rumbling. He stood quickly, forcing Richmond to move back. The effort made his head spin.

Richmond narrowed his eyes and stared at him.

"That's if they are looking for anyone's property in truth," said Fraunces. Hercules had almost forgotten he was there. "Many of these slave catchers are just opportunists with fake papers, taking their chances. Had they got Hercules here, they probably would have dragged him to the block just over in New Jersey for some quick coin. Or, more likely, negotiated with the president to quietly buy him back."

He said this pleasantly, as if he were discussing the best way to set a table or an interesting fact about grades of sugar.

Richmond seemed about to explode. Hercules glared at Fraunces.

Austin stepped forward and put a hand on Richmond's shoulder. The boy jumped.

"Time for bed, I think," he said. "Your pa's all right. You see so yourself. Let's go on now." He guided Richmond toward the door with a firm hand. Nate stood and followed them too.

Oney flounced over to the sideboard for a bowl, then retrieved the kettle and brought it back to the table, giving Fraunces a pointed look. She took the poultice from Hercules, wet it down again, and handed it back to him.

"I'll say goodnight too then," she said, looking only at Hercules and giving him a small curtsy before she returned the kettle to the hearth. He raised his hand in thanks.

Only Margaret was left standing at the other end of the table, practically cowering, as if she were stark naked to the world. She looked frantically from Hercules to Fraunces but made no move to go.

"Go to your rest, Margaret," Fraunces said. "You may leave now." He said it firmly and she jumped. She looked desperately at Hercules, her eyes shiny. He gave her the very smallest nod and she scurried off to the back of the pantry, where she rolled out her pallet each night.

When she had gone, Fraunces stepped to the table.

"It seems," he began as if he were musing out loud, "that after this little adventure you may have to stay in for your own good. I shall make the General aware."

Hercules readjusted the poultice and then looked at Fraunces.

"No," he said.

"No?" said Fraunces, feigning surprise. "I beg your pardon, Cook, but you mistake my meaning. I am not *asking* your leave. I am telling you what must be done."

"And I'm telling you that you will not," answered Hercules calmly.

Fraunces's expression hardened. "What has happened to you has proven, yet again, the folly of having . . . your *kind* as part of this household," he said through gritted teeth. "The General has long been sensible that there could be danger, and so it has come to pass. I shall recommend to him that this is reason, yet again, to send you all back to Mount Vernon."

Hercules put down the poultice and stood up, leaning heavily on the table.

"And if you do, I'll be sure to make him aware of the tavern you've bought down in Dock Street and that your lady oversees even now as we speak," he said.

Fraunces, ready with a reply, shut his mouth with a snap. He hadn't expected this.

"That is a lie!" he spat out.

"No, sir, it is not a lie," said Hercules, his voice low and angry. "But it is easily proven either way — with a word to the General's ear."

Now Fraunces composed his face and

smiled pleasantly.

"And just how would *you* possibly get a message to the General?" he asked with a snicker.

"I have my ways," Hercules said pleasantly. "But you mustn't take me at my word. You can always wait and see, but we know the General doesn't like surprises."

Fraunces studied Hercules now. He began to tap the table lightly with his index finger as he thought. Hercules sat back down and ignored him.

"Very well," said the steward. "But next time this happens, suffer the consequence as you may." Fraunces waited a moment for Hercules's reply. When one did not come, he turned and left the room without looking back.

Richmond watched him from the corner of the kitchen, taking care to look back down at the carrots he was scrubbing whenever Hercules looked his way. The bruise on Hercules's jaw was a swollen welt today, and the scullery maids stared at it when they came in that morning. Mr. Julien raised his eyebrows questioningly but Hercules only gave him a slight headshake, so the Frenchman did not bring attention to it again. No one else dared speak of it.

But Hercules was slower today. He called Richmond over to lift the pots bubbling on the hearth or to pull out baking dishes from the oven. It was Nate, though, whom he trusted to stand beside him chopping vegetables and herbs at his direction or trimming cuts of meat. Today, Hercules stood by and did not lift a knife or bowl himself, wincing when anything brushed him and resting his left arm on the table or on his leg when he sat down. He relied on Nate to be his arms and hands and the older boy worked beside Mr. Julien to produce dish after dish for the day's meals.

When Hercules looked at his son angrily drawing the knife over the carrots, his resolve momentarily faltered. Maybe he should call the boy over and have him work beside Nate, but whenever he thought about it, irritation rose up as he considered the bollocks Richmond would make of the thing.

Now the boy sat, legs splayed out so that when Margaret hurried by, basket of eggs in hand, she tripped over his foot and only just caught herself before dropping the whole thing.

"Richmond!" barked Hercules furiously. The boy blinked, as if he didn't know where he was.

"And you, Margaret, why aren't you minding where you are walking?" he snapped. Margaret stood, clutching the basket and looking nervously from him to Richmond. Sometimes her cow-eyed ways irritated Hercules almost as much as Richmond's half-wittedness.

Now those cow eyes filled with tears and she scurried away as Richmond narrowed his eyes.

Shaking his head, Hercules turned his attention back to Nate at the chopping block and began murmuring directions as the boy cut pastry shapes with the tip of a sharp knife. The lad had sure, deft strokes and Hercules smiled, praising him now and again.

With each word he could practically feel the fury emanating from Richmond, but there was naught to be done for it; the boy just would not learn. Hercules would have to think of another plan to keep his son out of harm's way. With each passing day, he was less sure that having him here in Philadelphia was the right course of action — especially after his own run-in with the slave catchers. He knew his son and nohow was a man going to put his hand on Richmond and drag him off in the street without the lad fighting or dying while trying to escape.

Hercules sighed and, after patting Nate on the shoulder, approached Richmond. Moving a basket of carrots to one side, he lowered himself next to the boy and put his hand out for the knife and carrot he held, saying,

"Here, son, let me show you a faster way."

Washington took his time assessing the man standing before him. He looked sober enough in a dark brown suit and light spring cloak. His head was completely bald, with a sheen of powder upon it. Washington had not laid eyes on him before, having engaged his services through the attorney general Edmund Randolph, who himself had fallen victim to the law in these particular matters.

The president gestured to the chair opposite his desk before seating himself. He would not offer the man any refreshment — this was not a social call.

"What report do you have for me, Mr. Kitt?" he said.

Frederick Kitt had taken his time observing the great Washington even as he was being observed. The man still stood tall in his perfectly tailored blue suit, but he moved his mouth oddly when he talked, as if his jaw pained him. He wore no wig and the once-red hair ran almost entirely to gray, but he had not bothered to powder it to be uniformly white, and where it was not braided tightly down his neck, the hair was frizzy and dry. He looked old.

"Your cook has been making visits to a house in Cherry Street, sir. There is a free woman there, a widow, who runs a school for their own kind. I believe he is — ah — courting her."

Washington's unblinking blue eyes didn't leave Kitt's face while he spoke. Now they squinted suspiciously.

"*Courting,* Mr. Kitt? Come now, let's not be so coy," he said with contempt. "Hercules is a slave, he cannot make associations. He is going there to bed her, is what you are insinuating?"

Frederick Kitt inclined his head slightly and smiled. "Just so, Excellency."

"You said she was a teacher?" asked Washington.

"Yes, sir." The president tapped his long fingers on the table light and considered this.

"I see," he said. "Anything else to report? Does it look like he is moving toward escape?"

"Hardly, sir," said Kitt. "Nothing about his movements show any inclination to flight. He seems quite content with his lot."

"He is treated well here," said Washington, more as an assurance to himself than to explain anything to Kitt. He focused again on the man across from him.

"Thank you for the report," he said. "My secretary has an envelope for you. You may collect it when you leave." Washington stood.

"Oh, one more thing, sir," Kitt said as he took his time rising. "The cook was set upon by some slave catchers from Georgia. A few days ago, when he left the woman's house."

Now Washington focused more sharply on him.

"Handled him a bit rough, they did. Each got hold of one of his arms and were like to have a tug of war. Landed a fair blow on his cheek and sliced his arm."

"Then how did he escape them?" Washington demanded.

"A man interfered and raised a fuss," said Kitt. "Others in the street crowded in and called out that he was your cook."

"Who was the man?" said Washington.

Now Kitt reached into his breast pocket and pulled out a small brass notebook polished to high shine. He carefully turned the pages until he found what he was looking for.

"I made inquiries, sir," he said. "Ah, here it is. The man is a painter. Lately returned from London — Gilbert Stuart he's called."

"I see," said Washington. "And what of the slave catchers? Were they apprehended?"

"Some tried to stop them when they ran off, sir, but failed," said Kitt.

Washington squinted again, his eyes taking on a hard anger.

"Make inquiries into this, Kitt," he said, his voice clipped. "I want names."

"Yes, sir," Kitt said, standing there in case the president said more. When he did not, Kitt spoke again.

"Another item, Excellency," he began. Washington raised his eyebrows. "About that stewardship . . ."

"Mr. Kitt," Washington said, sitting down at his desk once more. "Continue with these jobs I have given you and if you execute them well, we will have much to talk about by way of future work in my household. Of that, I assure you."

He leaned back in his chair and lifted a correspondence to read. For a moment Kitt watched the president, absorbed in his papers, before he bowed, unseen by the great man, and showed himself out.

Part II

CHAPTER 10

Summer 1794

"Margaret, please see to your packing." Hercules's voice rolled over Margaret. She had stepped out of the larder where she was putting preserves neatly into a crate and was just heading for the kitchen door. In the kitchen, people were flying around packing baskets and rushing out to the waiting carriages. The family was returning to Virginia for a month's time. Oney, Old Moll, the nursemaid to Lady Washington's grandson, and the coachmen were all going. Nate was going to help in the kitchens at Mount Vernon, since Hercules had to stay behind and help the new steward prepare the summerhouse in Germantown for their return. Margaret was to remain too, along with a few other day-helpers, to get the Philadelphia house put up for the season and the Germantown house properly dressed.

Earlier, as Hercules stood at the far end

of the kitchen speaking with Nate, Margaret had watched them a little too intently for his liking. Hercules clapped Nate on the arm and sent the boy out the kitchen door and Margaret had gone back to her work, but now she hovered again at the door, not attending her tasks. Hercules had not looked up from what he was doing when he spoke to her, but now he put his knife down and followed her gaze back out into the yard.

He glimpsed Nate near the stables, stepping up to test the position where he'd be sitting at the back of the carriage on top of the cases. Austin was already decked out in his livery. Another black servant who worked loading the cases was dressed the same way. He'd stand on the other side of the carriage when they departed. A matched set.

"Margaret!" Hercules said again, this time with more meaning in his voice. He couldn't imagine what the girl thought she was doing. He marveled at her lack of sense, mooning around the door when she had work to do. When she looked at him before hurrying back to the larder to continue packing the preserves, he gave her a hard eye.

In less than a month they would all be at Germantown to escape the sickening summer vapors of the city and the yellow death they carried. Hercules had heard Nate explaining it to her earlier in the day. Margaret didn't understand why the family was going so far away as Virginia only to return in a few weeks. When she asked Nate about it, he told her it was not her business, but Oney had blurted out in her heedless way, "They just moving us out of here before the six months run out."

Hercules had set the pan he was holding down loudly on the counter and given Oney a sharp glance. The girl needed to learn to shut her mouth. Didn't she know better than to say such things in front of this white girl?

He'd sent Margaret to the larder then to pack all the remaining put-by vegetables and fruits. Soon enough they'd use them all and then the fresh stores would start coming in.

When she finally emerged again from the small room, all was quiet. Hercules stood at his chopping block sharpening the knives on a stone.

Margaret turned slightly to each side, looking around.

"No need for 'em all to be in here what with most of the household gone," he said to her unasked question about the hired day servants who normally crowded the place. Margaret turned to face him and watched, mesmerized, as he drew the knife back and forth over the stone.

Hercules stopped and put the knife aside, breaking the spell. Margaret watched as he wiped down each of the knives before bringing them to their drawer in the kitchen dresser. He walked over to a shelf and started to reach up for a bowl and drew back in pain, grasping his left shoulder with his right hand. He uttered a low growl.

Margaret jumped slightly before moving forward. "Oh, sir, let me do it."

She was quickly at his side, reaching up for the bowl and bringing it down. When she held it in her arms and faced him, he realized how she had grown in these last six months. She was quite near his own height.

Margaret seemed to notice this fact for the first time too.

"Just set it there, then," he said, curtly, indicating the table where he usually worked.

Margaret quickly set the bowl down. She stood beside it, unsure of what to do next. She looked at him expectantly.

He walked over, still rubbing his shoulder, and stared at the bowl thoughtfully.

"Take this and go out to the garden," he said. "Cut me the most tender greens you can find — about half a bowl's worth."

When she returned with the greens he took them to the sink, where he pumped water over them and swirled them around with his hand.

"Bring me another bowl, please," he said over his shoulder. Margaret ran to get it. He lifted the greens out of the soil-clouded water and placed them in the clean bowl. Then he did it again. He poured out the dirty water, rinsed the bowl, and drew out the freshly swirled greens and put them inside. Margaret watched it all, fascinated.

"If you clean them this way, you will get all the grime out," he said, handing her the bowl. "Now, take this and spread these greens on a clean towel. Pat them dry — gently, mind."

Margaret took the bowl over to the other table where Mr. Julien usually worked.

When she came back, he was already chopping up cold chicken from the larder. He nodded toward an onion and some hard-boiled eggs that sat in another bowl.

"Take those and chop them fine — so all the pieces are the same size," he said.

Margaret hesitated before taking the bowl. Hercules stopped chopping chicken.

"Is the task beyond you, girl?" he asked, looking at her archly.

"No, sir," she stammered. "I used to —"

167

She stopped. "I cooked with my mother." She swallowed. "Before she died."

Hercules looked at her a moment, then jutted his chin toward the bowl. She grabbed it quickly and moved off to the other table.

When she was done chopping the eggs and onion, she came back and watched as he lay the lettuce leaves on a platter.

"We are doing a salmagundi for his Excellency's lunch," he said to her as he layered leaf over leaf. "Hand me that bowl of chicken."

She did and he layered the chicken on top of the lettuce.

"Now the onion and eggs," he said, and sprinkled them on top of the chicken.

"In the larder, you'll find some parsley that I have already chopped and a small bowl of those new peas — get them for me," he said.

Margaret turned and flew off. When she returned, he artfully arranged them on the platter.

He stood back and assessed the plate before heading to a low shelf where he kept vinegar and oil. He grabbed a small bowl within his reach on his way back to the table. Using his birch whisk, he mixed the oil and vinegar in the bowl, adding salt and pepper in tiny pinches. Dipping his pinky finger into the mix, he tasted the sauce after each addition.

Holding the bowl high, Hercules began to gently pour the dressing on the salad — and winced when he raised the bowl too far.

When he was done, he stood back and surveyed the platter, frowning. The girl watched him, fascinated.

"Go into the garden and cut the freshest-looking of the sweet pea flowers," he said. "Choose the ones that are the darkest pink."

Margaret headed out to the garden, where the fuchsia and light pink flowers climbed up a tall trellis fashioned out of bent and dried willow branches. Returning, she held her apron up and tumbled them out.

"In a bowl next time, Margaret," Hercules said sternly while he examined the flowers. "Always take care with every ingredient."

She blushed and stood watching as he picked the best flowers and arranged them on the salad.

He stepped back again and admired his work.

"Oh, sir, it looks like a Turkey rug!" she said. "It's that pretty. Almost too pretty for eating."

Her outburst surprised Hercules, and he laughed. She smiled at him shyly.

"Here," he said, sliding the platter toward her. "Wipe the edges of the plate with a towel — a *clean* one — and then put it on the side table there," he said. "The footmen will be down soon."

Hercules left her to wipe down the table and clean the bowls he had used for the salmagundi while he went into the larder for the other dishes for the General's lunch. He laid them out on the sideboard next to the salad.

When he was finished, he turned to find her standing quietly by his table. She was an odd girl, hovering about like an eager cur, but she did her work readily and without complaining. He often found that he felt sorry for her.

"You may continue packing the dry goods, Margaret," he said.

"Sir?" she said. He raised his eyebrows.

"I —" She hesitated.

"Yes?" he rumbled, looking at her more sternly now. It wouldn't do to encourage too much familiarity with this one, as sorry as she might be.

"What Nate said earlier — I keep thinking on it," she began.

Hercules took a step forward, a flicker of apprehension pricking him. "Yes?" he said, his voice more urgent. His mind raced over what else the girl might have heard. He'd have to warn Nate to take better care.

She took a step backward.

"Yes?" Now Hercules stood before her, his arms folded over his huge barrel chest.

Doubt shadowed her face and she hesitated but then blurted out, "What they said about being brought to Virginia because their six months was almost up. What did they mean, sir? Are they being sent away? Will they come back? Nate didn't tell me and . . ."

Her barrage of words trailed off as Hercules turned and began to cut bread slices and lay them on a wooden charger with some cold-cut meat for the servants' lunch.

"Ah," he said, gazed up at the ceiling, and blew out a breath. How to explain the particulars of the abolition law to her? Not that he even wanted to. He was saved from an immediate answer when they heard the footsteps of the new steward, Mr. Kitt, in the passageway.

Hercules quickly composed himself and straightened.

"Afternoon, Mr. Kitt," he said pleasantly. "You'll find all is ready for the servers on the sideboard."

Fraunces had gone to open his tavern — the president none pleased — and this Frederick Kitt was in his place. Where Fraunces was small and wiry, always elegantly turned out and brightly bewigged, Kitt appeared barely better appointed than a laborer. He wore no wig, preferring instead to completely shave his thinning hair. Hercules suspected he powdered both his pate and his face. It was easy to see the tracks where the rivulets of sweat trickled down the man's forehead.

Kitt was right peculiar — animally aggressive in his way — but Hercules supposed he was the best they could find on short notice. Hercules fervently hoped he wouldn't last. The man put him on edge and he wondered what the spiteful Fraunces had told Kitt about him before he left and how much of a problem the new steward might prove to be.

"Oh?" Kitt answered coldly, looking around. He didn't acknowledge Margaret who stood glued to the spot, clearly unsure of whether she should back away or stand still and be as small as she could.

Eyes narrowed, Kitt left the kitchen for the yard and Hercules said to Margaret, "Six months before they were free."

"I don't understand —"

"If any of us stay here in the capital above six months then the law says we are free," he said in a low voice. "Their time had come for that. Mrs. Washington takes them with her to Virginia where there are no laws against slaving, and then when she brings 'em back here, the time starts over again — see?"

He spoke calmly, evenly, just as if he were showing her how to properly lay out a dish.

Margaret sucked in her breath sharply and put out her hand, groping for the table to steady herself.

Hercules reached over and grabbed her wrist.

"Listen, girl," he said softly. "This is not for you to concern yourself with — hear? Not with this and not with Nate." Had she not realized that he saw how she looked at the young scullion? If she continued to carry on as she did — childlike and ignorant — she'd bring harm to herself and to the boy. She had to be made to see that. He looked into her eyes to be sure she understood, but her eyes were brimming with tears that threatened to fall. She gulped air like a fish out of water.

"But sir," she began nervously. "What about —" She stopped abruptly.

"What about me?" he said disgustedly. The girl's simpleness was annoying. "Is that what you were going to ask?"

Margaret nodded once. Hercules let go of her wrist.

"Don't worry about me. Go on now and see to that packing," he said, turning toward the hearth and taking up a broom to sweep back the ashes.

Margaret fled toward the larder but was caught back by the wave of his voice as she reached the door.

"Remember now, don't concern yourself — not with this and not with him."

"A shame to abandon such a robust garden."

Hercules straightened up and dusted his hands before turning to face the General.

"Afternoon, sir," he said.

Washington inclined his head politely.

"That's why we didn't plant much," Hercules went on. Washington liked little better than to speak about farming. "Just the peas and such, some lettuces. Only the spring vegetables. I've asked for some strong seedlings to be set aside for Germantown."

"Good man. I see the radishes are struggling," said Washington, walking over to the rows and nudging one of the sickly plants with the toe of his boot.

"Yes, sir," said Hercules. "Not sure why, though. The soil is good here."

"Too good maybe," said Washington thoughtfully. "They like a bit of sand mixed in with the compost. Try that."

"Will do, sir," said Hercules.

"Hercules," began Washington, turning to face him. "I have something I want to discuss with you."

"Sir?" said Hercules.

"It's about your boy, Richmond," Washington said. "He's not faring so well here. I am bringing him back to Mount Vernon to be with family. I think the farm suits him better than this place."

For a moment Hercules said nothing. His stomach lurched. It was hard to remain standing passively in front of the General when all he wanted to do was bolt for his son and hold him close and safe.

Even though he had suspected this day had to come, sending Richmond back meant that his son would be that much further away from freedom and back in the dank hovels they called quarters. There would be no more sleeping in an attic warmed by the chimney that kept the house fires going. He'd be working in a field sunup to sundown in the same pair of broken-down shoes until his feet were too blistered to walk, but still he would work.

His mind raced to think of something to

change the General's mind, even as he also knew that Richmond's own failings had caused this turn of events. Washington had brought Richmond here on Hercules's request, but would he let him remain upon it too? And was it worth it to trespass on the General's good nature for a boy who seemed hell-bent on causing trouble for them both?

Perhaps this was Hercules's own fault. He loved Richmond too much — enough to make him lazy and sullen, unable to cope with the life they had. The boy was always courting danger with his ways.

Hercules's mind jumped forward and back, weighing the thing. Richmond might be safer back at the plantation, after all — at least for now. His ready temper and churlish ways would get him into less trouble there because they didn't deal with the kind of whites they did here — the indentures or the hired folk that seemed pleasant enough but kicked up plenty of fuss when the boy got out of line. Down there, the rule was clear — every white man was your enemy, and if Richmond couldn't remember it and hold his tongue, then the other slaves, the older heads, would make it their business to remind him. And keep him safe.

In Philadelphia, he was constantly worried for the day Richmond would go too far and not even Hercules could protect him. Better for his son to be tucked away until the time came. Hercules would figure out how to get him back up here by then.

"Hercules?" said Washington, breaking into his thoughts. "Would your work be too burdensome without his aid?"

Hercules considered the man towering above him.

"No, sir," said Hercules, truthfully. "It would not."

"Good, have him be ready in a quarter of an hour," said the General. "We will leave directly after the servants take their lunch. He can sit at the back with the other kitchen boy — Nate, is it?"

Hercules bowed his head respectfully and stood watching as Washington retreated back to the house, pausing one more time to worry at the garden soil with the toe of his boot.

Chapter 11

The rain did nothing to cool the roof and the air inside the attic remained close and thick. Hercules lay on his pallet and stared out the dormer window pelted with driving rain. Had he been in the kitchen he would have propped open the garden door and let the damp breeze cool the room. But he wasn't going downstairs today.

He shifted on the pallet to ease the pain in his shoulder. It was bad but not nearly as much as he'd let on to Kitt that morning when the steward had shared his plan to travel across the river to Camden, New Jersey, for the afternoon "to look into some furnishings for the new house." He'd demanded that Hercules come to load any purchases onto a hired cart and then onto a waiting ship. It was, said Kitt, an express wish of the president.

They would have reached Mount Vernon by now, thought Hercules as he gazed at the rafters — but not so long as to have sent a letter that would have reached Philadelphia. No, Washington must have made this plan with Kitt before he left. The old fox was cunning.

New Jersey was a slave state and to carry Hercules there for but a minute would serve to reset his tenure in the capital, keeping him that much further from freedom. Hercules was not of a mind to oblige, especially since he had already effected his overstay in the capital back in '91. Technically he was free — a card he'd hold until he was ready to play it, so he had begged off, claiming pain in his shoulder. Margaret, bless her sorry little soul, had piped up then from where she stood polishing the silverware at the table.

"It's been ever so difficult for him, Mr. Kitt," she said earnestly. "Why, it's all he can do to reach upwards some of the time."

They both stared at her, Kitt's face twisting in annoyance and Hercules moving from anger that she should make him seem so weak to amusement at her bravery. Now he was grateful, pure and simple, because Kitt had retreated.

"I see," he had said, eyes narrowed suspiciously. "I imagine I can hire a man." Hercules wondered what Kitt was up to —

or, perhaps, whether the president had not drawn him into confidence. Although the steward gave up, the air between them crackled with his unspoken threat. Had he known the real reason for the trip, surely he would have had another pretense at the ready and insisted.

And he might still do, thought Hercules grimly on his pallet where he had repaired to "rest the shoulder for a short while."

He rubbed at it now, fury rising. The blasted pain would always be there, reminding him of that day. He'd run through the scene over and again in his mind. Why hadn't he been quick enough to break his walking stick down on their heads? Even as he imagined it with grim satisfaction, he knew that beating down a white man was impossible. His fury grew with each throb of his shoulder. The house was quiet. These few weeks before the family returned from Virginia offered perfect opportunities to slip away for hours at a time while Kitt spent more time out of the house than in it. He was allegedly organizing the move to Germantown, but Hercules had his doubts. The man was cagey.

Hercules sighed. Imagine lying down just so in the middle of the day! It was a luxury to be sure, but not one he particularly cared for. He'd rather be on his feet, out in the streets and dead tired, than spare a single free moment lying about in a hot garret — or even in one of the elegantly appointed bedchambers downstairs, come to that.

He'd get up in a little while when he was sure he'd heard the clatter of the carriage in the yard. Once Kitt was on his way, Hercules would be too.

The rain was beating on the roof in waves now, like an off-kilter drumroll. So far it had not been much of a summer with its cool, wet days. He wondered if the weather were any better at Mount Vernon and what Richmond might be doing. The ache for his son was almost as great as the ache in his shoulder.

Richmond had been angry when Hercules told him he was to go to Virginia with the others and remain there. The boy's eyes had narrowed with fury and Hercules had clapped him around the neck and shuffled him far out to the corner of the yard, behind the necessary, where they could talk undetected.

"I have no choice in this, you know that," he had hissed, trying not to breathe through his nose and get a lungful of the foul vapors that hovered around the outhouse.

"And Nate? What of him? Must he remain

in Virginia too?" his son had asked angrily.

"I have no idea," said Hercules smoothly.

Richmond had grunted and turned away, quickly wiping his eyes.

"Son," Hercules said, putting his hand on the boy's shoulder. "Sometimes it's better to be out of sight and mind for a while."

"What does that mean?" Richmond had asked, gulping angrily.

"It means that the General has taken notice of you — and not in a good way," said Hercules matter-of-factly. "That bodes no well. You — we — must choose our actions carefully."

Richmond looked at his father furiously, uncomprehending. He waved his hand in front of his tear-stained face to shoo the flies trying to settle there. Hercules watched him and was reminded of him as a tiny boy, struggling to walk, reaching his little hands in frustration at those who passed by. He'd cry and scream by turns, trapped in that place between anger and desperation. If only he'd learn the lesson of the middle road. Anger was a dangerous draught, though it could keep you alive in just the right dose. But it was Richmond's nature to drink too long and deep from that cup.

Hercules put his hand on his boy's shoulder, fighting the urge to grab him and run

as fast as he could away from this place —
toward certain disaster for them both.

"Trust me, son," he said instead, and the
boy nodded sullenly before Hercules had
sent him off to get ready for the journey.

Hercules drew another deep breath and
sat up. He thought of Waggoner Jack, who
the president had sold to the West Indies
for being churlish and disobedient. Jack had
kept a dog after Washington said no slave
could have one, its bark serving as a warning for the overseers' nighttime raids on the
cabins.

Jack had drunk his rum and cursed the
General's name and those of the men who
came searching for stolen goods, keeping
his dog long after the time they had all set
theirs free or given them away. The General
had hung the dog and put Jack on the next
ship leaving Alexandria for Jamaica, his legs
in shackles. They never did find anything
stolen in his cabin.

Hercules wiped his hand over his face and
prayed that Richmond was holding his
tongue at Mount Vernon. He tapped his
fingers restlessly on his knee, then reached
over the side of his pallet, felt along for the
place the seams were loose, and worked his
hand inside. He felt around until his fingers
touched the palm-sized leather book Mrs.

Harris had given him. Drawing it out, he opened it to the middle and stared at the drawing of a mug with a big letter M above it. Silently he made the sound of the letter, then the whole word, and stumbled through the rhyme written below. He went on to N, then O, and had gotten clear to T before he heard a door slam.

He crawled quickly over to the window and crouched down so he would not be seen. A carriage was waiting in front of the house, the driver hunkered down in his oilskin cloak, rainwater falling in streams off the brim of the hat jammed far down his head. The horses shook their heads, sending a spray of water toward a woman trudging by. She lifted her skirts with one hand and balanced a market basket in the other, her cloak and hood soaked through.

Improbably, and without regard to the actual weather, Kitt emerged attired in a light summer suit holding a ridiculously large umbrella aloft as he approached the carriage. The horses startled a little as the huge moving canopy came near.

Hercules snorted but quickly sobered. Kitt was an extremely odd and unpredictable fellow. That made him dangerous.

He watched as the steward negotiated closing his large contraption and getting into the carriage, then waited until the carriage had moved away from the house and was far down High Street before he returned his little book to its hiding place and made his way downstairs.

In the kitchen, Margaret still sat polishing the silver, her face red and her hair limp from sweat.

"Why do you not prop open the door?" he asked.

Margaret started.

"I — I didn't think of it," she stammered. She looked at him closely. "Do you want for anything? Shall I make you some tea?"

"No," said Hercules, waving his hand at her to sit back down. He walked over to his table and looked idly around.

"How is the packing coming?" he asked.

"Almost done now," she said, taking up a pitcher and beginning to rub at it vigorously.

"Hmmm," Hercules said and tapped his fingers on the table. He felt ill at ease and unable to focus. The close call with Kitt had unsettled his mind. He opened the door wide so a cool, wet breeze swept into the room, then stood and observed the yard with its mud puddles forming in front of the stables and the sodden vegetable patch. A thought was coming to him.

Humming a little, he turned away from the door, grabbed a wooden bowl from the dresser, then went into the larder where he tied on his apron. Rooting around in the basket of remaining potatoes, he grabbed six good-sized ones and placed them in his bowl, then took a stale half-loaf of bread from under a dishtowel and pulled a few springs of parsley, thyme, and sage from the dried herbs hanging from a string along the far wall. Hercules scrubbed the potatoes in the sink and brought them back to his table. When he reached down to lift a small Dutch oven, he winced in pain and stepped back, breathing hard. Margaret was suddenly at his side. "Let me, sir," she said, quickly snatching up the iron pot. She glanced at his ingredients at the table. "Water for boiling?"

Hercules nodded once and leaned on a stool pulled up to the table. He closed his eyes and rubbed the shoulder. He was grateful for the girl's help but a little put off at how closely she seemed to observe him now that Nate was gone. Margaret stoked the fire and set the pot to hang above it. She took the salt from the spice shelf and dropped a few good pinches into the water as Hercules watched. Once she glanced nervously over her shoulder at him. He nodded curtly, which made her pale cheeks burn red. After she placed the potatoes gently in the pot, she stood watching him expectantly.

"Cut a good slice from that bread and then rasp it into crumbs," he said. Margaret eagerly set about her task.

"Well done," Hercules said when she finished. Margaret half curtsied, then hurried over to her bench and the silverware. They worked for the next half hour or so in companionable silence, Margaret polishing and Hercules putting together a simple supper. He couldn't be sure if Kitt would be present for the evening meal, but he'd cobble something together in case.

As he peeled the boiled potatoes and smashed them with a fork, he glanced out the door. The rain was letting up to a fine mist. He cracked two eggs into the potato mash and added salt and pepper before crumbling up the dried parsley, thyme, and sage into it. He formed the potato mash into balls and rolled them around in the breadcrumbs, then brought them to the larder for frying later.

Coming out of the larder, he stood by Margaret's table.

"I have a hankering for some oysters," he said.

Margaret looked up at him curiously, then smiled.

"Come along then," he said.

Margaret was taken aback and stared at him, surprised, before looking nervously at the door.

"Kitt is away for the day," said Hercules, following her gaze. "He won't know that you are gone."

He watched as she considered this, the battling emotions written all over her plain, pale face. Perhaps she was even considering why he might want her company, though he doubted she was bright enough for that. In truth, he wasn't quite sure himself why he wanted her along, except that a small idea was beginning to itch at the edges of his mind.

Finally, Margaret stood and set her plate aside. She untied her apron and set it down.

Hercules gave one of his curt nods before striding out the door, leaving her to follow and close it behind her.

Even though the sun was hazy and weak-looking, it heated up the wet pavement and sent wisps of rising steam into the already thick air. The rain, which had smelled so cool and fresh as it fell, now mixed with the muck of the roads into a stinking, filthy soup.

Hercules strode easily down the pavement without a hat upon his kerchiefed head. Even as he moved purposefully through puddles and muck, Margaret hopped along beside him, striving to avoid them.

It seemed the whole of the town had waited for the rain to pass so they could flood out into the streets. Hercules sensed that Margaret was just barely able to keep herself from grasping at his sleeve as she did Nate's. He kept his stride two steps ahead and occasionally nodded politely at some passerby who called him by name or raised their hand.

When they got to the docks, Hercules headed to where Benjamin Johnson was using his hand to sluice the pools of water from his makeshift table. The waterfront was packed with stevedores and sailors making their ships ready now the squall had passed.

"The ones what have been floating aren't good just now, Master Hercules," the oyster-man said pleasantly after he returned Hercules's greeting. His Quaker accent seemed at odds with his brown skin. "They don't like the rain water falling upon them. Changes the taste it does." Johnson had rigged an ingenious system of cages that floated in the dock behind him, holding the oysters in the briny sea.

"And these?" Hercules said, gesturing to the large barrel by the oysterman's side.

"I pulled out these and covered them before the rain set upon us this morn," he said. "Thou shalt like them, I wager." He plucked a large oyster out of the barrel and quickly pried it open with his special knife before cutting the muscle from the shell and handing it back to Hercules.

The chef held it up to his lips and paused. "One too for the young lady, if you please, Mr. Johnson."

The oysterman selected another oyster and shucked it for Margaret, who eagerly plucked it from his hands and, watching to be sure that Hercules went first, quickly followed him in slurping down the briny bivalve.

"Very good, as always, sir," said Hercules happily. Few things gave him better satisfaction than a delectable morsel of food. He pulled a clean handkerchief from his pocket and wiped at his mouth.

"We'll have a dozen more each, then." Beside him Margaret gasped.

"Oh, no, sir, that's too much!" she said quickly.

"No?" said Hercules, his eyebrows rising

with amusement. "Six, then, for the girl and twelve for myself if you please, Mr. Johnson."

Johnson went to work opening the oysters and setting them on the table. Hercules picked one up and indicated that Margaret should do the same. Soon enough they were slurping them down as fast as Johnson could open them.

"I think you right well could put down twelve, my girl!" Hercules laughed, widely and broadly. Margaret grinned back at him.

"That's right, fill her belly with them oysters to get her randy enough to fill it with something else, eh?" a voice cackled behind them.

Hercules's face contorted with rage and Margaret shrank back in fear. He whirled around to face a ruddy-faced woman with wild orange hair and few teeth. Her bodice barely covered her meager breasts and the bottom of her cloak was crusted with the mud and filth of the road.

But when he set eyes upon the creature, his face changed. Here was the opportunity he had just realized he'd been seeking.

"Ah, Mistress Bolger," he said, his face curling into a terrible smile. "Rain ruin your trade for the afternoon?"

The woman's glared past Hercules toward

Margaret.

"So that's why my services ain't good enough for you, eh? Got yourself some fresh flesh?" she hissed. Hercules stepped into her line of sight and Margaret moved closer to Johnson.

"Why no, Mrs. Bolger, not at all. This girl, unlike you, is not a whore," he said as pleasantly as if he were chatting about the weather. "She too is in the General's employ."

"Employ, is it?" she cackled. "That's what you call it now?" Her face hardened.

"And you, Quaker? Still too godly for a good time?" she said to Johnson.

The oysterman pursed his lips and looked down. Margaret's cheeks were as red as if she had been slapped.

With a snort, the woman finally moved on. Hercules reached into his purse to pull out the coins for Johnson's payment.

"Do not pay her mind, Master Hercules," said the oysterman in a low voice. "Thou knowest she is a wretched creature."

Hercules, his face stony, handed the money to Johnson. "I do. Come along, Margaret," he said gently and guided her by the elbow down the wharf.

"Who was that?" the girl finally managed to whisper once they got to Front Street.

Hercules paused and faced her. He considered her a moment before speaking. This was the time.

"That woman is Mrs. Bolger, the wife of a free Negro chandler," he said, pausing a moment for his words to sink in. "Her people abandoned her when she married him and he lost work in every quarter when he married her. The good women of this town will not even let her wash their stairs."

He turned and began walking again, slowly enough this time for Margaret to keep up.

Hercules stopped and looked out to the farthest end of the harbor, where shipwrights were working furiously on new vessels. He went on, his voice becoming dreamy.

"She was pretty and young and fresh when she met Ward Bolger in her father's tavern. She fell in love but although her father was happy to take Negro money, he didn't want a Negro son-in-law. I'm sure you ken," he continued. "I suppose she thought love would carry them through."

"But how — how did she get like that?" asked Margaret, her voice quavering.

"They had to live somehow so he began to let other men have her favors — for money." He watched Margaret, whose face had now gone even whiter. She looked as if she were about to be sick. "Other black men who wanted to lie with a white woman because the whites wouldn't touch her after she had been 'soiled' by Bolger."

Margaret breathed in short, ragged bursts.

"I don't want you to think he's callous, my dear," Hercules went on sweetly. "No, he loves her very well. They have four or five half-breed children and of course Bolger can't know they are all his — still he keeps them all as his own."

Margaret stood stunned. Hercules turned and began walking again.

"Come along then, Margaret," he said. "A pity our jolly afternoon had to end such, but no need to concern ourselves about it anymore."

Margaret swallowed and trailed after him. He glanced over at her, walking quickly, head down as if she were being watched. For a moment he felt badly about the shock he had given her, but providence had offered an opportunity and he had to take it — for Nate's sake more than hers.

CHAPTER 12

Germantown, Summer 1794

Hercules stood by the fence of the house in Germantown. When he had last seen Thelma, she said the Chews were taking a house in Germantown as well — just on the other side of the square, though he did not know which one. When he went inside, Margaret was standing in the middle of the kitchen, holding the heavy basket with two hands and looking around in confusion as she waited for Hercules to tell her what to do.

"I believe the larder is through there," he said, pointing to a door at the back of the room.

The kitchen was much smaller than the one in Philadelphia and the larder nearly as big as the kitchen itself. Margaret squeezed through the boxes and crates, set the basket down, and picked her way out again.

"Go and find the well," Hercules said as

he pried open a crate and shuffled through the straw packing. When she left, he sighed in exasperation. The oven was inadequate and the kitchen entirely too small. At least there was a pretty orchard just past the kitchen door, and maybe the apples would prove something other than useless. He began to look for his cooking utensils. As soon as the foolish girl found the well, he'd set her to washing the dust and straw from his things.

His thoughts were broken by the yells of men calling horses to a halt in front of the house. Stepping outside the kitchen door, he saw Margaret turn from the well at the back of the property and rush toward the gate in the wall.

Ducking back inside, Hercules stepped into the front hall and slipped into the dining room. He could see the president's carriages and a baggage cart lined up at the door and he could see Margaret hiding behind the stone pillar so she could watch unseen.

Washington gingerly stepped out of the carriage. Austin hopped off the running board to offer his arm. Surprisingly, Washington leaned heavily upon it, slightly stooped over. Mrs. Washington left the carriage, twittering around him, calling for

Oney and for the other postilion to come around to help. The president held up his hand to hush her and then placed it on her shoulder. They proceeded slowly into the house, with Oney and Old Moll following with the children. Hercules quickly stepped back into the kitchen and slipped outside to watch Margaret from there. Nate emerged from around the cart and Hercules watched her face carefully and cursed silently when he saw hope there. Nate's face was serious as he brought a large leather satchel and set it near the steps. Margaret stood like a statue and watched him and Austin, returned from bringing the president inside, continue to unload the cart.

Hercules had to admit that the boy seemed different, more like a grown man than before, but that was hardly possible in a month's time.

Clearly Margaret had marked this too. She looked down at her own dress. Her arms stuck awkwardly out of the too-short sleeves and the hem came clear to the beginning of her shins. As if she were ashamed, she pulled at the sleeves and smoothed the skirt down as if doing so would make it grow long enough to hide her legs. Hercules could only hope Nate would see how drab she was with his travel-fresh eyes.

In the street, passersby had begun to stop. There wasn't much they could see with the carriages blocking the view, but many remained, buzzing as the carriages were unloaded and box after box brought into the house. Hercules stepped back inside and drew in his breath.

"Margaret!" he bellowed. A moment later she arrived, breathless, hands clutching her skirt.

"Sir, I —"

"The *well,* Margaret — where is it?"

She stepped back and pointed in its direction.

"Good, draw me enough water to fill the big tin washtub and get it set up," he said. "I don't like the look of these cauldrons they've left behind and they need a good scrubbing."

He waited with threadbare patience for her to catch her breath.

"They've returned!" she said finally. "And Nate, he's here —"

"The water, Margaret," he said abruptly, turning his back and retreating to the kitchen. His irritation was rising. Would he have to spend the whole of his time contriving ways to keep Margaret from mooning after his scullion? The girl was proving to be far more trouble than she was worth.

The next few hours felt like utter chaos, with servants carrying in boxes and Hercules shouting orders. More than once he yelled at a footman to stay out of his kitchen and Kitt closed the doorway into the house. That was about all the steward did besides standing to the side and eyeing them all critically as they worked.

The kitchen occupied the back of the house, not a separate building as it did in Philadelphia, but they would all be sadly mistaken to think he would change his ways even with the family close enough to hand to hear his bellows. They were worthless, the lot of them. Already he'd had to berate Oney for her laziness and she had stood sullenly, her pale cheeks flushed pink with anger. Next was Margaret who had watched the whole exchange, peering at them through the partly open larder door. He hated nothing more than a sneak. When Hercules turned away, Oney had flounced into the larder and, flinging the door open, said loudly, "His lordship says I am to help you."

Hercules could imagine Oney raking Margaret up and down with her sharp eyes and sharper tongue. Oney was pretty enough to make any lass feel poorly by compare. She had soft brown curls and her skin was the color of tea with plenty of milk. Her breasts swelled just enough over the top of her bodice to show off her slim and lovely figure. She made Margaret look like a scarecrow.

"I can manage, Oney," he heard Margaret say pleasantly. "Not much left to do."

Hercules pretended not to notice what was going on, though from the corner of his eye he had seen Oney take a tall cone of sugar from a crate and set it on a random shelf.

"Well, her *majesty* also says I am to help, so help I shall," she said and continued slamming sugar loaves wrapped in their indigo paper in a line along the shelf. Hercules stopped himself from going in and chastising her for misusing his goods. He wanted to see what would happen next.

"Chef likes one or two loaves left on the kitchen dresser," Margaret said meekly.

Oney stopped just before setting one down.

"Does he?" She looked Margaret up and down again before taking up another loaf and moving toward the door.

"Have you seen Nate yet?" Oney asked Margaret sarcastically.

"Yes. I mean, no," Margaret said uneasily. "That is, I saw the carriage draw up and he was unloading it but I've not spoken to him as yet."

"I see," said Oney. "Well, I'm sure you two will have time together soon enough, what with all the potatoes to be peeled and chickens to be plucked." She smiled sweetly.

Margaret just stared at her a moment, blushing more furiously. She turned back to her crates as Oney tripped triumphantly from the room past Hercules, who pretended to be concentrating on his chopping board.

Nate sat heavily down at the large table and wiped his forehead with his sleeve.

"That's the last of them," he said, taking the platter of green beans from Austin and forking some onto his plate.

"Good," said Kitt from the head of the table. "After lunch you can help Hercules set the kitchen to rights."

Hercules winked at Nate when the boy looked over at him. Kitt's commands bordered on comical to those who knew who truly ran this kitchen.

"Yes, sir," Nate said and picked up his fork.

Hercules watched Margaret, sitting across from Nate and staring like he'd come back from the dead. She held her fork in her hand, her food untouched.

Nate glanced at Kitt, who was busy with his plate. Oney smirked between bites. Austin and Moll were speaking to each other about the town market, but Hercules watched Nate and Margaret.

"Mr. Mueller's pigs will be happy to have your share, Margaret," he said pleasantly, his voice rolling over all of them. "When the dinner hour is over, we must get on with our business. No dawdling, so eat up."

Margaret jumped and looked guiltily at Hercules.

Lunch finished, and Oney, Moll, and Austin went off to attend to their various duties. Kitt and Hercules remained in the kitchen discussing an inventory of the stores, with the steward making a list of provisions for the market, while Nate and Margaret cleared the dishes and washed up.

"How was it?" Margaret asked softly so that, Hercules supposed, she thought he would not hear. She stood close beside Nate, scraping the leavings into the slop bucket.

He glanced at her and shrugged. "Fine, I guess."

"Is it as beautiful as folks say? Mount Vernon, I mean?"

"Dunno. I suppose," he said. "It's better here."

For a moment they continued working silently and only Kitt's voice filled the room. Hercules feigned interest in what the man was saying as he strained to hear the young ones' conversation.

"Were you able to, you know, keep up your studies?" she whispered.

Nate looked around quickly to be sure no one had heard. Hercules set his face in earnest attention to Kitt's droning.

"It was hard. You're never alone," he whispered back. "There's a lot more of us there. All packed into small cabins . . ." His voice trailed off.

"I —" she began but Hercules cut in. "Nate, please start the paste for the standing pies. Margaret, once you're done with the dishes, I need you to grate a half pound of chocolate for the tart and when you are done with that, collect whatever apples we have left and chop them along with some onions."

Nate thrust the dish he was scraping at Margaret and rushed off to do Hercules's bidding, leaving her to look after his retreating back.

Pistol-gray clouds brought the sky down low

over the garden where Nate and Margaret kneeled, pulling weeds and hoeing between the plants. The air didn't move, and from time to time when Hercules came out and inspected their work, it felt like the very heat from the kitchen was rising off his clothes as he towered over them before storming back inside.

Hercules was irritable. It seemed he spent more of his time watching over these two than anything else. And it was time he didn't have. He wished he could leave them to their fate and was annoyed with whatever it was in him that could not let it alone. He didn't care what happened to the girl, but Nate — he reminded him of his boy, Richmond. Or, truth be told, of what he wished his boy could be. No, he couldn't let this orphan flotsam ruin Nate's life — whether she meant to or not. Who knew what foolish and unpredictable thing she might do, dragging Nate down with her?

As he worked in the kitchen, he watched them through the door. Nate stopped his hoeing now and again and spoke to the girl, who sat back on her heels and wiped her face with her sleeve. She said something and Nate shook his head and leaned over the hoe again. Margaret stood up and put her hands on her hips, looking thoughtfully toward the kitchen door before bending over and taking up a stick. She turned her back to the house and started on another patch of garden behind them before the first one was finished. Hercules slammed down his knife and made for the door, furious — they couldn't even grub out a patch of dirt the right way — then something made him stop. Narrowing his eyes, he watched a moment longer as Nate walked over to stand beside her.

She had taken up a stick and was making marks in the dirt. Nate looked at her and then at the house. Hercules stepped back in the shadow of the door. Margaret stared at Nate expectantly and tapped at the dirt with the stick.

Nate whispered something and she nodded before rubbing her marks out with her foot and writing another. His lips moved until finally she nodded and rubbed out the markings again. They did this over and over before she handed Nate the stick.

He took it from her hesitantly and clumsily moved the stick through the dirt. She put a hand over his to guide him, then squeezed his arm, meeting his eyes and broad smile with her own before pulling back bashfully.

Now Hercules moved swiftly from the kitchen, praying that no one was at the upper windows of the house.

When he reached them, he saw the word FREE etched in the dirt.

He stomped upon it with his buckled shoe, its high polish becoming a golden blur as he rubbed it out vigorously.

Startled, Nate stepped back, pushing Margaret slightly behind him.

"Best not let anyone see you doing that," said Hercules, putting one beefy hand on Nate's neck. He could feel the boy flinch. "Margaret, go on into the kitchen and start peeling the cucumbers." She remained dumbly frozen where she stood. He didn't glance her way. The girl did not seem sensible of how things stood here, no matter how he tried to school her, and if he looked at her, his rage might explode.

He watched Nate and felt the same old tinge of worry that dogged him when Richmond had been here.

He looked down at the marred dirt. "Free, indeed. You'll be sold away south if they catch you playing at this." He made sure to keep his voice casual and steady, but he squeezed Nate's neck as he said it.

Now, Margaret's eyes were wild with a sort of panic. Hercules leaned forward across Nate.

"Be easy, girl," he said. "Let this be forgotten. Least said, soonest mended. Just go into the kitchen as usual and start peeling those cucumbers."

She gave a half curtsy before fairly running back into the house.

When she had gone, Hercules let go of Nate's neck and grabbed his arm. He walked him quickly to the orchard and pointed out a tree laden with apples.

"Look to where I point, lad, act like you are taking instruction," said Hercules in a normal tone of voice. "We won't be heard here, and if we are seen, I am merely instructing you on picking the best apples for a sauce. Do you understand?"

"Yes," said Nate, looking up to where Hercules pointed.

"You are playing at dangerous business," he said. "And so is the girl. If you are found out, there is no good end for either of you." He leaned forward and pulled down a laden branch between them.

Nate met Hercules's eyes through the leaves.

"I'll not tell you to stop — you have a right to improving yourself as much as any man — maybe more so. You are a good and quick study," said Hercules. "But I'll tell you to be more discreet — especially with a teacher such as she, lest your interest be taken for something else."

Now Nate's eyes narrowed. "Who could think such, Chef? I have made no improper move —"

Hercules let the branch go and then squatted down to pick up an apple. He gestured to Nate to squat down beside him.

"No, son," he said in a low voice. "I know you haven't. But that doesn't mean she doesn't wish for you to."

The younger man now stared at Hercules in shock. "I — I —" he stuttered.

"Let us say no more," said Hercules, rising and putting his hand out to help Nate up. "Just take good care."

"How did you know?" said Nate, looking at Hercules across the table where they were gutting chickens. Hercules paused, his hands red with the blood and gore of the bird's innards.

"Know what, son?" he said mildly. They were alone in the room.

"The word," said Nate. "The word in the soil." Hercules had hoped his own faux pas would pass unnoticed in the heat of the moment, but he, of all people, should have known his apprentice was too quick for that. He wiped his hands on a dishtowel and brought the gutted chicken to a waiting bowl of water to wash it off.

"Put those entrails in that slop bucket there," he said to Nate over his shoulder. "Then wash down that board well. Use lye."

When Nate finally returned from his tasks, Hercules was chopping onions to add to the chicken, which was already submerged in a large pot of water with herbs.

"Take this over to the fire," he said without looking up. Perhaps if he didn't answer, the boy wouldn't have the courage to persist. But no, Nate did as he was told and then came back to stand expectantly.

Hercules weighed his words and spoke. "As I said, Nate, to want to learn is a natural thing. I don't begrudge it any man. But we must be careful in how we let those aspirations be known." He lowered his voice and leaned a bit over the table. "I made an error in my haste that day," he said. "One I shall not make again — nor, I expect, will you."

Nate nodded uneasily.

"Good," said Hercules in a louder voice this time. "Go and see what Margaret has gleaned, if anything, from those blackberry bushes. Once you've cleaned them and set them to simmer with some sugar and spices, you and I shall go to the market."

The boy hurried out of the room, aware

209

that Hercules's gaze followed him clear through the doorway and into the yard.

Carrying a large basket, Hercules stepped into the garden and paused. Washington was in the orchard meandering through the stand of old trees. Now he stopped and watched Nate and Margaret worrying at the old blackberry bush across the yard. He appeared very interested in how they carried the overfull basket between them back to the kitchen.

When they had gone, the General put his hand on the trunk of the largest of the apple trees and stared into the distance.

Hercules closed the door loudly and Washington looked up.

"Excellency?" Hercules said as he neared the spot where Washington stood.

"Ah, Hercules. What make you of this fruit?"

Hercules looked up at the tree, which had been left to grow too tall.

"I reckon it's good for cider," he said. "At least, I mean to try some for that."

"A good idea," said the General seriously. "That which we've purchased in town has not served us well."

"No, sir," said Hercules. "And apples have been too dear to buy a sufficient quantity to make our own."

"Just so, Hercules," said the General, eyeing him. "You have more sensible care for my resources than most who surround me." Washington muttered this softly more to himself, so Hercules pretended not to hear.

Hercules bent down to retrieve a fallen apple, wincing with pain as he extended his arm. Pushing on his shoulder with the opposite hand, he straightened up, holding the apple to smell.

"The aroma is good, Excellency," he said after inhaling deeply. "I believe they'll make a crisp cider with a good nose."

Washington closed his eyes and leaned forward to gently sniff the apple Hercules held out. "I have no doubt you are right, Hercules," he said, opening his eyes. "What of your shoulder?" Washington asked suddenly. "It pains you, I see — and this is not the first I've noticed."

Hercules was startled. "I pulled it somehow, sir," he said quickly. "It is of no consequence."

"Oh, but it rather is," said Washington, looking up at the tree canopy again. "Kitt tells me you were unable to accompany him to New Jersey because of your pains."

"That is true, sir," said Hercules slowly. What was the old fox up to? And that bastard Kitt . . . "But I am better now."

"I see," said Washington, turning to walk the length of the orchard. Hercules followed.

"We are two of a kind, you and I," said the president, walking with hands clasped behind his back. Hercules raised his eyebrows at this ludicrousness but remained silent. Washington paused and turned to look at the smaller man, his eyes narrowed.

"My back, your shoulder — two old warhorses hobbled by our injuries." He looked inquisitively at Hercules.

"Made stronger by them, sir," Hercules said. "At least, Your Excellency is made stronger by them." Hercules smiled. "My labors are not in comparison to yours." He bowed.

Washington observed him a moment before turning to walk again.

"I note you were carrying a basket," he said after a bit. "More blackberries to glean?"

"Ah, no, sir, the others have done a good job at that," said Hercules. "I am for the market."

"Are you?" Washington raised his eyebrows slightly. "Is not Kitt laying in the supplies adequately?"

Hercules hesitated. The truth was Kitt did

nearly nothing adequately except hover and observe Hercules like a skulking rat. Still, it was always a tricky business to speak against a man that the General had placed in service himself.

"He is — adequate, sir," said Hercules. "I simply like to see what is on offer. I am" — he paused, looking for the appropriate word — "*particular* about what is sent to your table."

Again, Washington stopped walking and turned to look at him.

"Yes, Hercules, I believe you are," he said. "Well, I'll not delay you further."

Bowing again, Hercules turned to take up his basket when the president called.

"Cook, I have a taste for those hoecakes you make for tomorrow's breakfast," he said.

Hercules looked back at the tall man, now stooped, standing under the canopy of branches. He seemed far older and feebler than Hercules had ever seen him. Putting his hand to his chest, Hercules bowed again, more deeply this time, ignoring the searing pain in his shoulder.

CHAPTER 13

The market was winding down its business for the day and there was little left for Hercules and Nate to choose from.

"It's fish that I'm wanting," said Hercules to his assistant. "But we won't buy it here, not after it's been sitting out all day like this. We'll find the seller with the cleanest stall and the best variety. We'll ask him where he fishes and how often and then strike a bargain to bring his wares direct to the house."

They walked on through the rows, pausing at the stall of a butter vendor in the cool of the market house.

"Ask her what cows have given the cream for the butter," Hercules said to Nate as they faced the Quaker woman behind the table.

"What cows do you keep, mistress?" Nate asked politely.

"Jerseys," she said, looking from one to

the other. Hercules asked to look inside the crock.

She opened one of the clay crocks nearest her and moved it forward at an angle for him to look inside.

"Good," he said. "Please give us five pounds." Her eyes widened.

"I have only four left," she said. "Thou can have that."

"Fine, four then," he said, counting the money from the small bag at his waist.

"Next week I shall have five, however, and I'll not collect it here," he said. "Please deliver it before you come to market to the gray house fronting the market square — the house where president and Lady Washington are living at present. Do you know it? Good." Now the woman busied herself drawing the lumps of butter from the small barrel of buttermilk behind her and pressing them into a fresh crock that she held out to Nate.

'Take that back to the house, son," said Hercules, nodding at the woman. "It's too hot to walk with butter in hand. Madam," he said, bowing slightly to her.

Hercules walked on after Nate had left, looking idly at what was on offer. He passed by a table of nice-looking honey but the house was overloaded with the stuff, brought by admirers to the president, who was partial to it. Finally, he came upon a fish vendor he liked and spent some time questioning the man and bargaining with him for a delivery of fish twice a week.

"Make sure to send your absolute best," he said sternly. "President Washington is extremely fond of fish."

His business done, Hercules walked through the rest of the stalls, stopping to purchase the last of a fruiterer's apricots and figs. When he turned, his basket laden, he caught his breath. Thelma was walking toward him, a chattering white girl holding fast to her arm. This must be Harriet Chew. He had not seen Thelma once since they'd been in Germantown, though he was ever aware that she was nearby.

The surprise halted him and he stood observing her. She was looking down and appeared to be listening to her companion, but Hercules knew her too well. Her mind was elsewhere.

She was ravishing in a pink silk dress with gauzy ruffles at her breast and sleeves. Her small waist was deliciously wrapped in a wide fuchsia ribbon. Hercules felt his loins rise as he thought about untying that ribbon. He held the basket lower in front of his pants. Making a swift decision, he walked toward them.

"Good afternoon, ladies," he said in his deepest voice when he was within a few feet of them. He bowed grandly.

Thelma startled and drew her breath. She looked at him wildly. Beside her, the chattering girl stopped mid-sentence and gasped.

"Don't be afraid, Thelma!" she said quickly, pulling Thelma along with her. "I know him — he is General Washington's cook." Hercules straightened and watched them hurry away. He could still hear Harriet Chew's chatter.

"I know the General sets quite a store on him, but he is impertinent," she twittered. "I can't imagine why the General lets his people go about as he does. What with all the free blacks *influencing* them. I mean, even Attorney General Randolph lost his slaves to that terrible abolition law. And now all the French planters from the West Indies fighting to keep their people, as if it weren't bad enough they had to flee their country . . ."

Harriet stopped talking when she heard Thelma gasp.

"Oh! Forgive me, my dear, I did not mean to frighten you," she said earnestly. She studied Thelma a moment. "You — you did not lose anyone to the abolition law, did you? How thoughtless of me not to ask! I just assumed given your circumstance . . ."

"*Non,* my dear, I did not," Thelma answered. "It is just that I am as shocked as you."

Satisfied, Harriet began to pull Thelma farther away, her voice fading as they exited the other side of the market.

When he reached the other edge of the square, Hercules paused and considered what to do. The prospect of a reunion with Thelma seemed more remote than ever. There was no question of going after her, but he needed to know where she was staying. Maybe he could follow without being seen. But what if he could contrive to meet her only to find that Harriet had set her against him? Nonetheless, he began to turn back the way he had come.

"*Mon taureau . . .*" said a breathless voice from behind him. He swung around to face her, a grin pulling at the corners of his mouth. She was breathing hard, her bosoms heaving above her bodice as if she had run back the whole way.

"The Chews have taken that house, across there." She flicked her head in its direction. "If you come tonight, after they are abed, I will come out. *Oui?* You can manage this?"

She searched his eyes. "I can," he said under his breath. "Go now before someone takes note."

Although they were in the center of the village, Germantown was such a small burgh that even on a market day, there weren't enough crowds for Hercules to blend in. He had to wait until the family was properly abed and the town quiet before he made his way to the Chews'. He only hoped that Thelma would not have retired as well.

Nate and Austin had long gone up to their attic room, which was far less commodious than their quarters at the presidential mansion. Here the roof sloped so low that they had to crawl to their pallets to sleep and crawl out again. It wasn't so much an issue for Hercules, who was short, but Austin had banged his head on the rafters more than once when he sat up too quickly upon waking.

Hercules made good use of the time he had to wait, studying the letters in his small book by the light of the dying fire. He had prepared two pies for the next day and had them cooling on the table should anyone come down to the kitchen at the late hour, and he had mixed the batter for the president's corn cakes, which sat in the larder covered with a cloth.

When he could finally sense no more movement in the rooms overhead, Hercules stood and slipped the small book into his boot before going out the garden gate. He paused a moment, adjusting his eyes to the moonless night. The town watch was clear at the end of the main road — he could see his lantern bobbing far in the distance. Glancing up, he saw no lights in the windows of the house.

Hercules crossed the square, keeping well to the edges where there were trees and shrubs for cover. When he reached the wide stone gambrel-roofed house where the Chews were staying, he slipped around the back and stood across the street, stepping into a small shed there and peering out from the shadows.

He couldn't be sure if it was the right side of the house for Thelma's room, but he guessed that, her being a paid companion, it would be nearer the back stairs. He stood for almost a half hour before he saw a side door open and a cloaked figure move toward him.

Hercules stepped backward into the open doorway of the shed. It was hard to make out whether the approaching figure was a man or woman. It could easily be one of the footmen who would wonder why a Negro was lingering across the way.

The figure stepped into the shed and pulled back the hood.

"Mon taureau," Thelma breathed, moving to cover his mouth with her own. She pressed up against him and he reached under the cloak to pull her close.

"What are you wearing?" he said, surprised.

"My nightdress, what else?" she said simply, running her tongue down his neck. "How I've longed for you," she groaned. He felt himself stiffen.

"You might be missed," he said, holding her away from him.

Thelma stepped toward him again. "Do you not want me?" she said coquettishly.

Hercules glanced out the door of the shed and shut it with a soft click before lunging toward her and backing her up against the wall. In a flash, he was inside her and she wrapped her legs around his back.

"Have you got your answer?" he said into her neck.

Once he was done, she smiled impishly, she pulled down the nightdress and tied the cloak tighter. Outside the sentry called the two o'clock hour.

"We cannot meet here again," he said, tak-

221

ing her hand. "It's not safe."

Thelma was now no longer smiling.

"But —" she began.

He held up his hand. "You're at risk," he said. He opened the door and glanced out. "There's no one in the street now, you can go back quickly."

Thelma caught at his sleeve and pulled him back into the shadows. She put her hand on his face. *"Mon taureau . . ."*

Hercules caught her wrist and kissed her palm.

"Don't worry," he said, leaning up to kiss her mouth. "I will find another way."

They kissed and nuzzled for a few seconds more before he held her away again.

"Which one is your window?" he said, nodding toward the house. Thelma pointed to a small window on the top floor near the rear of the building.

"Good," he said. "Look out your window every day at the noon hour. If you see me that means I have news and will be here, in this spot, that night when I can get away."

"I can do this," she said, moving toward him again.

"Beautiful Thelma," he said, grabbing her arms and looking at her before kissing her hard. "I want you a thousand ways but you must go while it's safe."

Nodding, she kissed him one last time before dashing across the street, her pale skin a flash in the inky night.

Hercules gently closed the door when he slipped back into the kitchen. Margaret would be sleeping on her pallet in the larder. He moved quietly toward the stairs when he heard a sickly groan. Standing, he waited. The sound was something between a whimper and a gag. It was coming from the larder where Margaret slept.

Hercules moved to the larder door and eased it open. Margaret lay there on the pallet in her shift. She had kicked off the light blanket and sweat coated her absurdly pale arms and legs, which were splayed out like those of a broken doll.

Squinting at him, she rose up on one elbow but then flopped down again and collapsed on the pallet.

Hercules uttered a curse and moved closer into the room. What the devil was wrong with her? Kneeling, he felt her face. It was burning hot.

"Father?" she muttered and tried to reach for him, but then her eyes fluttered up in her head.

Alarmed now, Hercules made his way quickly up the stairs to the hall where Oney slept outside the Washingtons' room. He would need her help. Shaking her awake, he told her what was wrong and to alert her mistress.

Oney scowled, furious at being awoken, but eventually she nodded. Hercules returned downstairs and waited, unsure what to do. Finally, he went to the well and drew a bowl of cold water and wet down some clean kitchen rags.

A long time passed while he patted down Margaret's head and legs, feeling peculiar the whole time. He could see that she was somewhere between a child and a woman and it felt wrong to be doing this, but worse to let her lie and suffer. Finally, to his relief, he heard Oney come into the kitchen, calling softly. She reached him in the larder and her mouth fell open.

"Well?" said Hercules gruffly, ignoring her shock.

"Uh, Lady Washington says to lay her out in the box room upstairs. There's an extra cot there . . ." Her voice trailed off as she stared at Margaret's thin white arm in Hercules's hand.

"Fine," said Hercules, scooping the girl up and standing. His injured shoulder screamed in pain. In his arms, Margaret tried to say something but the words were just a gurgle.

Once he lay her down on the small cot, he went up to his room. Lady Washington had sent for the doctor and he lay awake a long time listening until he heard the sound of voices at the front door and then footsteps on the stairs.

Loud voices and heavy footsteps sounded overhead, then a high-pitched scream followed by total silence. In the kitchen, Nate bolted up from his bench where he sat shelling peas.

"Sit down," said Hercules from where he stirred the pot over the fire.

"They're hurting her!" Nate said angrily. He did not sit down.

"They're not hurting her," said Hercules calmly. "The doctor is bleeding her. She is getting the best of care. Same as Lady Washington's granddaughter would."

Nate balled his hand into a fist before sitting heavily down.

"Besides," Hercules went on as he buttered a tart pan, "what is it to you?"

Nate shrugged. "She is my friend," he said, trying and failing to sound nonchalant.

"Friends, is it?" Hercules rumbled. He could see he was going to have to use harsher tactics to make the boy face the truth. He opened his mouth to say something more when there was the noise of many feet in the hall. Oney bustled in, carrying a bowl of bloodied water that she flung outside the kitchen door.

She turned toward them, her hand on her hip, looking ready for a fight.

"Now, I'm to be nursemaid to a *servant*?" she began. Voices entered the kitchen from the hall through the door that Oney had left ajar.

"Do you think it's the yellow fever?" they heard Lady Washington ask in shrill tones.

"That girl isn't worth her keep —" Oney was going on.

"Hush!" hissed Nate, straining to hear what was being said in the hall.

Oney closed her mouth with a snap and gave him an evil look.

"I doubt it," the doctor was saying. His voice sounded tired. "It is an ague of some kind. Others in the village have had it but it passes within a day or so. Just keep her still and see if someone can get some willow bark tea down her — that should help with the pain and fever. Some broth too if you can manage it."

"So there is no concern for the others in the house?" Lady Washington asked nervously. "My grandchildren —"

"No, Mrs. Washington, I don't think so," he said. "Does she spend much time with them?"

"Heavens, no!" she answered. "She's a scullery maid, an orphan girl. She's only with the other servants."

"Ah, I see," they heard the doctor say. Their voices were getting farther away as Mrs. Washington showed the doctor to the door. "She has no people then. You are doing her a great kindness."

He murmured something else that they could not make out before they heard the door shutting firmly and her heavy footsteps coming back down the hall.

They all busied themselves with something by the time her ample frame filled the doorway.

"Hercules?" she said, looking toward him.

"Madam?" he answered politely, stepping around his table and wiping his hands on a cloth. "How may I help?"

"Could you make a short broth? Something for the girl upstairs?"

"I believe so," he said. "There are some lamb shank bones I was saving to make pocket soup."

"Good, good," she said, wiping her hands down the front of her skirt. "Oney, please mix up some willow bark tea. You'll have to go to the apothecary for the bark."

Oney curtsied and made for the door. "And be quick about it!" Mrs. Washington said after her. "We are to have ten for supper tomorrow, Hercules," she said, turning back to him. "Can you do well enough without the girl? Should we hire in for the day?"

"I think I can do well enough with Nate here, Lady Washington," said Hercules, nodding toward the boy. Mrs. Washington turned to examine the young man critically.

"Well, if you are sure . . ." she said nervously.

"I have ordered sweetmeats from the confectioner already," he said. "Nate has a light hand with his pie crusts and he will get started on the tarts as soon as we are done preparing the meal for tonight. I'll slice one of our Mount Vernon hams as well and that will help fill the table."

Now Mrs. Washington smiled. "Good," she said, and bustled out of the room.

The rest of the evening was filled with supper preparations and getting ahead of the work for the next day. Oney flounced in with the apothecary packet and made the willow bark tea, complaining all the while.

"Here, add this to your tray," Hercules

said to her, ladling some broth into a porringer.

"Madam better recover soon," she said nastily. "I'll not be her handmaiden."

"Oney," began Austin, just come in from the stable. "Have a care . . ."

She turned on him in a flash, ready to bicker, but before they could begin — she shrill and he calm — Nate straightened up from garnishing a standing pork pie with dough cutouts and set his knife down. He crossed over to where Oney was holding the tray and grabbed hold of its handles.

"I'll take it," he said, pulling the tray from her so a bit of the soup slopped over the side of the porringer.

"Well, well," said Oney, smirking. "Miss your little shadow, do you?"

Nate opened his mouth to answer but Hercules cut in first.

"Be quick about it, then," he said sharply. Behind Oney's shoulder, he gave Nate a pointed look. "Oney, you best get on."

Oney looked at Hercules over her shoulder and gave a sly grin.

"Yes, I reckon I best be," she said, giving her brother an arch glance before walking out of the kitchen, head held high.

Nate turned with the tray to follow her out as quickly as he dared without the contents of the bowls being completely lost.

CHAPTER 14

Hercules glanced out the door at Margaret and Nate working in the chicken yard. He was mucking out the coop and she was sitting in a chair picking through a bowl of hominy and throwing the marred grains to the birds. Although it had been nearly two weeks since her illness, she was still pale and winded easily.

Nate had told him how he'd found the girl on the cot, delirious with fever, the counterpane splattered red from the blood-letting. She had mistaken Nate for her father and then cried when he was not. The boy had spent the better part of an hour up there until Hercules had bounded up the stairs in a rage, looking for him.

Unseen, Hercules had stood there looking at the pathetic creature lying there with Nate holding a spoon uselessly up to her mouth. Her skin looked clammy, like a plucked chicken carcass. Her hair was plastered to her forehead in greasy wisps.

For a moment he felt sorry for the girl, then quickly felt foolish. She was young, and as soon as her indenture was over her lot in life would be a damn sight better than his own. He'd returned to his kitchen and worked Nate hard for the rest of the afternoon and night until the boy, nearly falling from exhaustion, made his way to his own pallet and collapsed there.

Now the two were inseparable and Hercules had tired of making tasks to keep them apart — a difficult proposition in a kitchen where they all had to work together. All he could do now was hope to intervene when anyone of import might take note. Austin just shook his head when he walked by them and Oney had taken to calling Margaret Nate's "specter" on account of her sickly pallor. Even Old Moll had watched them curiously as they sat together upon a bench, speaking in low tones as they snapped green beans.

Annoyed, Hercules grabbed a wooden bowl and headed out to where some wild strawberries clustered against the outside of the garden wall. There might yet be some that had survived the pelting rain of the last few weeks, and he would use them for an iced cream.

"Good afternoon," a voice said pleasantly behind him as he stretched forward.

Hercules briefly looked up from where he squatted. There stood the scribbler who had been dogging him all those days in Philadelphia.

"Afternoon, sir," he said politely but without any warmth.

"Perhaps you don't recall," the man went on. "I am Gilbert Stuart — we know each other."

"I recall," said Hercules, pushing aside leaves to see if he had missed any of the small red berries.

The other man did not seem to have an answer for this.

"I've just been to see your master," he tried again.

Hercules paused for a split second before resuming his work.

"Yes, sir," said Hercules, his mind racing. Had Stuart told the General about the incident in the city? If Washington believed any of his slaves were in danger he would certainly ship them all back to Virginia. They all knew he was already nervous about them taking advantage of the freedom law. Damn this man.

"I want to paint him, you see," Stuart went on. "I am a painter."

Hercules moved farther down the fence and forced his voice to remain calm. "There's many as want to paint the General, sir."

"Indeed so," Stuart said. He followed Hercules's progress by a few steps, hovering annoyingly as he gleaned the last of the strawberries from the patch.

"He refused me as a matter of fact," said Stuart finally. "Rather a recalcitrant old fellow, isn't he?"

There was no good answer for this, and Hercules didn't want to give one, so he kept on at his work, hoping the irritating man would leave. Instead, the painter followed him along, watching as he worked.

"I didn't tell him about the last time we met," Stuart said finally. Hercules stood slowly and brushed the dust from the knees of his britches. Finally, the man had come to his purpose.

"And why is that, sir?" he said, trying to keep the relief out of his voice.

"I'm sure I can't say," answered the other man pleasantly. "I imagine it would not help my case."

"I couldn't speak to that, now, could I?" said Hercules, leaning over for the bowl.

"You are called Hercules, are you not?"

asked Stuart, blocking the smaller man's way.

Now Hercules narrowed his eyes. "It seems you are more of a detective than a painter, sir," he said calmly. "First you follow me about the town and now we find you here."

"So you knew —" said Stuart, his eyes widening, but then he stopped abruptly and smiled what Hercules supposed was the man's most charming smile.

"I suppose I find you interesting, Hercules," he said.

Hercules studied him a long moment. What did the man really want?

"Do you?" he said sarcastically. He'd had his fill of this crazed fool.

"Yes, I do," said Stuart. "I should like to paint you, as a matter of fact."

Now Hercules smirked openly. The man was truly insane, spouting mad thoughts, as if his wild hair and disheveled clothes hadn't proved that enough. "I doubt you'll be getting a commission from the General to paint the likes of one of his slaves. His horse maybe, but not one of his slaves."

Stuart smiled again. "I don't mean as a commission," he said. "I would like to paint you for myself, Hercules." He paused and leaned in closer. "I like the look of you."

The man was a complete lunatic, thought Hercules. But then, that was often the way of white people — subject to whims and strange desires they expected to be fulfilled.

"And even if I agreed, how would you suppose a person such as myself could simply put aside the time to be painted as if he were a gentleman?"

Stuart's face became serious. "Oh, I know you come and go quite freely, remember, Hercules? That's how we met the last time."

Hercules's jaw hardened. The man was threatening him.

"I'm not sure I'd care to," he said in a low growl.

"No, I expect you wouldn't," said Stuart, taking a step toward him. "But I suggest you consider it, or I might have to have a conversation with the General."

Hercules hoped the panic wouldn't show in his eyes. He forced himself to smile easily. "I suggest you do so then," he said, bowing slightly. He made to move around the artist, hoping he would not call his bluff.

Stuart put his hand on Hercules's arm as he passed. "Wait," he said. "I wouldn't care to do that — as a first resort. I doubt it would serve either of us."

Hercules looked at the hand grasping his arm. The nails were bitten down to the quick and the skin was raw and red.

"Perhaps there is something else you want," said Stuart. "Just think on it. I am at the small stone house about a quarter mile down the road on this same side of the street. There is a barn in the back that I use partly for my studio. There's a weathervane upon it of an Indian drawing back a bow."

Hercules stood stock-still, staring straight ahead, until the painter finally released his arm and went on his way.

He balanced the package of shirts newly made for him and Austin on top of his market basket. Kitt had been happy to let Hercules run this errand, preferring, as always, to use his time on whatever he did during his many trips out.

The tailor's shop stood close enough to Stuart's house that Hercules could gaze upon it easily. It was a small house sur-rounded by a rather large yard, set back from the street. The barn-studio was tucked away into the corner, fairly far from the road. As he watched, a charwoman emptied a slop bucket into the yard, sending an arc of dirty water high into the air.

Hercules studied the house a bit longer. Few people came down this part of the road unless they had business at the tailor's or the apothecary, but that was daytime trade. The town tavern was at the opposite end of High Street.

There were no animals in the yard, not even a single chicken. Clearly Stuart did not mean to keep this house in German-town long — no doubt only for the few weeks required to stay close to possible patrons during the summer.

Hercules doubted the painter was in enough coin to hire live-in help, and the charwoman he saw was probably a local who only came in during the days.

This could work.

Hercules turned, smiling, and headed back down the street toward the President's House. He might have to pay Mr. Stuart an evening visit after all.

Chapter 15

Mr. Kitt had retired to his room, leaving the kitchen staff to finish clearing away the supper things. The night had been a long one, with the Washingtons returning the invitations of several of the prominent families in town who had entertained them during the summer.

Nate and Margaret stood at the deep washtub, shoulders touching. He was scrubbing the dishes and then handing them to her to rinse and dry. They murmured together in low voices, their words occasionally loud enough to float across the room to where Hercules was grinding cornmeal and Oney was sewing a mobcap. Beside her, her brother Austin was polishing his boots, stopping occasionally to tease his sister about her fussy stitching and talking about what he had seen and heard in the capital earlier in the day.

"Like a ghost town it is," he said, taking

up a soft cloth to rub on the boots. "Guess folks haven't forgotten about what happened last year."

"Is the fever back?" Oney asked her brother.

"Not much as I've heard," said Austin, shrugging. "A few cases. Can't be too bad if the General keeps coming and going."

Oney considered this. "Still and all, you should try and stay away from folks as much as you can — sit up there on the carriage, away from the vapors, until he wants you."

Austin smiled and nudged her playfully, "Yes, little mama."

Margaret and Nate began to move about the kitchen putting away pans and crockery.

Oney swatted Austin away and then eyed them before going on. "I heard Mrs. Washington telling Nelly that terrible Betsey wants to come for a visit when we go back to Philadelphia," she said.

Betsey, Mrs. Washington's granddaughter, was Nelly's older sister. She was known for her bossy ways and high temper. She stomped around the house and picked on everyone and everything. The only person she had eyes for was her step-grandfather, and the only time her voice didn't reach a shrill pitch was when she spoke to him.

Austin only grunted and continued polishing his boots. Hercules kept grinding his corn.

Oney looked from one to the other of them and then pursed her mouth. "Y'all have nothing to say?" she said snappishly. "You know what a misery that Betsey is, and I'm the one that will have to tend to her. She's a tribulation to be sure."

Behind her Hercules saw Margaret raise her eyebrows at Nate, who shrugged.

"My dear Oney, everyone is a tribulation to you. Work is a tribulation to you," said Hercules, amused. "You seem to forget that is the only reason why we are here."

Austin smirked and put the boots on the floor.

"Lord knows that's true," he said. "Anyhow, why you working yourself up already? Betsey ain't here yet."

Oney gave her brother a narrow-eyed look. "Betsey ain't here yet," she mimicked him.

"Betsey might not be here for a year, but just the thought of her being here *ever* is enough to sour my stomach from now until then," she said, standing up and clutching her sewing.

"Aw, Oney, don't take on so," said Austin, standing too. "I can't imagine she could be any worse than any of them."

"What do you know, Austin?" Oney said,

pushing her face up close to his. "The clos-
est you get to one of these uppity white
ladies is to hand her into a carriage and out
of it. You don't have to hurry and fetch and
arrange their clothes and clean their chamber pots and pretend it don't stink worse
than what comes out of your own black ass."

"Oh!" Margaret burst out. Oney turned
to her in fury.

"Don't you act scandalized, *Miss,*" Oney
hissed. "Floating around here like a sorry
little cur. You may have this one feeling sorry
for you" — she jabbed her finger toward
Nate — "but the rest of us nigras ain't
fooled." She took a step closer to Margaret
and Nate moved forward.

"Be careful what you playing at, girl," she
went on in a low, threatening voice. She
spoke to Nate. "Mind, one day she'll walk
on outta here free and you and me will still
be cleaning shit and flinging slop. You think
she's gonna remember you then?"

"Oney! That's enough!" Hercules boomed
behind her. She was on the edge of going
too far. "Go on now, get on upstairs. I'm
sure Lady Washington will be looking for
you."

Oney didn't answer. She stood there looking at them a minute more, breathing hard
with anger. Nate looked like he was about

242

to slap her, and Austin moved closer to the trio, ready to protect his sister. Margaret stood there, her face red and her eyes welling with tears.

Finally, Oney turned and marched out of the room. When she had gone, Margaret collapsed against Nate's side. She buried her face in his sleeve.

"Don't mind her," he murmured, putting his arm around her. She sobbed against his chest.

Hercules caught Austin's eye and gave a tiny head shake. Austin blinked to show he understood before both men turned away. Oney had said what there was to say for all of them.

Hercules tapped lightly on the low door, keeping one eye on the yard and road beyond. Gilbert Stuart's studio was little more than a hovel. The artist had divided his stable with a crude wall and Hercules could hear the man's horse snuffling just on the other side of it.

When there was no answer to his second knock, he walked around to look in the rough window cut into the side of the building. Light shone through the shutters, so the artist must be inside.

Hercules returned to the door and gently

scraped it open and was almost hit by a lantern swinging wildly in front of him. "Who's there?" said Stuart, squinting as though blinded by the lantern he wielded so recklessly.

"Mr. Stuart!" Hercules said. "Sir! It's Hercules — General Washington's cook."

Stuart lowered the lamp and peered at him.

"Well, come in, man, don't just stand there in the doorway," he said, leaning forward and pulling at Hercules's arm.

Hercules resisted the urge to shake off Stuart's hand and moved farther into the room, glancing around. The cheap lath and plaster that was used to coat the walls and turn the stable into a usable room was already crumbling away in spots. Hercules looked at him more closely now. Again, it occurred to him that the painter was quite mad. Brushes sat in a neat row on the table next to his easel. Sketch after sketch was flung onto the floor and every surface of the room. Country scenes, market day, ladies walking. Even Hercules knew that such things were worthless. In the new America those who could afford art — the new class of middling merchant — wanted portraits of famous men like Washington or Jefferson or even Hamilton, to hang in his parlor and gaze upon as he sipped his after-dinner port.

"I, ah —" Hercules looked at Stuart with his wild hair and over-bright eyes. The man stank too. "I've thought about your offer."

"Yes?" Stuart said, leaning forward excitedly.

"I should like to be painted, I think," said Hercules simply.

Stuart broke into a hysterical smile. He came forward and clapped Hercules on the back, pulling him farther into the room. Hercules struggled not to show his distaste.

"Here, sit — sit," he said excitedly. "Ale?" he asked, holding up the tankard.

"Ah, no," said Hercules. "I thank you."

"So," said Gilbert, drawing a chair opposite him. "When can we start? I'm eager to experiment with your tone. I haven't painted a Negro before, it will be a new experience for me —"

He stopped. Hercules was looking at him as if he were the curiosity.

"There is something I want," said Hercules when Stuart paused. "You said — you said that perhaps there was something I wanted, and I do."

Gilbert's eyebrows rose. "Money? I don't have much, but surely I can pay you something."

Hercules held up his hand. "Forgive me,

Mr. Stuart, but I have plenty of ready money," he said, working hard to keep the disdain from his voice. "No doubt this surprises you, but the General does allow me to earn some coin of my own in various ways."

Gilbert cocked his head, looking both amused and perplexed.

"Interesting," he said. "So, what is it you want?"

"I want the use of your studio," said Hercules.

"My studio?"

"Yes, of an evening here and there — when you have finished for the night."

"But what could you want with it?" said the artist. "Surely you must be in your quarters at night."

"That is true," said Hercules. "The sun must rise upon me in my quarters at the President's House."

Stuart looked carefully at Hercules.

"So then, I ask you again, what could you possibly want with my studio?"

"There is someone I must meet from time to time," said Hercules. "The circumstances make it imprudent to do so where we might be seen."

Hercules could almost see Stuart's brain working. Who could he be meeting? A woman? Someone who could help him to freedom? A smuggler? Was Hercules stealing from the Washingtons?

"I assure you, Mr. Stuart, the meeting is nothing more than *intimate* in nature," said Hercules, cutting into the man's thoughts.

Stuart considered this and finally smiled.

"I think, Hercules," he said, "that we can come to such an agreement."

Hercules smiled and stood. He bowed slightly.

"I am glad to hear you say that, Mr. Stuart," he said. "When do you want me to come to you next?"

"Why not tomorrow?"

"Why not tomorrow indeed?" said Hercules, a small smile playing at the corners of his mouth. "I'll bid you goodnight."

". . . and then we'll serve the ratafia cakes with elderberry jellies," Hercules was saying as he and Nate made their way out of the market. Nate shifted the basket filled with pig feet to his other hand. "Some pocket soup is probably in order as well . . ."

Hercules went on talking cheerfully about all the things they'd make with the trotters they had just bought, but he could tell the scullion's mind was somewhere else.

Normally, Nate would be eager enough

for the conversation but Hercules had found it hard to get him to focus since Margaret had been sick. Something had changed again between them and Hercules wasn't sure what — or even how.

He had hoped the run-in with Oney would have knocked some sense into the boy's head and that he would have seen the truth in what she'd said in spite — that Margaret would eventually be free and he would not. And that even if Nate were free too, they did not belong together.

Hercules stopped walking and watched as Nate wandered on, staring at the ground, unaware that Hercules's deep voice wasn't washing over him. Finally, sensing that something was amiss, he paused his stride. He turned around quickly, basket swinging, to see Hercules, hands on hips, standing twenty feet behind. Nate rushed back.

"Your mind is elsewhere, son," said Hercules sternly when Nate had come up to him panting. He clapped a hand on the boy's shoulder. "Let's walk a little," he said, gesturing toward a road that ran along the side of the market, away from the house. "It's a fine day and no need to rush back just yet."

They walked a few paces without speaking until Hercules came to a stop in front of a shed.

"Never let your thoughts run away like that, Nate," he said seriously. Nate looked down at the ground. "Look at me, son. People like us, we need to be aware at all times," Hercules said to the boy who was now a few inches taller than him. Hercules glanced around, his eyes flickering to the grand house across the road from where they stood. "Do you understand?"

Nate had followed Hercules's gaze to the house and then back again. "Yes, sir," he said.

"Good," said Hercules, looking at him a long moment. Again, he glanced over to the house, trying to see if Thelma might be at the window taking notice of him.

"We can't afford to be going along dreaming — there's danger in it," he said, looking back at Nate.

When Nate nodded, Hercules turned back toward the square, leaving the boy to follow, but not before he had noticed a flutter of the curtains in the upstairs rear window of the house across the street.

It had been three days since Hercules had first walked with Nate to the shed across from the Chews' house and he had faithfully shown up every day just after the noon hour. He'd leaned on the shed for a few minutes so that she might see him, but she hadn't come out.

Today, he had slipped out again after the luncheon was served. He walked slowly around the square and down the Chews' street, forcing himself to hunch a bit to be less noticeable. He didn't want the drivers sitting on the carriages that lined the road in front of the house to mark his presence. The Chews must be receiving callers today.

When he was about halfway up the block, Hercules saw Thelma step out onto the stair and he breathed a sigh of relief. He began to speed up but then slowed again as a man emerged and offered her his arm. Hercules cursed under his breath.

She looked quickly down the street, spotting him, and met his eyes before turning toward her companion.

"Have you seen this little building here, Captain Grayson?" she said, loudly, her voice carrying across the road toward Hercules as she dragged him across the path.

The man looked at her uncertainly. What possible interest could there be in a falling-down shed?

"I have . . ." he said.

"It is so odd, is it not? What is it for?" she

kept chattering.

"I imagine it is . . ." he began.

Thelma did not let him finish but continued to walk quickly now that she was on the same side of the street as Hercules, who started to move slowly toward them, staring at the trees and the buildings as if he were confused.

"I might sketch it, perhaps," she continued, talking more loudly now.

"Are you quite all right, Miss Blondelle?" Grayson said, attempting to slow down. "Perhaps the heat — ?"

"Heat?" Now she laughed, loud and shrill. "*Non, monsieur!* On my island it is always far hotter than this."

Grayson's pale — almost white — eyebrows knit together, perplexed. "What island, Miss Blondelle?"

Hercules's heart stopped. She had made a fatal error. He dared not look at her as he heard the panic in her shrill voice, but instead, she took the offensive. "Island? I did not say island."

She pressed on. They were close enough now that surely he would be able to say something quickly before the man intervened. He looked around as if he were lost.

Now they were quite close and Hercules scratched his head as if puzzled.

" 'Scuse me, suh," said Hercules in his best imitation of a country pickaninny. "I'se lookin' fer Gilbert Stuart's place? I got to deliver a message from my master but I can't find it." He turned around looking more confused and nervous. "Folks say it's a barn-like thing but I ain't see no barn . . . I got to deliver this message, see . . ."

Grayson moved to the side, forcing Thelma along with him.

"I'm sure I don't know," said Grayson coldly, trying to go around him.

"Miss, do you know?" Hercules said, wringing his hands and looking at Thelma, willing her to understand.

"No! She does not!" Grayson said angrily. "I've told you already, be along your way."

"Is this the main road, sir? Only as I know the place is on the main road." He turned around again, still looking confused.

Now Grayson exploded. "No, you fool! The main road is farther on! Don't you see the public market there?"

Hercules looked around wildly. "Oh! There it is. I see it now! Thank you, suh! Thank you! I supposin' I didn't recognize it being as I only markets on Wednesday," he said nonsensically, then bowed deeply and caught Thelma's eye as he straightened. She blinked her eyes slowly to show him she understood him: Gilbert Stuart's barn in the main road on Wednesday night.

"Be on your way!" said Grayson angrily.

"Yes, suh!" said Hercules, smiling a wide fool's smile, before he turned and nearly ran down the road, doing his best to keep down his loud laugh.

Gilbert Stuart put down his charcoal stick and held his sketchpad away from his face. "Can you turn and face the other way?" he asked.

Hercules stood, turning his neck this way and that until Stuart seemed satisfied.

"I didn't realize what hard business this was," Hercules said as he sat down again. He couldn't even enjoy the time simply sitting because of Stuart's constant chatter.

"It can be," said Stuart, sitting down again himself. He sketched a few minutes more, mumbling to himself as he did.

"Ah, yes, that's better," he said, looking over at Hercules and smiling. "Tell me, Hercules, what's it like to work for the president?"

Hercules swallowed a laugh and instead stared at Stuart with something between amusement and disgust. He raised an eyebrow. "It's not as though I have much choice in it, is it, Mr. Stuart?" he asked mildly.

Stuart opened his mouth then shut it again. "Ah — I suppose not," said the artist sheepishly. "Well, do you like to cook?" He turned the sketchbook to a clean page and moved a bit to the right to capture another angle.

Hercules's eyes followed him. "I do," he said simply.

The man began to talk, filling the space between them with noise. "When I was in England — I was there for nearly twenty years, you know — when I was there I had the occasion to eat in many fine houses. I always remember thinking that we had much finer ingredients here in America, much finer." He paused and smiled at Hercules. "Not, that is to say, that good ingredients can make a poor cook skillful, but I imagine it helps."

Hercules made a sound that was something like a snort. Finally, the man had said something sensible. "This is what I tell my assistant," he said. "You must start with the best ingredients you can get, otherwise your skill is for naught."

"Seems very sound," said Stuart, his charcoal moving quickly on the page. "Now in France, they take their cuisine very seriously indeed. Some of my patrons spoke of the parties and fetes they attended there and if they are to be believed, the nature of the dishes were more like art than food."

"Yes, I have heard the same," said Hercules, thinking about his many conversations with James Hemings. "A friend told me as much."

Thelma rolled off Hercules's lap, breathing hard. She lay flopped beside him on the settee until she caught her breath, then stood and walked over to the water pitcher on a small side table.

"I wish you'd dress yourself," said Hercules, watching Thelma pour herself some water.

"Why? Do you not like to see me *au naturel*?" she asked, coming back and holding out the mug.

He sat up to button the flap of his trousers.

"Naturally," he said, smiling and rising. He pulled her shawl from the settee and wrapped it around her. "But it always pays to be able to escape or hide oneself quickly, and that is harder to do when one is naked." He took the water from her hand and drained it.

"Besides," he said, after the last swallow, "how would it look for Mr. Stuart if a Negro slave was found in his studio with a naked white woman? That would be the end of us, of course, and what of that poor bastard?"

Thelma smiled and turned away toward her clothes on the floor. "Stop calling me a 'white woman,' " she said, slipping on her bloomers, pulling her shift over her head, and pulling on her petticoat.

"Isn't that what you're passing for?" said Hercules easily, without accusation. It was just a statement of fact.

Thelma turned to look at him for a few seconds before picking up her stays and slipping her arms through. She walked over and turned her back to him.

"Pull the strings, please," she said, holding her long, heavy hair up off her neck.

Hercules grabbed the strings and pulled hard enough for her to draw a sharp breath.

"That man — who was he?" he said, pleasantly, as he tied a tight bow.

"Captain Grayson? He is no one — a guest in the house," said Thelma, turning to face him. Her chest heaved as she drew breath in the tight fittings.

"I believe he rather fancies you," he said, putting his large hands around her cinched waist.

"Perhaps, but I don't like him. He's a pompous fool," she said, shrugging, but her eyes were troubled.

She laughed as she told him that no matter how many people crowded the Chew parlors, there was Captain Grayson through every meal and every tea staring at her like a hungry dog. Thelma marveled at how the Chews took no notice of this, except for Harriet, who babbled endlessly that the "handsome Southerner" was "smitten" with Thelma — a fact that annoyed Harriet's sisters particularly.

"Mind yourself," Hercules said. "He might get the wrong idea."

She smirked at this. "The wrong idea — he already has this, *non?*"

She turned away from him and picked up her dress to pull over her head. When she had buttoned the lace stomacher onto the bodice and checked that her matching sleeve ruffles were still secured, she went to Stuart's drawing table and studied the sheets there. She looked at each one a long time before turning it aside.

"They are a good likeness," she said, taking one of the sheets over to the candle to better see it.

"Watch the flame!" said Hercules, stepping toward her quickly and grasping her wrist.

Thelma raised an eyebrow before stepping

back out of his grasp and away from the light. "His technique, it is good, I think."

"I imagine it would be, if the better sort in Europe ask him to paint them," he answered dryly.

Thelma smirked again. "The better sort?" she said sarcastically. "Now who has — as you say — the *wrong idea*?"

She tossed the sketch upon the table. When she turned back to face Hercules after tying on her cloak, her eyes were defiant.

"Next week, then?" she asked before kissing him hard on the mouth and rushing out the door, her cloak hood pulled far forward over her face.

CHAPTER 16

Gilbert Stuart paused, his brush in midair, and listened. The sounds of horse's hooves approached. Hercules rose up a bit from the seat across from the painter and looked uneasily at the door while Stuart went to the window.

"Someone's coming," spat Stuart in a panic. He rushed to the easel and lifted the canvas, quickly replacing it with another that leaned against the table. "This way!" He gestured frantically to Hercules, who rose and followed him quickly to a door in the wall that adjoined the rest of the stable.

Hercules stepped through and nearly into a pile of steaming manure just dropped by the horse. The painter started to speak when a loud knock rattled the door. He rubbed his hands over his face in a panic and, gesturing to Hercules to be silent, closed the door.

Holding his kerchief to his face, Hercules

pressed himself against the door, his ear against the rough wooden slats, and listened.

"Mr. Stuart?" The raspy voice barely reached Hercules's ears but it was familiar. He moved his face closer to the narrow gap between the door planks and strained to look in at a sliver of the room.

"Yes?" answered the painter.

"May I enter?" the man said, moving forward purposefully without waiting for agreement. Stuart was forced to take a step back as the caller shut the door behind him.

As the man moved farther into the room, Hercules could make him out. General Washington. The tricorn on his head added to his great height; it seemed that the president stooped slightly as if to avoid the rafters that were still a good foot above his hat. He turned from side to side, assessing the room, until the cold blue eyes settled on the door behind which Hercules stood.

Hercules jerked his head away from the door. What was Washington doing here? He peered in again though the slats. In the small, cluttered room, Washington looked more like his large, imposing legend than the stooped old man Hercules had become accustomed to seeing.

Washington cleared his throat lightly. "Mr. Stuart?" he finally said, breaking the painter out of his reverie.

"Forgive me, Excellency," said Stuart, dashing to fetch the one straight-backed chair. "Will you sit? Or perhaps you prefer the settee?" He gestured toward the small sitting couch and then, focusing on it, realized it was draped with shawls and all manner of paper. He began clearing away the mess, turning back to his table with the piles in his arms, and stopped short.

Washington stood there, looking at the sketches, one hand still holding his riding crop behind his back. With the other he lifted a leaf here or there to examine the drawing underneath.

As Washington stretched his arm farther to another pile, Stuart lunged forward, panicked. Hercules knew the many sketches Stuart had made of him — character studies, he called them — were somewhere in that avalanche.

"Sir?" he said, dumping the pile he had removed from the settee on the table in front of Washington in a way that Hercules knew would surely irk the General. Washington stepped back and gave the painter an exasperated look.

"Please, please do sit," said Stuart, gesturing toward the settee, which Hercules could not see from his narrow vantage. Stuart tried to put the other hand jovially on the president's shoulder and earned a deadly glare. The older man stepped widely out of the way of his hand. Now the room was quiet. Hercules felt dread rise up in his gut as the silence went on.

"A good likeness," the General said finally.

"Van Rensselaer," Stuart answered "One of your generals, I believe?" Relief made Hercules feel woozy. They must be looking at the painting that Stuart had hastily placed on the easel to replace his own.

"Just so," came Washington's answer.

"Will you take tea, sir? Or perhaps something stronger?" said Stuart. "I'll send to the house."

"No, thank you," said Washington.

Hercules heard the dragging of a chair nearer the settee where Washington must have been sitting and then its creak as the painter sat heavily down.

"To what do I owe the honor, sir —" Stuart began, but Washington cut him off.

"Mrs. Washington is desirous of my portrait," he said. "She has heard of your work favorably and I recalled your visit the other day."

"An honor, sir," said the painter. "I am at your disposal."

Now Hercules heard Stuart's chair scrape

the rough floor. Washington must have stood.

"Good," the General was saying. "My secretary shall inform you of the particulars. I might send for you at any time my schedule permits. I shan't waste your time, sir, nor do I expect you to waste mine. I shall sit for a length of time and be entirely at your disposal. I expect you will complete your work satisfactorily and not impress upon me to return at your leisure, which I will not do."

"I understand, Excellency," said Stuart, following as the General made his way to the door, once again in sight of the small opening through which Hercules peered.

"I submit very reluctantly to this business of portraiture, but it pleases my wife and so I must do it," he said, turning back to face Stuart one more time. The painter had been so close at his back that he had to quickly take a step back.

"Very good, sir," Stuart said.

Washington looked at him a moment more, then nodded curtly and ducked his head as he went out the short door. Inside the stable, Hercules counted to one hundred, picturing the General's long strides out to his horse Prescott and the time it would take him to mount the horse. He was ready to slip quickly back inside when he heard Washington's cluck to his beast.

Once he was back inside, he and Stuart looked at one another without speaking, both listening to the hoofbeats of Washington's horse until it was the faintest thud in the far distance.

Thelma's eyes flew open and her gaze darted around the room, panicked. It was a relief when the lightning flashed harshly into the unkempt chamber and she found herself able to make out the shapes of Stuart's easel and table. Beside her, Hercules slept soundly through the thunder that she had mistaken in her sleep for the sound of cannon fire. She sat up and exhaled before reaching for the shawl that lay beside them on the floor, then moved to the window. Rain was lashing the nearby willow tree, its long, thin branches moving back and forth across the ground like a broom. It was nothing compared to the sea-storms they'd endured back home.

Thelma walked over to the table and lit a candle before taking up a piece of paper and charcoal. She glanced over at Hercules — they could not remain here much longer. She studied her lover while he slept, skin glowing in each flash of lightning, stretched taut over bulging muscles.

Her fingers began to fly across the page, trying to capture his form, but soon other images took over — not of the man lying beside her but of what she had seen before. The things she wouldn't speak of with the General's cook. The blood-run roadways and paths of her island, the wild dogs gnawing on the human limbs flung into the fields. Through the black smoke from the burning plantation houses, Bastien, the voodoo priest, had emerged, ambling easily, using his long, twisted stick for purchase, as if he were taking a stroll through the forests.

Thelma had seen him from where she stood at the shore, soaking rags to drape over the window holes of their little house, to catch the smoke and soot.

"Ki kote ou se manman ou ye?" he'd asked in his pidgin French. *Where is your mother?*

She'd gestured toward the house, then dropped her rags into a bucket and followed him up the small dune.

"Blondelle mouri. Nou te pran I. Fanmi I' tou," he told her mother. *"Ou anyen pa rive Et poko men tifi ou dwe ale. Blan sou po se yon mak pou touye koulye a. Dènye batiman an a pwal. Mete I' sou li."*

Blondelle is dead. We've taken him. His family too. You are safe and you are free but

265

your girl must go. White skin is a death mark now, the last ship is going. Put her on it.

Maman had looked wildly from him to Thelma, pain crumpling her face.

"Who will escort her?" she asked. "How can I be sure she will be safe?"

"I will take her myself," the priest answered. He turned toward the door. "I will return with a cart. *Pare.*"

Be ready.

She had fallen on her knees on the hard dirt floor and clung to her mother's legs. "Come with me," she begged.

Maman had stood stock-still, halted for a moment in her mad rush around the small room, flinging Thelma's three dresses and her few books and art supplies into a small trunk. She placed her worn, rough hand on Thelma's smooth head. "My darling girl," she had murmured. "There is no place for me where you must go. You can pass into the white man's land. I cannot."

Thelma had buried her face in her mother's skirts and sobbed.

"I would drag you down," Maman said. "Alone, you could find your way. Find respectable work. With me you would be a Negress, something to barter and use."

Thelma had screamed into her mother's lap. Screamed and screamed until her throat was raw and until she had felt the priest's vise grip on her shoulders, ripping her away. He had pulled her roughly with one arm and hoisted the small trunk on his shoulder with the other.

Outside a donkey cart waited, piled with gunny cloth sacks and barrels. "Climb up there and stay down," said the priest. Maman's hand slipped into Thelma's and she pressed a small brocade bag into it. All the money she had spirited away over the years.

"Hurry now, no time," said the priest, holding up a length of sacking for Thelma to climb under. She clung to her mother.

"Go, *mon petite ange,*" she murmured in Thelma's ear. *"Se souvenir: je t'aime au-delà où l'univers se termine."*

Remember: I will love you past when the universe ends.

Thelma swallowed hard now and breathed through her nose. The tears came anyway, falling heavily onto the page and making blotches on the charcoal images.

She looked down at what she had drawn. A white woman, naked, her mouth a gaping gash from which a soundless scream erupted. The scream was endless.

At first, under her sacking, Thelma thought she herself was screaming again, beyond her senses with grief. When she had peeked out above the edge of the cart, she saw a woman, shrieking like a pig at slaughter, unsilenced even by the heavy blows falling around her face and head from the slaves in their rags who surrounded her. Two of them held her arms while another raped her. Blood ran down her legs.

Fear had gripped her so badly she wet herself, and in her confusion mistook the warm wetness running down her legs for blood as well. She had known the woman — her half sister Monique. She had last seen her sipping wine at their father's table while Thelma had cleared dishes and poured out the port.

When they reached the ship, she felt half dead. The priest had dragged her up the gangplank and handed the captain some coins, no doubt provided by her mother. How much had he kept for himself?

They were quite at sea when she came to herself again, huddled with a mother and her two girls below decks, their eyes still wild from terror.

She had stayed with them for the remainder of the voyage to Philadelphia, sharing rations, never moving about without one another — protection against the women-hungry sailors.

When they had arrived in the capital city,

their relatives had come to collect them and Thelma was left alone to fend for herself, barely able to walk on dry land from being so long on a rolling, pitching ship.

A lady from the Quaker church had approached her, speaking terrible French, and Thelma had answered in halting English. It was the first time she had actually used the language her father had taught her to converse with a real person. The lady was from some sort of society organized to help the "poor, unfortunate victims of Saint-Domingue."

The victims. Thelma had said nothing and allowed herself to be bustled along to a clean room in a private home to bathe and eat a hot meal. It had been January and Thelma had never felt such cold. The trees were so curious too — not one of them had a leaf.

Only when months had passed did she learn about the seasons, her artist's heart learning to delight in the flamboyant colors of spring and then, later, like a surprise jewel at the bottom of the box, autumn.

Later, another refugee boat had come with the reports of the gruesome massacre, setting the whites in Philadelphia on edge.

Her father had been strung up by his feet like a goat. His guts had been cut out. He had drowned in the blood that ran out of his stomach down his face. Then they had cut him up and fed his body to the hogs.

Thelma put the last few lines of shading around the scene before she put aside the charcoal and wiped her hands on a rag. Turning toward the flame, she held the edge of the paper to it and watched, expressionless, as the flames licked up the page and nipped at her fingers. She did not drop the leaf until it was no more than a cinder ash.

Thelma couldn't have wished a better end for the man. Not since he'd turned away from her mother and started rutting her in the field or the scullery or anywhere he had a mind to. Once, he even shoved her up against the well as she dragged on the rope to draw up water. That time was in plain sight of the others working in the garden.

It was a fine end for one such as him. She'd only wished she'd been there to see it.

Hercules turned in his sleep, reaching out to where she had been lying behind him. He awoke when he felt the space was bare and sat up suddenly.

"What is wrong, love?" he said, focusing on her.

"Nothing," she said, drawing the shawl over her lap.

He rubbed his hand over his face and stretched.

"It's late," he said. "We better be gone."

"Oui," answered Thelma, rising to kneel before him. "Just one more thing first," she said, letting the shawl drop and pressing her body against his.

■ ■ ■ ■

PART III

■ ■ ■ ■

CHAPTER 17

Philadelphia, Autumn 1794

Hercules set a box down on the long wooden table. Through the small window he could see the commotion in the yard as the servants rushed to unload the dray carts carrying the furniture back from Germantown.

"Hercules?" The voice fluttered through the kitchen.

"Yes, Lady Washington?" he said smoothly, turning to bow. The violet scent she wore overpowered the room.

"The president will be entertaining guests before supper this evening," she said. "Do you have anything for refreshment?"

She looked around the kitchen in despair. "Oh my, nothing is ready," she said more to herself than to him. "So inconvenient . . . I imagine we could send to the grocer, but then . . ." She looked at him pleadingly.

"Not to worry, madam," Hercules said. "I

know of an excellent cake seller who usually has lovely confections to hand. I will set the others to putting the kitchen to rights and will go into the city to buy the cakes. Will that suit?"

"Oh, that will be fine," said Lady Washington, giving Hercules an indulgent smile. "Thank you."

"And I have some hams from Mount Vernon to slice for a cold supper — along with whatever greens we may have in the garden," he said. "I'll procure some loaves of bread when I go out as well."

Again, the First Lady heaved a sigh of relief. "I really don't know why I worry so, Hercules, with you here," she said, smoothing her skirt. "You always have everything in hand."

He bowed once again. "I try, madam," he said.

Mrs. Washington smiled before turning and making her way out of the kitchen.

Kitt came in after Mrs. Washington had passed. Hercules ignored him and stepped around a particularly large crate that sat on the floor.

"Nate," called Hercules, loudly. The scullion appeared from the back of the kitchen. "Unpack these first," he said, gesturing to the smaller boxes on the table.

"You should find at least two hams in them. Slice half of one thinly and set it upon the large charger, which I believe is in the crate Austin is prying open now." He gestured toward where the postilion, his fine jacket removed, was working on a larger crate. "When you are done with that, go over whatever Margaret can find from the garden and slice it all very thinly — like paper. Dress it with salad oil, vinegar, salt, and pepper and set it aside. Then continue with the unpacking. I'll return shortly."

Nate, who had been listening intently to Hercules's instructions, stopped mid-nod.

"Return? Shortly?" he said. "I'm to prepare this alone?"

"I must procure some cakes from Mrs. Brummage and then see if there is any bread to be found in the capital at this hour," he said. Hercules paused and looked at the young man, whose eyes had become wide. "You can do this," he said, putting his hand on Nate's shoulder. It was time the boy tried his hand at a few things on his own. One day, Hercules meant to be gone from this place, but the General would have a fine cook in his stead. "These are easy tasks you have done many times."

"But you've always been here while I did them," said Nate.

"Indeed, and Mr. Kitt is here if you need aid," said Hercules, looking pointedly over at the steward, who was suspiciously counting the silverware, even though he'd already done so that morning before they were packed away for the short journey back to the capital.

Hearing his name, Kitt turned around. "What's that?" he said.

"I must away to buy some items for the General's guests this afternoon," said Hercules. "Nate will prepare the supper in my stead — and of course you are here to make sure all goes smoothly."

Kitt looked from Hercules to Nate. "I should come —" he said firmly.

"I've promised Lady Washington that I would attend to this myself, Mr. Kitt," said Hercules easily. "No need to trouble yourself."

The steward stared at him overlong, a malicious snarl lifting his upper lip before he finally said, "I see." He said nothing for a moment, then barked at Nate, "Get to it then."

Nate looked from Kitt to Hercules nervously, then bowed to the steward. Hercules gave Nate another clap on the back, then turned for the door.

When he was outside the garden walls, he

drew a deep breath. Even the stench of horse shit, rotting waste, privies, and unwashed slatterns — the smells of the city — were delightful after the fresh open air of the country where he could not move about as freely.

Hercules crossed High Street and headed down Sixth. He paused every now and again to pretend he was looking at a shop window or feign interest in something going on in the road. Once he stopped in front of a woman selling nosegays and spent a longish time choosing among them until he settled upon a small bouquet of blue lobelia.

His pauses had purpose, for each time he stopped he scanned the streets and alleyways to be sure he was not taken unawares again. He walked on, shrugging his injured shoulder as he made his way to Mrs. Harris's home in Cherry Street.

He rapped upon the door twice, waiting a good length of time between each, and was turning away when the door opened behind him.

"Master Hercules?" said the teacher, her voice trilling with delight.

He turned and bowed gallantly. "None other, madam," he said, straightening up and smiling.

She glanced down the alleyway and then

back at him. "You were not —"

"Followed? No, I was not," he said, putting his booted foot upon the short stair.

Mrs. Harris stepped aside so he could pass into the house.

Once he was in the hall, he could hear the low murmur of a group of people talking. Startled, he looked at Mrs. Harris, who only smiled and gestured him into the schoolroom.

"Do come in, Master Hercules, it is most fortunate you happen by just now," she said. "There are some people here I would have you meet."

He followed the schoolteacher into the room, where a strange group sat in chairs formed into a close circle. An old white woman — a Jewess by her head wrap and the star brooch at her throat — sat by an old Negro who, bizarrely, wore the skull cap of a Jew. Two white men in expensive clothing sat side by side and a tall, muscled, nut-brown Negro wearing mariner's clothing completed the circle. There were two open chairs, one of which Mrs. Harris must have vacated when she came to answer the door.

Hercules hesitated as Mrs. Harris moved toward the circle. They all stopped talking and watched him with interest. A look passed across the face of one of the white gentlemen as if he were trying to figure something out. The mariner stood and gestured for Hercules to sit.

"I was unaware you had company, Mrs. Harris," Hercules said, looking at each person in the room and then settling his gaze on his teacher. He turned toward the door. "I'll come back at another time."

"No!" she said swiftly, taking a step toward him, then stepping back. "That is to say, you are most welcome here, Master Hercules. These are" — she gestured vaguely toward the circle — "my friends," she finished awkwardly. Hercules uneasily allowed himself to be drawn forward by Mrs. Harris to a chair set out by the mariner, whom she introduced as James Brown.

"And this is Mistress Levi," she said, gesturing toward the old woman. "And her servant, Solomon."

Hercules nodded, not caring a whit who they were. He began to absently tap his cane upon the floor.

"And allow me to present Mr. Winters," she said, gesturing to the younger of the two white men. "And this is Dr. Rush."

Hercules looked at the man introduced as Dr. Rush more closely and suddenly felt queer. Benjamin Rush. Of course, he knew him. He was well known to the president, this doctor who had believed Africans could not get the yellow fever and had convinced so many to minister to the sick and dying, until they too eventually fell ill. Those who survived were spat upon by society, accused of being opportunists, preying on white victims.

"Apologies for my tardiness." A voice came in from the back hall. A side door to the room opened and there stood the Reverend Allen. He stopped just as he was about to say more and looked at the group and then at Hercules before breaking into a huge smile.

"Well! If it isn't the General's cook!" he said loudly, moving to shake Hercules's hand. Hercules returned the handshake silently, giving Mrs. Harris a curious sideways look.

"The General?" asked Dr. Rush, leaning forward now.

"The president, I should really say," said Allen.

Understanding passed across Rush's face and Mistress Levi leaned over to whisper in her servant's ear. Why was a servant sitting in a group with one of the city's most prominent ministers and doctors? And who was this seaman?

When they had all settled in, no one spoke

for what seemed a long time. Hercules smiled pleasantly at Mrs. Harris, but he hoped the question — and the anger — in his eyes was clear.

"Master Hercules," began Mrs. Harris, looking around at the others. "We are a society of . . . helpers."

He raised his eyebrows, willing her to hurry up and say her piece so he might leave.

"Yes," cut in Reverend Allen. "We give aid to those who would make a better life for themselves but are barred from doing so on their own."

Dr. Rush had propped his reading spectacles up high on his forehead and now looked from one to the other of them, his eyes shining. With his beaky nose he resembled a bald eagle about to strike its prey.

Beside Hercules, the mariner, James Brown, crossed his arms.

"Mistress Levi, here, for example, is in the business of buying souls in order to set them free," said Mrs. Harris, nodding toward the old woman.

"My Solomon was one such," said the old lady, putting her hand on the arm of the old man beside her. Large, expensive rings encased her gnarled fingers. Hercules doubted she could take them off now even if she wanted to. The old man put his dark hand over her white one and smiled gently at her. Hercules felt something go funny in his head. Surely, there was never a stranger scene.

"Stop with de mincing," said James Brown suddenly in a heavy West Indian accent. Hercules was curious about what he had to say. "We is abolitionists. Pure and simple — help folk escape they masters." He leaned forward then and tapped Hercules on the knee. "Get them away from some pretty important folk — but none so important as you own."

Hercules's head pounded as if he had run too long and too far, but he made himself look Brown in the eye calmly before smiling widely and standing up.

"Gentleman — and ladies." He bowed politely to Mrs. Harris and then Mrs. Levi. "I'm afraid you mistake my presence here. I have come only to pay my compliments to Mrs. Harris. I'll take my leave now."

Dr. Rush sat back, his cheek resting in his palm, one long finger extended along the length of his jaw.

"There is nothing to fear here —" began Reverend Allen, standing as well.

Hercules turned to him, his eyes hard and glittering. "And nor am I afraid," he said with an edge to his voice that he hoped was unmistakable.

"Let he go," said Brown behind him. "You can lead a horse to water . . . He go come back when he time right."

Hercules ignored him and stepped away from the circle.

"I bid you all good day," he said, thrusting the bouquet he had purchased toward Mrs. Harris before turning toward the door.

When he reached the front hall, Mrs. Harris was close behind him.

"Master Hercules —" she began, but he opened the door and stepped through. "Hercules!" she said loudly, following him into the alley. He turned quickly and closed the few steps between them quick as a cat.

"Hush!" he hissed angrily. "Keep your voice down, woman."

"I'm sorry," she said. "I thought it would be good for you to —"

"To what?" he spat out. "To be in the company of known abolitionists? How do you think Washington would take to hearing that? And make no mistake, there is little he does not know."

"I assure you, we are discreet," she said desperately. "Lives are at stake if we are not."

He turned to walk away from her and then

turned back.

"Mistress Harris," he began, forcing himself to sound more kindly this time. "I have no doubt that you are, but I make it a policy to never underestimate General Washington and I advise that you do the same."

He stood looking at her a moment more, searching her eyes and willing her to take in the seriousness of his words.

"Will you risk coming back?" she said finally. "For your lessons?"

Hercules looked back toward the house and then at her. "I will, but not when they are here," he said. "Do you always meet on Saturday?"

"Yes," she said. "The students only come for half of a day of lessons then."

"Good," he said curtly and then as if it were an afterthought, gave her one of his particular smiles. "Mrs. Harris." He bowed and quickly made his way from the alley and into the city in search of cake.

CHAPTER 18

Weeks had passed, with all resuming their regular activities. Hercules had begun to relax. He hummed to himself, taking pleasure in reading the signs that hung from the buildings as he walked toward the New Market on the other side of town. He entered just in time to see Nate point at the small trout that the fishmonger was about to put in his basket.

"Not that one," Nate said. "No trickery from you — I'll not pay for a measly one without flesh on its bones."

Beside him, Margaret gave him a surprised look. The fishmonger's dirty fingers halted in midair and then closed into a fist.

"You'll take what you get and like it, nigra!" he growled, his left hand curling around the scaling knife on the table.

Nate's expression hardened and Hercules's stomach sank as the boy leaned in closer to the man instead of away.

"None of that," Nate said in a low and nasty voice. "Or I'll have to report to my master how you tried to cheat him."

The man snorted and showed his gray teeth. "Even your master won't make me heel to a nigra boy, now git before I gut you!"

Nate watched him, a smile twitching at the corners of his mouth.

"And you'll put an extra on that pile, no charge — for good measure," he said in a friendly tone.

Margaret tugged at Nate's sleeve to get him away.

The man's eyes widened and then he guffawed, stopping almost as soon as he started. He pulled the knife out of the butcher's block on the table and pointed it at Nate.

"This nigra's trying to rob me!" he said loudly so that the people milling about could hear. "You all are witness! I'll defend my trade!"

Mumbling went through the crowd and a few other merchants stepped around their tables and stood, arms crossed, ready for trouble. Hercules began to shove his way through the crowd that had gathered around the table.

"This man is trying to cheat the President

of the United States!" Nate shouted.

In the crowd Hercules heard the words "Washington" and "General" thrown about. Now, more strongly, the murmur of doubt rippled through the chatter, but still they pressed in farther — just as Hercules reached Margaret.

"What goes on here?" he rumbled, low and threatening. Margaret turned and nearly collapsed with relief at the sight of him.

Now the pitch of the crowd grew louder as they chattered among themselves. One of the merchants shook his head and returned to his table. The fishmonger looked at Hercules, who stared at him without blinking, then back at the crowd, which started to fray around the edges and disperse. Hercules was relieved to see the fishmonger was losing their sympathy.

"I'll not be threatened!" he said louder now, toward the crowd, and turned back to where Hercules stood, arms crossed, observing the scene.

Another vendor, wearing a long apron smeared with blood, moved closer to the fishmonger's side. He murmured something in a low voice, watching Hercules the whole time. Through it all Nate stood, smiling pleasantly as if he were insensible of any danger.

The fishmonger put down the knife. His friend put a hand on his shoulder and then returned to his stall, leaving the fish man to glare at Nate across the table.

Hercules stepped around Margaret until he was standing behind Nate.

"I don't think we'll be needing any fish today," he said smoothly, looking scornfully at the trout. "Leastways, if we do, there are better to be had elsewhere."

He clapped a hand around the base of Nate's neck. He meant for it to hurt.

"Good day, sir," said Hercules, bowing slightly at the man and giving him a pleasant smile. "Come along, Margaret," he said over his shoulder as he propelled Nate forward and out of the market at Second Street.

They walked in silence past the fine houses down Pine Street but Hercules never moved his hand from Nate's neck. Abruptly, he turned into a small alley and Margaret faltered behind them before recovering herself and following.

She stopped short when she saw that Hercules had Nate smashed up against the brick side of the house and his face inches away from Nate's own.

"What did you think you were about in there?" he snarled, barely able to control himself. Margaret shrank back.

"He was trying to cheat us," Nate gasped out, for Hercules had his hand around the front of the boy's neck now, holding him up off the ground.

"You should have walked away," spat Hercules. His fingers twitched; he longed to squeeze harder.

"I thought —" began Nate.

"Don't," said Hercules viciously. "Don't think. *Walk away.*"

Margaret pressed herself against the opposite wall, too terrified to speak. Hercules could hear her breath coming out in fast bursts. To his surprise, she bolted forward and darted between them.

"Let him go!" she shrieked, inches from Hercules face.

Hercules looked down at her and his eyes got wilder and his lips curled back. It took all his will not to strike her with his free hand, but he let go and Nate fell forward upon her, coughing.

Hercules watched with his hands on his hips until the boy regained his composure, just behind Margaret. Finally, moving around her, Nate squeaked out, "*You* never walk away!"

"I am me and you —" said Hercules, his eyes narrowing. He paused for a minute, then said, "Are not."

"He thought I was a stupid rube!" said Nate angrily.

"And so let him," said Hercules, his voice equally angry.

"But —"

Hercules put his hand up to stop the boy from speaking. He stood a moment, collecting his thoughts. It was like Richmond all over again. When had this boy become so heedless? Out of the corner of his eye, he saw Margaret moving again to the side, trying to make herself small. Nate's nemesis — though neither of them saw it.

"If I hadn't come along, he would have gutted you and that crowd would have let him," he said.

"But the president —"

"Yes. The president would have had him punished — hung," said Hercules simply. "But not because of any other reason than his property was destroyed. And in the end you'd still be dead, wouldn't you?"

Nate closed his mouth and said nothing.

"And you," said Hercules, whirling to face Margaret, who was now nearly to the mouth of the alley. "Protecting your little cur, here. Did you ever give a thought to what would have become of you if those men had their way? What do you think they would have done to the likes of you, consorting with this little nigra, so close at his side so you may as well be one?"

Margaret's breath caught in her throat and her eyes filled with tears. She looked over to Nate but he was looking sheepishly at the ground.

Hercules turned back to Nate.

"It's better when they take no notice of you," he said more calmly now. "If you are unseen, there's some freedom in that." Nate didn't answer, and Margaret was crying openly now, tears streaming down her face. Surprising him, the boy rushed past and out of the alley. As he passed Margaret, she instinctively reached out to grab his sleeve, but he pulled away just before her fingers touched the cloth, leaving her to snatch her hand back to her mouth to stifle her sob.

Hercules observed her silently shaking with tears before he too walked furiously out of the alley, forcing her to move aside as he walked past.

CHAPTER 19

"Nate, come in now please," Hercules called from the kitchen door. The scullion crouched among the garden rows, pulling off the dried bean pods and filling baskets that he brought over to set by Margaret.

She also looked up from shelling the dried cowpeas into the waiting bowl and tossing the dried husks into another basket for the compost.

Every time Hercules glanced out the door for the last hour he had seen her steadily talking and nodding to herself, like a mad-woman. Nate, working beside her, barely moved his lips. Hercules had been gratified that ever since that day in the market, Nate hardly spoke to her. He did not know what had become of their reading lessons — they were over now, he supposed, but that was all to the better, given the danger they would be in if they were caught.

As Nate stood and left, Margaret bit her

lip. She split another pod with her thumb-nail and slid the beans into the bowl before stopping to press the heels of her hands to her eyes.

When she came into the kitchen, the wooden bowl heavy with shelled peas propped against her hip, Hercules barely glanced at her. He was keeping one eye on Nate, who spooned filling into small tart pans while he himself was stuffing a pheasant with herbs and ground meat. Mr. Julien, who had returned to them when they came back to Philadelphia, was slicing a large fish into steaks and the hired scullery maids were scrubbing pots and peeling vegetables.

"Don't just stand there, girl," snapped Hercules, when Margaret stood foolishly while everything around her operated at a steady hum. "Take those peas to the storage bin in the cellar, then come right back up and start peeling pears for poaching in wine."

For the briefest moment, an expression like hatred twisted Margaret's face and she opened her mouth to say something. Hercules waited, interested in what she might be brave enough to do, but just as quickly her expression changed. No doubt she remembered that no good would come from one such as her sassing him. Instead, she nodded and quickly picked up her bowl before heading back out to the cellar. Hercules was gratified to see that when she tried to catch Nate's eye as she passed, the boy did not look up.

Hercules stroked Thelma's arm as she lay with one cream-colored leg thrown over him.

"Mmm," she murmured, nestling her face into his neck.

"We must go soon," he said softly into her hair.

Thelma sighed and rolled away to sit up. She hugged her knees to her chest and traced the pattern on the Turkish rug in Gilbert's new Philadelphia studio. The artist had secured an ideal location in Chestnut Street — just near Congress Hall and all the merchants of note. Society Hill, where he would no doubt get many a wealthy commission, was steps away as was the President's House — which particularly suited Hercules. Now that Stuart had secured a commission to paint Washington, his fortunes had changed for the better.

Hercules sat up and kissed the side of Thelma's head. Her hair smelled of lemon verbena.

"You've changed your scent," he said, breathing deeply and relishing the light perfume, which, he imagined was the smell of places where all was right and good in the world.

"What? Oh . . ." she said. "Yes. A gift . . . from Harriet."

"Hmmm," he murmured, suddenly suspicious at her hesitation. Was it really a gift from Harriet or that ferret-faced Grayson?

Thelma, oblivious to his dark thoughts, smiled at him over her shoulder before rising and walking to the canvas upon the easel. Hercules glanced at the windows to be sure there was no gap in the drapes before turning his gaze back to her.

Thelma lifted the cloth covering the painting and peered at it, her head cocked sharply to the side.

"It is a good likeness . . . but so dark," she said, turning to look at him. The flickering firelight made his skin shine gold, then red and deep black when it receded.

"And so am I," he said with a chuckle at his own joke.

Thelma clucked her tongue at him and went back to looking at the painting.

"*Non,* it needs something," she said, studying it.

"Yes, Stuart says the same," said Hercules,

reaching over to where his shirt lay a few feet away and pulling it over his head.

"It needs some light, I think," she said. "Here . . . and here." Her fingers grazed the image of her lover across his chest and in the space above his head.

Now Hercules was standing, pulling up his britches.

"He told me about a special white jacket and hat that chefs in Europe wear," he said, walking over to the painting and standing beside it. "With buttons like so." He gestured down the length of his torso. "And the hat is tall and white."

"Vraiment?" said Thelma. "How peculiar. It would seem to become soiled in the kitchen, *non*?"

"Oui," he said, smiling and leaning over to kiss her. "Now put on your clothes."

After she had rolled up her stockings and pulled on her bloomers, she slipped on her corset and turned her back to him to tie it.

"I wish," she sighed. "I wish we could be together always."

Hercules put his hands on her shoulders and turned her gently to face him. These were dangerous waters into which he did not want to wade. He'd long ago learned to stop imagining the world of wishes and dreams. That world would never materialize, given who they were.

"A pretty dream, my love," he said, lifting her hand and kissing it.

She smiled sadly at him and turned again to face the picture.

"I wish I could have it," she said.

Hercules chuckled. "Yes, it would make a lovely adornment for your boudoir," he said. "A reminder of my . . . talents." He grinned at her.

"Don't be silly," she said, pouting. "Anyway, what will he do with it? Who would buy such a thing?"

"Oh, so now you are saying I am too ugly for anyone to buy my portrait?" he teased.

"Oh you!" She slapped at his arm. "You're being too foolish, now."

"In truth, I don't know," said Hercules, smiling less. "Nor do I care. I can't imagine why he even wants to paint me at all, but as long as he does, we benefit." He lifted her hand and kissed it again. "Not so?"

"Yes," whispered Thelma, turning away and sitting heavily on the settee. She picked at her dress.

Hercules, surprised, walked over and knelt by her side.

"What is it, my love?" he said. Surely, she wasn't still dwelling on the impossibility of a future together. He had never taken

Thelma for a foolish girl.

"I —" She shook her head, unable to continue.

"What is it, dear?"

"Captain Grayson asked me for my promise," she whispered.

"The fool from Germantown?" he said, his voice becoming hard.

"Do you mean to say that you have been keeping his company all this time?"

"No. I mean yes. That is —" Thelma stopped miserably. "He follows me everywhere when he comes to Philadelphia for his business. He does not leave me alone."

Hercules studied her for a moment, fury rising. "Well? What did you say to him?" he asked, knowing even as he did that he had no right.

"That I must think on it," she said and grasped at his hand. "But I only said this, so he would stop his pestering of me. I do not want to marry him."

Hercules stood. He walked to the window and drew the curtain aside a little to look into the street. He tried to marshal his thoughts, which ran furiously in all directions.

"Does he know?" he said without turning around.

"Know?" said Thelma, confused.

"About you?" said Hercules, his eyes still scanning the street below. Across the way, a driver dozed in his coach in front of a tavern. Farther down the road, he could hear the noise of the crowd pouring out of the Chestnut Street Theater. The president had his own box there. Hercules himself enjoyed a show there now and again, sitting among the "quality" in ground floor seats. He always made sure to never find himself at the same show the General was attending.

Now he turned to face Thelma, noting that she looked particularly fetching in the glow of the fire.

"That you are a Negress," he said baldly. "Are you sure he does not know? He might expose you."

Thelma colored pink.

"I am not sure, he has said things . . ."

"What things?"

"He drops the hints that make me think he does not forget what I said that day, about my island, and . . ."

"And?"

"He does not want for me to meet his family."

"So you have not told him the truth."

"I never lied —"

"But you never told him," he said.

She shook her head silently and for a minute or two neither of them said anything. Finally, Thelma stood and came toward him.

"This — it doesn't matter what he knows," she said. "I made him no promise. I don't even like him!"

Hercules put his hand around the bottom of her face and drew her close. He leaned in and ran his tongue over her lips.

"Keep it that way," he said before kissing her hard and backing her up to the couch, reaching below her skirts.

CHAPTER 20

"I can't imagine how you wear through your shoes so quickly, Hercules," said Kitt irritably. "Your shoes are not above four months old if I recall, and quite costly too." He turned some pages in his ledger and looked back at the entries.

The steward sat behind a desk strewn with papers and quill pens. In one corner, candle wax had melted down the brass holder onto the desk. Hercules stood there watching him. Kitt would have a long time to wait if he expected Hercules to act humble.

"Fine," said Kitt, finally closing the book with a snap. "Here you are." He took seventy-five cents from the locked drawer in his desk.

Hercules stepped forward and took the money the other man held out.

"What have you planned for tonight, cook?" he asked as Hercules turned to go. "It's a levy night, you know."

As if Hercules didn't know that it was one of the nights Mrs. Washington entertained the ladies of society — which meant a large crowd of admiring females hoping to get a glimpse of the president.

"Cold leg of mutton, forced mushrooms, sweet potato buns, and pears stewed purple," he said, keeping his voice pleasant. "The usual course of nuts, fruit, and sweetmeat. The president received a shipment of pineapple from the West Indies, so I shall make a molded ice from them as well."

"Very fine," said Kitt, and absentmindedly patted his stomach. Hercules held back a smirk. He knew that the greedy steward would come sniffing around like a dog when the platters came back, barely touched, from the dining room.

"Mrs. Bingham will be in attendance," Kitt said. "She is particularly fond of your carrot pudding. Is it too late, you think, to add that to the menu?"

Hercules smiled and gave the steward a gallant bow. "Certainly not, Mr. Kitt," he said. "Mistress Bingham's wish is my command."

When he returned to the kitchen, he set Nate to shredding the carrots for the pudding and Margaret to assembling the other ingredients while he attended the roast. As he worked, he observed them closely when they didn't notice.

Interesting. They no longer stood so close together. In fact, few, if any, words passed between them. Nate had to ask Margaret twice to pass the bowl of eggs before she obliged and did not acknowledge his polite thank-you.

So, it would seem that they had heeded his warning. Finally. He added spices to the port wine he was using to poach the pears. Things were starting to settle back to normal.

"Nate my boy, you will mix that pudding yourself," he called jovially to his assistant. "After you grate the carrots, tell me — what comes next?"

Once the party was well under way, and the last dish removed by the footmen, Hercules untied his apron and laid it on the bench near the door. He shrugged into his waistcoat and pulled off his head kerchief, running a hand through his hair before perching his cockade hat on his head. Taking up his walking stick, he turned to the others in the kitchen and touched it to the rim of his hat before heading out.

He turned up his collar against the damp chill as he hurried through the garden gate and past the front door, politely touching his hat to the footmen who stood guard there.

"Evening, Master Hercules," said the taller of the two. Raymond, he was called. He was a lanky country fellow who sometimes came and sat in Hercules's kitchen in his free hours, whittling a piece of wood. He said the noise and rush of the kitchen reminded him of his big family home.

"Oh, so you got black folks in you family?" Oney had snapped at him. Hercules had to turn his back on them and busy himself with the tin oven to hide his smile.

"Evening, Raymond," he said pleasantly now, as he hurried on.

Even though he walked quickly he didn't have a particular plan. He had already visited Mrs. Harris this week and he was not due at Mr. Stuart's for another few days. He'd just wanted to walk and think.

His last meeting with Thelma lay heavy on his mind. Captain Grayson, that pathetic, girl-faced, white man, was courting Thelma. He felt rage. The kind of rage that would make him do something rash if he didn't get a hold of it.

Grayson was away on the China Trade, Thelma had said, and she didn't know how long before he'd return. That was something at least. Surely the girl couldn't possibly entertain his offer? She was not stupid and nor, Hercules thought, was she greedy enough to be lured by Grayson's promises of wealth. But of course he couldn't really know that, could he? He didn't actually know her very well at all.

Hercules tapped his stick meaningfully on the ground as he walked along and willed his thoughts elsewhere. Even if Thelma could remain free, he was not. They could never be together. He had no way to support her. Worse yet, she looked like a white woman.

He let his mind imagine a bit. Would he want to marry Thelma even if he could? He couldn't really say. What did he know of her beside the intricacies of her delightful body?

He found himself panting from walking too fast. He was already close to the water at Second Street. Turning right, he realized where it was he meant to go.

Samuel Fraunces's tavern was quiet even while the City Tavern, just a block beyond Dock Street, was loud and busy as ever. Mariners and seamen crowded the street but no one came in or out of the place. Hercules headed to the door. It was time he saw firsthand what the snake Fraunces had done for himself.

Inside, only a few tables were filled. An elderly couple sat together at one eating their supper, and at another a genteel lady dined alone, though she kept glancing at the door as though waiting for someone. Alone as she was, she could only have been a high-priced whore.

No one was behind the bar, although he heard sounds from the kitchen. He walked forward and rapped on the wooden counter with his stick. It took a few moments but eventually the door behind the counter opened and Black Sam stepped out. He wore a long apron and his wig was slightly off-kilter. He seemed harried — far more than warranted by three patrons.

His smile faltered a bit when he saw Hercules, but then he composed himself and stepped forward.

"Hercules, by my eyes," he said, smiling stiffly. "To what do I owe the pleasure?"

"Some claret, please, master stew— that is, Master Fraunces," he said, relishing the other man's discomfort. "And I should like to sample what's on the menu this evening."

Confusion passed over the former steward's face for a moment.

"Are you not sent by the General?" he asked. "No, no, you wouldn't be. He wouldn't send a slave . . ." The last he murmured to himself, but Hercules caught it.

"Alas, I am not," said Hercules, somewhat loudly. So the old bastard was, perhaps, regretting his move. "Are you expecting word from him? Meaning to leave this place, are you?" he went on, feigning innocence.

"Shhh!" Fraunces hissed at him, leaning forward. "No, I am not," he went on priggishly. "And I'll thank you to keep your voice down. I just thought — well, never you mind. Take a seat if you must."

Hercules smiled broadly at his old nemesis and took a seat near the window. Clearly, the steward could not afford to turn him away with the house so empty.

Fraunces reappeared with a plate of mutton stew dressed with potatoes and apples, which he set before Hercules with some bread and butter. He poured out the claret in a small glass and placed it beside the plate, barely hiding his annoyance.

Hercules closed his eyes and let the aromas meet his nose.

"A fine cook you always were, master steward," he said.

Fraunces was surprised. "How did you know I made that?" he said. "There was — *is* — a cook here, you know. You can't imagine I am managing this establishment and also at the hearth."

Hercules said nothing, because that was exactly what he imagined. He took another bite of food and looked around the room appraisingly. Things did not look to be going so well here at the Fraunces Tavern.

"I know your hand, sir," Hercules finally said, raising his glass in a toast. "A masterful way with the spice box."

"Taught you all you needed to know," said Fraunces, a touch of his usual smugness creeping into his voice.

Hercules only smiled at this, taking up his knife and fork. "That, indeed, you did."

Fraunces seemed surprised by this response and stood there. He looked around at the others in the dining room. The couple were engrossed in their own chatter and the strumpet was busy at her plate, perhaps having given up on the night's assignation.

"Tell me, cook," he said, his voice softer. "How goes all at the President's House? Are they well there?"

"Well enough," said Hercules, swallowing his food and taking up the wine. "The new steward isn't a patch on you." He said this last not only because it was in fact true, but also because he knew it would flatter.

Now the old man smiled broadly. "Is that so?" he said with a chuckle.

"How goes with all this?" said Hercules, gesturing vaguely around the room.

"Oh, fine, fine," said Fraunces, puffing his chest up in the old way. "It's just slow tonight, you see. A concert over at the City Tavern . . ." His voice trailed off.

Hercules watched him carefully. He doubted the place was ever full, but he said pleasantly, "I imagine you are flocked with trade from the mariners during the day hours."

"Oh no," said Fraunces, haughty again. "We don't encourage *that* kind of trade. Only persons of quality here — travelers to the city and the like." His gaze flicked involuntarily to the woman in the corner.

That was typical Fraunces, thought Hercules, forking some more of the tender meat into his mouth — he'd cut off his nose to spite his face. Here he was, hard on the water, and he refused the seamen's trade. Foolish.

"Well, I will leave you to your supper," said Fraunces after a moment. Hercules raised his glass again. "Let me — let me know if you require more," he said so gently that Hercules looked at him sharply, but he had already turned and was walking toward the kitchen door, his gait slower and more stooped than Hercules had remembered.

311

He sat back in the chair and allowed the food to settle, staring out the window and thinking about Fraunces. How much had an ill word from the General figured into the man's poor fortune? A figure passed below on the sidewalk that he thought he recognized. He leaned forward to get a better look at the hulking form. It was the man from Mrs. Harris's house. James Brown.

Before he could think why, Hercules rapped on the window to get the man's attention and he held up his hand in greeting. James Brown stepped forward, squinting to get a better look behind the glass. When recognition dawned, he made his way up the steps.

Fraunces met him at the door. Hercules could see him struggle with welcoming trade or putting the man, who was obviously a common mariner, out. Hercules stood up.

"Mr. Fraunces, this is Mr. Brown," he called. "An acquaintance."

Fraunces squinted at the black sailor in his woolen hat and striped trousers.

"Would you be so kind as to bring him some of your delicious stew?" said Hercules, stepping forward and opening his arm toward the table. "What will you drink, Mr. Brown — ale, porter? Something stronger?"

Brown glanced at the table. "Another of dat is fine," he said, nodding toward Hercules's glass.

"Claret then," said Hercules, smiling at Fraunces, who was beside himself. He turned on his heel and headed into the kitchen.

At the table, James Brown sat wide-legged and looked at Hercules expectantly.

"So you deck-off, eh?" he said finally. "You real dress up," he clarified when Hercules looked at him uncomprehendingly.

"I suppose," he said evenly. Was the man mocking him?

"What I can do fuh yuh?" said Brown, nodding to Fraunces as he put the plate down in front of him. "Obliged," he said politely before taking up the spoon and taking a taste. He looked thoughtful and took another.

"This real good," he said. "You have cassareep in here?" he called to Fraunces's back. The steward turned in surprise and returned to the table.

"Yes — how did you know?"

"Common thing where I'm from," he said, looking closely at Fraunces. "You too, I expect." Hercules recalled that Fraunces had been born in Barbados, where the treacle-like cassareep was a common ingredient.

The old steward looked at the sailor with his rheumy eyes for a longish time before nodding slowly and hobbling away. When, thought Hercules, had he gotten so old?

"So," said Brown. "I ask what it is I can do fuh yuh?"

"Do for me?" said Hercules, taking up his own fork again. "Nothing. I just saw you and —" Hercules paused. He wasn't actually sure why he had called out to the other man; maybe an instinct that the sailor was a useful person to know in these days where he felt the press of the General's household on him like a box about to close.

"Mmm-hmmm," said Brown, drawing out the syllables as he chewed slowly.

"Do you travel far in your trade?" asked Hercules to make conversation and get the man's intent stare off of him.

"New York mostly," he said. "Alexandria. I ain't like to go farther south than dat. Obvious reasons."

He said the last pointedly and took a sip of his wine.

"You from down Alexandria way, not so?" he asked next.

"Yes," said Hercules carefully.

"Uh-huh," said Brown, watching him. He

turned his gaze to the room. "Dis a real fine place."

Hercules looked around as well. "Yes, it is," he said. "Mr. Fraunces knows what he's about."

"I aim to have such a place one day," said Brown, tucking into his food again.

"You do?" said Hercules, surprised.

"Yep," he said between chews. "Ran a tavern for my master in Grenada. I real good at it."

Hercules eyed the man with new respect.

"Why did you turn your fortunes to the sea?" he asked.

"Escape," said Brown, lowering his voice. "I stowed away on a trade ship, bribed de ship cook to take me on as a scullion." He shrugged. "We got here and I made my way."

Interesting. The man was clever and industrious. Hercules was feeling more sure that James Brown was a useful man to know.

"Where will you open your tavern?" asked Hercules between bites.

Brown looked out the window at the crowd that had spilled over from the City Tavern before he answered.

"Plenty taverns mash up together here," he said. "Too much of competition. I aim to make fuh New York."

Hercules considered this a moment.

"But isn't the capital more —" he paused to find the right word. "Welcoming for those such as us to conduct business?"

Brown's lips twitched at the corners.

"So it may be," he said. "But den, when you free, you can make you way anywhere, not so?"

Hercules stopped short of putting another bite to his lips and searched Brown's face. Again, he wondered if the sailor was having fun at his expense. Shrugging slightly and smiling, he continued eating.

"Besides, there's more good I can do dere," said Brown, watching Hercules carefully. "In my other line, dat is."

Hercules let this pass. He wasn't about to be drawn into that conversation until he was good and ready.

"What is New York like?" he asked instead.

Brown thought about this before answering.

"Hodgepodge like. As big as Philadelphia but not so well put up," he said. "But de city expanding, inching north and north every time I does go there. Ain't but a few Quakers dere so anything goes." He smiled to himself as he said this.

Hercules nodded, encouraging Brown to go on while he continued eating.

"I mean to make my place on de water at de west end, just above de press of de old city," he said. "Maybe in Desbrosses Street or Spring, somewhere in dere. Dere's plenty trade to be had by dem such as myself."

Hercules raised his eyebrows curiously.

"Mariners," Brown clarified. "The city is full-up of men who go to sea."

Hercules had stopped eating while he listened and considered this.

"Nowadays, it possible to get almost as many a fine thing dere as it is here in Philadelphia," Brown said, taking up his drink again. "But none of that does trouble me — my fare go be plain and simple. A good bar and a better hand at cooking is all I need — someone more in your way of skill." Brown smiled at his companion. "But here I talking too long," he said. "Boring you wit my rambling."

"Not at all," said Hercules mildly. In fact, he had found all Mr. Brown had to say more than interesting.

"A toast," said Brown suddenly raising his glass. "To new acquaintances."

Hercules's hand clasped around his own glass and hesitated before raising it to meet Brown's own.

"May they soon be old friends," he said.

■ ■ ■ ■

Hercules came back into the yard and saw Nate go down the cellar stairs with Margaret, holding the lantern aloft behind him. At first, he thought nothing of it — no doubt they were assembling the next day's supplies. Besides, he knew there had been a chill between them since that day she flew at Hercules and shamed Nate, as if he were a little boy who needed her protection.

But just as he reached the kitchen door, something nagged at his mind and he turned back toward the cellar and listened at the top of the step. For a minute or two he heard nothing but the sounds of them moving about and filling baskets, but then her voice broke through suddenly, cracking the silence of the cellar.

"Why have you come to hate me?"

"What?" he said, surprised.

"You hate me — why?"

"Keep your voice down," Nate said, low and angry.

"I won't," she said in a normal tone. "I have a right to know."

Hercules heard Nate snicker.

"You don't have 'a right.' Nor do I," he said spitefully. "Now let's get on with this."

"No," she said, her voice snapping out into the dark like a gun crack. "At least tell me what I've done."

"Nothing," he said. "Why must you carry on so? Let us be about our business."

"NO!" she said, even louder now and banged her hand on something — the top of a barrel, probably.

"Dammit, shut your gob!" he hissed at her and Hercules could hear his angry steps. "Stop this!"

Hercules started down the steps, fearful that Nate would strike the wench and seal his fate, but then all was silent.

"Please, Nate," she whispered. "I thought we were —"

"Thought we were what?" he said, clearly struggling to hold on to his anger.

She was sobbing now.

"I don't know — friends," she said between gulps of air.

"People like us can't be friends, Margaret."

"But I don't care what anyone says about me!" she exclaimed. "You are all I have! What is there left if you turn away?"

"Listen to me!" he growled. "This is not about *you*. Do you understand?"

Hercules heard her whimper.

"Do you know what it means for *me* to

be seen with you? To have you hovering at my side? Someday someone — some *white* someone — isn't going to like that. Then what?" He spat out the last.

The girl whimpered again. "I'm sorry," she whispered. "Oh dear God, I'm sorry."

For a while, there was only the sound of the girl crying and Hercules, gratified, began to walk quietly up the step and into the yard, but then Nate spoke again.

"Shhh shhh," he murmured. "I'm sorry. Shhhh."

Slowly, the sobs turned to sniffles and then, as Hercules strained to hear, there was some snuffling and a low moan. Alarmed, he moved quietly down the steps again, afraid of what he might see.

When he reached the bottom, it took a moment for his eyes to adjust to the light. When they did, he felt his stomach lurch with fear and fury. There against the side wall, dimly lit by the lantern light, Margaret was pressed against the wall with Nate pushed up against her. She was kissing his lips, his face, grasping at his hands and kissing them too.

The boy pulled aside the cloth at her neck and kissed her there and then down to her collarbone before the little strumpet curiously, cautiously reached out and put her hand against the swelling in his pants.

He moaned and put his hand over hers, pushing it down, rubbing hard. She pressed her body closer into his but not before unbuttoning his trousers and reaching inside. A little gasp came from her lips when she felt him without the cloth.

They stood pressed together, his face buried in the rise of her meager bosom, as he guided her to stroke him back and forth until finally there was an explosion of wet in her hands.

Through it all Hercules had stood frozen to the spot. He was too ashamed for them both — and for himself — to cry out, and now he didn't want to retreat so they would know he had been watching. He stepped backward into the shadows at the base of the stair.

Now, Nate pulled away and quickly buttoned his pants. Searching the cold stone room, he found a scrap of rag wedged between the wall and a barrel. She was staring at the thick fluid on her hand and he grasped her by the wrist and scrubbed at it with the dirty cloth.

"Forgive me," he said to her hand, too ashamed to look at her.

Margaret put her hands on each side of his face and forced him to meet her eyes before she kissed him gently on the lips for what seemed a long time.

"No," she said when she pulled away. "I cannot forgive when there is no offense."

He looked at her and touched her face, where Hercules knew he would see the veins beneath the thin skin.

Hercules slunk quietly up the stairs, anger and despair warring in his heart. As he reached the top, he heard Nate say hoarsely as if amazed, "I do love you."

CHAPTER 21

Early 1795

"I'll thank you for your full attention when I speak to you," snapped Kitt. Hercules paused, his knife in midair. All noise in the kitchen stopped as they watched to see what he would do.

Hercules raised the knife high and brought it down smoothly on the head of a fish, separating it from the body. He tossed it into a bowl with several others.

"Nate," he said to the scullion, who had been kneading dough for rolls at the far end of the kitchen, "these are ready for the broth. Add a bit more savory this time, please."

Wiping his knife on a cloth, he stuck it straight up into the cutting board and then wiped his own hands carefully before turning to face Mr. Kitt. The steward was becoming more of a problem, and it seemed that Washington meant to keep him in service for the long term. Lately, his constant presence around Hercules had made it more difficult for him to come and go as he pleased.

"I am at your service," he said with a tight-lipped smile.

Kitt had watched him stiffly through the whole performance and did not once turn his head toward the rest of the kitchen.

"Good," he said shortly. "Are we understood? You'll check with me upon the menu?"

"Certainly," said Hercules.

"The General wants his table well laid for this event but not extremely so," he went on, as if Hercules were new to the house. "This means I will attend every detail."

Hercules continued to look at him, a slight smile plastered on his face.

"Well, then, as long as we are settled," said Kitt, "You may proceed." He watched for a moment, expecting Hercules to take up his knife. When Hercules continued to stand there smiling like a half-wit, he finally turned to leave the room.

When he was quite to the door, Hercules called out. "Oh, Mr. Kitt?"

The steward turned around expectantly.

"I'll need more sherry for cooking by tomorrow's end," he said. Kitt nodded and turned again to leave.

Hercules picked up his knife and began to pick at the fish's innards. "Oh! But I forgot — of course you'll need to ask the General's secretary for that," he said, making his voice friendly. "Since the General doesn't allow the stewards control of the wine room."

Kitt hesitated in the doorframe, his shoulders inching up. Even from the back Hercules could see he was deciding whether to turn around or not. Finally, he chose to proceed out of the room without answering.

At the butchering table, Hercules began to hum to himself just as Oney came into the kitchen carrying Lady Washington's tea tray, which she set on the washing board. She was subdued, moving listlessly these few months since Austin had been killed in a carriage accident on his way back to Mount Vernon just before Christmas.

At his chopping block, Hercules didn't stop working, but his eyes followed Oney as she made her way from the room.

"You going out for Lady Washington today, Oney?" he asked.

Oney looked limply at him. "Yes, to deliver a letter to Mrs. Chew — why?"

"If you'd stop at the apothecary for some liniment for my shoulder, I'd be much obliged," he said. The shoulder had been troubling him worse since he had carried Oney from the hall to the kitchen after she had fainted when Lady Washington told her of her brother's death. She'd sat in the kitchen in a trance for the rest of the afternoon, mumbling with tears streaming down her cheeks.

Oney, her gaze dull, acknowledged his request before she turned and passed like a specter from the room.

"Chef? Chef?" He could barely make out the words. "Master Hercules?" He struggled to open his eyes. Someone was crouching over him. Richmond? The face came closer. No. Nate. He drifted off again.

A loud rude voice broke through next. "How long has he been like this?" There was a mumble. Another voice asked, "What was in those pills?" Before he could hear the answer, he was gone again.

The sunlight slanting through the attic window made his eyelids twitch. He cracked one eye open, holding his hand up to his face. His body felt so stiff.

Squinting, he could make out a form sitting on a chair at the edge of his cot.

"How you goin', Master Hercules?" It was Old Moll, Lady Washington's grandson's nanny.

When he tried to open his mouth to speak, he found his voice came out in a croak.

"Hold on there," said the old lady, standing up and making her way to small clay jug on the room's one table. She poured out some water into a tin tankard and came back to him.

He tried to sit up and sharp pain shot through his shoulder before he collapsed back down.

"What you got to do is roll over to the good side and then push yuhself up," said Moll, standing near the cot.

Hercules grunted with the effort of rolling to the side until eventually he was sitting up. He took the cup gratefully, sucking down the liquid and holding it out for more. Moll refilled it for him.

When he was done drinking, he handed back the mug and cleared his throat.

"What are you doing up here, Moll?" he said, his voice still sticking.

"You was out near fourteen hours," said the old lady, peering at him. "Them pills what they gave you for that shoulder really cut you down."

Hercules ran a hand over his face. The liniment he'd sent Oney for hadn't worked and his shoulder was still aching something fierce when the steward sent to the apothecary for some pills. He tried to stand.

"I have to get downstairs . . . the Thanksgiving banquet," he said. It was an important event — proclaimed last year to be held now, in February. It wouldn't do for Hercules to be absent. But as soon as he was upright, dizziness felled him again. He sat down on the cot with a slump.

"The General like as took a fit when he found out you was up here laid out," said Moll, sitting back in her chair. "Mmm hmmm."

"He's angry?" asked Hercules.

"Good and angry — but not at you," she said. "No, he gave that Mr. Kitt an earful, sending for medicine to put you out than for a doctor what could help you."

Hercules lay back on the pillow, relief etched on his face.

"Well, I'm fine now," he said. "I'll be down shortly."

"No, son, no you won't," said Moll, leaning over and tapping him on the leg. "The General, he say I'm to sit up here with you and make sure you rest that shoulder — a couple days at least. He say he'd rather have you out the kitchen for two or three days than for God knows how long if that shoulder stopping you from work."

Hercules closed his eyes as he considered this. Once he would have thought it kindness from a master who was not cruel, now he felt like Prescott, the General's favored horse, stabled for a few days for a bruised hoof lest he push the animal too hard and lose him — and his investment — altogether.

"But Mr. Julien and Nate can't manage that dinner alone and the hired-in women aren't much of a hand," he fretted out loud.

"Don't matter," said Moll, taking up her sewing from the basket by her feet. "The General say they have to make do. Mr. Kitt, he hired in some cooks."

Hercules exhaled slowly. Beneath the covers his leg started to twitch. The last thing he could stand was other people in his kitchen, especially people put in place by the devious Kitt.

"Maybe I should just go and check . . ." he said, swinging his legs back over the edge of the cot.

"No, sir, you won't," said Old Moll, looking up from her sewing. "The General told me to sit up here and stop you from running around. 'That's an order, Moll,' he say. So that's what I'm set up here to do."

Hercules felt the annoyance rising up his chest. Damn this old woman. She was like a dog with a bone.

"He say the onliest thing I'm to leave for is so you can use the chamber pot," she said, looking at him pointedly.

He squinted at her and looked away.

"Where is Nate sleeping if you are up in here, nannying me?"

Old Moll chuckled at this. "Now, don't get testy there," she said. "Lotta folks would be happy to stay in they bed on the General's say-so. Nate been sleeping in the landing."

Hercules grunted and looked back out the window. Must be about ten in the morning from the way the sun was slanting in. It had snowed in the night and white powder had collected in the corners of the window and frost covered the panes, mirroring the sun like crystals. At least with the fires in the house going, the chimney that came through this room was throwing off plenty of heat.

"Time for you to step on out, Miss Moll," said Hercules, putting his feet on the floor and rising. "I have to do the necessary."

Three days later he felt well enough to get dressed and come down to the kitchen. Before he could leave his room, though, Old Moll had gone down to the president's study with a full report. He was only allowed out when she had come back and given him the go-ahead.

Tying his neckerchief as he made his way down the stairs, Hercules considered how Kitt might have used his illness for his own advantage. Being laid out might have given the steward what he needed to further argue that it was best for him to remain at home in the evenings — lest his shoulder be injured further, of course.

Except for the pain, it had been nearly impossible for him to lie in that bed, with Moll yammering and sewing, sewing and yammering the whole time. All he could think of was the disaster that was being made of his kitchen. Nate had stopped in every evening and told him all that was going on in great detail, but he knew the boy was leaving things out — the things that would send him flying down the three flights of stairs in a fury.

". . . and you have seen, Lady Washington, my cooks have everything well in hand." Kitt's voice came through the closed kitchen door. Hercules hesitated and drew his hand back from the knob. They must be standing right in the vestibule between the kitchen and the passage. Mrs. Washington said something he couldn't quite make out and then Kitt spoke again.

"I'm sure his Excellency would consider it a great relief to be able to return those members of your — ah, family — back to Virginia and allow for these white cooks instead."

Now, Hercules could make out the First Lady's response quite clearly. "The General was not satisfied with the Thanksgiving dinner, Mr. Kitt," she said sharply. "And the breakfasts that your cooks prepare are far too elaborate. Hercules —"

"I know that the General is accustomed to the style of his cook, but that is not to say that it is most superior," he cut in. "With a little time —"

"Mr. Kitt!" said Lady Washington sharply. "Are you suggesting that the president learn to accept your choice of cook when he has his own?"

Now, Kitt mumbled unintelligibly before his voice rose again. ". . . and what if Hercules remains unwell? What then? We need to be able to organize ourselves appropriately."

"There is nothing whatever to suggest he shall remain unwell," said Lady Washington irritably. "And if he does, we shall cross that bridge when we come to it. Clearly, you are quite capable of finding people to your liking when the situation arises."

Her voice grew fainter and Kitt's replies less clear as they moved away from the door farther into the kitchen. Hercules stood there a moment longer to be sure they were well away before grabbing the handle and turning it purposefully. He strode into the kitchen cheerfully and made to reach for his apron upon the peg, then feigned delight at seeing the First Lady in the kitchen.

"Lady Washington," he said, smiling and bowing. "Mr. Kitt." He nodded at the steward after he straightened.

"Hercules!" said Mrs. Washington, relief clear upon her face. "But you look much recovered! How do you feel?" She peered at him as if she could see his affliction by staring hard enough.

"I am indeed much recovered, madam," he said politely. "Thanks to the kind ministering of Old Moll — I thank you for sparing her to be at my side."

Mrs. Washington twittered and smiled happily.

"I understand that we have been graced with some fine cooks in my absence," said Hercules jovially, going to his worktable in front of the hearth and looking at the roast sitting on a board. One of the hired cooks, a heavyset woman with red hair and a sweaty forehead, stood over it with a carving knife. The other cook, an equally heavy-set man with black hair tied in a queue, stirred something in a pot hanging over the fire.

"That roast is dry," said Hercules pleasantly, looking at it resting on the block.

The woman cook snapped disdainfully, "Not likely!" and went back to sharpening her knives.

Nate watched from the other side of the kitchen where he was picking over some dried beans, then cut a glance over to Margaret, who was washing pottery at the sink. Hercules resisted the urge to wink at the boy.

The male cook turned from what he was stirring with a look of disbelief at Hercules. He straightened up and came over to the table as well.

"Go on and cut into it then," said Hercules, his voice measured, but he stared at her coldly.

The woman cook looked at him like he was crazy while the man snorted and shook his head before going back to stirring the pot.

"Shall I do it then?" said Hercules, heading for the drawer where the knives were kept.

"Now, see here!" she exclaimed, looking

at Kitt. "I'll not be told what to do by the likes of —"

"Mistress Webb —" cut in Kitt nervously, glancing at Mrs. Washington.

"I would like to see the quality of the roast, as a matter of fact," said the president's wife suddenly. "The president has not been satisfied with the joints that have come to table."

Giving Hercules an evil look, Mistress Webb took up the carving knife and began to slice into the roast.

The cook cut thin, even slices of meat that fell prettily to the board in a fan pattern, stopping when she had reached midway through the roast. Hercules took up a wooden spoon from the table and pressed upon the meat. No juice came out.

"As I suspected — dry," he said. "You cannot let it cook completely to brown, madam. It will continue to cook when removed from the fire, and so you must remove it sooner lest it dry out — like this one."

"No one's ever complained of my cooking!" she snarled. "And what would one such as you know of good food?"

At the hearth, the man chuckled to himself.

"I can smell from here that your pottage

requires salt, sir," said Hercules to his bent back. The other cook stopped stirring and turned around angrily.

"What the devil," he began.

Now Kitt moved forward. "May I remind you, Mr. and Mrs. Webb, that you are in the presence of Lady Washington?" he said to the two cooks, who glanced quickly at the General's wife and then at Kitt.

"Begging your pardon, madam," said the woman, half curtsying to Martha, knife still held aloft. "What is it you'd have us do?" she asked Kitt.

"I am quite well to take over now," said Hercules mildly, walking over to the hook and finally getting his apron. "No doubt the General would like to spare any extra expense." He paused and watched Kitt's face turn red.

"Yes," said Mrs. Washington. "The General will be relieved to know you are at your duties again, Hercules." She turned to Kitt. "Please settle accounts with Mr. and Mrs. Webb, Mr. Kitt."

Then, nodding to the hired cooks who stood, mouths agape, she headed toward the door, with both Hercules and Kitt bowing as she went past. As they rose from their bent positions, Kitt narrowed his eyes at him threateningly.

"Oh," said Mrs. Washington, her hand on the doorknob. "Hercules — the president has a hankering for your hoecakes. Please have them ready for his breakfast tomorrow."

"As you wish, madam," he said, bowing deeply again as she swept through the door, leaving the four of them to look at one another. Nate sat forward on his bench nervously. Margaret, who had not turned around from her scrubbing through the exchange, paused in her work, listening.

"Very well then," Kitt said crisply. "Come along with me, Mr. and Mrs. Webb."

The two cooks untied their aprons and flung them onto the bench in the corner before angrily following Kitt out of the room. Hercules began to whistle and walked around the table to point at the dry roast with the tip of his knife.

"Nate!" he said loudly. "Come over here and take the rest of this meat off the bone and chop it finely. We will mix it with suet and use it to force some vegetables. Margaret — leave that now and see if there are any cabbages and small squash in the cellar."

Margaret quickly dried her hands and turned to do his bidding.

"Oh, and take those aprons out of here

with you and drop them at the laundress on your way," he said, gesturing dismissively to where the Webbs had flung the soiled items.

"When you're done with that, I want you to chop some parsnips for this pottage, and add some salt and savory, then we'll see what I need next," said Hercules, going to the larder to check the stores.

"You," he said, pointing to one of the hired scullery maids who had stood agog at the action between cooks. "I want this place cleaned top to bottom. Every surface wiped with hot water, floor scrubbed with lye. Set a cauldron to boiling outside."

With that he disappeared into the small storage room and began to take stock.

Oney dashed into the kitchen and dumped an armful of wet things — a lady's overcoat and gloves — by the hearth and dashed out before Hercules could bellow after her.

Furious, Hercules looked around the kitchen until he spotted Margaret.

"You! Take those things out of here, now!" he said, turning back to his table while she scurried to the task. Oney hadn't been right since Austin died but this was going too far.

In another ten minutes, Oney was back. She wasn't running now. Instead, she began to pace the room, wringing her hands.

Hercules sighed in exasperation. "What are you doing, Oney?" he said, his voice rising with irritation. "And why are you doing it here?"

Oney stopped pacing, her forehead creased with worry and fear.

"Miss Betsey's arrived," she said.

"Oh," he said, studying her face. "Were they expecting her?"

Oney shook her head miserably. "She just showed up — said a lady from down their way in Virginia was traveling and she went along." Hercules wasn't surprised. Betsey was clever and conniving and she would have jumped at a suitable chaperone to get herself up here. Everyone knew that she was attached overmuch to Washington, hanging on his every word and look. Her jealousy that her younger sister, Nelly, was being raised here was legendary.

"Miss Nelly saw her carriage through the parlor window. It was a real shock. She just stormed in and started bossing people around —" Oney's words came out so fast that they were almost hard to make out. She didn't look at anyone while she talked but moved around the room, touching things and rearranging them. The others in the kitchen looked from her to Hercules, and he saw the uncertainty in their eyes.

"She shrieked at me to take off her wet shoes — see?" Oney turned to Hercules and lifted her apron. There was a muddy footprint there.

"Oney, becalm yourself," said Hercules. He moved around his table and grasped her shoulders. "How long will she be here?"

"I don't know," she said, staring up desperately into his face. "Until the weather clears at least. Mrs. Washington said it was a risk for her to have even got here and they couldn't tempt providence like that again. She's going to share Nelly's room and I'm to attend her and you know how evil she is and —"

"Oney!" Hercules gave her a shake. "This won't do. What do you think Mrs. Washington will do to you if you carry on so?" He led her to a bench by the fire and sat her down.

"Just sit for a moment, girl," he said and went to the sideboard and poured water into a pewter cup. The others in the kitchen were now watching openly.

"Here," he said, returning and handing her the water, but Oney just stared at him dumbly.

"Take it," he said, his voice more forceful this time, startling Nate, Margaret, and the others from their intense scrutiny of the scene. Everyone made a show of going back to their tasks, although he could tell that their ears still pricked to what was happening by the hearth.

Oney took the cup.

"Drink," said Hercules. Nodding miserably, she took a sip.

Hercules squatted in front of her. "Hear me, Oney Judge," he said, his voice too low for the others to hear. "Get ahold of yourself lest you bring that old cow's anger down on your head."

Oney cut her eyes to the others and then back to him.

"Do you understand?" he said again, his voice low. She nodded.

"Are you sure?"

Oney nodded once more and brought the cup to her lips again.

Hercules studied her a moment more then stood, smoothing his apron and returning his table.

The problem was he wasn't sure she understood at all.

Chapter 22

Spring 1795

Hercules paused and observed the pair heading toward him a block down Chestnut Street. Betsey Parke Custis charged forward like a common housewife rushing to get the best fish at the market and Oney Judge skipped hurriedly along, her feet slapping the pavement in a near run to keep up.

Betsey's bonneted head bobbed like a fat, angry pigeon, her face pinched, as she marched past other people on the sidewalk with her long manly stride. Hercules began to smirk but then set his face to rights. Oney may as well not have been chaperoning Betsey for how little the girl cared for propriety.

Soon enough, the space between them narrowed and the pair stopped while Betsey looked furiously around her. Oney wrung her hands until she spied Hercules. Her brows shot up.

Hercules moved forward before Oney

could make a move that would set the ever-shrewish Betsey off and said, "Ladies," bowing deeply.

Betsey's head snapped forward and her face twisted in fury.

"May I be of help?" he said as he straightened.

"Oh! Hercules," said Oney, relief making her voice breathy. "We are looking for Gilbert Stuart's house, might you know it — ?"

"Oney!" snapped Betsey, raising her hand and slapping the girl on the side of her head, then turning to him, her hands on her sturdy hips. Her thick, sow-like frame reminded Hercules of her grandmother, Lady Washington, and he longed to shove the woman in the gutter.

"How dare you share my private business with this nigra," she went on shrilly. "Besides, how would he know where Gilbert Stuart's house is?" She raised her hand again and Oney cowered.

Now Hercules stepped forward and made his voice as deep as he could to get her attention.

"The fault is all mine, Miss Betsey," he said, looking at her uplifted hand pointedly. Somewhat cowed, she let her hand drop and then started to crane her neck around him as if looking for aid from a passerby.

"You may not remember me — I'm your grandfather's cook."

Now Betsey turned to stare at him.

"Uncle Harkless?" she said, her eyes beady with suspicion. "But why are you here in the road? I am about to keep Grandfather company as he sits for Mr. Stuart and I shall apprise him —"

He wished he could tell her it was none of her blasted business, but instead he said politely,

"I'm just returning from meeting the ship from Alexandria with our Mount Vernon goods."

"Oh," she said and pressed her mouth into a firm line, then opened it again, and closed it.

"I believe that Stuart's house is just there," he said, pointing to a building a few doors down.

Betsey turned and looked at where his finger indicated, then without saying any more, she grabbed Oney's arm roughly and started charging toward Mr. Stuart's house. Oney looked at him beseechingly over her shoulder as they went.

Hercules continued on his way, musing about the General sitting for Stuart in the very same studio where he bedded Thelma.

He passed the doorway just as a black servant opened it to Betsey, who demanded, "Where are they?"

"Who, Miss?" she said politely but with a chill.

"Why, who lives here?" snapped Betsey.

Hercules shook his head and kept walking. Pity gurgled in his chest. He didn't envy Oney Judge at all.

Hercules leaned over the elaborate pie decorated with a pastry cutout of a pheasant standing beneath a tree. He placed the last bay leaf in the small slit he had made around the branches so that it filled out the tableau with the fullness of green.

"There," he said, straightening up and bringing the dish over to the side table for the footmen. "Nate, spoon out the ragout of green beans and garnish it with the sliced egg."

Wiping his hands, Hercules set about cleaning his work area and inspecting the crockery that Margaret had already washed.

"This isn't clean enough," he said to her after examining a large bowl. "I see the sheen of butter grease still upon it — wash it again."

"Perhaps if you spent less time looking after Nate and more time tending to your business you would not have to do your work twice," he murmured so only she could hear. Margaret looked up, startled, and met his eyes. He kept his face impassive but he hoped she could see the hardness there. He'd been extra demanding of her work in the months since witnessing the scene in the cellar. She was making a brave show of it — he had to give her that. Hercules didn't think she had it in her. She made him want to wring her scrawny neck.

Everyone returned to their business until the last dish had been removed and Hercules untied his apron and hung it on the peg.

"I'm for the city," he said, slipping on the light coat that he wore against the chill that could still come on in the evenings of early May. Satisfied that all was in order, he took up his cane and hat and slipped out the door before Mr. Kitt could come into the kitchen and delay him.

Walking the city streets usually calmed his mind, but not tonight. His thoughts kept wandering to Thelma and this business between Margaret and Nate. He had been foolish to hope he could separate them for good. He thought of Richmond, back home in Virginia. Well, at least he would see his son in a few months' time when they traveled back for the summer visit.

The thought of Virginia crowded out all else and he was back at Mansion Farm again, trapped by all the outlying acreage of holdings that made up Mount Vernon. There was the little daughter he had fathered on one of the housemaids some five years ago. He hardly knew the girl, being in Philadelphia nearly all the while since she was born.

Hercules knew he should long to see her and Richmond and his older girls Delia and Evey too, but he could feel the air being choked out of him at the very thought of Virginia. When he was there he was not as a father should be, consumed as he was with the idea of getting out, and this made him ashamed. It was better for them all when he was not there. But when the president went home he had no choice but to go too. The thought threw his spirit into a dark place, for soon enough Washington would want to return to his farm for good.

Hercules took a deep breath in the chilly air. The street was quiet except for a few people tripping into taverns and some late-night oyster sellers huddled in the alleyways to sell their wares to the prostitutes and their patrons who conducted business there. He turned toward Fraunces's tavern, the docks to his left crawling with as much activity as if it were broad daylight. Stevedores unloaded cargo onto waiting dray carts under the glow of torchlight.

He turned right, up Dock Street, and passed the Man Full of Trouble Tavern, which was doing fair enough trade. He hadn't gone there for more than a year now — since that last time he saw James Hemings. Hercules wondered about his old friend and whether that mongrel Jefferson would keep his word about the freedom contract. He doubted it.

He rounded the bend and could already hear the noise of the carriages dropping off "the quality" in front of the City Tavern up the block, but here no streetlamps illuminated the road. Fraunces's tavern sat quietly in a dark pool. Hercules walked closer and saw that the door was shuttered tight and there were no lights in the windows. The sign that had swung from the yardarm had been whitewashed.

"You friend choose a poor spot fuh he tavern." A voice from behind startled him. He stood very still so as not to show that he had been taken unawares, and instead leaned more heavily on his cane and studied the building.

"It was a tavern before he took it on," said Hercules. "I seem to recall that much."

"T'was that, but it were fuh the working-men — the dock folk," the other man said. "Hard to compete with de City Tavern for de quality."

Hercules knew the voice, with its lilt and falls. He turned to face the mariner James Brown.

"Mr. Brown," he said by way of greeting.

"Master cook," said Brown, bowing. "Hard luck about you friend," he said, nodding toward the tavern.

Hercules followed his gaze. "He wasn't a friend exactly," he said thoughtfully. "I am sorry that this didn't work out for him, though."

Brown grunted, "Oh, I think he all right. Some of de mariners tell me he take over de Tun Tavern near de docks in Water Street."

"Has he now?" said Hercules, turning away from the building.

"Wouldn't know it except de boys say he turn a fine hand to shad," said Brown.

Hercules smirked. Fraunces and that damned fish. The lengths he would go to put a shad in front of the General, who favored the bony and oily fish. Folks said it was the shad runs that saved the troops at Valley Forge from total starvation back in the spring of '78.

Ah well. Hercules would have to find some other place to spend his evening. He touched his cane to his hat. "Good evening, sir," he said to the sailor before walking away.

"A moment!" said Brown, moving forward to walk alongside him. "I know another place — a respectable one," he continued in response to Hercules's raised eyebrows. "It time I return your hospitality."

Hercules didn't slow his pace and said nothing as he walked. What the devil did the mariner want? To press him again about his abolitionist trade? Curiosity bested him and finally, without looking over at Brown, he said, "I should be delighted."

"Good," said Brown. "It just this way," he said, walking around Hercules and moving down an alley to the left. "It small but it clean and de food decent enough."

Hercules changed his course to follow the sailor.

"You know," Hercules said musingly, "I know another man called James and we used to frequent this part of town together."

"Oh?" said Brown. "What become of he?"

"He was bound to return to Virginia with his mas—" Hercules stopped suddenly. The word he was about to say turned in his stomach like sour food. "He was obliged to return home," he finished quickly.

Brown considered this silently. "Ah," he finally said, "well, now you has *two* friend called James. One for de other — until you meet again, perhaps."

Hercules glanced over at the other man who walked along purposefully, his eyes scanning the streets. Sensing Hercules watching him, he looked over and smiled.

As Hercules crossed the yard, market basket in hand, he noticed the General at the stables, standing at Prescott's head, rubbing the huge horse's ears with each of his great hands. He seemed to be talking to the beast, leaning in toward the horse's face. The white stallion flicked his ears and shook his head slightly as if he were answering, and the president leaned his forehead against the animal's nose for a moment.

Hercules felt strange witnessing this moment, what with the way the General was with the horses, like they were his only true friends. Maybe they were. Washington straightened up and gave the horse a final rub and held out one of last fall's apples in his open palm. Prescott leaned down and nibbled it delicately.

The General stood patiently, smiling and holding his hand steady as Prescott ate.

When the horse was done, the General accepted the rag that Postilion Joe, the stableman, gave him and wiped his hand.

Washington turned and began to pace the garden. Hercules knew him in these moods — somber and restless. He watched as the General crossed his arms and walked with eyes downcast around the bricked yard, pausing in front of the kitchen garden. He looked over and spotted Hercules standing there.

Hercules bowed quickly and headed toward him.

"Excellency?" he said. "May I be of service?"

"Ah, Hercules, no, I was just —" He stopped, looking weary. "Are you off to market then?"

"Why yes, sir, but if there is something you need —"

"No," said Washington, turning away as if looking around for something. "I'm fine."

"As you wish, sir," said Hercules. He hesitated a moment, waiting to be formally dismissed, but Washington continued to stare at the trees, lost in thought. Washington was hard to read as a rule but even more so when he was in one of these moods.

"I'll walk with you then," said the General suddenly.

"Sir?" said Hercules, confused. Had the old man gone mad?

"Yes, I'd like to step out. The market might be just the thing — that is if you don't mind my company," he said, raising his eyebrows.

"It would be an honor, sir," said Hercules, smiling deferentially to hide his annoyance. Mentally, he ran through the list of vendors at the market, making note of where to avoid or not linger too long, lest the General see more than he need.

"Lead on then," said Washington. "And be about your business as if I were not present. If you can do that, I assure you it will be more than the others we encounter."

Hercules lifted the side of his mouth in a smirk that he halted before it fully bloomed. As if such were possible. The General was right — his stepping out as a common citizen would cause a stir. They left through the garden gate, Hercules holding the door for the president.

"Tell me, Hercules," the General said in his raspy voice, causing Hercules to fall in step with him so he might better hear. "There was, I remember, an old woman who sold pepper pot — I went there with his Excellency, Mr. Franklin, back in '74. I imagine she must long have died."

"I believe her daughter is there, Excellency," said Hercules, thinking of his friend Polly Haine and the shock upon her face should he arrive at her stand in the company of the president. "We might go see her if you like."

Washington nodded at this and continued silently, worrying over something in his mind.

Hercules had seen him like this before, those times he came home to Virginia during the war when he wandered the property on horseback, his body servant Billy Lee riding at his side.

It was just a block before they stepped into the market shed at Fifth Street, and Hercules hesitated. The crowd was thick today. It didn't seem the president had noticed or, if he had, he was undeterred. He strode on without pause and Hercules hurried to follow as they entered the dark of the shed with its stink of farm animals and blood and rotten vegetables. The General's face relaxed and he seemed not to hear the murmurs that were rising up around him.

A ragged woman came up to them and blocked their way. She held the hand of a snotty-faced little boy in raggedy clothes, dragging him to the ground as she made a low curtsy.

"Your Excellency, sir, please," she said breathlessly, looking up at the cold blue eyes. "This bairn is named for you."

Washington looked down at the child who had stuck his thumb in his mouth, although he was too old to be doing so. Hercules only just stopped himself from screwing up his nose from their smell.

"Are you called George or Georgie then?" Washington said, smiling and putting his hand on the child's head. The boy, who might have been dull, didn't take his thumb out of his mouth and kept twisting his head up to see what was resting there.

"Oh no, sir, it's George it is," said the woman proudly. "He's to grow up strong and brave like you. No baby names for him."

Washington smiled a little at this and then patted the boy, who acted as if he hadn't noticed what was going on or the small crowd that had formed around him. The president reached into the leather pocket sewn into the inside of his coat and pulled out a coin that he pressed into the mother's hand.

"That's to buy something for your boy," he said sternly. She curtsied again and thanked him profusely even as he walked past her.

They pushed on, with a trail of people following them now. Those few brave enough to step forward and try to shake the president's hand were made quickly wiser by the nod of his head and that his hands remained clasped behind his back.

As Hercules stopped at the cheesemonger and the meat seller, Washington strode alongside, standing silently and watching the proceedings while the proprietors stood agog.

At a stand selling jams, Washington picked up a crock of honey and handed it to Hercules who dutifully purchased it, knowing there was a full cupboard at home. He startled the broom maker by pausing overlong to watch him at his craft and fascinated the pear seller by advising Hercules as to which ones looked fairest.

They were only halfway through the sheds and Hercules was finding himself wearied and peeved by their slow procession, so when Washington lingered at an oyster seller, he spoke up.

"Excellency, sir," he said in a low voice. "I procure your oysters from the best man in the city — keeps them in baskets in the seawater to stay fresh. I am sure these will not compare."

Washington considered this before moving on.

"Why, Excellency!" a voice called from behind them. They both turned to see a tall man with white hair approach them in the company of a young lady.

Washington turned and, noting the man, smiled genuinely for the first time. "Mr. Peale," he said. "A pleasant surprise." He turned toward the young lady and bowed. "Miss Peale."

Hercules stepped back and busied himself by scowling at the crowd of imbeciles dogging them.

"What brings you to market, sir?" said Peale. Hercules supposed he could only be the famous artist. He had heard Stuart speak bitterly of him and his houseful of artistic children who, together, captured every good commission in the city.

"Some fresh air," answered the General. He nodded his head toward Hercules. "My cook has been kind enough to allow me to step out with him. I'm afraid my presence has delayed him in his tasks."

Peale peered around Washington and acknowledged Hercules, but the girl — his daughter, he presumed — stared at him, perplexed.

"We were fortunate enough to see your lady not more than an hour ago at the milliner," said Peale. "We were happy to see her looking quite well — well enough that her portrait should be painted again."

"Well then, be painted she must," said Washington pleasantly. "I'm sure the chance of looking so well for all eternity upon the canvas will prove too great a temptation for Mrs. Washington."

As they chatted, Hercules let his mind roam to the trip back to Virginia, which was coming fast upon them. The night he saw James Brown in front of Fraunces's closed tavern, they'd had drinks and for the first time Hercules unburdened his thoughts to another person. The thought of Virginia made him feel shackled, he'd told the mariner, and as the day grew closer, he could practically feel the chafe of iron around his hands and feet.

And here was the General standing but inches away from him in this, his domain. Next, he'd want to set up his study in the kitchen and steal his peace there too. Hercules smiled at this insane thought but quickly set his face back to stone. Yes, Virginia was weighing heavy on his mind.

". . . I've been meaning to come by your museum," Washington was saying. "Are there any new exhibits?"

"A few," said Peale. "Some interesting fossil specimens from Connecticut."

After some more pleasantries, the pair passed on and Washington nodded to Hercules that they should proceed.

"Hercules," he said as they moved through the press of people. "What of that pepper pot? I believe, even hot as it is, I should like to have some."

CHAPTER 23

Mount Vernon, Summer 1795

"Start with inspecting the cookware. Re-wash anything that looks dirty," said Hercules to Margaret as he perused the shelves at the Mount Vernon cookhouse. "Nate, come with me, please."

The scullion followed him out the door toward the kitchen gardens. The slaves working on the grounds around the house stopped to raise their hands. Even the children, running around in their gangs, changed course to follow as Hercules and Nate walked along the path that led around the bowling green in front of the house.

Hercules waved now and then in return, but otherwise generally took no notice of the awe that followed him. He was used to it — nay, had come to expect it, for when they were at Mount Vernon there was even less doubt who was the most valued among them.

"Mind you don't run through the General's gardens," said Hercules, placing his hand solemnly on the head of the eldest boy, who was about eight. "And stay away from the house or it's a switch for you all."

The boy stood looking up at him in wonder.

"Where's Richmond?" Hercules asked.

"Dunno," shrugged the boy. The others did the same.

"Well, if you see him send him to the kitchen for me, hear?"

The boy nodded.

"Off with you then," said Hercules, patting the child on his shoulder as he continued past.

Waving at him and Nate, they ran off — toward the house. Hercules sighed and shook his head.

At the lower gardens several women and the younger children worked, harvesting squash and peppers. They all smiled and greeted Hercules as he walked around examining the various plots.

"What have you of cucumbers?" he asked the most elderly of the women.

"A good bunch over there." With her little shovel, she indicated a plot by the garden wall.

Beckoning to Nate, Hercules headed to

the area she had pointed to. The scullion pulled several of the large fruit off the trellised vine and placed them in the basket he carried.

"Now to the greenhouses," Hercules said, striding purposefully across the bowling green instead of taking the path around it while Nate looked nervously up at the house as if someone were going to fly out and shoo them off the grass. They might do, thought Hercules grimly, but not to him.

The weather was particularly fine that day. The river glittered behind them like a blue satin ribbon. Several boats moved steadily along at full sail. The smell of cook fires tumbled out of the chimneys at either end of the bunkhouses, which extended out long on either side of the greenhouse. From somewhere inside, a baby wailed.

The greenhouse rose up before them, all ornate brick and windows. They stepped inside the building with its slate floor, fancy worktables, and shelves. Most of the plants were out for the summer except for a huge lemon tree that took up an entire corner.

"Evey?" Hercules called out, his voice bouncing off the slate and echoing back to them. The room was oppressively hot even though the rear door had been flung open.

A short and slender girl appeared in that

doorway, a watering can in her hand. Shielding her eyes to adjust them from the harsh sunlight, she gazed in to see who had called.

"Papa!" she cried and set the can down to run into Hercules's open arms.

"My girl . . ." he murmured, embracing her and kissing the top of her head. It felt good to hold his child in his arms. "Let me see you — practically grown. A mirror to your mama." Hercules stopped, his voice catching in his throat.

Evey beamed at her father's compliment. "Truly?" she said, her eyes flitting over to the scullion. "Nate," she said with a happy nod. The boy looked odd — like he'd swallowed a stone — but he gamely smiled back.

"Papa, Delia is working here with me too, now," she said. Hercules's eyebrows furrowed, then relaxed. Yes, of course, he thought bitterly. Delia was now ten — old enough for the General to benefit by her labor.

Of all the jobs on the plantation, tending the greenhouse and assisting the gardeners was a choice one. The labor was not too hard and it was well out of sight of those in the house. He was glad to hear both of his daughters were here rather than up in the mansion.

"Is Miss Easter still minding you all,

then?" he said.

Evey laughed. "No, Papa! I'm old enough for that now!" She raised her chin proudly. "Richmond is working over here at the blacksmith's so he doesn't have to travel. I cook for us and Delia helps with the garden and to look after Baby. Sometimes Richmond brings home some squirrel or fish, if the mood takes him."

Hercules didn't say anything, but sadness was unfurling inside him like a miasma. His children had a life without him. A life he didn't know. It was better that way, he supposed, better that they learn to make their own way, yet it made his heart hurt.

"Papa!" A smaller girl ran pell-mell toward him, knocking him backward with the force of her embrace. "Papa!" she said again, practically climbing him, until he lifted her and twirled her around before gathering her up.

"Soon you'll be too big for that," said Hercules. "Like Evey."

"But I'm not too big yet!" giggled Delia, hugging him again.

"All right then," he said, laughing and twirling her once more and setting her down with a wince. He rubbed his shoulder gingerly.

"What is it, Papa?" asked Delia, watching him.

"Nothing, it's nothing. Say hello to Nate," he said, looking down at his shirt that the girl had smudged with her muddy hands. "What were you doing? Burrowing like a groundhog?"

Delia laughed. "No! I was filling the plant pots with soil for seedlings, silly!" She beamed at her father and wiggled her fingers at him. "Oh, hello, Nate," she said as an afterthought.

"There are trowels for that task, my girl," Hercules teased. "No need to use your hands. Where's Baby?" he asked, looking around as if she might also be in the greenhouse.

"Probably with the other little ones," said Delia, shrugging, as if she hadn't just been part of the children's gang herself only months before. "We had best be back. I will come see you all tonight," he said, kissing each of his daughters on their heads.

"Will you stay with us, Papa?" asked Delia eagerly.

Hercules hesitated. He had no desire to be in their small part of the communal living space with its hard-packed dirt floor and meager cots. He far preferred the room above the kitchen, with its clean wood planks and windows, that he would share with Nate when they were there.

"Perhaps," he said pleasantly if a little too quickly. "It depends on our work. This place has become practically an inn what with the visitors coming and going. A lot of cooking to do!" He said the last too jovially, clapping Nate on the shoulder.

The boy managed a weak smile at the girls, whose faces fell.

"Oh, it's always like that," said Evey. "Even when the General isn't here. Worse, of course, when he is."

"Yes, well —" Hercules hesitated, at a loss for what to say. "We will go see Richmond on our way back. But before I go, I'll have some of those lemons — I'm amazed the tree is bearing at all now."

Evey smiled broadly and headed over to the tree with Delia, who held out her apron as her older sister climbed up a small ladder and plucked the few remaining fruit to be found.

■ ■ ■ ■

PART IV

■ ■ ■ ■

CHAPTER 24

Richmond took off his leather apron and hung it on the peg. Sweat bathed his bare chest. Hercules, standing in the doorway, was surprised to see how much he looked like a man already, developing the broad shoulders and muscled torso of a blacksmith.

Richmond had scarcely come to see Hercules in the many weeks since they arrived, until finally the time to return to Philadelphia was upon them and, longing to see more of the boy, Hercules had been forced seek him out. Now, ignoring him, Richmond went out to the rain barrel at the back door of the blacksmith shop and scooped a tin of water and poured it over his head. He stood there a minute, cooling down, before he did it again.

"We can't go without permission," said Richmond, stepping in and taking up a rag to dry off before pulling on his shirt. "And

Mr. Allistone will be at his supper now —
he won't care to see one of us at his door
for leave to gad about."

Hercules had come to the blacksmith shop
with the intention of spending the evening
with his eldest child. His boy. There was, he
had heard, a social club in town where
slaves and free blacks gathered. Old Sam,
the only one of them who had hailed from
Africa, had told him. "The whites know
about it, they do," said the old man, his tat-
tooed and symmetrically scarred cheeks
now hanging with age. "Only, they don't
know what it is we do there. Singing and
dancing mostly — so they think."

Hercules had raised his eyebrows and
leaned forward. "How's that?" he said pleasantly.

"There are other things," said the old man
mysteriously, pulling one of his copper-
ringed ears. He had a heavy lisp since he
had no front teeth — sold them, he said, to
Washington to use in his dentures.

"The old fool is an older fool than me,"
he had chuckled to Hercules. "Them teeth
were practically no good."

But Hercules could get no more out of
him about the "social club." Still, he was
resolved to see for himself — and bring
Richmond along for good measure. He

wanted to spend time with his son and to learn how he had come along since he had left Philadelphia. Hercules had hoped his temper had eased. But the boy was not inclined to go.

"I have the General's leave to go about as I wish," said Hercules, mildly. "You know this."

"But I do not," said Richmond, nastily. "And I'm not about to trail along behind you like them others — Son of Head Nigra."

Hercules felt his blood get hot in that old familiar way. Richmond was still up to his old tricks, except now instead of just being worthless he was old enough — and brave enough — to bait his father.

"Suit yourself," he said, shrugging and turning quickly so Richmond would not see his anger and disappointment. He left the blacksmith shop without looking back, crossed back over the bowling green, and then ambled down the pathway to the dock where a small skiff was unloading barrels.

"Heading back to Alexandria?" he asked one of the black boatswains when got close enough.

"Yup."

"Hitch a ride?"

"Yup," said the boy.

Hercules stood to the side and waited for them to finish their business. He could hear the sound of visitors walking the grounds and the shouts of servants running to and fro to get ready for the evening's party. Hercules had more than exerted himself putting on a feast for this, the president's last night in Virginia. He deserved a night out.

"Hand up?" the boy on the deck called.

Hercules turned to face him and accepted the offered hand. He settled down on a bench near the stern and watched as the peachy gold of the setting sun reached across the shore and crawled up through the woods to set the red roofs of the farm buildings aglow. As they rounded the bend to where the house faced the slope, the fading light bathed the back veranda, with its tall white columns, in a pinkish light.

He tried to remember when this was the whole of his world and how he felt tracking these woods and cooking his fish on an open fire. He hadn't known there was more than that. And when he had become the General's man he had thanked God every day for a kind and good master. Now every day that passed here was a hellish eternity.

Hercules drew a deep breath. The breeze smelled faintly of fish. The cool weather would be hard on their heels as they made their way back to the capital. He couldn't wait.

The chilly drizzle drove sideways right into his face as Hercules made his way up High Street from the harbor. Sodden leaves sped along with the wind and plastered themselves to his legs. No matter; he bent his head and pressed on. Better a miserable day in Philadelphia than a fine one in Virginia.

"Master cook! Hercules!" He heard the call somewhere off to his left but ignored it. He was eager to get back to his warm, dry kitchen with the basket of oysters he lugged.

"Hercules! Stop!" The voice came more urgently now. He stopped and squinted through the rain. The Reverend Allen came toward him from White Horse Alley, holding his hat upon his head with one hand and flagging Hercules down with the other.

"I'm glad I caught you," he said, breathlessly, when he reached him.

Hercules looked at the tall, thin man in his minister's collar and recalled their meeting at Mrs. Harris's home some months before, forcing himself to answer without impatience, "Hello, Reverend. Bad day to be about."

"What? Oh yes, yes it is. An ill parishioner . . ." He stopped and peered at Hercules. "That is no matter. I saw you happen by and wanted to take the chance to speak with you."

"If it's about your meetings, I —" began Hercules, holding up one hand.

"No, it's not about that," he said, looking around. "Here, let's stand under this awning." He pulled Hercules toward the overhang of a small tavern situated in the alley.

Hercules wiped the water from his face and looked at the minister expectantly.

"It's about Fraunces," the man began. "What of him?"

"Have you not heard?" said Reverend Allen, frowning.

"We've only just arrived from Virginia — heard what? I know his tavern failed and that he's at the Tun . . ."

"He's dead."

Hercules closed his mouth. He felt as if he'd been slapped and he wasn't sure why. There was no love lost between him and the steward, yet he felt knocked back by this news.

"Dead?" he said, bewildered. "Why?"

"Why must any of us die?" said the Reverend gently. "It is the Lord's way —"

"No, I mean by what measure?" said

Hercules, cutting him off. He wasn't in the mood for any preaching.

"Age, I suppose," said Allen. "He was an old man, you know. Just didn't wake up one morning."

"When?"

"October the tenth," said Allen. "Been buried over at St. Peter's."

"I see," said Hercules, thoughtfully. He felt peculiar. It was odd to think of Fraunces gone. Then there was the business of that failed tavern. Even though he was free, Fraunces hadn't mastered his own fate after all.

"Does the General know, do you think?" said Allen.

"Couldn't say," murmured Hercules, his mind elsewhere.

"Should I pay him a call?" asked the minister thoughtfully.

"I imagine it doesn't matter now," said Hercules, looking up at him. "The man is buried. He'll come to know soon enough, I'm sure."

Would he even care? Hercules thought. Washington didn't forget a slight — not even after death — and Fraunces's leaving had put the steward on the other side of friendship. Was that why his business had failed? Was there no escaping the grip of

General Washington's good — or ill — word? Hercules wondered.

"I better be back," said Hercules, nodding toward his basket. He started to walk down the alley, then turned back, the rain pelting him again. "Thank you, Reverend, for letting me know."

CHAPTER 25

Early 1796

The breeze that came in through the open kitchen door had the smell of the soil, already thawing in the unusually warm February. Fog rose up from the frozen ground soaked by rain, shrouding the garden in slips of mist. The lights from the windows of the neighboring house visible over the far wall glowed orange through the haze. Even as cannon fire punctuated the air, Hercules unflinchingly creamed the butter and sugar together with his fingers.

"You need to make your wrist looser," he said, looking over to where Nate was whipping egg whites to froth with the birch whisk. "How are the peels coming, Margaret?" he called over to where she was chopping candied fruit peels. Putting down her knife, she gathered some into her palm and brought them over for the master cook's inspection. "Finer, Margaret," he said.

"Every mouthful should have a little piece of peel to flavor it."

Hercules watched Nate's gaze follow Margaret back to the table. A little smile twitched the boy's lips and he gazed at her hungrily. Hercules wanted to reach over and slap him hard, but it wouldn't do to let on that he knew about them.

Feeling Hercules's eyes on him, Nate tried to change his expression.

"She doesn't have the skill for it, Chef," he said loudly, sneeringly. Margaret looked up at him, startled. "I'll do it when I'm done here."

Hercules narrowed his eyes and said nothing. He did not look over at Margaret, who dropped her eyes, her cheeks burning red. At the sink, the hired scullery maids snickered.

"She'll do just fine, Nate," said Hercules dryly, but irritation pricked around his thoughts. He never expected Nate to question his authority and then try to play him for a fool. Nate made a disgusted sound in his throat, as if scornful of Hercules's assessment of Margaret's abilities. The boy must truly be besotted to attempt a ploy that made him flout Hercules's word. No more could be said because Mr. Kitt bustled in carrying a sheaf of papers.

"How go the preparations, cook?" he said to Hercules.

"Just fine, master steward," said Hercules, accepting the egg whites Nate handed him and jiggling the bowl to test their firmness. "Now whisk together the flour, mace, and cinnamon in another bowl," he told Nate before turning back to Kitt. "All the roasts are nearly done, and the standing pies are well in hand. The weather has turned against us for molding the iced creams, but they are in the ice house now," he said, picking up a bowl of egg yolks and adding them one at a time to the butter and sugar and mixing them with a wooden spoon. "Oh, and the oysters will be here soon — Postilion Joe will help shaving the ice for those."

"Good, good," said Kitt, looking around, looking none too happy. He liked nothing more than to give orders or to find something awry — a chance he rarely got in Hercules's kitchen. Finally, his eyes settled upon the open door and he strode quickly across the room to shut it.

"How can you work with all that racket?" he said loudly. "Those cannons have been going since early this morning."

"And I imagine will do until the last of the day," said Hercules mildly. Kitt turned around to face him. "That is how it is on the president's birthday. We are accustomed."

Kitt narrowed his eyes. Hercules hand made sure his words were mild enough but he knew the steward would take his true meaning. *We belong here. You do not.*

"Yes, well . . ." He turned around and let his gaze fly around the kitchen. "Everything must be ready ahead of time. I imagine many will arrive early."

Kitt turned to smile at Hercules, who did not look up but paused just slightly as he mixed his batter. Now it was his turn to understand the hidden meaning in the other man's words: This would be the last Birth Night ball, since the president had announced his plans to retire by the end of the year.

"All will be ready, Mr. Kitt," said Hercules smoothly and resumed slowly adding the flour mixture that Nate brought him. "As it always is."

Kitt let the breath out slowly through his nose.

"Good to hear, cook," said Kitt, bowing slightly with the same affectation Washington used toward his lessers. "Good to hear." With that, he swept imperiously from the room.

■ ■ ■ ■

Hercules remained at the sideboard, examining each dish before footmen carried it off, wiping a rim here or moving a garnish there. Only when the cake, newly iced in white and garnished with sugared cherries from Mount Vernon, left the room did he remove his apron and survey the kitchen. All was in tight order. Nate and Margaret were drying and putting away the last dishes and the hired scullery maids had taken their suppers.

"You may take your suppers now, before the first of the dishes come back to wash." He looked over at Jane and Mathilda, just wiping their mouths at the table. "You begin, then Nate and Margaret will take over."

Mathilda grunted. No matter how many years had passed, Hercules knew she still resented taking orders from him. He went to the kitchen door and lifted his cockade hat from the hook and shrugged himself into his blue velvet coat. "I'm for the city," he said, saluting with the gold-headed cane.

Once outside, he breathed the warming air deeply. The garden had become a rut of muddy puddles and no doubt the streets would be slick with muck kicked up from the horses' hooves. But that wouldn't stop anyone from enjoying the night's festivities. The president's Birth Night and the Independence Day celebrations were the two times of the year when the whole of Philadelphia reveled together.

He stepped through the garden wall that gave onto High Street and watched for a moment as the fine carriages deposited ever more guests at the front door of the mansion. There would be the fireworks later, and many an open and welcome tavern. He thought of Fraunces, buried in an unmarked grave at St. Peter's church. Fraunces with his fastidious demands for decorum on what he called "this auspicious day." Hercules watched as a small white carriage regally trimmed in gold pulled up to the door.

A man got out and handed down a young woman with reddish-brown curls. Her hands were tucked into a red muff that matched the cloak from which the curls cascaded. Hercules saw a flash of white silk under the cloak as she stepped forward onto the carriage step.

As she stepped down to the pavement she looked up at the man, her lips inches from his chin, and he paused, looking hungrily down at her face. Raymond, standing at the carriage door, looked away, embarrassed.

The cloak fell back from her upturned head and a diamond hairpin caught the light of the torches burning nearby. Hercules took a step closer to better see, but she had turned her head fully to the man now.

Raymond murmured something, and the man stepped aside to allow him to close the door. As he did, the woman took his arm and faced forward. The man leaned close and said something in her ear and she laughed, throwing her head back and drawing her gloved hand to cover her mouth. She giggled some more, this time looking side to side to see if anyone had heard, her face now fully visible to Hercules. His breath left his chest in a rush. He shrugged his shoulders violently, the memory of the slave catchers' hands on his body coming unbidden to his mind. His gold-headed cane clattered to the brick walk.

The noise caused Thelma to turn her head, eyes panicked and searching until she caught sight of her lover. For the merest moment, she froze. Hercules could see it took all her effort to force herself not to dart her eyes over to Grayson. She made her face blank and unseeing before she rearranged her smile and brightly turned back to face the man beside her.

CHAPTER 26

Thelma stepped into the studio, a little out of breath. She wore the same red cloak as when Hercules had last seen her entering the Birth Night ball. Her eyes flitted from one part of the room to another, searching.

Hercules watched from the shadows that collected in the corners of the vast space. He hadn't even been sure she would come when he had affixed the sign that morning to the garden wall across from the Chew house. Finally, he stepped forward.

She smiled, drawing back her hood. The flash on her left hand drew his attention and his eyebrows came together.

"My love . . ." she said breathlessly, moving toward him.

He did not move forward to meet her.

"So you are to marry him then," he said, his voice hard. "Or is that bauble for some other service rendered?"

"Yes, we are to be married," she said, looking at him warily.

"I see."

Thelma moved toward him and began to talk quickly. No, he didn't see, she said. She had been waiting anxiously for a sign from Hercules that they might meet, each day getting more and more nervous about what she had to say. Grayson had been corresponding with her these many weeks, each letter more revealing than the last with hints that he knew her secret. She pulled a stack of letters from her drawstring purse and held them out to Hercules, who only raised his eyebrows.

"What would you have me do with those?" He hadn't even shared with Thelma that he had been learning to read. "You know they are no more than marks on a page to me."

Thelma dropped her arm and licked her lips before chattering again. What was she to do? she asked Hercules. Grayson had arrived at the Chews' house, ring in hand, with a proposition more than a proposal.

The good captain, it seemed, was in need of a wife for a very particular purpose. There had been, he'd told Thelma, an incident with one of the stable hands at his father's plantation. It was not the first time. Marriage was the best solution possible.

It wasn't that he didn't like women, he'd

told Thelma. No, it wasn't that at all. It was just that he liked, well, everything, and the more exotic the better: stable boys, slave girls, sailors, Chinese prostitutes, and Moroccan eunuchs. Or upper class "French" girls without connections, who were not what they appeared to be.

"He leered at me like a jackal," said Thelma, studying Hercules's face. "I was in terror, there was no choice." Hercules only stared at her. She went on, her voice edged with strain.

She and Grayson had come to an agreement. Thelma would gain security and protection and Charles would go on as he pleased with the respectability of marriage to protect him — and without her interference.

Now that there was a wedding to plan, it had been hard for Thelma to sneak out and see Hercules. Harriet was constantly at her with swatches of cloth and menus even though the affair was going to be a small one — after all, Thelma had no one to invite and Grayson's people were in South Carolina. But she was here now and she had a plan.

"This doesn't mean we — this — has to end," she said carefully, moving toward him again.

"Oh?" said Hercules, deliberately keeping his face bland, though he longed to spit at her.

"No," she said eagerly, moving closer. "Charles — Monsieur Grayson — he is quite wealthy and there is a way, I believe . . ."

He watched her, shocked at what he was sure she was about to suggest but willing his eyes to betray nothing.

"We will have our own house," she went on quickly. "And we will need our own cook —" She hesitated now. "Everyone has heard of the great Hercules, I am sure I could convince Charles to approach the General . . ." Her voice trailed away under his steady gaze.

"Approach the General?" he said, raising his eyebrows as if intrigued. Now it would be his turn to play her for the fool she had taken him to be. "To what end?"

"To have you cook for us —"

"You mean to buy me," he said, cutting her off viciously, never looking away from her face.

"It would not be like that," she began.

"No?" he said, smiling indulgently as if he were intrigued by what she might say. "What would it be like?" He moved forward languidly, tapping his cane lightly upon the floor with each step. She knew him well enough to hesitate; his easy movements were like a cat about to strike.

"It would —"

"— be a hovel in which to live, with straps across the back, trapped in a putrid backwater." He cut her off, the words stinging like lashes. "Or do you not remember?"

Thelma shut her mouth, then opened it, but Hercules spoke over her again.

"And what will happen when you spawn a little black mongrel? How will you explain that?" he sneered. "Oh!" He widened his eyes in faux surprise and snapped his fingers as if he just remembered an important fact. "But I am forgetting myself — that will happen anyway, won't it? Because even without me bending you over, and even though your fiancé may not know it for sure, you belong in one of those little hovels yourself."

He moved forward threateningly. "You have no business in the big house, playing mistress, or did you forget?" He was gratified to see Thelma cringe as if he had slapped her.

"I did not lie to him," she said.

"No?" he said, moving close to her. "It doesn't bother him, then, that you're just as nigra as them who clean out his chamber pots?"

Thelma shook her head, then began to nod, and stopped. Tears rose in her eyes. "Ah!" he said. "I see. You didn't have to lie — you just let him think what he would — like the rest of them."

Thelma had turned from him and toward the far wall — the now complete portrait of her lover stood on an easel, next to the nearly finished one of the General. The style was virtually the same.

She stepped around Hercules's solid form and crossed over to see them better — Washington with his white skin and dark coat and Hercules in that odd, tall hat, with his dark skin and white coat.

"So how will you hide it when that first child comes?" he said to her back.

She did not answer, choosing instead to cock her head to study the paintings more closely. Finally, she turned around.

"There will be no children."

"And how do you think you'll manage that?" he sneered.

She whirled on him with furious eyes. "Why is it this never troubled you before? All this time you've been bedding me?"

Now he stood in angry silence, regarding her.

"I had a child when I was twelve," she said, her voice low and bitter. "The man who was my father started to rut me when I was ten." She spoke through gritted teeth. "When the baby came it tore me apart and the midwife said there would be no more. I was lucky to live." She spoke through gulps of air while Hercules watched her from across the room. His jaw pulsed.

"Please, *mon taureau,* I love you, or I would not have suggested such a thing," she said. He made a rude sound in his throat. Thelma swallowed and sized him up.

Without taking her eyes off him, she leaned forward slightly and reached into her bodice to scoop out her breasts. They perched over the edge. Licking her finger, she circled a nipple then pinched it rigid before cupping the breast and nodding toward it. When he did not move, she put her foot on the settee and drew up her skirt so he could see that she wore no bloomers. Still he made no move toward her.

Thelma smiled. Dropping her skirt, she approached him and pressed herself against his rigid body. He refused to move the cane, so she had to angle herself against his side.

"Mon taureau," she murmured, running her tongue along his jawline and placing her hand over his groin. He would have welcomed the chance to cruelly take his pleasure from her and then leave her there

like a rag doll in a heap, but now she sickened him and there was no rising in his loins. Putting her hand on the front of his pants, she realized this soon enough and froze, surprised. Undeterred, she massaged him while kissing his neck lightly, but still nothing happened.

Finally, she pulled away angrily.

"What would you have me do? Live always as someone's maid? Or tutor? Or companion?" she hissed.

"You can do as you like — *you* are free," he said, shrugging. He was becoming tired of this little game. He no longer had use for her and wished she would just go.

"Free to starve? To be ill used to earn my keep?" she spat.

"Isn't that what you are doing? What are you going to be but a rich man's toy?" he growled at her.

She flew at him but he caught her raised hand before it could meet his face.

"You are not better," she said, her voice rising, shrill and hysterical. "Why do you not run? You could disappear into the city *comme ca!*" She snapped her fingers violently in the air, causing her still-exposed breasts to bounce. "*Mais non,* you enjoy being the General's man — strutting and preening through the streets!"

Thelma darted toward the paintings standing side by side on their easels.

"You are just like him!" She spat the words and pointed violently toward Washington's image. "Giving the orders so everyone will scurry like the little mice. You enjoy for the people to have the fear of you. But you are no better than the cows or pigs he owns on his farm."

Now Hercules narrowed his eyes, took two steps toward her, and looked her up and down. He drew air through his nose and closed his eyes for a moment. He would not risk his future by throttling the bitch.

"Cover yourself," he said when he opened his eyes again, keeping his voice frighteningly steady. "You look like a common whore."

Thelma's eyes widened with rage. Turning her back on him, she tucked her breasts back into her dress — in full view of Washington. She snatched up her cloak on her way to the door and stormed through it without another word.

When she had gone, Hercules walked over to the pile of letters she had let fall on the floor. Taking them up, he settled himself by the fire and began to carefully read each one before tossing it onto the waiting flames.

■ ■ ■ ■

Margaret quickly set down the bowl of cut parsnips and scurried away from him.

"I need more potatoes," he said sourly to her retreating back. "Flour too. Take Nate and bring me some."

Nate was turning pigeons on the spit. He sighed loudly and stood up, grumbling.

"Do I inconvenience you, young master?" said Hercules sarcastically, tiring of the boy's idiot game of pretending he had no interest in the girl. Clearly, he took Hercules for a fool and that was something Hercules didn't take kindly.

"No, no, Chef — it's just that —" he hesitated and glanced at Margaret. "I don't see why she can't take two trips. I am tending those —"

Before he could finish, Hercules exploded. "Because I have told you to do it!" He stuck his knife into the chopping board where it wobbled stiffly back and forth. "Do you question me further?" he said furiously.

"No, no, sir," Nate stammered and moved to the door, where Margaret hovered. "Come on!" he said rudely.

She meekly followed the boy out of the room and Hercules went back to his work before anger itched at him again. Damn them! Wallowing in his own feelings, he'd given them the perfect opportunity to be alone. Slamming down the knife, he headed out of the kitchen toward the stairs. Ahead of him, Margaret's foot hadn't yet reached the bottom step when Hercules saw Nate turn on her swiftly and grab her waist, hungrily covering her mouth with his own.

"Nate!" Hercules bellowed from the open door. "I've changed my mind, I need you to gut these pheasant for me." There was only tomb-like silence.

"Now!" he roared.

"Yes, Chef!" the boy yelped and dashed back up the stairs, taking them two at a time.

CHAPTER 27

Spring 1796

Hercules prided himself on his imperturbability, but he was taken by surprise when Oney walked into the middle of the kitchen and opened her mouth wide like a banshee, screaming, but no sound came out.

He had reared back at the wretched sound of the breath she dragged into her lungs before making the silent scream again. Horrified as he was, watching the veins bulging dangerously in her neck, he almost did not come around his worktable in time to catch her as her eyes rolled up in her head and she collapsed to the floor.

Margaret dropped the silver bowl she was polishing and ran forward while Nate bolted up from his place at the hearth. The loud clatter of the falling bowl even drew the housekeeper, Mrs. Emerson, from the small office she shared with Mr. Kitt on the days she was there.

Hercules held up his hand, palm facing them as if calming a skittish horse, while he crouched down, his arm encircling Oney who lay there, eyes rolled up in her head.

"Oney!" he said, shaking her. "Oney! What's wrong?"

She began mumbling gibberish, oblivious to him and the others. Hercules scooped the girl up and moved toward the door, which Nate rushed to open. He carried her to the stable and kicked the door. Postilion Joe came running and quickly opened it.

"What happened to her, boss?" he said, helping Hercules carry her to an empty stall.

"Don't know," he grunted as he held her head so it wouldn't knock against the floor. "A shock of some kind. Seen it before at funerals."

"Did someone die?" said Joe, his voice rising fearfully.

"Not that I know of — not recently anyhow," Hercules replied, looking at her thoughtfully. Could it be she was overtaken again with grief for Austin? But why now? The anniversary of his death had passed some months ago.

"Help me bring her to her senses," he said, grabbing one of Oney's arms and nodding to Joe to take the other one. Together they rubbed until her light brown skin was red.

"Joe, you have any liquor?" asked Hercules, looking at the coachman.

Joe hesitated — they weren't supposed to have liquor — before he rose to clomp up the ladder to his living quarters above the stables. In the stall next to them, Prescott snorted, his ears twitching.

"I brought these too," said Joe when he returned, clutching a small bottle in his huge fist. "Keeps 'em in case some of the ladies gets to fainting when we is on the road." He uncapped the smelling salts and held them out to Hercules's outstretched hand.

"NO!" shrieked Oney, coughing and spluttering after he passed the vial under her nose. "No!" she screamed again and tried to push Hercules away, but he held her fast within his arms. He nodded to Joe, who stepped forward with a tin mug. "Here — have some of this," he said. Hercules took the mug and, holding Oney firmly across his chest with his other arm, held it to her lips.

"Go on," he said, trying to hold the cup steady as she turned her face away. "Oney Judge!" growled Hercules, giving her a hard shake. "Calm down now, you hear? Don't make me slap sense into you."

Oney stopped thrashing, her eyes mooning up at him.

"Drink," he commanded. Still watching him, she took a drink and then spluttered. She took another and this time got it down without gagging. When she looked up at Hercules and Postilion Joe, her face crumpled into tears and she moaned, low and hopeless.

"What's happened, Oney?" said Joe. "Is it about Austin?"

She shook her head.

"What then?" asked Hercules.

"She means to give me to Betsey," she said, tears filling her eyes.

Clutching Hercules's arm, she told him about going to Mrs. Washington's room to gather the laundry things. Then the old bitch had told her happily that she was to be a wedding gift for Betsey, who had recently found some fool to marry her. They were living in Washington City and Betsey was now expecting a baby.

Hercules considered this grimly. They had all seen Washington City when they passed through it to and from Mount Vernon so that the General could see its progress. It was still nothing but a muddy, deserted swamp, and Oney would be trapped there with that nasty Betsey and whatever monstrous brats she brought into the world.

"She told me I should be delighted to have a baby to take care of!" Oney whispered viciously, spittle forming on her lips. "Hercules, I would have killed her right then, I would, but there wasn't so much as a letter knife within reach. It'd be worth it to hang just to kill that old sow first."

Hercules looked quickly up at Joe, judging whether he was able to keep his own counsel. Joe loomed over them, shaking his head sadly.

"Not much different than being here, I expect," said Hercules, hoping she believed him.

"That Betsey is evil-mean, Hercules, and you know it!" said Oney, ignoring Joe, her voice rising. "She like to slap and pinch and hit — you've seen her! She even beat Old Moll!"

She stopped talking a minute and gulped air.

"That house at Washington City is way out the way of other folks." She stopped talking and left the rest unsaid: with no one to see. Without Betsey's grandparents around to pass a comment or two.

"Hercules," she said, grasping at his arm. "I'm not crazy and anyways it's no matter if you think I am — I'm not going."

"Can't see as there's much choice," said Joe, his voice getting sadder. Hercules said nothing.

"Still one choice no matter what *they* say," she muttered, looking at Joe disdainfully. Then, in a whisper so low that Hercules wasn't even sure he'd heard it, she said, "I still have the *me* part of me — and I go kill myself 'fore I got to give it to Mrs. Betsey Law." She began to sob again.

Hercules looked sharply at Joe to see if he had heard. Prescott sensed the agitation of the creatures in the stall beside him and began to snort and move nervously in the small space. Closing his mouth into a thin, hard line as the depth of her despair washed over him like a bitter wind, Hercules gripped Oney tightly to his chest.

He closed the book he had been reading aloud to Mrs. Harris and sat back. The teacher looked at him for a long moment, her black eyes never moving from his face.

"I am impressed by how far you've come, Master Hercules," she said. "Especially since I can't imagine you have much time to practice."

He smiled and tapped the cover of the book lightly with his forefinger. "It *has* been two years," he said, feeling supremely happy in that moment. "Besides, now that I can make them out, I've come to see that words are everywhere, madam. On shops signs and apothecary labels — the markings upon the barrels of provisions — and so much more," he said, pride bubbling under his words. "I move about more freely than the others so I have ample opportunity to make the city my teacher."

"And it has taught you well," Mrs. Harris answered, smiling. Usually, he did not stay above an hour with her and it was nearing that time now.

"Mrs. Harris — a moment, if you please," Hercules said. He had been waiting for the right moment to speak to her about the thing most troubling his mind. Her eyebrows rising questioningly, she took her seat opposite him once again.

"Sir?"

"The meeting I happened upon — your meetings," he began, then stopped. "I would like to know more about the — er — work that you do."

Mrs. Harris narrowed her eyes and studied him warily.

"And why is that, sir?" she asked easily. "You led us to understand that it is not a subject in which you have interest."

"You are correct, madam," he said, conceding the point. "I led you to believe the same, but you are mistaken that I have no interest in the topic."

"I see," Mrs. Harris said. "Where does that interest lie, sir? Surely, given our activities here" — she gestured at him and back at herself — "you cannot mean to expose us? That would hardly seem gentlemanly." She said this last easily, as if making small talk, but he could see that she was nervous. He knew that, to her, he was a potentially dangerous man, considering to whom his allegiance was expected.

"A fair question," said Hercules. He didn't blame her for being suspicious; they all had to guard their secrets closely. "And I suppose I deserve no more than suspicion after my — er — reaction that day. But I am sure you must understand that a person in my very particular circumstance cannot afford to have his business known by too many."

Mrs. Harris considered this a moment.

"Those such as us — as me — would do well to know all of our options, should the need ever arise," he said, examining her carefully as he said this. "However, I should better like to understand how you go about this trade."

The teacher leaned forward a bit and

looked into his eyes for a long time. With each slow blink it seemed she was consuming some bit of information about him and deciphering it. He forced himself to gaze back at her steadily without flinching until she finally sat back.

"We have a number of ways," she said. "Mistress Levi buys slaves as she can and then manumits them. Solomon helps them to find apprentice work among the network of free black and sympathetic white tradesmen in the town — and north." She stopped and observed him listening attentively before going on. "There is a couple who are man and wife but live as lady and servant, for she is white and he black." The schoolteacher watched him closely to see if he would betray any shock. He did not. "We depend up on their network to help with families if the need arises — or with those like themselves, if you understand my meaning." His thoughts briefly, disturbingly, fluttered to his scullion and Margaret.

"Mr. Brown uses his connections upon the waterways to bring many to safety in the Northern states," she said. "And of course, we use the law to our advantage wherever we can. We have men who work with us — white men, prominent men — who make it their business to steal back

Negroes taken by slave catchers and bring culprits into the courts. We've had some successes there as well."

Now he was surprised. "And the courts found in your favor?"

"They have done, yes," she said, folding her hands on the table in front of her. "But we only pursue that route if we can be very sure of winning. If not, we find other ways to remove these souls from the way of harm."

Hercules sat and digested all of this, his mind churning.

"Mrs. Harris, I thank you greatly," he said, standing up and bowing. "What you've said has been most interesting. I assure you that your confidences are safe with me. And, madam, with your leave, there is someone whom — as time and circumstance permit — I would very much like for you to meet."

The teacher cocked her head curiously at this, but asked no more questions. He was relieved she made no attempt to pry it out of him.

"As you wish, sir," she said, following him to the front door. "I shall look forward to making that acquaintance."

After he took his leave, he walked out into Cherry Street and breathed with deep relief. It was time to enact his plan.

■ ■ ■ ■

As the time to depart for Mount Vernon again drew near, Oney was becoming more difficult to manage. Betsey's letters to her grandmother were filled with demands for goods from the capital city and directions for Oney to begin sewing the child's layette. Plus, Mrs. Washington herself had a never-ending list of things for the girl to attend before she left Philadelphia for good.

Hercules watched her from his place behind the worktable and said nothing. The others, made nervous by Oney's hovering presence, missed his orders or failed to carry them out in time. Nate burned a roast because he was watching Oney rather than the spit he was turning. Hercules's own ears were always pricked for the screams that never came forth.

No one had asked him what had gone on that day when he took her to the stable. Once she had calmed enough, she had gone ahead of him to the cookhouse, walking as usual, head high as if nothing had happened. When Hercules returned, he made sure that his face betrayed nothing and he went back to work, but not before glancing meaningfully around the room to be sure they were all about their business. He noticed that the others looked at each other with wide, questioning eyes behind Oney's back as she passed.

Now it was only four weeks before they must leave and Oney, though quiet, was no better. Her eyes went from blank to panic in a split second and when she got close enough he could see the prick marks upon her cream-colored fingers where the needle had gone awry, unguided in the absence of its mistress's mind.

"Something on your mind, son?" Hercules's voice rolled like distant thunder over Nate, who was watching Oney nervously from where he worked chipping at an ice block.

"No, sir," he said, trying to look sharp, chipping faster at the block before him.

"That's enough ice then," said Hercules as soothingly as he could. It wouldn't do for them all to react to Oney's nervousness and bring Kitt's or Mrs. Emerson's attention to the goings-on in the kitchen. It was critical, in fact, that they did no such thing. "Bring it here." Nate cradled the huge bowl of ice in his arms and set it on the table. He held the iced cream maker steady as the chef poured the chipped ice around the cylinder, then held the cylinder itself while Hercules poured in the custard he had ready.

"Go on and start," he said, putting the bowl down. Nate began to turn the cylinder.

Hercules watched him closely before going back to his own table. Now and again, he glanced around the room until he was sure that, becalmed by the mundane actions of the kitchen, each was concentrating enough on their own tasks not to pay them any particular mind.

"Nate — please come with me to the gardens," he finally said, waving Margaret over to continue turning the cylinder.

When they reached the garden, Hercules squatted down and began pushing aside the leaves of the plants as if he were examining what was underneath. He gestured to Nate to join him. Nate squatted and watched Hercules's busy hands, waiting for instruction. Finally, he said, "What are we doing, Chef?"

"Look at the leaves, Nate, turn them over and pull off any grubs," said Hercules, resuming his work.

"There is nothing there. I saw when you turned them over."

"Just do it, son."

Once Nate seemed engrossed in the task, Hercules sat back on his haunches and looked up at the brick house rising before them. In a low voice he said, "When we return to the cookhouse, I will say I am going to the harbor to seek out Mr. Johnson the oyster seller."

"But you said never to buy oysters this time of year —"

Hercules held up his hand and continued, "And I will be taking Oney with me to help carry the basket."

"Oney!" exclaimed Nate. "But surely she isn't to do kitchen work now? What of Margaret?"

Hercules looked at him calmly before he spoke again. "Nate, listen to me with some care." He stopped turning over leaves. "I'm not really going to see Mr. Johnson, but you must pretend otherwise. I need you to remain here and manage the others in the kitchen."

Nate closed his mouth and looked at the chef in shock.

"When I return, I will say that the oysters did not look good at this time of year and that is why I brought none back," said Hercules. "Do you understand?"

Once Nate nodded, he said, "Good, I will speak to Oney." He stood up. When Nate followed suit and they were but inches from each other, the boy asked, "But where are you going, Chef?"

"I cannot tell you that now. Perhaps one day," Hercules said soberly. "I know it's hard to understand, but I am trusting you with this, Nate. Do not let me down."

"This way," said Hercules, heading straight for the market sheds and toward the docks. If anyone happened to see them, better to appear to be going about regular business.

Oney licked her lips. She was starting to take on the same look as Sister Seer, who wandered around Mount Vernon talking to herself and hovering on the edge of things, eyes wide and watching. She was no good to anyone and folks let her be — they said she could see into the other world. The General allowed her to wander around the farms as long as she didn't trouble anyone or interfere with a day's work. But that wouldn't do for Oney at Betsey Law's house, where her young mistress might take it upon herself to beat the crazy out of her.

The market wasn't too crowded since it was near to closing time. Some sellers had already packed their carts for home. Hercules walked purposefully through the sheds, stopping now and again to inspect some produce or a piece of cheese, making sure that people saw them. When they passed a woman selling ribbons and feathers, he nudged Oney and said loud enough for those nearby to hear, "There's the stand with sewing notions. You should look them over for your work."

Oney looked at him peculiarly and then dully back at the stand. "Go on," he said, nudging her toward the seller. Oney moved over to the stand and looked listlessly at all that was laid out there before turning back to him, her eyes troubled.

"Nothing you fancy? Well, come on then," he said cheerfully and guided her under the elbow with the hand that did not hold the market basket.

Eventually they made it out of the sheds at Front Street and he pointed her to the left along the harbor as if he were seeking something out. When they reached Chancery Lane, she hesitated.

"This is Helltown," she said, her eyes fearful.

"I know it is. But you have nothing to fear — you are with me."

Oney's eyes cut away from him, up the notorious road and back. She turned as if she were going to head back toward the harbor.

"No, my girl," said Hercules firmly, catching her arm. "Mind me now."

She stood still a moment, looking toward

the crowds at the waterfront and then back at the street with its dark alleys and wafting stench. Lifting her chin a bit, she nodded and turned back.

"Here, take my arm," said Hercules in a low voice, "and look at no one. We just have to cross three blocks to the other side into Cherry Street."

Hercules pulled his hat low over his head and pulled Oney close to him as they walked through the crowd of evil-looking, already-drunk sailors clogging the road in front of the infamously depraved Three Jolly Irishmen.

"Lean into me," he instructed her softly as he snaked his arm around her waist. "And giggle, like I said something amusing." Oney looked at him in shock.

"Just do it, Oney," he said, his voice gravelly and threatening. "Do not look over at those men."

She did as she was told and Hercules leaned into her and nuzzled his face into her neck while propelling them past the pub as though they had too much to drink.

A few men guffawed.

"Look like she's ready for you," one called out, then cackled loudly. "There's an alley just there, friend."

Hercules raised a hand in thanks without

turning around and ducked into the alley.

He looked at Oney, whose eyes were wild with terror, and held his finger to his lips. They stood still for a moment listening. When the crowd of drunken men hurtled down the street, laughing and singing bawdy songs, Hercules pushed Oney into the wall and pressed his body against hers.

"Don't say anything," he whispered hoarsely and pressed his mouth against her neck.

Some of the men spotted them and hooted and cackled out encouragement to Hercules so he raised up her skirt and hiked her leg around his waist, feigning the act of love-making.

Fat, fast tears began to drop from the girl's eyes and fell onto the side of his face as he pressed it into her neck. Her tense body had fairly collapsed against him like a rag doll. Hercules felt sick.

When the sound died away, he pushed away from her and smoothed down her skirt, making every effort to arrange the fabric without touching her skin through it.

"I'm sorry for that, my girl," he said as gently as he could. "But it had to be done."

Still crying, Oney looked at him with a mixture of relief and terror. Her eyes were wide and crazed. Once again he held his finger to his lips and leaned out of the alley before beckoning her forward.

Once in the now-empty street they walked quickly, Hercules forcing her forward with his hand under her elbow. Oney kept her eyes on her feet as she walked quickly beside him. Eventually they crossed Fourth Street and stepped into a different world.

"Here," he said, nodding toward a small alley with a little gray house at the back.

Mrs. Harris answered the knock before they could sound another and looked from Hercules to Oney, her face still wet with tears and her clothes badly disheveled.

Recovering herself quickly, Mrs. Harris moved aside and opened the door wide.

Hercules surveyed the plates he had prepared for Lady Washington's light luncheon. He'd laid out platters of cut roasted beef and pickled radishes, chicken pudding, apple fritters, and a small mince pie for the dessert.

There was plenty enough here to keep the old lady satisfied while the others finished the preparations for their summer trip to Mount Vernon. To Hercules's enormous relief, the Congress and Mr. Adams had convinced the president to stay through one more term. That gave him to time to make a plan of his own. In the meantime, there was this short trip to consider and all he had to achieve beforehand.

Oney had been jumpy and barely listened to direction, and Hercules had been forced to take her aside and speak to her in a low voice more than once, especially after the old woman had threatened that a few straps across the back would set Oney to rights. They all knew the General would not allow the slaves to be punished in that way — but that protection wouldn't last long. Oney could well expect a few good lashes at the Laws' if she got out of line.

Once the luncheon dishes went up to the dining room, Hercules continued managing the business of packing up the kitchen. He could hear the noises of the servants running to and from the yard, bringing out trunks and boxes and loading carriages. Mr. Kitt's voice carried from somewhere in the house, snappishly barking directions.

Just about now, Hercules knew that Oney Judge would be handing up Mrs. Washington's toiletry trunk to Postilion Joe, who was loading the dray cart with the luggage. She'd have exclaimed that she had left one of the First Lady's hairbrushes behind and rushed back to the house to get it.

Hercules waited in the kitchen, knowing

that Oney Judge's footfall on the stair or voice calling out to Mrs. Emerson would not be among the din of the house all around him. He knew that soon she would round the corner of the house, well out of sight of the dining room and all the doings in the yard. Oney Judge, clutching her traveling bag, would slip out of a side gate in the wall surrounding the house and into the fray of the city without so much as the smallest look back.

CHAPTER 28

Mount Vernon, Summer 1796

"I wouldn't do that if I were you," Hercules said in a low, solid voice through the dark room. Nate halted, crouched at the side of his bed, his clothes in one arm and lifting his shoes with the other hand.

Hercules swung his legs over the side of his cot and leaned forward in the dark.

"Don't try it, son," he said again. Inside, he marveled at the boy's mixture of boldness and stupidity. It irked him that Nate, as sharp-minded as he was, persisted in playing the idiot when it came to Margaret. "There are too many people in that house and none will take kindly to you going up there and ferreting about for the girl."

"I was just going out for a walk," Nate stammered into the darkness.

"They wouldn't take too kindly to that either," Hercules said, making his voice solid even as he spoke in a whisper. "A slave wandering about at night? To what end? Escape maybe?"

"I wasn't —" Nate began before Hercules cut him off.

"I know that," he said as kindly as he could. "But they don't. Especially after what's happened. Go back to sleep, Nate."

The boy was young and he would learn in time, no need to gut him with it now, but he must still heed the message. Hercules lay back down, rolled over, and stared at the wall, listening to see what the boy would do next. He'd stop him bodily if he had to. Nate's persistence exhausted him. He reminded Hercules of a moth dancing madly around a candle flame, becoming more crazed even as its wings singed. The boy's blind desire led him to take dangerous risks with grave consequences. They had all seen Washington's high fury after Oney had gone.

It had taken a good half hour for the maids to calm the red-faced Lady Washington when the alarm went up, only to have her explode again in rage when Mrs. Emerson had returned to say the General's secretaries' canvass of the neighborhood had turned up nothing. Throughout the house they could hear her shrieking for an armed guard to turn out every house. She'd had to be given a sherry and taken to her room to have her temples bathed in perfume by Old Moll.

By then crucial hours had been lost and General Washington had been obliged to oversee what must be a discreet search, lest the public take note that he was hunting one of his slaves. And it had all been for naught except to lose them a full day on the journey home and make a particularly annoying stop at Betsey's in Washington City to explain the loss of her gift. Margaret had been brought into the house to learn the service of lady's maid, should Mrs. Washington choose to use her when they returned to Philadelphia.

Just two days ago Hercules had stood with Nate in the pantry and read the notice the General had put in the paper, hoping to hunt Oney down.

Absconded from the household of the President of the United States, ONEY JUDGE, a light mulatto girl, much freckled, with very black eyes and bushy hair. She is of middle stature, slender, and delicately formed, about 20 years of age . . . She has many changes of good clothes, of all sorts, but they are not sufficiently recollected to be described — As there was no suspicion of her going off, nor no provocation to do so, it is not easy to conjecture whither she has gone, or fully, what her design is . . . Ten dollars will be paid to any person who will bring her home, if taken in the city, or on board any vessel in the harbour; — and a reasonable additional sum if apprehended at, and brought from a greater distance, and in proportion to the distance.

They'd burned the paper when they were done, lest anyone wonder why two illiterate slaves had a newspaper in the kitchen. Hercules had hoped that the whole affair would scare Nate off Margaret but that hadn't happened, and so while he didn't approve what was going on between them, all he could do now was make sure they didn't take a misstep that could cost them far dearer than they could comprehend.

He could feel now that Nate remained crouched where he was in the dark, probably still considering his chances.

Hercules spoke again softly. "The house is big and you have no business to be inside it," he said. "Who do you know there to trust to take a message to Margaret and hold tongue about it later?"

Finally, Hercules heard Nate rise and he lay there, tensed, to see what move he'd make. He heard the boy slowly letting out the air he had held in his lungs and then settle back down on his cot.

"How long have you known?" Nate's voice came softly across the room. Hercules could hear the shame there.

On his own cot, Hercules let his body relax and said nothing, purposefully making his breathing steady as if he were already asleep. Eventually, he heard Nate sigh and move around to get comfortable.

How long had he known? There were too many things that Hercules knew, and the burden was getting heavy to bear. He let his mind wander back to that day he brought Oney to Mrs. Harris. When they had gotten inside, the schoolteacher had asked a few questions and listened carefully to Oney's answers.

"Have you been beaten?" she asked, peering into the girl's eyes.

When Oney shook her head no, she asked. "Have you been ill used?"

Then, to Hercules's surprise, Oney had started talking all in a rush about Miss Betsey and how *she* would beat a person easy-like, and Virginia, and being a slave and, well, everything.

Mrs. Harris only listened, glancing briefly at Hercules from time to time.

Finally she spoke. "It's not for us to judge *why* a person aims to be free. It's all of our right to want that, I reckon. We just have to be sure that your request is" — she paused, searching for the right word — "a genuine one." She looked now at Hercules, without blinking. "You can appreciate the delicacy of the matter given the household from which you come," she finished.

Oney looked at Hercules, who'd nodded curtly.

"Good," said Mrs. Harris, apparently satisfied. "You'll find your way back to me two more times, Miss Judge, and we'll make our plans accordingly."

Then came the day to go back to Virginia, and there was no Oney to be found. They had been delayed a whole day while the president demanded a search of the city. Nate had been sent among some of the hired men to scour the town, since he knew what she looked like.

All that time, Hercules had remained in his kitchen, focused on his cooking. He'd made his face a perfect mask of surprise and then concern when Mrs. Washington had come down to question them all.

Hercules smiled as he drifted to sleep. Soon he'd make his move too. It was time for him to plan for himself.

Hercules placed the last of the peaches in syrup and closed the crock tightly.

"That anise should impart an interesting flavor," he said with satisfaction as he handed Nate the jar to put into the cellar. He wiped down his worktable.

As he scrubbed away the thick syrup from the surface, he thought about the coming evening. Evey had visited as she did most every day of the last two months that they had been at the farm and asked him when he would come by. He'd usually spend an hour or two, bringing some food from the General's kitchen with him. At least while he was there, his children could eat better than what they were provisioned or could grow in their little kitchen garden.

But he found it hard to remain much longer than what was required to take a meal and play a little with Baby. It depressed him to answer their eager questions about Philadelphia, for he would rather be there than here and he was sure they knew it. It was worse when Richmond came down instead of remaining above the blacksmith shop as he usually did. He hardly spoke and answered Hercules's questions with a barely civil tongue.

It pained him too to know that these might be his last days with them, planning as he was. The General had announced in the papers he'd be leaving the presidency by early next year — this time for sure, no delays, he'd said, not even from God himself. That meant Hercules would soon have to take his chance. Sometimes he'd dream of bringing them all to Philadelphia, but it was a dream that faded fast when he considered how he might try to move with three children and an angry young man on his coattails.

He must have sighed; Nate asked if he was all right.

"Yes, fine," he said, smiling at the boy. "You best start packing the crates with hams and the pickles we put up to go back with the General next week. Do you think you can remember what all else has to come when you follow us with Mrs. Washington next month?"

"Maybe I could make a list —" Nate began.

"Shhhh!" Hercules hissed, coming around the table and standing close. "Don't ever say a thing like that again," he said, gripping the boy's arm roughly. "You don't know who might hear. Never forget where you are. Ask up at the house for them to send one who can write to make a list to call out to you later — Margaret maybe."

Nate nodded. It was an act of kindness on Hercules's part. Nate met his eyes and managed a weak, grateful smile before each turned to his own work as the sound of voices approached from outside the cook-house.

"Cook — a word?" John Allistone, the overseer, stuck his head through the kitchen door but did not enter. Behind him a servant hurried by, not wanting to linger in the man's path.

Hercules raised his eyebrows just as Nate's own shot up in alarm. He stepped out of the hot kitchen. He'd rarely had to deal with Allistone, his truck being mostly with the steward and Lady Washington herself. The overseer was a common laboring sort with a stained shirt opened at the collar to show a few white-blond hairs curling forth on the sun-baked skin.

"The General asked me to speak with you," said Allistone, dirty hands on hips. "It's about your boy Richmond." He stared hard at Hercules's face. He felt a sharp pang of alarm but struggled not to show it and continued to look at the man with polite interest.

"He stole some money from Mr. Wilke's saddlebag," said Allistone. "He's been sent to River Farm."

River Farm functioned independently with its own overseer who worked his slaves as he pleased. It would mean hard labor and beatings. The fool! Hercules felt the rage rise in his chest but he kept his face bland.

"I see," he said, his mind racing.

Allistone was talking again and this time it took Hercules a moment to follow. He stared at the man's fleshy mouth and tried to focus.

"I said do you know whether your boy had plans to run away, Uncle Harkless?"

Hercules did his best not to show fury. "No, sir," he said truthfully. "None at all."

Allistone looked at him overly long, hoping to catch him out in a lie. He moved closer to Hercules so his stinking breath came hot in his face. "Are you sure about that, boy?"

Hercules clenched his jaw down harder. He willed his hand to hang loosely at his side instead of forming into a fist. He stared straight through the overseer toward the mansion as if the man weren't there. Behind him he heard Nate shuffle nervously. He'd have to find a way to see the General — Allistone broke into his thoughts. "The General feels it's best if you don't accompany him back to the capital this time," said the overseer, gloating. His voice trailed off as his eyes followed one of the mulatto girls rounding the corner from the laundry. He licked his lips. Hercules itched to backhand him across his rotten-toothed mouth. "He thinks it's better for you to stay here, being as they only will be gone a few months this time."

The man smiled broadly at Hercules, showing his full mouth of blackened teeth. Hercules tried to swallow but his mouth had gone too dry. Stay here. What had Richmond brought down upon his head? He'd kill the boy if he ever clapped eyes on him again.

"But who will do the cooking?" asked Nate, his panicked voice reaching into the rafters of their room above the kitchen.

"You will go back in my stead, along with Margaret," said Hercules. "And I imagine they will hire someone — Mr. Julien perhaps — to manage the kitchen."

"This isn't right!" said Nate, tears rising in his eyes. He turned and brushed them away roughly.

"Many things aren't right, son," said Hercules. His voice was raspy and tired. "But you better get used to that in this life."

Nate didn't say anything for a while. "What will you do here, then?" he asked finally.

"Cook — what else? There's still Lady

Washington and the rest of the family —
she doesn't join him for another month at
least. Then there are always the guests . . ."
The weariness of these last days suddenly
pressed on him and he let his voice trail off.
He watched as Nate angrily packed his
satchel.

"Take care about how you are with the
girl," he said softly. "Folks notice things,
even when you think they don't."

Nate stopped packing.

"Be most mindful of Kitt," Hercules went
on. "He's got his own ideas about folk like
us."

Nate put the last shirt in the satchel and
buckled it closed. "I will, Chef," he said.

"There's something else," said Hercules,
getting up to stand close to Nate.

The younger man looked questioningly at
Hercules.

"If you should find yourself in . . . trouble," Hercules whispered, his face inches
from Nate's own, "there is a woman I want
you to see."

"A woman?" Nate said, surprised. His
voice was loud in the empty room.

"Quiet!" Hercules hissed, moving closer
still. "Her name is Mrs. Harris. She has digs
in Cherry Street. A gray clapboard house at
the end of an alley. If you find yourself in

any kind of trouble, go to her and tell her that I've sent you."

Nate's eyes grew afraid but he nodded.

"Good," Hercules said in a normal voice. He clasped the boy on the shoulder. Nate was now a full head taller than he was.

"You are a fine cook, son," he said, giving his arm a firm squeeze.

Now Nate could not stop the water from rushing up to his eyes.

"Have the best teacher," he whispered, the tears overtaking his voice.

Hercules gave him a tight-lipped smile as Nate angrily rubbed his face.

"It's only for a few months," Nate said, searching Hercules's face for confirmation. Hercules pulled the boy forward in a fierce hug as the boy cried desperately into his shoulder. "Only a few months, right, Chef?"

"It will be all right, I expect," murmured Hercules, holding him tight, clamping his teeth down hard so tears wouldn't come to his own eyes. How did this one become dearer to him than his own son?

He released the boy and clapped him on the back before sticking out his hand. Nate looked down at it in surprise and then took it in his own. After silently shaking it, he hoisted the satchel on his shoulder and headed for the stairs. Hercules hoped it would be a good long time before the boy realized that he'd never answered his question.

CHAPTER 29

Fall 1796

"Papa?" Hercules turned away from the fire toward Evey. He smiled gently. "Yes, child?"

"Would you like for me to rub your shoulder?" she offered.

"I'd be much obliged," he said.

As she kneaded her small hands into the shoulder that burned and ached from breaking rocks, he stared idly at Baby, who was playing with the rags she called her "dolly" by the fire. Why hadn't he at least tried to get them away from this place? The answer needn't be said. To be caught trying to escape was not a risk worth taking, for their lives thereafter would be far worse than the ones they led now. His jaw ached from clamping down as he considered his youngest child, playing happily without knowledge of the wretched life that would soon enough be hers.

"Do you miss the kitchen, Papa?" asked

Delia, who was sewing beside the fire, just a few steps away from the hearth. The cold seeped through the chinks and cracks of the poorly made cabin.

"Shhh," Evey hissed at her sister, with a quick glance at him.

"It's all right," said Hercules, patting Evey's hand upon his shoulder.

"I miss it, yes," he answered, carefully keeping the anger out of his voice. It wouldn't do for them to see him railing against the impossible, lest they get their own dangerous ideas the way Richmond had. "But not much to do about that."

"But you'll be cooking again when the General returns, won't you?" Delia asked, her brows coming together. Hercules shrugged. "Couldn't say," he said mildly, although in truth, the answer to that question had plagued him plenty these past months. "Don't know what the General plans."

If someone had asked him a few months ago whether he'd miss something so simple as peeling a potato or mixing a sauce, he'd have laughed. Who would long for such mundane things? But now that he was crushing rock to plaster the house and grubbing out weeds from the gardens, he realized he missed those simple tasks with a powerful longing.

The other day Cyrus and Frank, who were working with him, laughed at the way he'd mixed the rock powder with the paint, folding it in like egg whites into a batter.

"You not making a fine cake there, boss," Cyrus had guffawed, grabbing away the trowel and mixing the thick mass as hard as he could. For a moment, Hercules had stood with his hands at his sides, bewildered, until Allistone had barked at him to get back to work. While he worked, the man was usually at his side, haranguing and cursing him, trying to get him to admit he had plotted with his wretched son. One day he would snap and brain the bastard with a rock. And then they'd fall on him like a pack of wild dogs.

Now he looked down at his hands. The glow from the fire illuminated all the hard cracks that were there now.

"Papa," came Evey's voice from over his shoulder. "What of Richmond — any news?"

Hercules grunted and shook his head. He'd had no news of his son, nor had he sought it out. He still couldn't trust himself not to thrash the boy for what he'd done, but if he beat Richmond senseless as he wanted, he'd be damaging Mrs. Washington's property, wouldn't he? Then what would become of them all? He snorted bitterly, then stood abruptly.

"Just going out for a little air," he said to his daughters.

"Now?" said Delia, looking fearfully toward the door at a dark outside world that was not theirs to traverse.

"Not far," he said, forcing himself to give her a gentle smile. He stepped through the flimsy door.

"I'll help!" exclaimed Margaret quickly, setting aside the dish of dried peas she was picking over.

"I hardly think —" began Mr. Julien from his place behind Hercules's old table, but Margaret had already leapt up to follow Nate to the cellar where the cook had asked him to collect some beetroots. At the table the Frenchman shrugged. He had enough to think about, what with the First Lady determined to outdo every one of her Friday night receptions in order to show off her granddaughter Nelly to society.

Not for the first time he wondered why they left Hercules at Mount Vernon if this was such an important time. Neither Nate nor Margaret would speak of it, but he had heard the rumors that Hercules had been planning to escape with his son.

It made no good sense to Julien. Why escape from Virginia when it would have been so much each easier to do so here in Philadelphia? The Frenchman could only wonder. The steward had only smiled evilly when he had asked him. Julien wrinkled his nose at the thought of Kitt. Certainly Fraunces had been petty, but he was unparalleled at his job. This one was barely equipped for doing much more than listening at doors and squirreling away whatever he'd learned. He even looked like a rodent, thought Julien. With Hercules gone, Kitt had run unchecked. Even Julien was surprised to realize how much power the General's cook had really had.

At least there were Nate and Margaret. Whatever their peculiarities, Hercules had taught them their business well and for that he was grateful. Julien hadn't understood just how in hand Hercules had this kitchen until it was under his own command. What with Lady Washington's constant changes of mind and the worthless hired staff, he'd have more than he could handle were it not for the two young ones.

In the basement, Nate headed over to the bin with the beets, calling over his shoulder teasingly, "I think I can handle a few beets,

Margaret. Or was there something else you had in mind?"

Margaret stood stock-still in the middle of the cellar as Nate went into the gloom and came back out again, balancing several large beets in his splayed fingers. They fell from his hands with a dull thud when he saw the look on her face — the same dull-eyed stare she'd had when she had been so sick that time in Germantown, the same look that had haunted Oney before she ran away.

"What is it? What's wrong?" he said, rushing to her. As he did, her face crumpled and the tears came so hard she couldn't speak. Her hands pressed against her stomach with such force that Nate grasped at her arms, trying to make out the words she was choking out.

"With child," she croaked.

"What child? With what child?" he said.

Margaret shook her head violently. "No," she gulped. "No. I am with child. *Our* child." She broke down with more sobs while Nate stood in shock. His hands slipped from her arms and he took a step back before he raised both hands to his head and squatted down on the dirt floor.

From the cellar door one of the scullery maids was calling down into the gloom, unaware of their catastrophe. Mr. Julien had need of those beets.

Hercules jumped onto the dock and stood shivering with the others while the hold was being emptied of the Mount Vernon goods that would be sold here in Alexandria. His hands were already stiff from the November sleet, but he grasped the barrels that were being handed down as best he could.

When he dropped one, his hands too cold to work properly, the Negro overseer cuffed him hard at the back of his head.

"Watch what you're doing, boy!" he snarled, spittle landing from his mouth onto Hercules's face.

He swallowed his anger although it would almost be worth pushing the mongrel bastard into the river, even though the rest of them would stand by while the white sailors descended on him like a pack of hunting dogs, ready to tear him apart. He glanced over at the pilot, who was often willing to be bribed to give Hercules a lift downriver to the town some evenings. The man held his gaze and gave him a slight shake of his head.

"Get to the back of the line," spat the overseer. Hercules took his place by the cart.

By the time it was loaded, twenty minutes later, his chill had turned to sweat and he was breathing hard. The overseer gestured for them to follow the cart as it moved toward the warehouse and they started the process of unloading it. Passing each barrel, hand to hand.

As he worked, Hercules let his mind wander to Philadelphia and the household there. He prayed the boy Nate was minding his steps. Hopefully the scullion had taken a lesson from how quickly Hercules's fortunes had shifted and sufficiently scared off the white girl, but he doubted it.

Once they were done in the warehouse, they sat on the piled boxes and barrels and ate the cheap meal of bread and gristly meat that the overseer doled out to them. Hercules could barely gag it down but it was all he'd get today, so he forced himself to swallow.

When they were finished, they trudged back to the docks and the boat waiting to take them back to Mount Vernon. The sleet that had fallen earlier had frozen into a slick path of ice. Hercules felt himself go down hard on his back, his shoulder slamming into the ground.

He groaned and closed his eyes. Seconds later he felt a vise-like grip on is arm, hauling him up. Shrugging the hand off, he rose to his feet, ready this time to take a swing

— consequence be damned. He'd had enough. Anything would be worth it to level a blow against the head of that step-and-fetch nigra who'd been beating him down for massa these many weeks.

But when he turned it was into the face of James Brown, the mariner from Philadelphia. He dropped his hand in surprise.

"Well, I'll be damned!" said the man. "If it isn't the General's cook."

Hercules glanced at the others who were well ahead of him by now and then back at James Brown.

"I looked fuh you in de capital," Brown said quizzically.

"And so you've found me. What brings you to Alexandria?" said Hercules, his voice tense and surprised.

Brown waved away the question. "Regular business. You been here de whole of dis time?"

"Since the summer, yes," he answered.

"And doin' hard labor by the looks of you . . . Dem don't need you in de kitchen no more?" Brown peered at him.

Hercules shrugged and smiled. "Different work now," he said and made to move off. The last thing he wanted was to speak about his reversal of fortunes, nor had he the time to do it with the others waiting and the

438

overseer itching to use his whip.

"Good to see you, James."

As he tried to get by, Brown grasped him on the shoulder.

"Now hold a minute," he said. "What happen? The General is yet in Philadelphia, not so?"

Hercules feigned an easy smile. "It's too long a story for right now."

James Brown looked at him steadily and then at the gang moving down the road.

"De social club at the edge of town — do you know it?" said the sailor.

Hercules nodded.

"Good, meet me there as soon as you can get away," said Brown. "I go be here for de next t'ree nights."

Hercules glanced nervously away and then back at his friend before running on to catch up, slipping and sliding on the icy road.

Two nights later, Hercules stepped off the boat onto the dock at Alexandria. It was a risk coming out, but the ferryman was again willing to be bribed and he'd bet his skin on the fact that Allistone wouldn't be out checking the cabins on a night like this. More likely he'd have a slave girl warming the bed in his cozy cabin while the winter wind barreled through the chinks and holes in the slaves' quarters.

The wind slapped his face sideways with needle-sharp ice pellets whisked up from the river. The sun was already dipping below the horizon with one last blast of orange against the sky.

He bent his head and headed up King Street past the taverns with glowing windows. He burrowed his nose into his collar and shoved his hands down into his pockets, turning left on Henry Street toward the Bottoms, where the Negroes lived and where the social club was. Here the buildings were meaner and poorer than the grand brick warehouses and homes closer to the river.

The social club was nothing more than a lean-to on the back of an old stable. As he approached he could clearly hear the rise and fall of voices and a fiddle wavering above them. Light flickered through the chinks in the wallboards.

Hercules stepped inside and was stopped in his tracks by the pulse of heat that filled the room. Heat from the warm bodies and the small hearth in the corner. It made him realize how long it had been since he had felt truly warm.

A young woman with dark skin and reddish hair hoisted a tray of tankards above the crowd. He scanned the room for faces from the farm, only recognizing a few here and there. He squeezed through into a corner near the far wall from which he could see the door but wouldn't get taken up in conversation.

He leaned his back against the boards and closed his eyes. The wall felt cold through his coat even as the warmth of the room radiated around him. He was weary. A shout rose above the crowd, but since no one seemed alarmed, he didn't open his eyes. He could feel the bodies shift around him.

"Master cook!" The shout drew nearer. Hercules opened a searching eye. The crowd shifted and swayed in front of him. Somewhere in another part of the room the fiddle paused before taking up a tune.

"Hercules!" The voice came more insistent now, and closer too. He leaned up off the wall and blinked. James Brown was pushing toward him.

"I ready to hear you story," he said after shaking hands.

Hercules shrugged. "Not much to tell. The General decided I should stay here — for safekeeping."

Brown raised his eyebrows. "Come on," he said, pushing Hercules forward toward the girl with the tankards. He tossed a coin on the tray and she lowered it to allow him to pull a couple down.

He handed one to Hercules and guided him into a dim corner. "I always in market fuh a good tale. So go on — tell me."

Mrs. Harris put down her fork at the sound of a knock at her door.

A black boy and white girl, servants by the look of them, stood on her doorstep. "Yes?" she said.

"Are you Mistress Harris, the schoolteacher?" the boy said nervously.

"I am."

"We are sent by Master Hercules, General Wash—"

"I know who he is," Mrs. Harris said, cutting him off. She stepped to the side of the door to allow them to pass. "You had better come in."

CHAPTER 30

Winter 1796

Hercules filled the brush with paint and sand and slapped it on the side of the house. The others talked while they worked, painting the glop on the house's wood shingles to make it look like stone. Nothing was ever what it seemed here, he thought bitterly. All this time he'd thought himself an almost free man. But almost free wasn't the same as being free, was it?

He let his mind wander to the second time he saw James Brown at the social club, when the mariner had come back down to Alexandria at Christmastime.

"I believe opportunity will soon come," James Brown had said in low tones. Even in that place it was better to be circumspect. There were those among them who would trade information for coin. And neither man would blame them for it. You did what you must to make your own lot a little better.

"Happy Christmas," he said more loudly, so others could hear, and raised his glass toward Hercules, who sat across the small table from him. The social club was nearly empty, most folks being home with their families. Hercules had remained in his quarters until the girls were asleep.

"And to you," he said now to Brown before downing his drink in one go.

"I'll be back this way in two months' time, taking shipments from the warehouses up to the capital," Brown said, now softly again. "Some of them from Mount Vernon."

Hercules had often met the ship from Virginia when it arrived in the capital city with hams bound for market and supplies for the President's House.

He gestured to the girl and bought them another round. James Brown took a long sip and set the cup down. He did not speak again until the girl moved away from the table. Hercules had leaned in closer to better hear.

"Good," Brown had said. "Here's what I want you to do."

Hercules brought his thoughts back to the present. As he told Nate so long ago, it was a dangerous business to let your mind wander too long. Now the others were laughing and talking about what they'd get up to on the General's birthday when the slaves were given rum and a few nights to celebrate.

"What about you, Uncle Harkless?" said one of the younger men with a jeer. They used the hated nickname as often as they could — a reminder that he had come down in the world to be just like them. "What you got planned?"

Hercules shrugged and made himself smile pleasantly.

"Oh, nothing much," he said and bent to dip the brush in the bucket once more.

CHAPTER 31

February 22, 1797

Folks passed rum bottles around crowded campfires near the slave quarters and in some of the fields. Hercules could hear the cries of "To the General!" and "Washington's health!" from outside the cabin door. Their celebrations would go on at least two days or more — ample time before anyone noticed Hercules was gone. He only hoped his girls would have the sense to hold their tongues.

He sat next to Baby's cot and stroked her chubby cheek. Soon she would be six years old, old enough to remember him but young enough to maybe not miss him.

Her sisters, now — that was another story.

He swallowed down the lump in his throat as he stood and went over to where they lay huddled together next to the fire, choosing the hard floor so the little one could have the one pallet. They were good girls. He

446

only hoped the General wouldn't punish them for what he would see as Hercules's treachery. Maybe one day the General would even see fit to sell his children to him when he raised the money to purchase their freedom.

Hercules set his jaw in a hard line, grinding the back teeth together so that pain would overtake sorrow. He'd earn the money — he would — as soon as he got to New York. He'd do nothing but work until they too were free.

Reaching into his pocket, he pulled out the leather drawstring purse in which he had saved his coins. There were enough to make a good start somewhere else. He took out a handful and put them under Evey's pillow and kissed her on her forehead.

He turned his back on his children and quickly put on his one good shirt over the one he wore, tattered and filthy as it was. He did the same with his good britches. At the very least the extra layers would keep him warm as he crossed the miles of estate on his way toward Alexandria.

At the door, he looked at his walking stick with its elegant head. He was going to leave it for the girls as a remembrance or, if worst came to worst, to sell when the coins ran out. He hoped that Evey had the sense not to let on that she had them.

On second thought, he snatched it up again. He could use it to lean upon during the trek, or to protect himself if it came to that. Tucking the coins well into the inside of his coat, he jammed his hat on his head and stepped out the door. The cold was already reaching out for him as he moved quickly away from the house into the woods near the river, until he could double back in the forest toward Alexandria, where there was no one to see his footprints in the snow.

"Almost done here, sir," said Nate over his shoulder as he scrubbed out the last pot. Margaret moved around the kitchen putting things away.

"Good," said Mr. Julien, smiling. "Then you have leave to celebrate a little. Here —" He stepped toward the table and put two coins upon it. "These are from Mrs. Washington. Should you like to step out and see the fireworks displays, you might have a little refreshment."

"Thank you, sir, much obliged," said Nate. He dared not meet Margaret's eyes.

Margaret stepped forward and picked up one of the coins. "That is very kind of her," she said. "I hope his Excellency might have a very happy birthday indeed."

"Yes, I imagine he will," said Julien, smiling. "Don't stay out too late; tomorrow we had better go through the stores and consider what we may send on to Virginia. Only a few weeks to go . . ."

"Yes, sir," said Nate, nodding.

"Good," said the chef again, heading for the door and raising his hat. "I'll bid you goodnight, then."

For a moment, Nate felt strange. Hercules used to do just that. It occurred to him that he would never see the cook again, now that he and Margaret were running away with Mrs. Harris's help. He swallowed and forced himself to give a jaunty salute. "Goodnight, Chef!"

Once the door had closed, Nate continued his scrubbing while Margaret took up the broom and worked it around the room. He rinsed the pot and began drying it just as the scraping of the broom against the brick floor stopped. They couldn't have been handed a better chance.

As Margaret slipped into the cellar where they had hidden the small cloth tied up with their few things, Nate put on his hat and coat. When she came back into the room, her cheeks were already red from the brief moment in the cold.

"Not that hat," she said softly, looking at

his head. He snatched off the livery cap and looked at it a moment before tossing it onto Hercules's old worktable.

"Shall we go?"

Margaret nodded and went out the door first — they were to separate at the stone wall surrounding the garden and take different routes to where Mrs. Harris's agent would bring them well outside of the city in his cart.

"Ah, Nate, there you are." A voice echoed through the darkened kitchen just as he was about to step through the door.

He turned toward Mr. Kitt. "Sir?"

"I need you to bring up some more cider from the cellar," Kitt said, moving toward him, holding a lantern aloft.

Nate's eyes flicked involuntarily to the door. He prayed that Margaret had pressed on and into crowds clamoring in the street, their voices rising up between the sudden blasts of cannon fire saluting General Washington from the ships in the harbor.

Kitt leisurely walked toward the worktable and set down his lantern, bathing Nate's cap in a pool of light.

"Why is this here?" he asked, looking at Nate.

Nate stared at the hat and swallowed.

"I — I must have set it down on my way

out, sir," he said, hesitating. "Mr. Julien said it was all right to go out and see the fireworks . . . that is, Mrs. Washington told him so, sir."

Kitt looked at him for a longish time. "Where's the girl?" he said suddenly.

Nate felt his stomach pitch. "The girl, sir?"

"Margaret — where is she?"

"I — I don't know, sir, Mr. Julien said she was to go out too if she liked." Nate's mind raced. "Maybe she did?"

Kitt took a step toward him and examined his face. Something wasn't right here, but he couldn't figure what. It wasn't like Margaret to be brave enough to go out alone. "Why didn't you go with her?" he asked suspiciously.

Nate swallowed fearfully and willed himself to think. What would Hercules do? He'd shift Kitt's attention to where he wanted it.

"Me? Why would I want to go about with her?" Nate said, trying to make his voice sound contemptuous. He swallowed. "It's not often I get out to . . . enjoy the town." He went on hurriedly before he lost his courage. "Lots of things to get up to without that milk-faced girl clinging on my sleeve." He blurted the last out and tried to leer, imagining he was copying that slow terrible smile that Hercules affected when he

451

wanted to frighten someone without saying a word. Kitt could well cuff him for the impertinence, but he'd take the blow if it helped Margaret get away.

"Why you filthy —" He pulled at Nate's arm. "Come on then." Kitt shoved him roughly. "Get on down and bring me up that cider."

"Ready?" said General Washington, looking down at his granddaughter Nelly happily as the swirl of ballgoers moved about them.

"Yes, sir," she answered with a curtsy.

"You may not be able to keep up," he said with a wink. "I mean to out-dance you all this evening even if I am now sixty-five."

Nelly laughed, happy to see the old gentleman in such high spirits. "Of that, sir, I have no doubt," she said just as the music started and, true to his word, he stepped lively out to the floor.

"Ready?" said Mrs. Harris's driver, a Scotsman called Seamus, who sat beside Margaret on the cart bench, clutching the horse's reins.

"Can we not wait a moment more?" she begged.

"You know the plan, girl. Have to keep moving, no matter what," he said, beginning to twitch the reins. Before he could, the horses tossed their heads and stamped their feet, spooked.

Seamus looked around, his hand reaching for the gun at his feet. A shape burst out of the woods by the side of the road just as Seamus drew up the revolver.

"No!" yelled Margaret, pulling down his arm as Nate stumbled, panting up to the cart. A bruise was rising on the side of his cheek.

"Nate! What happened?"

"Nothing," he said quickly and climbed into the back of the cart, where he picked up the burlap sacking and burrowed under it as planned. He had to trust in this man, because he was an agent of Mrs. Harris and Hercules trusted her. It was all they had to hold onto.

"Hold tight," said Seamus, after he saw that Nate had flattened himself well. "I mean to go fast this night but I will bring you safely to your destination."

Margaret cast a worried glance back to where Nate had disappeared under the cloth and cargo. She nodded tightly.

"Of that, sir, I have no doubt," she said, just as he clucked at the horse and the cart moved forward with a jolt onto the road.

■ ■ ■ ■

The first day had been the hardest. He'd walked steadily through the night and he wasn't even tired when the sun started to break over the horizon. His blood was pumping like it hadn't for months and even the cold, wet cloth of his britches and hose, sodden from wading through the creeks and ponds in his path, hadn't bothered him. The stiff cloth was freezing into place, scraping at his skin, but it had been necessary to walk through the water to throw Allistone's dogs off the scent.

He'd found a bramble that was large and thick enough to hide him when he'd crawled inside, the burrs pulling and tearing at his skin. He sat there too afraid to start a fire, not only because the smoke could be seen but that it would have stifled him dead in that closed space.

Reaching into his bag, he pulled out the crusts of bread he'd put aside from every one of his meals for the last week. The pieces were hard and most had green mold but he ate them anyway. He needed the strength. They weren't much better when they were fresh anyway. He'd already had enough to drink — scooping up snow as he walked and eating it, picking small twigs and leaves out as it melted in his hand. Still, he considered these sorry victuals a banquet — the first meal he'd eaten as a free man.

Hercules closed his eyes and tried to rest. His mind wasn't tired but he knew he had to keep up his strength. His thoughts raced crazily — to his girls and then to them in Philadelphia. Nate and Margaret.

He must have dozed for a moment because he was startled awake by the sound of barking dogs. He lay still, his heart banging hard in this throat.

"This way!" a voice called and Hercules crawled on his stomach to a space in the bramble and peered outside.

Three white men with muskets and dogs were splashing across the creek some few hundred yards away. Hercules closed his eyes and willed himself not to thrash out of the bramble in a panic. Maybe the dogs wouldn't pick up his scent.

The barking got closer; one of the hounds sniffed around the edge of the bramble. Hercules wondered if he could reach out fast enough to grab the animal by his neck and slit his throat with the knife he had in his boot.

"Buster! Here, boy!" The call came from farther away now. The dog lifted his head from sniffing and bounded toward the sound.

Hercules held his breath, not moving while the sounds of the men and their dogs faded into the distance. Bird hunters. Not slave catchers.

Hercules breathed out slowly and lay back down on the ground. He'd wait a little longer and find a new place to hide.

He bent down and untied the branches from his ankles and surveyed the town. It had taken him two days to make the walk through the woods to his rendezvous with James Brown in Alexandria. Two days of hiding in the daylight, sleeping a few hours at a time.

On the second day he'd found a small rock crevice that he crawled into and made a small fire that wouldn't be noticed. He'd scurried to hide from poachers on the General's land more than once, trying not to breathe lest they see his cold breath and take him for a deer — or worse.

He had been holding his piss for hours at a time, not wanting to leave its strong scent behind for the dogs that the overseer would surely send after him. He finally relieved himself over the side of a hill, watching the droplets freeze as they flew through the air.

For two nights he'd trudged on, the branches he tied to his boots in order to hide his footprints dragging his gait.

Now he squatted, panting, and stared at the warehouse by the dock. The night was cold enough to have driven even the watchmen indoors. Still, he waited a good quarter of an hour before he made his way toward the brick building and looked for the door with the small chalk mark above the handle, which James Brown had left open for him. Fortunately, the moon was high enough for him to see.

The warehouse was crowded with barrels and crates that mostly blocked the windows. Inside it was too dark to make anything out clearly. He stood still, trying to get his bearings. Brown had said to walk to the back wall near the loading doors and wait there. He squatted, lest his form be made out by anyone peering into the window at the gaps and spaces that the crates did not cover. Slowly he edged along the wall behind him to a stand of large barrels. He sat down to wait.

"Ready?" said James Brown, holding the barrel lid open.

"Yes," said Hercules, looking doubtfully at the large barrel that he was meant to climb into. The mariner had shown him where he drilled air holes for him to breathe but still he did not relish the idea.

"It only fuh a short while," said Brown. "Until I can roll you onto the ship. I have a place fuh you to hide in the hold and then we gone to Philadelphia."

Hercules tucked the roll of old clothing under his arm. He ran his hand over his scalp, which Brown had made smooth with a straight razor. The newly shaven head was a precaution to prevent him from being recognized, as were the new clothes he wore.

"You go have to leave this," said the seaman, holding up the stick.

Hercules nodded and Brown broke the stick over his leg. He pocketed the gold handle. "We go sell it when we make New York." Hercules took a deep breath and hoisted his leg to climb into the barrel with the sailor's help.

"Don't worry, master cook, I go bring you to safety this night," Brown said seriously as Hercules crouched down, waiting for the lid to be placed over his head.

"Of that, sir," Hercules said in a soft voice, "I have no doubt."

EPILOGUE

Maine, Summer 1797

Margaret grabbed the bedpost and panted. "Come now, come on," said Mrs. Jacks, reaching under her arm and hoisting the girl from where she squatted.

Margaret lumbered up and gasped as the pain shot through her.

The two looked enough alike with their blond hair and blue eyes to be mother and daughter, or aunt and niece, which is what they'd tell folks when Margaret was ready to come out of hiding. The baby, should it live, would go to the black family at the edge of town if it looked Negro. It would be taken for just another of their brood and they'd earn good coin for its keep. And if it looked white, Mrs. Jacks would claim it and Margaret as the children of her sister in Georgia who had died in childbirth.

Outside the door, Nate paced the room until Mr. Jacks, who had been calmly filling his pipe, called him outside to have a look at an apple tree that was sickened by some rot.

Nate didn't give a jot about the tree but he reluctantly followed, starting back for the door when Margaret's scream ripped the air.

"Come along, son," said Jacks, grabbing his arm.

As the two walked toward the orchard on the ridge behind the house, Jacks made small talk about this and that.

"Many a woman's had a baby before your missus," said Jacks amiably. "My Molly has her well in hand. Not to worry."

Nate still couldn't believe how easily these people in Mrs. Harris's network referred to Margaret as his "missus" and he as her "husband." He hadn't known, before, how much of a miracle a small word could be.

"How are you finding the tavern?" Jacks was saying.

"It's all right, I guess," said Nate, pulling at a tall stand of grass as he passed. "Pretty easygoing."

In truth, cooking at the tavern was so boring a simpleton could do it, but it was work and he was grateful for it.

"I can well imagine, given the victuals you've turned your hand to," said Jacks, puffing at the pipe.

They reached the ridge and stood looking down at the house where Margaret struggled to bring their child into the world.

"Have you given thought to what you'll do when the child is old enough?" Jacks asked.

Nate shoved his hands into his pockets. He had thought of nothing else this whole while, for despite the Jackses' kindness, every day here was still a day on tenterhooks.

"You know he won't leave off hunting you down," said Jacks, giving voice to Nate's thoughts. "There's many a man eager to earn the president's bounty by dragging you back — especially now that another has gone off."

Nate stopped walking. "Another?" he said, his mind running through those left at the President's House. Moll was too old to run and Joe too witless. Perhaps someone at the plantation — His thoughts raced to the only one who mattered and he impulsively grabbed Jacks's arm.

"Who? Do you recall who?" he asked urgently.

"His cook, I believe," said the other man. "Yes, that's right. I read the notice in the paper. It was the cook. They say the old man's even more angry than when that girl ran off — has scores of men trying to hunt him down." He paused to puff at his pipe while Nate stared dumbly into the distance. "Why, you knew him, of course," Jacks said as if the thought had just occurred to him.

Nate swallowed. "Yes, I knew him."

Hercules had escaped. He was free. Nate felt strangely light-headed.

Jacks was moving forward up the hill and talking about the baby again. ". . . and when the child is old enough you'll be able to travel north into Canada; there are some free black settlements there. That would be the best thing," said Jacks thoughtfully. "As long as both you and the missus can work and put aside your coin, perhaps you'd get there in a year's time." A year's time. Until then they'd live in separate houses, with Margaret posing as the Jackses' niece and them seeing each other on the sly. If the child were sent to the other family, there'd only be occasional visits with it. Margaret was already taking it hard, but there was nothing to be done. It was their only chance. He found himself wishing, not for the first time, that the child would look white — for all of their sakes.

"I thank you, sir, for all you and Mrs. Jacks have done," said Nate, looking at the older man who Nate now realized must be at least as old as the president.

"Nothing to thank me for, son," he said, puffing thoughtfully and staring off into the distance where the sun began to dip. "Them that's able must turn their hands to setting things to rights."

Nate lifted his eyes to the reddening sky. He thought of how the sunsets made the brick walks and buildings of Philadelphia glow as if they were fresh from baking-fire and how Hercules would walk those streets as if they were laid out just for him no matter what color he be.

Hercules was *free*. Nate closed his eyes and prayed for his child to be a boy, for he already knew the name with which to bestow him.

Thelma Grayson put the stopper back in the bottle of French perfume after lightly dabbing it behind her ears and in her décolletage. The peach-colored satin suited her nicely, although the day had not cooled when the sun had dropped behind the horizon. She would have to wear the white gauze tonight instead.

"Thelma, are you in here?" Grayson tapped gently on her bedroom door and poked his head around. She arranged her face into the kind of pretty smile she knew he expected as he crossed over to her.

"I have something for you," he said, bending to kiss not her cheek but her bosom, deeply inhaling the scent she had applied. "Very nice," he said, "Verbena?"

"Yes."

He held out a small box. "Go ahead, open it."

Thelma hesitated a fraction of a second. If Charles was giving her a present, that meant he wanted something. In the year they had been in New Orleans he had managed to find every house of debauchery there was, and it did not seem he meant to leave any time soon.

Once Thelma asked him if he did not long for America.

"I prefer it here," he had said of the French territory. "I can sail just as easily — easier — from this port, and with you as my emissary — what more could I want?"

She had smiled, as expected, and inclined her head. Thelma had proved an able translator with her refined French that the colonials could not easily pick apart.

She knew she should be happy. They had taken a lovely house. Grayson had bestowed her with all she wanted. And if he had cottoned to what she really was, here in this city full of octoroons and quadroons like herself, he hadn't revealed it to her. Except, of course, in the ways he had demanded she satisfy his hungers — ways that she was sure he would never degrade a real white woman into doing. But they did not speak of such things.

"Thelma, you're dreaming again." His voice broke into her thoughts. She looked up at his glittering eyes and swallowed before easing the hinged box open.

Two large teardrop diamond earrings lay there. Involuntarily, she gasped.

"Mon Dieu," she whispered.

"They are beautiful, are they not?" he said, smiling. "I want you to wear them tonight. I have found a singularly special place for us."

Thelma felt her stomach turn. What would the special place be this time? Like the salon where a woman wearing a false member penetrated her while Charles and another man watched, sipping wine and having their dinner before they had a go at each other? Or the place where he had forced her to kneel like a dog while man after man had placed himself inside her mouth?

"I should be delighted, of course, husband," she said, smiling up at him.

"Of course you will. Have Emily make

your corset tighter before we leave," he said, moving toward the door. "I'll wait for you downstairs."

Thelma let out a slow breath and looked at the earrings. She would cast her mind elsewhere, as she always did during Charles's entertainments. She found herself thinking about the General's cook more and more these days. What would her life have been like if she had never met Harriet Chew and, through her, Charles Grayson? She had been stupid to give up her simple room and her pupils. She had been stupid to give up those afternoons and evenings with the General's cook. Had she not been so greedy, they could have gone on as they were forever.

She closed her eyes. Another thing that was best not to think about. All she could do now was continue to pray that Charles would be run through by a well-placed knife in the hands of the rough trade that he picked up by the docks. She would imagine them gutting him like a fish as they had done to her father and watching him drown in his own blood.

It was what got her through. That and the knowledge that each expensive bauble he gave her added to a treasure trove that would, one day, buy her freedom to walk onto a ship leaving New Orleans harbor, the New World fading rapidly behind her.

Louis Philippe d'Orleans walked down the piazza from Mount Vernon with his notebook in hand. Washington always proved himself a most gracious host, but he seemed preoccupied today.

"I beg your pardon, Monsieur Orleans," he had said, standing abruptly during the luncheon. "I have some business to attend." The General had hurried out somewhere to the recesses of his house.

D'Orleans welcomed the president's departure so that he would not have to finish the barely edible food upon his plate. The victuals at Mount Vernon had not proven true to the stories of elegant meals prepared there. At least the wines were fine, he thought, draining his glass.

His secretary had said the reason was because the cook had run away — a scullion and a kitchen maid too. D'Orleans could not pretend sympathy. When would these Americans give up the idea of holding other humans in bondage? It was rumored that the president felt himself forced to perhaps purchase another slave to attend his kitchens, having not found a suitable cook for hire.

Now d'Orleans meandered toward the

river and stood awhile looking at it. There was the group of black children that seemed to rove in gangs about the place. They played at skipping stones across the river.

"Look! I'm the General!" said one little boy, heaving a great stone into the water, where it fell with a great splash.

"Aww, you ain't throw'd that two feet," said another little boy, picking up his own rock and heaving it not much farther. It fell into the river with a plop.

"At what are they playing?" d'Orleans asked his secretary, who had come up to his side.

"The Americans have a legend — they say that the General threw a stone clear across the river when he was a lad," the other man said with a smile. "I imagine they are playing at that."

D'Orleans watched a few minutes more before moving toward the house.

"Let us go see the place where the slaves live," he said to his secretary, who raised his eyebrows slightly but obligingly followed.

They came upon the long building adjacent to the greenhouse and stood there looking at it. There was one door at either end and the windows were rudely cut holes in the wall with wooden shutters to seal out the rain.

D'Orleans walked around to the back of the building where several more children played while the older ones tended some cook fires, it being too hot to cook inside. As meager as it was, it was far better than some he'd seen in this godforsaken land.

A little girl wandered out of the quarters clutching a rag bundle that she cooed to as if it were a doll.

"I believe that is a child of the General's cook who recently ran away," said the secretary, as if she were a point of interest on a scenic tour.

"Is she?" said d'Orleans thoughtfully. He squatted down and gestured for the little girl to come closer, reaching into his pocket for a coin.

" 'Allo," he said in his heavily accented English.

Her little fingers closed around the coin and she held it in her palm, examining it. She smiled up at him. "Hello, sir."

"What is your name?" he asked.

Her little eyebrows furrowed together. "They call me Baby," she said.

"And are you the baby?" d'Orleans said seriously.

"Yes, sir," she said.

"Where is your mama, Baby?"

Again, the little eyebrows creased. "Don't

have none. She went to heaven."

"Ah," said the nobleman and glanced up at his secretary, who was watching the exchange.

"And your papa, he is not here either, is he?"

"No, sir," she said guilelessly. "He left."

"Where did he go, Baby, do you know?"

"No, sir." She fidgeted, becoming bored by the conversation. A lot of other men like this one had already asked her and her sisters the same things over and again since Papa had gone.

Louis Phillipe grasped the little hand. It was already worn with work.

"Tell me, Baby, do you miss your papa?" he asked gently.

Baby focused on him looking at her dark hand in his soft white one. She nodded.

"You must be deeply upset that you will not see your papa again," he said gently, shaking the little hand.

Baby looked sharply up from his hand into his eyes. He could see the lashes curling up and away from her very black pupils. She pursed her little mouth.

"No, sir," she said, pulling her hand gently away and straightening up like a little woman. "I am very glad — for now he is free."

■ ■ ■ ■

"Full house tonight," said James Brown, coming through the door to the kitchen where Hercules stood over one of the scullions, directing him to cut an apple thinner.

"This pork roast is good with Madeira — push that, it will fetch a higher price," said the chef. "And I've a standing pork pie for those with thinner purses."

Brown grinned at his business partner. "Yes, sir!" he said, saluting.

"And now get out of my kitchen," Hercules said, laughing. "But, tell me, any news from Virginia?"

"You family seem well — from what I gather in Alexandria. He hasn't harmed dem in any way," said Brown, matching Hercules's low tone.

Hercules's jaw clenched but he nodded. No, that at least wasn't Washington's way. He wouldn't harm little girls for what their father had done. Richmond, however, might be another story.

"He still out fuh you though," said Brown. "Been sending agents around Philadelphia to rout you out." He handed Hercules a newspaper, which he scanned quickly, reading his own description and the posting for a reward for his apprehension.

"Well, he'll have a time of it, won't he?" said Hercules, smiling.

"Dat he will," Brown replied with a grin. "I best be back to it. It getting rowdy in dere with de crowds pushing in fuh a taste of you cooking."

Hercules turned back to the tavern kitchen as Brown went out to the taproom. Around him everyone was at their tasks, just as he liked it. The only sounds were the spit of the fire and knives hitting the chopping board. Satisfied that all was running tight, he stepped out the kitchen door to the alley between the tavern and the warehouse beside it.

Hard upon the end of Spring Street, the Hudson River was choked with ships more numerous than what he had seen in Philadelphia. Behind him the city crouched, bursting its seams, pushing ever northward.

He stood a moment and watched the hurly-burly of the docks. Men shouting orders to one another, unloading barrels like the one that had carried him aboard the ship to Philadelphia and then on to New York. The ships were larger and taller here, bound for England and the Far East. Maybe one day he'd find himself upon one, seeing more of the world.

But for now, he turned toward his tavern
and his kitchen. After the night's business
was over, there was a city of delights to
behold.

HISTORICAL NOTES

I first heard about George Washington's celebrated enslaved chef, Hercules, from former Clinton aide turned culinary scholar Adrian Miller, who had dedicated a good deal of time to writing about black cooks in the White House for his book *The President's Kitchen Cabinet,* which was ultimately published in 2017. Hercules came up in our conversation as the "grandfather" of all African American presidential cooks, and he entered my imagination forever.

For four years, Hercules became my all-consuming passion, taking me from Philadelphia to Mount Vernon and through thousands of pages of historical records and scholarly documentation about the lives of President Washington and the enslaved persons he owned. Much of what you have read in *The General's Cook* is based on historical fact. Actual recorded incidents are reproduced faithfully where possible — like the fact that President George Washington came to serve his tenure in Philadelphia in 1790 bringing enslaved "servants" with him from his household in Virginia. Most were eventually sent back to their estate, Mount Vernon, because the First Couple feared they would take advantage of Pennsylvania's 1780 Gradual Abolition Act, which allowed for enslaved people to petition for freedom after six months of continuous residency. In fact, it was US Attorney General Edmund Randolph who advised the Washingtons on exactly how to keep their people enslaved through a "rotation system," moving them out of Pennsylvania and into slave states to reset their tenure. Randolph, a fellow Virginian, had himself lost enslaved people to the law and was well versed in how to subvert it.

This rotation of enslaved people lasted throughout the Washingtons' seven years in Philadelphia, carrying them back on visits home to Mount Vernon but also on shorter trips across the Delaware River to New Jersey, where slavery was legal.

As I read through the period documents — most notably after the escape of Oney Judge — it was clear enough that Washington's enslaved people knew what was going on. These included Hercules, Oney Judge,

Old Moll, Austin, and later Postilion Joe, a groom and carriage driver.

Of these souls, Hercules seemed the savviest, not only about his situation but about rectifying it — or at least so it appears to me after reading period accounts in which Hercules declares himself mortified by an accusation — from Washington's secretary Tobias Lear — that he might take advantage of the abolition law. Just as I write in the first chapter of the book, Mrs. Washington was so touched by Hercules's show of fealty that she allowed him to remain in the capital beyond six months — thereby actually, if unintentionally, handing him the tools for his freedom — although he did not use these tools as one would have imagined, a fact which historians and scholars still ponder, and the potential reasons for which I've attempted to explore in this book.

Like most Americans, I realized that the Founding Fathers were complicit in keeping the "peculiar institution" of slavery going even if they were not actually slaveholders themselves. I knew too that Washington, as a Virginian, was a slaveholder, but this new information about how far he and his wife went to hold onto their human chattel both repelled and fascinated me enough to start examining their world — particularly their time in Philadelphia.

Philadelphia's population at the time of this story was roughly five percent African American and most in that number were free people. Indentured servitude was also common in the city as it was throughout the colonies and early Federal America. Orphans, like Margaret, and those dependent on the state were often indentured for a period of eight, twelve, or twenty-eight years as determined by their color, legal status, age, or physical condition. Black men, women, and children were indentured for the longest tenures and white men, women, and children for the least time.

President and Mrs. Washington made use of the indenture system a fair amount while they were in Philadelphia — primarily to make up for the lack of their own "servants" (enslaved people) in the capital. There was, in fact, a Margaret Held indentured in the president's house, but nothing is known about her beyond her name. I chose to create a story around her in these pages.

A major point in favor of holding indentures over enslaved people revolved around a serious concern for masters: Slave owners, especially those living in Pennsylvania, were, like the Washingtons, ever fearful that those they had enslaved would not just escape but revolt.

The slave uprising and revolt in Saint-Domingue (present-day Haiti), which brings the fictional character of Thelma to Philadelphia and into Hercules's sphere, drove many white planters and their enslaved people from the island to the refuge of Philadelphia. In the American capital, society folks banded together to support them as refugees, but their presence also fanned the flames of the fear of an American slave revolt.

To add to the feeling of race-related chaos, many of the enslaved people who came with the refugees of Saint-Domingue's planter class quickly took advantage of the 1780 law, leading to a bustling trade in slave-catching funded by those who aimed to get their "property" back.

For his own part, Washington donated money to one of these white refugee societies while refusing to comment on whether refugees had a "right" to retain the people they had enslaved. This was consistent: Washington wanted to keep his own slaves but did not want the public to turn against him for it. Instead, he opted to keep mum on the issue whenever possible.

But just as the society refugees had backing, their enslaved people who wanted to be free were not without supports. The Pennsylvania Abolition Society operated as one of the first formal organizations to help African Americans seek freedom. Their activities included sending enslaved people north as well as using the court system to petition on their behalf — particularly against the activities of slave catchers who roamed cities seeking both runaways and even free people who might be kidnapped and sold for bounty. The most famous of these stories is that of Solomon Northup, recounted in his book *Twelve Years a Slave*.

Mrs. Harris's early "underground railroad" is patterned on groups like the PAS, but even they had to work around laws that existed in every one of the original thirteen states, except for Pennsylvania, against interracial marriage and sex, which was in some cases punishable by death. It should be noted that although amalgamation — as intermarriage between races was called — was not illegal in Pennsylvania, it was far from being socially accepted. In later years, "amalgamation" was replaced with the post-Civil War term "miscegenation" (literally, Latin for "race mixing") and was used in the most malicious manner possible, including as a lynching rallying cry in the Jim Crow South.

One of the major themes in this book — and probably the one dearest to me — is that Hercules and Nate both have the desire to read. To us in the modern day, this may seem like a small enough desire, but it's important to remember that education and learning was carefully kept away from the enslaved because in knowledge there truly is power.

The ability to read and write represented a step closer to freedom for enslaved people because it not only opened up greater opportunities in business but also allowed them to advocate on their own behalf. Something so simple as being able to read one's own manumission papers — and using them as a means of protection under the law — meant the difference between being returned to slavery or continuing on to a free life.

With respect to the characters in this book pursuing their own literacy, Oney Judge learned to read later in life — long after her escape. In a newspaper interview she gave when she was a much older woman, she bitterly complained that the Washingtons did not allow her to learn to read while she was with them. We do know that Washington's body servant Christopher Sheels could read and that the Washingtons were well aware of this, but where he obtained that skill is unknown.

Nothing is known of Hercules's literacy, but as I researched slavery and enslaved people and the power of the written word and juxtaposed this knowledge against Hercules's powerful personality — and later escape — it seemed inconceivable to me that he would be immune to the desire to read. So, while his lessons with Mrs. Harris are a pure fabrication, I feel they add a possible, or even probable, element to his story.

On the topic of Mrs. Harris: she too is a dynamic but wholly made-up character, although the 1790 census does list a "Mrs. Harris, black, schoolteacher" in Cherry Street. Throughout much of the book I did insert real people from the 1790 census document, along with their professions, so that these early pioneers of free black American life might yet live again — if only for a line or two. They include not just the famous formerly enslaved abolitionist preacher Richard Allen but Polly Haine, the pepper pot seller, Charles Sang, the confectioner, and Benjamin Johnson, the oysterman. Their lives might have been humble, but they were forging an integral part of the new American culture just by going about their daily existence.

One particularly notable real-life character is James Hemings, the enslaved cook of Thomas Jefferson who accompanied Jefferson not just to Paris when he was Secretary of State but lived with him in Philadelphia upon their return from France, where Hemings had been apprenticed to a master French cook and learned the cuisine that Jefferson so favored. While in France, where slavery was illegal, Jefferson paid Hemings a salary, a practice he continued when they reached Philadelphia.

By all account James Hemings had a brilliant mind — not just in the kitchen. He could read and write both French and English and often served as Jefferson's translator in Paris as Jefferson could not master the language. Like Hercules, James Hemings could have taken advantage of being legally free in France and not returned to America with Jefferson. Scholars have surmised that he returned to prevent retaliation toward his enslaved family at Monticello, the most famous of whom was his sister Sally, Jefferson's enslaved paramour. Jefferson reluctantly granted Hemings his freedom in return for teaching of his French cooking skills to his younger brother. He was manumitted in 1796, leaving behind written recipes and an inventory of utensils.

After Jefferson became president in 1801, he summoned Hemings from the Baltimore tavern where he was working to cook for Jefferson at the White House — Hemings refused. James Hemings died later that year in an alleged suicide which Jefferson immediately ascribed to excessive drinking — although neither allegation has been proven true.

While there is no definitive historical record that James Hemings and Hercules were friends, it is likely that they would have interacted given their condition of being enslaved by the nation's two most important men, sharing the same profession, and living within a block of one another. It is within the realm of possibility that the fact that James Hemings could read and write might have influenced the real-life Hercules.

Next to learning to read, Hercules's secret meetings with Gilbert Stuart — and, through him, with Thelma — are my other pure fabrication in this book, but Gilbert Stuart did presumably paint George Washington's cook and that painting, though unauthenticated, is now in the Museo Thyssen-Bornemisza in Madrid, Spain. Like much of Stuart's work, it is unsigned but very clearly painted in his signature style. In fact, although I am no art critic, I see an uncanny resemblance in form and composition to Stuart's famed Athenaeum portrait of George Washington himself.

Turning from the imagined to the real, I have to say a few words on Hercules's actual family. The cook really did have four children, Richmond, Evey, Delia, and a little girl whose name is unknown. She is the child referred to as "Baby" in this novel — a name I gave her drawing on African American and Afro-Caribbean heritages in which it would not have been uncommon for a youngest daughter to have this nickname.

As in *The General's Cook,* Hercules's eldest child, Richmond, did spend a short time in the capital with his father as a scullion, but left in 1791, not 1794 as I've written for the purposes of story. There is no record of the children's lives after their father's escape from Mount Vernon past the account written by the future French King Louis Philippe d'Orleans during his visit to Mount Vernon, where he spoke with Hercules's youngest daughter, who proclaimed herself very happy that her father was gone "because he is free now."

What we know of Hercules's actual life is from letters written by George Washington, Tobias Lear, and others, household account books, and a biographical sketch written by the first president's step-grandson, George Washington Parke Custis ("Washy"), in his book *Recollections and Private Memoirs of Washington.* There he painted the cook as a notable personage on the Philadelphia scene who was a master chef much valued by the Washingtons, and it is from this work that I built most of my personal image of Hercules as a larger-than-life figure. The dishes described in this novel, from the salmagundi to chocolate pie to oysters and standing pork pie, are all those that Hercules would have prepared.

After his escape on the president's birthday in 1797, Washington did attempt to get his cook back, hiring detectives to try to discover him in his "haunts" in Philadelphia and to leave no stone unturned. Washington was unsuccessful in apprehending his cook, whom he wished to be returned "unharmed." Hercules was spotted again in New York City in 1801, by then-mayor Richard Varick, two years after the president's death. Varick wrote to Mrs. Washington, asking if she would care to have him apprehended.

By that time, Hercules was a free man twice over — first because he had stayed above six months in Philadelphia and was technically a free man even though he remained in Washington's household, and then by the terms of General Washington's will, freeing all the enslaved people in his personal possession. However, the prideful First Lady wrote back that there was no need because *"I have been so fortunate as to engage a white cook who answers very well. I have thought it therefore better to decline taking Hercules back again."*

So what happened to Hercules? No one knows. Many have speculated that perhaps he wound up in Europe because that's where his painting has been for the last many decades, but that doesn't necessarily follow.

In the novel, I chose to give Hercules a firmer hold on a successful new life — not in small part because I myself could not bear to see him go — and Hercules finds himself a co-owner of a tavern along with the character of James Brown. Those who know New York City will recognize the location of the tavern as the site of the Ear Inn or the "James Brown House." The real Mr. Brown was a free African American Revolutionary War veteran who purchased the house and ran a tobacco shop there — later selling it to owners who eventually turned it into a tavern. I've taken the liberty to use

Mr. Brown's name and home (built some twelve years after this story ends), but there is no evidence that he knew the General's cook or was in the tavern business himself.

As to General and Mrs. Washington: George Washington died in 1799 at the age of sixty-seven and his wife just two years later. By the time the president died, he had altered his views on slavery considerably — the culmination of a slow evolution. I like to think that as the General lived through the horrors of war and the fierce work of building a new nation, he came to see the value of each person for their own merit and so valued Hercules's clear talents as individual achievement. Perhaps this is what led him, bit by bit, to personally reject the idea of slavery although he, self-admittedly, did not see how the nation could do without it.

Still, in an act of personal evolution, Washington did attempt to sell his own real estate holdings during his life to make provision for the freedom of whatever enslaved people he personally owned at his death. He even went so far as to command that his freed slaves not be turned out of Mount Vernon as a retaliatory measure when the time came to exercise their manumission.

Had our national father had taken a

stronger stand against slavery while he yet lived, he was probably the one American who could have ended the practice of slavery and changed history. But Washington was truly a man of his time, not a visionary for all humankind. Just as he undeservedly enjoyed wealth and comfort predicated on enslaved labor in his lifetime, so too did his contemporaries and the nation as a whole. He believed the fledging nation could not do without enforced labor of African Americans and still maintain an economy that unjustly advantaged the few. Certainly, scholars have well established that the free labor of the enslaved gave America a financial jumpstart, the residual effects of which the United States economy still benefits from today. And so the viciously cruel and morally corrupt institution of slavery continued for 66 years after his death and the nation continued to be built upon the backs of those robbed of their own freedom.

BIBLIOGRAPHIC NOTES

In order to recreate the late eighteenth-century world of Hercules, George Washington's enslaved cook, in both Philadelphia and in Virginia, the following sources were invaluable. The archives of the National Park Service, Independence Hall district, provided extensive detail on the President's House site, what it looked like, who lived there, and in what condition. While the house is no longer standing, a curated plein air exhibit serves as a memorial to the enslaved persons of African descent who labored there. It's well worth a visit.

Ron Chernow's Pulitzer Prize–winning biography of the first president, *Washington: A Life,* proved the best examination of the first president's evolving mind-set on slavery. Edward G. Lengel's *Inventing George Washington* was helpful in this as well.

Events in the lives of Hercules and the household at large were largely reconstructed with the help of the historians at Mount Vernon and their aid in my reading of *The Private Affairs of George Washington* by Stephen Decatur Jr., which included the household accounts for the President's House in Philadelphia.

Books such as Billy G. Smith's *The Lower Sort: Philadelphia's Laboring People, 1750–1800* and *Life in Early Philadelphia: Documents from the Revolutionary and Early National Periods* as well as Gary B. Nash's *Forging Freedom: The Formation of Philadelphia's Black Community, 1720–1840* allowed me to reconstruct the lives of everyday folk in Philadelphia during this time period.

Birch's Views of Philadelphia 1800 provided actual glimpses into the physical structure of the town in this era before photographic evidence. *Slavery at the Home of George Washington,* a series of scholarly articles edited by Philip J. Schwarz, was quite useful for understanding how the peculiar institution of African enslavement worked at Mount Vernon. The George Washington Papers collection at the Library of Congress offered insight into the man himself as well as some of the excerpts of the letters and period papers in this book.

Volumes such as *Independence: A Guide to*

Historic Philadelphia by George W. Boudreau and *Sex Among the Rabble: An Intimate History of Gender and Power in the Age of Revolution, Philadelphia, 1730–1830* by Clare A. Lyons rounded out my understanding of the most intimate aspects of daily life among all classes and races in the City of Brotherly Love at this time. *Washington in Germantown* by Charles Francis Jenkins helped my descriptions of the family's time in Germantown during the summer of 1794.

The food and culinary information in this book was dependent on fine works as such as *Food in Colonial and Federal America* by Sandra Oliver, *Martha Washington's Booke of Cookery* annotated by Karen Hess, *Dining with the Washingtons: Historic Recipes, Entertaining, and Hospitality from Mount Vernon* by Stephen A. McLeod, *The Virginia Housewife* by Mary Randolph, and *The First American Cookbook* by Amelia Simmons, as well as "History is Served," the website of Colonial Williamsburg Historic Foodways (recipes.history.org/).

Finally, the weather in the novel is accurately portrayed thanks to *A Meteorological Account of the Weather in Philadelphia, From January 1, 1790, to January 1, 1847,*

Including Fifty-seven Years; With an Appendix, by Charles Peirce.

ACKNOWLEDGMENTS

Over the course of five years researching and writing this book I had immeasurable help and support from many people whom I wish to thank here.

First and foremost is culinary scholar Adrian Miller, author of *The President's Kitchen Cabinet* (University of North Carolina Press). Adrian not only introduced me to Hercules but has done remarkable work deeply researching and sharing the true stories of the African American cooks who have fed the American presidents from Washington through President Obama.

Thank you, Adrian, for bringing Hercules into my life — for even now he remains my silent daily companion. I immediately felt a kinship to Hercules on many levels. Our most obvious similarity is that we are both chefs but we are also people who are not what we may immediately appear to be. I can't overstate the extent to which Hercules' ability to maintain his dignity in the most unimaginably inhuman circumstances, has awed me as I've researched and written about him.

Thank you to my editor Lilly Golden for her sharp eye in fine-tuning the manuscript and most of all to my agent and first editor Jane von Mehren who worked with me on many drafts of the book over the course of multiple years.

I am extremely grateful to Arcade Publishing for letting me share Hercules' story as I always meant to tell it. Editorial Director, Mark Gompertz was open-minded enough to give me — and Hercules — a chance following the controversy around the offensive illustrations for my picture book about Hercules, and over which I had no control.

While no one alive today or for many generations past can fully understand the lives or know the feelings of those who lived centuries ago, research through primary source material help us paint a more accurate picture. The help of skilled historians was seminal to writing this book. I wish to thank Anna Coxe Toogood, Historian at the National Archives, Independence Hall National Historic Park, for helping research the site of the President's House in Philadelphia and the Germantown White House.

Ms. Toogood's aid in guiding me toward resources to reconstruct African American life in late 18th century Philadelphia was invaluable. Thanks, too, to the Germantown Historical Society for aiding my understanding of that area, particularly the role of the Chew family.

Mary Thompson, Historian at Mount Vernon was instrumental in providing detailed information about Hercules within the historical record as well as larger context for the lives of those people enslaved by George and Martha Washington. Leni Sorensen, Ph. D and retired African American Research Historian at Thomas Jefferson's Monticello, helped me contextualize figures like Samuel Fraunces early on in my research as well the lives of enslaved people and Southern plantation culture — particularly as cooks and kitchen workers.

Dr. Sorensen also offered moral support and courage when it seemed that, because of the picture book controversy, *The General's Cook* would never see the light of day although it had been completed long before the other book came out. Like Dr. Sorensen, there were others who also believed that Hercules' story was too important to remain untold and these dear souls never let me give up on him. They include my brother Ramesh Ganeshram, who has forever been my champion in matters large and small; my dear friends Lorilynn Bauer, Victoria Kann, Andrea Kalb and Renee Brown whose love and support make all things possible; and my husband, Jean Paul Vellotti, who has always backed my fight to give Hercules his rightful due.

There are many more too numerous to name here. Heartfelt thanks to them all for insisting Hercules' truth be spoken so he may yet live again. They know who they are.

ABOUT THE AUTHOR

Ramin Ganeshram is a veteran journalist, who has written features for the *New York Times* and for *New York Newsday.* As a professionally trained chef with a Master's degree in Journalism from Columbia, she is a celebrated food columnist who has been awarded seven Society of Professional Journalists awards for her work and an IACP Cookbook of The Year Award. Ganeshram is the author of several cookbooks. As an American of Trinidadian and Iranian heritage, she specializes in writing about multicultural communities as a news reporter and about food from the perspective of history and culture. Her work has appeared in *Saveur, Gourmet, Bon Appetit, National Geographic Traveler, Forbes Traveler, Forbes Four Seasons,* and many others. Born and raised in New York City, she lives in Westport, Connecticut.

The employees of Thorndike Press hope you have enjoyed this Large Print book. All our Thorndike, Wheeler, and Kennebec Large Print titles are designed for easy reading, and all our books are made to last. Other Thorndike Press Large Print books are available at your library, through selected bookstores, or directly from us.

For information about titles, please call:
(800) 223-1244

or visit our website at:
gale.com/thorndike

To share your comments, please write:
Publisher
Thorndike Press
10 Water St., Suite 310
Waterville, ME 04901